SACRAMENTO PUBLIC LIBRARY

# Strange Brew

## Also edited by P. N. Elrod

*My Big Fat Supernatural Wedding*
*My Big Fat Supernatural Honeymoon*

# Strange Brew

Edited by P. N. Elrod

 St. Martin's Griffin New York

These stories are works of fiction. All of the characters, organizations, and events portrayed in each story are either products of the author's imagination or are used fictitiously.

SEEING EYE copyright © 2009 by Patricia Briggs. LAST CALL copyright © 2009 by Jim Butcher. DEATH WARMED OVER copyright © 2009 by Rachel Caine. VEGAS ODDS copyright © 2009 by Karen Chance. HECATE'S GOLDEN EYE copyright © 2009 by P. N. Elrod. BACON copyright © 2009 by Charlaine Harris. SIGNATURES OF THE DEAD copyright © 2009 by Faith Hunter. GINGER copyright © 2009 by Caitlin Kittredge. DARK SINS copyright © 2009 by Jenna Maclaine. All rights reserved. Printed in the United States of America. For information, address St. Martin's Press, 175 Fifth Avenue, New York, N.Y. 10010.

www.stmartins.com

Library of Congress Cataloging-in-Publication Data

Strange brew / Jim Butcher . . . [et al.]. — 1st ed.
p. cm.
ISBN-13: 978-0-312-38336-7
ISBN-10: 0-312-38336-3
1. Occult fiction, American. I. Butcher, Jim, 1971–
PS648.O33S77 2009
813'.0876608—dc22

2009007370

First Edition: July 2009

10 9 8 7 6 5 4 3 2 1

# Contents

# Strange Brew

# Seeing Eye

Patricia Briggs

THE DOORBELL RANG.

That was the problem with her business. Too many people thought they could approach her at any time. Even oh-dark thirty, even though her hours were posted clearly on her door *and* on her Web site.

Of course, answering the door would be something to do other than sit in her study shivering in the dark. Not that her world was ever anything but dark. It was one of the reasons she hated bad dreams—she had no way of turning on the light. Bad dreams that held warnings of things to come were the worst.

The doorbell rang again.

She slept—or tried to sleep—the same hours as most people. Kept steady business hours, too. Something she had no trouble making clear to those morons who woke her up in the middle of the night. They came to see Glinda the Good Witch, but after midnight, they found the Wicked Witch of the West and left quaking in fear of flying monkeys.

Whoever waited at the door would have no reason to suspect how grateful she was for the interruption of her thoughts.

The doorbell began a steady throbbing beat, ring-long, ring-short, ring-short, ring-long, and she grew a lot less grateful. To heck with flying monkeys, *she* was going to turn whoever it was into a frog. She shoved her concealing glasses on her face and stomped out the hall to her front door. No matter that most of the good transmutation spells had been lost with the Coranda family in the seventeenth century—rude people needed to be turned into frogs. Or pigs.

She jerked open the door and slapped the offending hand on her doorbell. She even got out a "Stop that!" before the force of his spirit hit her like a physical blow. Her nose told her, belatedly, that he was sweaty as if he'd been jogging. Her other senses told her that he was something *other*.

Not that she'd expected him to be human. Unlike other witches, she didn't advertise, and thus seldom had mundane customers unless their needs disturbed her sleep and she set out one of her "find me" spells to speak to them—she knew when they were coming.

"Ms. Keller," he growled. "I need to speak to you." At least he'd quit ringing the bell.

She let her left eyebrow slide up her forehead until it would be visible above her glasses. "Polite people come between the hours of eight in the morning and seven at night," she informed him. Werewolf, she decided. If he really lost his temper, she might have trouble, but she thought he was desperate, not angry—though with a wolf, the two states could be interchanged with remarkable speed. "Rude people get sent on their way."

"Tomorrow morning might be too late," he said—and

then added the bit that kept her from slamming the door in his face: "Alan Choo gave me your address, said you were the only one he knew with enough moxie to defy them."

She should shut the door in his face—not even a werewolf could get through her portal if she didn't want him to. But . . . *them*. Her dream tonight and for the past weeks had been about *them*, about *him* again. Portents, her instincts had told her, not just nightmares. The time had come at last. No. She wasn't grateful to him at all.

"Did Alan tell you to say it in those words?"

"Yes, ma'am." His temper was still there, but restrained and under control. It hadn't been aimed at her anyway, she thought, only fury born of frustration and fear. She knew how that felt.

She centered herself and asked the questions he'd expect. "Who am I supposed to be defying?"

And he gave her the answer she expected in return. "Something called Samhain's Coven."

Moira took a tighter hold on the door. "I see."

It wasn't really a coven. No matter what the popular literature said, it had been a long time since a real coven had been possible. Covens had thirteen members, no member related to any other to the sixth generation. Each family amassed its own specialty spells, and a coven of thirteen benefited from all those differing magics. But after most of the witchblood families had been wiped out by fighting amongst themselves, covens became a thing of the past. What few families remained (and there weren't thirteen, not if you didn't count the Russians or the Chinese, who kept to their own ways) had a bone-deep antipathy for the other survivors.

Kouros changed the rules to suit the new times. His coven

had between ten and thirteen members. . . . He had a distressing tendency to burn out his followers. The current bunch descended from only three families that she knew of, and most of them weren't properly trained—children following their leader.

Samhain wasn't up to the tricks of the old covens, but they were scary enough even the local vampires walked softly around them, and Seattle, with its overcast skies, had a relatively large seethe of vampires. Samhain's master had approached Moira about joining them when she was thirteen. She'd refused and made her refusal stick at some cost to all the parties involved.

"What does Samhain have to do with a werewolf?" she asked.

"I think they have my brother."

"Another werewolf?" It wasn't unheard of for brothers to be werewolves, especially since the Marrok, He-Who-Ruled-the-Wolves, began Changing people with more care than had been the usual custom. But it wasn't at all common either. Surviving the Change—even with the safeguards the Marrok could manage—was still, she understood, nowhere near a certainty.

"No." He took a deep breath. "Not a werewolf. Human. He has the *sight*. Choo says he thinks that's why they took him."

"Your brother is a witch?"

The fabric of his shirt rustled with his shrug, telling her that he wasn't as tall as he felt to her. Only a little above average instead of a seven-foot giant. Good to know.

"I don't know enough about witches to know," he said. "Jon gets hunches. Takes a walk just at the right time to find five dollars someone dropped, picks the right lottery number to win ten bucks. That kind of thing. Nothing big, nothing anyone would have noticed if my grandma hadn't had it stronger."

The *sight* was one of those general terms that told Moira precisely nothing. It could mean anything from a little fae blood in the family tree or full-blown witchblood. His brother's lack of power wouldn't mean he wasn't a witch—the magic sang weaker in the men. But fae or witchblood, Alan Choo had been right about it being something that would attract Samhain's attention. She rubbed her cheekbone even though she knew the ache was a phantom pain touch wouldn't alter.

Samhain. Did she have a choice? In her dreams, she died.

She could feel the intensity of the wolf's regard, strengthening as her silence continued. Then he told her the final straw that broke her resistance. "Jon's a cop—undercover—so I doubt your coven knows it. If his body turns up, though, there will be an investigation. I'll see to it that the witchcraft angle gets explored thoroughly. They might listen to a werewolf who tells them that witches might be a little more than turbaned fortune-tellers."

Blackmail galled him, she could tell—but he wasn't bluffing. He must love his brother.

She had only a touch of empathy, and it came and went. It seemed to be pretty focused on this werewolf tonight, though.

If she didn't help him, his brother would die at Samhain's hands, and his blood would be on her as well. If it cost her death, as her dreams warned her, perhaps that was justice served.

"Come in," Moira said, hearing the grudge in her voice.

He'd think it was her reaction to the threat—and the police poking about the coven would end badly for all concerned.

But it wasn't his threat that moved her. She took care of the people in her neighborhood; that was her job. The police she saw as brothers-in-arms. If she could help one, it was her duty to do so. Even if it meant her life for his.

"You'll have to wait until I get my coffee," she told him, and her mother's ghost forced the next bit of politeness out of her. "Would you like a cup?"

"No. There's no time."

He said that as if he had some idea about it—maybe the *sight* hadn't passed him by either.

"We have until tomorrow night if Samhain has him." She turned on her heel and left him to follow her or not, saying over her shoulder, "Unless they took him because he saw something. In which case, he probably is already dead. Either way, there's time for coffee."

He closed the door with deliberate softness and followed her. "Tomorrow's Halloween. Samhain."

"Kouros isn't Wiccan, any more than he is Greek, but he apes both for his followers," she told him as she continued deeper into her apartment. She remembered to turn on the hall light—not that he'd need it, being a wolf. It just seemed courteous: allies should show each other courtesy. "Like a magician playing sleight of hand, he pulls upon myth, religion, and anything else he can to keep them in thrall. Samhain—the time, not the coven—has power for the fae, for Wicca, for witches. Kouros uses it to cement his own, and killing someone with a bit of power generates more strength than killing a stray dog—and bothers him about as much."

"Kouros?" He said it as if it solved some puzzle, but it must not have been important, because he continued with no more than a breath of pause. "I thought witches were all women." He followed her into the kitchen and stood too close behind her. If he were to attack, she wouldn't have time to ready a spell.

But he wouldn't attack; her death wouldn't come at his hands tonight.

The kitchen lights were where she remembered them, and she had to take it on faith that she was turning them on and not off. She could never remember which way the switch worked. He didn't say anything, so she must have been right.

She always left her coffeepot primed for mornings, so all she had to do was push the button and it began gurgling in promise of coffee soon.

"Um," she said, remembering he'd asked her a question. His closeness distracted her—and not for the reasons it should. "Women tend to be more powerful witches, but you can make up for lack of talent with enough death and pain. Someone else's, of course, if you're a black practitioner like Kouros."

"What are you?" he asked, sniffing at her. His breath tickled the back of her neck—wolves, she'd noticed before, had a somewhat different idea of personal space than she did.

Her machine began dribbling coffee out into the carafe at last, giving her an excuse to step away. "Didn't Alan tell you? I'm a witch."

He followed; his nose touched her where his breath had sensitized her flesh, and she probably had goose bumps on her toes from the zing he sent through her. "My pack has a witch we pay to clean up messes. You don't smell like a witch."

He probably didn't mean anything by it; he was just being a wolf. She stepped out of his reach in the pretense of getting a coffee cup, or rather he allowed her to escape.

Alan was right: She needed to get out more. She hadn't so much as dated in . . . well, a long time. The last man's reaction to seeing what she'd done to herself was something she didn't want to repeat.

This man smelled good, even with the scent of his sweat teasing her nose. He felt strong and warm, promising to be the strength and safety she'd never had outside of her own two hands. Dominant wolves took care of their pack—doubtless something she'd picked up on. And then there was the possibility of death hovering over her.

Whatever the ultimate cause, his nearness and the light touch of breath on her skin sparked her interest in a way she knew he'd have picked up on. You can't hide sexual interest from something that can trail a hummingbird on the wing. Neither of them needed the complication of sex interfering in urgent business, even assuming he'd be willing.

"Witchcraft gains power from death and pain. From sacrifice and sacrificing," she told him coolly, pouring coffee in two mugs with steady hands. She was an expert in sacrifice. Not sleeping with a strange werewolf who showed up on her doorstep didn't even register in her scale.

She drank coffee black, so that was how she fixed it, holding the second cup out to him. "Evil leaves a psychic stench behind. Maybe a wolf nose can pick up on it. I don't know, not being a werewolf, myself. There's milk in the fridge and sugar in the cupboard in front of you if you'd like."

She wasn't at all what Tom had expected. Their pack's hired witch was a motherly woman of indeterminate years who wore swami robes in bright hues and smelled strongly of patchouli and old blood that didn't quite mask something bitter and dark. When he'd played Jon's message for her, she'd hung up the phone and refused to answer it again.

By the time he'd driven to her house, it was shut up and locked with no one inside. That was his first clue that this Samhain's Coven might be even more of a problem than he'd thought, and his worry had risen to fever pitch. He'd gone down to the underpass where his brother had been living and used his nose through the parks and other places his brother drifted through. But wherever they were holding Jon (and he refused to believe Jon was dead), it wasn't anywhere near where they kidnaped him.

His Alpha didn't like pack members concerning themselves with matters outside of the pack ("Your only family is your pack, son"). Tom didn't even bother contacting him. He'd gone to Choo instead. The Emerald City Pack's only submissive wolf, Alan worked as an herbalist and knew almost everyone in the supernatural world of Seattle. When he told Alan about the message Jon had left on his phone, Alan had written this woman's name and address and handed it to him. He'd have thought it was a joke, but Alan had better taste than that. So Tom had gone looking for a witch named Wendy—Wendy Moira Keller.

At his first look, he'd been disappointed. Wendy the witch was five foot nothing with rich curves in all the right places and feathery black hair that must have been dyed, because only black Labs and cats are that black. The stupid wraparound mirrored glasses kept him from guessing her age exactly, but he'd bet she wasn't yet thirty. No woman over thirty would be caught dead in those glasses. The cop in him wondered if she was covering up bruises—but he didn't smell a male in the living-scents in the house.

She wore a gray T-shirt without a bra, and black pajama pants with white skull-and-crossbones wearing red bows. But despite all that, he saw no piercings or tattoos—like she'd approached mall Goth culture, but only so far. She smelled of fresh flowers and mint. Her apartment was decorated with a minimum of furniture and a mishmash of colors that didn't quite fit together.

He didn't scare her.

Tom scared everyone—and he had even before their pack had a run-in with a bunch of fae a few years ago. His face had gotten cut up pretty badly with some sort of magical knife and hadn't healed right afterwards. The scars made him look almost as dangerous as he was. People walked warily around him.

Not only wasn't she scared, but she didn't even bother to hide her irritation at being woken up. He stalked her, and all she'd felt was a flash of sexual awareness that came and went so swiftly, he might have missed it if he'd been younger.

Either she was stupid or she was powerful. Since Alan had sent him here, Tom was betting on powerful. He hoped she was powerful.

He didn't want the coffee, but he took it when she handed to him. It was black and stronger that he usually drank it, but it tasted good. "So why don't you smell like other witches?"

"Like Kouros, I'm not Wiccan," she told him, "but 'and it harm none' seems like a good way to live to me."

White witch.

He knew that Wiccans consider themselves witches—and some of them had enough witchblood to make it so. But witches, the real thing, weren't witches because of what they believed, but because of genetic heritage. A witch was born a witch and studied to become a better one. But for witches, real power came from blood and death—mostly other people's blood and death.

White witches, especially those outside of Wicca (where numbers meant safety), were weak and valuable sacrifices for black witches, who didn't have their scruples. As Wendy the Witch had noted—witches seemed to have a real preference for killing their own.

He sipped at his coffee and asked, "So how have you managed without ending up as bits and pieces in someone else's cauldron?"

The witch snorted a laugh and set her coffee down abruptly. She grabbed a paper towel off its holder and held it to her face as she gasped and choked coffee, looking suddenly a lot less than thirty. When she was finished, she said, "That's awesome. Bits and pieces. I'll have to remember that."

Still grinning, she picked up the coffee again. He wished he could see her eyes, because he was pretty sure that whatever humor she'd felt was only surface deep.

"I tell you what," she said, "why don't you tell me who you are and what you know? That way I can tell you if I can help you or not."

"Fair enough," he said. The coffee was strong, and he could feel it and the four other cups he'd had since midnight settle in his bones with caffeine's untrustworthy gift of nervous energy.

"I'm Tom Franklin and I'm second in the Emerald City Pack." She wasn't surprised by that. She'd known what he was as soon as she opened her door. "My brother Jon is a cop and a damn fine one. He's been on the Seattle PD for nearly twenty years, and for the last six months he's been undercover as a street person. He was sent as part of a drug task force: there's been some nasty garbage out on the street lately, and he's been looking for it."

Wendy Moira Keller leaned back against the cabinets with a sigh. "I'd like to say that no witch would mess with drugs. Not from moral principles, mind you. Witches, for the most part, don't have moral principles. But drugs are too likely to attract unwanted attention. We never have been so deep in secrecy as you wolves like to be, not when witches sometimes crop up in mundane families—we need to be part of society enough that they can find us. Mostly people think we're a bunch of harmless charlatans—trafficking in drugs would change all that for the worse. But the Samhain bunch is powerful enough that no one wants to face them—and Kouros is arrogant and crazy. He likes money, and there is at least one herbalist among his followers who could manufacture some really odd stuff."

He shrugged. "I don't know. I'm interested in finding my brother, not in finding out if witches are selling drugs. It sounded to me like the drugs had nothing to do with my brother's kidnapping. Let me play Jon's call, and you make the determination." He pulled out his cell phone and played the message for her.

It had come from a pay phone. There weren't many of those left, now that cell phones had made it less profitable for the phone companies to keep repairing the damage of vandals. But there was no mistaking the characteristic static and hiss as his brother talked very quietly into the mouthpiece.

Tom had called in favors and found the phone Jon used, but the people who took his brother were impossible to pick out from the scents of the hundreds of people who had been there since the last rain—and his brother's scent stopped right at the pay phone, outside a battered convenience store. Stopped as if they'd teleported him to another planet—or, more prosaically, thrown him in a car.

Jon's voice—smoker-dark, though he'd never touched tobacco or any of its relatives—slid through the apartment: "Look, Tom. My gut told me to call you tonight—and I listen to my gut. I've been hearing something on the street about a freaky group calling themselves Samhain—" He spelled it, to be sure Tom got it right. "Last few days I've had a couple of people following me that might be part of Samhain. No one wants to talk about 'em much. The streets are afraid of these . . ."

He didn't know if the witch could hear the rest. He'd been a wolf for twenty years and more, so his judgment about what human senses were good for was pretty much gone.

*He* could hear the girl's sweet voice clearly, though. "Lucky Jon?" she asked. "Lucky Jon, who are you calling? Let's hang it up, now." A pause, then the girl spoke into the phone. "Hello?" Another pause. "It's an answering machine, I think. No worries."

At the same time, a male, probably young, was saying in a rapid, rabid flow of sound, "I feel it. . . . Doncha feel it? I feel it in him. This is the one. He'll do for Kouros." Then there was a soft click as the call ended.

The last fifty times he'd heard the recording, he couldn't make out the last word. But with the information the witch had given him, he understood it just fine this time.

Tom looked at Choo's witch, but he couldn't tell what she thought. Somewhere she'd learned to discipline her emotions, so he could smell only the strong ones—like the flash of desire she'd felt as he sniffed the back of her neck. Even in this situation, it had been enough to raise a thread of interest. Maybe after they got his brother back, they could do something about that interest. In the meantime . . .

"How much of the last did you hear, Wendy?" he asked.

"Don't call me Wendy," she snapped. "It's Moira. No one called me Wendy except my mom, and she's been dead a long time."

"Fine," he snapped back before he could control himself. He was tired and worried, but he could do better than that. He tightened his control and softened his voice. "Did you hear the guy? The one who said that he felt *it* in him—meaning my brother, I think. And that he would do for Kouros?"

"No. Or at least not well enough to catch his words. But I know the woman's voice. You're right: It was Samhain." Though he couldn't feel anything from her, her knuckles were white on the coffee cup.

"You need a Finder, and I can't do that anymore. Wait—" She held up a hand before he could say anything. "—I'm not saying I won't help you, just that it could be a lot simpler. Kouros moves all the time. Did you trace the call? It sounded like a pay phone to me."

"I found the phone booth he called from, but I couldn't find anything except that he'd been there." He tapped his nose, then glanced at her dark glasses and said, "I could smell him there and backtrail him, but I couldn't trail him out. They transported him somehow."

"They don't know that he's a cop, or that his brother is a werewolf."

"He doesn't carry ID with him while he's undercover. I don't see how anyone would know I was his brother. Unless he told them, and he wouldn't."

"Good," she said. "They won't expect you. That'll help."

"So do you know a Finder I can go to?"

She shook her head. "Not one who will help you against Samhain. Anyone, *anyone* who makes a move against them is punished in some rather spectacular ways." He saw her consider sharing one or two of them with him and discard it. She didn't want him scared off. Not that he could be, not with Jon's life at stake. But it was interesting that she hadn't tried.

"If you take me to where they stole him, maybe I can find something they left behind, something to use to find them."

Tom frowned at her. She didn't know his brother, he hadn't mentioned money, and he was getting the feeling that she couldn't care less if he called in the authorities. "So if Samhain is so all-powerful, how come you, a white witch, are willing to buck them?"

"You're a cop, too, aren't you?" She finished her coffee, but if she was waiting for a reaction, she wasn't going to get one. He'd seen the "all-knowing" witch act before. Her lips turned up as she set the empty cup on the counter. "It's not magic. Cops are easy to spot—suspicious is your middle name. Fair enough."

She pulled off her glasses, and he saw that he'd been wrong. He'd been pretty sure she was blind—the other reason women wore wraparound sunglasses at night. And she was. But that wasn't why she wore the sunglasses.

Her left eye was Swamp Thing–green without pupil or white. Her right eye was gone, and it looked as though it had been removed by someone who wasn't too good with a knife. It was horrible—and he'd seen some horrible things.

"Sacrifice is good for power," she said again. "But it works best if you can manage to make the sacrifice your own."

Jesus. She'd done it to herself.

She might not be able to see him, but she read his reaction just fine. She smiled tightly. "There were some extenuating circumstances," she continued. "You aren't going to see witches cutting off their fingers to power their spells—it doesn't work that way. But this worked for me." She tapped the scar tissue around her right eye. "Kouros did the other one first. That's why I'm willing to take them on. I've done it before and survived—and I still owe them a few." She replaced her sunglasses, and he watched her relax as they settled into place.

TOM FRANKLIN HADN'T brought a car, and for obvious reasons, *she* didn't drive. He said the phone was only a couple of miles from her apartment, and neither wanted to wait around for a cab. So they walked. She felt his start of surprise when she tucked her arm in his, but he didn't object. At least he didn't jump away from her and say "ick," like the last person who'd seen what she'd done to herself.

"You'll have to tell me when we come to curbs or if there's something in the way," she told him. "Or you can amuse yourself when I fall on my face. I can find my way around my apartment, but out here I'm at your mercy."

He said, with sober humor, "I imagine watching you trip over a few curbs would be a good way to get you to help Jon. Why don't you get a guide dog?"

"Small apartments aren't a good place for big dogs," she told him. "It's not fair to the dog."

They walked a few blocks in silence, the rain drizzling unhappily down the back of her neck and soaking the bottoms of the jeans she'd put on before they started out. Seattle was living up to its reputation. He guided her as if he'd done it before, unobtrusively but clearly, as if they were waltzing instead of walking down the street. She relaxed and walked faster.

"Wendy." He broke the companionable silence with the voice of One Who Suddenly Comprehends. "It's worse than I thought. I was stuck on Casper the Friendly Ghost and Wendy the Good Little Witch. But Wendy Moira . . . I bet it's Wendy Moira Angela, isn't it?"

She gave him a mock scowl. "I don't have a kiss for you, and I can't fly—not even with fairy dust. And I *hate Peter Pan*, the play, and all the movies."

His arm moved, and she could tell he was laughing to himself. "I bet."

"It could be worse, Toto," she told him. "I could belong to the Emerald City Pack."

He laughed out loud at that, a softer sound than she'd expected, given the rough grumble of his voice. "You know, I've never thought of it that way. It seemed logical, Seattle being the Emerald City."

She might have said something, but he suddenly picked up his pace like a hunting dog spotting his prey. She kept her hand tight on his arm and did her best to keep up. He stopped at last. "Here."

She felt his tension, the desire for action of some sort. Hopefully she'd be able to provide him the opportunity. She released his arm and stepped to the side.

"All right," she told him, falling into the comfortable patter she adopted with most of her clients—erasing the odd intimacy that had sprung up between them. "I know the girl on your brother's phone—her name used to be Molly, but I think she goes by something like Spearmint or Peppermint, somethingmint. I'm going to call for things that belong to her—a hair, a cigarette—anything will do. You'll have to do the looking. Whatever it is will glow, but it might be very small, easy to overlook."

"What if I don't see anything?"

"Then they didn't leave anything behind, and I'll figure out something else to try."

She set aside her worries, shedding them like a duck would shed the cool Seattle rain. Closing her senses to the outside world, she reached into her well of power and drew out a bucketful and threw it out in a circle around her as she called to the essence that was Molly. She hadn't done this spell since she could see out of both eyes—but there was no reason she couldn't do it now. Once learned, spells came to her hand like trained spaniels, and this one was no exception.

"What do you see?" she asked. The vibration of power warmed her against the cold fall drizzle that began to fall. There was something here; she could feel it.

"Nothing," his voice told her he'd put a lot of hope into this working.

"There's something," she said, sensations crawling up her arms and over her shoulders. She held out her right hand, her left being otherwise occupied with the workings of her spell. "Touching me might help you see."

Warmth flooded her as his hand touched hers . . . and she could see the faint traces Molly had left behind. She froze.

"Moira?"

She couldn't see anything else. Just bright bits of pink light sparkling from the ground, giving her a little bit of an idea what the landscape looked like. She let go of his hand and the light disappeared, leaving her in darkness again.

"Did you see anything?" she asked, her voice hoarse. The oddity of seeing anything . . . She craved it too much, and it made her wary because she didn't know how it worked.

"No."

He wanted his brother and she wanted to see. Just for a moment. She held her hand out. "Touch me again."

. . . and the sparkles returned like glitter scattered in front of her. Small bits of skin and hair, too small for what she needed. But there was something. . . .

She followed the glittering trail, and as if it had been hidden, a small wad of something blazed like a bonfire.

"Is there a wall just to our right?" she asked.

"A building and an alley." His voice was tight, but she ignored it. She had other business first.

They'd waited for Tom's brother in the alley. Maybe Jon came to the pay phone here often.

She led Tom to the blaze and bent to pick it up: soft and sticky, gum. Better, she thought, better than she could have hoped. Saliva would make a stronger guide than hair or fingernails could. She released his hand reluctantly.

"What did you find?"

"Molly's gum." She allowed her magic to loosen the last spell and slide back to her, hissing as the power warmed her skin almost to the point of burning. The next spell would be easier, even if it might eventually need more power. Sympathetic magic—which used the connections between like things—was one of those affinities that ran through her father's bloodlines into her.

But before she tried any more magic, she needed to figure

out what Tom had done to her spell. How touching him allowed her to *see*.

SHE LOOKED UNEARTHLY. A violent wind he had not felt, not even when she'd fastened on to his hand with fierce strength, had blown her hair away from her face. The skin on her hands was reddened, as if she held them too close to a fire. He wanted to soothe them—but he firmly intended never to touch her again.

He had no idea what she'd done to him while she held on to him and made his body burn and tremble. He didn't like surprises, and she'd told him that he would have to look, not that she'd use him to *see*. He especially didn't like it that as long as she was touching him, he hadn't wanted her to let him go.

Witches gather more power from hurting those with magic, she'd said . . . more or less. People just like him—but it hadn't hurt, not that he'd noticed.

He wasn't afraid of her, not really. Witch or not, she was no match for him. Even in human form, he could break her human-fragile body in mere moments. But if she was using him . . .

"Why are you helping me?" he asked as he had earlier, but the question seemed more important now. He'd known what she was, but *witch* meant something different to him now. He knew enough about witches not to ask the obvious question, though—like what it was she'd done to him. Witches, in his experience, were secretive about their spells—like junkyard dogs are secretive about their bones.

She'd taken something from him by using him that way . . . broken the trust he'd felt building between them. He needed to reestablish what he could expect out of her. Needed to know exactly what she was getting him into, beyond rescuing his brother. Witches were not altruistic. "What do you want out of this? Revenge for your blindness?"

She watched him . . . appeared to watch him, anyway, as she considered his question. There hadn't been many people who could lie to Tom before he Changed—cops learn all about lying the first year on the job. Afterwards . . . he could smell a lie a mile away an hour before it was spoken.

"Andy Choo sent you," she said finally. "That's one. Your brother's a policeman, and an investigation into his death might be awkward. That's two. He takes risks to help people he doesn't know—it's only right someone return the favor. That's three."

They weren't lies, but they weren't everything either. Her face was very still, as if the magic she worked had changed her view of him, too.

Then she tilted her head sideways and said in a totally different voice, hesitant and raw. "Sins of the fathers."

Here was absolute truth. Obscure as hell, but truth. "Sins of the fathers?"

"Kouros's real name is Lin Keller, though he hasn't used it in twenty years or more."

"He's your father." And then he added two and two. "Your *father* is running Samhain's Coven?" Her father had ruined her eye and—Tom could read between the lines—caused her to ruin the other? Her own father?

She drew in a deep breath—and for a moment he was afraid she was going to cry or something. But a stray gust of air brought the scent of her to him, and he realized she was angry. It tasted like a werewolf's rage, wild and biting.

"I am not a part of it," she said, her voice a half octave lower than it had been. "I'm not bringing you to his lair so he can dine upon werewolf, too. I am here because some jerk made me feel sorry for him. I am here because I want both him and his brother out of my hair and safely out of the hands of my rat-bastard father so I won't have their deaths on my conscience, too."

Someone else might have been scared of her, she being a witch and all. Tom wanted to apologize—and he couldn't remember the last time that impulse had touched him. It was even more amazing because he wasn't at fault: she'd misunderstood him. Maybe she'd picked up on how appalled he was that her own father had maimed her—he hadn't been implying she was one of them.

He didn't apologize, though, or explain himself. People said things when they were mad that they wouldn't tell you otherwise.

"What was it you did to me?"

"Did to you?" Arctic ice might be warmer.

"When you were looking for the gum. It felt like you hit me with a bolt of lightning." He was damned if he'd tell her everything he felt.

Her right eyebrow peeked out above her sunglasses. Interest replaced coldness. "You felt like I was doing something to you?" And then she held out her left hand. "Take my hand."

He looked at it.

After a moment, she smiled. He didn't know she had a smile like that in her. Bright and cheerful and sudden. Knowing. As if she had gained every thought that passed through his head. Her anger, the misunderstanding between them was gone as if it had never been.

"I don't know what happened," she told him gently. "Let me try re-creating it, and maybe I can tell you."

He gave her his hand. Instead of taking it, she put only two fingers on his palm. She stepped closer to him, dropped her head so he could see her scalp gleaming pale underneath her dark hair. The magic that touched him this time was gentler, sparklers instead of fireworks—and she jerked her fingers away as if his hand were a hot potato.

"What the heck . . ." She rubbed her hands on her arms with nervous speed.

"What?"

"You weren't acting as my focus—I can tell you that much."

"So what was going on?"

She shook her head, clearly uncomfortable. "I think I was using you to *see*. I shouldn't be able to do that."

He found himself smiling grimly. "So I'm your Seeing Eye wolf?"

"I don't know."

He recognized her panic, having seen it in his own mirror upon occasion. It was always frightening when something you thought was firmly under control broke free to run where it would. With him, it was the wolf.

Something resettled in his gut. She hadn't done it on purpose; she wasn't using him.

"Is it harmful to me?"

She frowned. "Did it hurt?"

"No."

"Either time?"

"Neither time."

"Then it didn't harm you."

"All right," he said. "Where do we go from here?"

She opened her right hand, the one with the gum in it. "Not us. Me. This is going to show us where Molly is—and Molly will know where your brother is."

She closed her fingers, twisted her hand palm down, then turned herself in a slow circle. She hit a break in the pavement, and he grabbed her before she could do more than stumble. His hand touched her wrist, and she turned her hand to grab him as the kick of power flowed through his body once more.

"They're in a boat," she told him, and went limp in his arms.

SHE AWOKE WITH the familiar headache that usually accompanied the overuse of magic—and absolutely no idea where she was. It smelled wrong to be her apartment, but she was lying on a couch with a blanket covering her.

Panic rose in her chest—sometimes she hated being blind.

"Back in the land of the living?"

"Tom?"

He must have heard the distress in her voice, because when he spoke again, he was much closer and his voice was softer. "You're on a couch in my apartment. We were as close to mine as we were to yours, and I knew I could get us into my apartment. Yours is probably sealed with hocus-pocus. Are you all right?"

She sat up and put her feet on the floor, and her erstwhile bed indeed proved itself to be a couch. "Do you have something with sugar in it? Sweet tea or fruit juice?"

"Hot cocoa or tea," he told her.

"Tea."

He must have had water already heated, because he was quickly back with a cup. She drank the sweet stuff down as fast as she could, and the warmth did as much as the sugar to clear her headache.

"Sorry," she said.

"For what, exactly?" he said.

"For using you. I think you don't have any barriers," she told him slowly. "We all have safeguards, walls that keep out intruders. It's what keeps us safe."

In his silence, she heard him consider that.

"So, I'm vulnerable to witches?"

She didn't know what to do with her empty cup, so she set it on the couch beside her. Then she used her left hand, her seeking hand, to *look* at him again.

"No, I don't think so. Your barriers seem solid . . . even stronger than usual, as I'd expect from a wolf as far up the command structure as you are. I think you are vulnerable only to me."

"Which means?"

"Which means when I touch you, I can see magic through your eyes . . . with practice, I might even be able just to see. It means that you can feed my magic with your skin." She swallowed. "You're not going to like this."

"Tell me."

"You are acting like my familiar." She couldn't feel a thing from him. "If I had a familiar."

Floorboards creaked under his feet as his weight shifted. His shoulder brushed her as he picked up the empty cup. She heard him walk away from her and set the cup on a hard surface. "Do you need more tea?"

"No," she said, needing suddenly to be home, somewhere she wasn't so dependent upon him. "I'm fine. If you would call me a taxi, I'd appreciate it." She stood up, too. Then realized she had no idea where the door was or what obstacles might be hiding on the floor. In her own apartment, redolent with her magic, she was never so helpless.

"Can you find my brother?"

She hadn't heard him move, not a creak, not a breath, but his voice told her he was no more than a few inches from her. Disoriented and vulnerable, she was afraid of him for the first time.

He took a big step away from her. "I'm not going to hurt you."

"Sorry," she told him. "You startled me. Do we still have the gum?"

"Yes. You said she was on a boat."

She'd forgotten, but as soon as he said it, she could picture the boat in her head. That hadn't been the way the spell was supposed to work. It was more of a "hot and cold" spell, but she could still see the boat in her mind's eye.

Nothing had really changed, except that she'd used someone without asking. There was still a policeman to be saved and her father to kill.

"If we still have the gum, I can find Molly—the girl on your brother's phone call."

"I have a buddy whose boat we can borrow."

"All right," she told him after a moment. "Do you have some aspirin?"

SHE HATED BOATING. The rocking motion disrupted her sense of direction, the engine's roar obscured softer sounds, and the scent of the ocean covered the subtler scents she used to negotiate everyday life. Worse than all of that, though, was the thought of trying to swim without knowing where she was going. The damp air chilled her already cold skin.

"Which direction?" said Tom over the sound of the engine.

His presence shouldn't have made her feel better—werewolves couldn't swim at all—but it did. She pointed with the hand that held the gum. "Not far now," she warned him.

"There's a private dock about a half mile up the coast. Looks like it's been here awhile," he told her. "There's a boat—*The Tern*, the bird."

It felt right. "I think that must be it."

There were other boats on the water; she could hear them. "What time is it?"

"About ten in the morning. We're passing the boat right now."

Molly's traces, left on the gum, pulled toward their source, tugging Moira's hand toward the back of the boat. "That's it."

"There's a park with docks about a mile back," he said, and the boat tilted to the side. "We'll go tie up there and come back on foot."

But when he'd tied the boat up, he changed his mind. "Why don't you stay here and let me check this out?"

Moira rubbed her hands together. It bothered her to have her magic doing something it wasn't supposed to be doing, and she'd let it throw her off her game: time to collect herself. She gave him a sultry smile. "Poor blind girl," she said. "Must be kept out of danger, do you think?" She turned a hand palm up and heard the whoosh of flame as it caught fire. "You'll need me when you find Molly—you may be a werewolf, but she's a witch who looks like a pretty young thing." She snuffed the flame and dusted off her hands. "Besides, she's afraid of me. She'll tell me where your brother is."

She didn't let him know how grateful she was for the help he gave her exiting the boat. When this night was over, he'd go back to his life and she to hers. If she wanted to keep him—she knew he wouldn't want to be kept by her. She was a witch, and ugly with scars of the past.

Besides, if her dreams were right, she wouldn't survive to see nightfall.

SHE THREADED THROUGH the dense underbrush as if she could see every hanging branch, one hand on his back and her other held out in front of her. He wondered if she was using magic to see.

She wasn't using him. Her hand in the middle of his back was warm and light, but his flannel shirt was between it and skin. Probably she was reading his body language and using her upraised hand as an insurance policy against low-hanging branches.

They followed a half-overgrown path that had been trod out a hundred feet or so from the coast, which was obscured by ferns and underbrush. He kept his ears tuned so he'd know it if they started heading away from the ocean.

*The Tern* had been moored in a small natural harbor on a battered dock next to the remains of a boathouse. A private property rather than the public dock he'd used.

They'd traveled north and were somewhere not too far from Everett, by his reckoning. He wasn't terribly surprised when their path ended in a brand-new eight-foot chain-link fence. Someone had a real estate gold mine on their hands, and they were waiting to sell it to some developer when the price was right. Until then, they'd try to keep out the riffraff.

He helped Moira over the fence, mostly a matter of whispering a few directions until she found the top of it. He waited until she was over and then vaulted over himself.

The path they'd been following continued on, though not nearly so well traveled as it had been before the fence. A quarter mile of blackberry brambles ended abruptly in thigh-deep damp grasslands that might once have been a lawn. He stopped before they left the cover of the bushes, sinking down to rest on his heels.

"There's a burnt-out house here," he told Moira, who had ducked down when he did. "It must have burned down a couple of years ago, because I don't smell it."

"Hidden," she commented.

"Someone's had tents up here," he told her. "And I see the remnants of a campfire."

"Can you see the boat from here?"

"No, but there's a path I think should lead down to the water. I think this is the place."

She pulled her hand away from his arm. "Can you go check it out without being seen?"

"It would be easier if I do it as a wolf," Tom admitted. "But I don't dare. We might have to make a quick getaway, and it'll be a while before I can shift back to human." He hoped Jon would be healthy enough to pilot in an emergency—but he didn't like to make plans that depended upon an unknown. Moira wasn't going to be piloting a boat anywhere.

"Wait," she told him. She murmured a few words and then put her cold fingers against his throat. A sudden shock, like a static charge on steroids, hit him—and when it was over, her fingers were hot on his pulse. "You aren't invisible, but it'll make people want to overlook you."

He pulled out his HK and checked the magazine before sliding it back in. The big gun fit his hand like a glove. He believed in using weapons: guns or fangs, whatever got the job done.

"It won't take me long."

"If you don't go, you'll never get back," she told him, and gave him a gentle push. "I can take care of myself."

It didn't sit right with him, leaving her alone in the territory of his enemies, but common sense said he'd have a better chance of roaming unseen. And no one tackled a witch lightly—not even other witches.

Spell or no, he slid through the wet overgrown trees like a shadow, crouching to minimize his silhouette and avoiding anything likely to crunch. One thing living in Seattle did was minimize the stuff that would crunch under your foot—all the leaves were wet and moldy without a noise to be had.

The boat was there, bobbing gently in the water. Empty. He closed his eyes and let the morning air tell him all it could.

His brother had been in the boat. There had been others, too—Tom memorized their scents. If anything happened to Jon, he'd track them down and kill them, one by one. Once he had them, he'd let his nose lead him to Jon.

He found blood where Jon had scraped against a tree, crushed plants where his brother had tried to get away and rolled around in the mud with another man. Or maybe he'd just been laying a trail for Tom. Jon knew Tom would come for him—that's what family did.

The path the kidnappers took paralleled the waterfront for a while and then headed inland, but not for the burnt-out house. Someone had found a better hideout. Nearly invisible under a shelter of trees, a small barn nestled snugly amidst broken pieces of corral fencing. Its silvered sides bore only a hint of red paint, but the aluminum roof, though covered with moss, was undamaged.

And his brother was there. He couldn't quite hear what Jon was saying, but he recognized his voice . . . and the slurring rapid rhythm of his schizophrenic-mimicry. If Jon was acting, he was all right. The relief of that settled in his spine and steadied his nerves.

All he needed to do was get his witch. . . . Movement caught his attention, and he dropped to the ground and froze, hidden by wet grass and weeds.

MOIRA WASN'T SURPRISED when they found her—ten in the morning isn't a good time to hide. It was one of the young ones—she could tell by the surprised squeal and the rapid thud of footsteps as he ran for help.

Of course, if she'd really been trying to hide, she might have managed it. But sometime after Tom left it had occurred to her that if she wanted to find Samhain, the easiest thing might be to let them find her. So she set about attracting their attention.

If they found her, it would unnerve them. They knew she worked alone. Her arrival here would puzzle them, but they wouldn't look for anyone else—leaving Tom as her secret weapon.

Magic called to magic, unless the witch took pains to hide

it, so any of them should have been able to feel the flames that danced over her hands. It had taken them longer than she expected. While she waited for the boy to return, she found a sharp-edged rock and put it in her pocket. She folded her legs and let the coolness of the damp earth flow through her.

She didn't hear him come, but she knew by his silence whom the young covenist had run to.

"Hello, Father," she told him, rising to her feet. "We have much to talk about."

SHE DIDN'T LOOK like a captive, Tom thought, watching Moira walk to the barn as if she'd been there before, though she might have been following the sullen-looking half-grown boy who clomped through the grass ahead of her. A tall man followed them both, his hungry eyes on Moira's back.

His wolf recognized another dominant male with a near-silent growl, while Tom thought that the man was too young to have a grown daughter. But there was no one else this could be but Lin Keller—that predator was not a man who followed anyone or allowed anyone around him who might challenge him. He'd seen an Alpha or two like that.

Tom watched them until they disappeared into the barn.

It hurt to imagine she might have betrayed him—as if there were some bond between them, though he hadn't known her a full day. Part of him would not believe it. He remembered her real indignation when she thought he believed she was part of Samhain, and it comforted him.

It didn't matter, couldn't matter. Not yet. Saving Jon mattered, and the rest would wait. His witch was captured or had betrayed him. Either way, it was time to let the wolf free.

The change hurt, but experience meant he made no sound

as his bones rearranged themselves and his muscles stretched and slithered to adjust to his new shape. It took fifteen minutes of agony before he rose on four paws, a snarl fixed on his muzzle—ready to kill someone. Anyone.

Instead he stalked like a ghost to the barn where his witch waited. He rejected the door they'd used, but prowled around the side, where four stall doors awaited. Two of them were broken with missing boards; one of the openings was big enough for him to slide through.

The interior of the barn was dark, and the stall's half walls blocked his view of the main section, where his quarry waited. Jon was still going strong, a wild ranting conversation with no one about the Old Testament, complete with quotes. Tom knew a lot of them himself.

"Killing things again, Father?" said Moira's cool disapproving voice, cutting though Jon's soliloquy.

And suddenly Tom could breathe again. They'd found her somehow, Samhain's Coven had, but she wasn't one of them.

"So judgmental." Tom had expected something . . . bigger from the man's voice. His own Alpha, for instance, could have made a living as a televangelist with his raw fire-and-brimstone voice. This man sounded like an accountant.

"Kill her. You have to kill her before she destroys us—I have seen it." It was Molly, the girl from Jon's message.

"You couldn't see your way out of a paper bag, Molly," said Moira. "Not that you're wrong, of course."

There were other people in the barn, Tom could smell them, but they stayed quiet.

"You aren't going to kill me," said Kouros. "If you could have done that, you'd have done it before now. Which brings me to my point: Why are you here?"

"To stop you from killing this man," Moira told him.

"I've killed men before—and you haven't stopped me. What is so special about this one?"

MOIRA FELT THE burden of all those deaths upon her shoulders. He was right. She could have killed him before—before he'd killed anyone else.

"This one has a brother," she said.

She felt Tom's presence in the barn, but her look-past-me spell must still have been working, because no one seemed to notice the werewolf. And any witch with a modicum of sensitivity to auras would have felt him. His brother was a faint trace to her left—something his constant stream of words made far more clear than her magic was able to.

Her father she could follow only from his voice.

There were other people in the structure—she hadn't quite decided what the cavernous building was: probably a barn, given the dirt floor and faint odor of cow—but she couldn't pinpoint them either. She knew where Molly was, though. And Molly was the important one, Kouros's right hand.

"Someone *paid* you to go up against me?" Her father's voice was faintly incredulous. "Against us?"

Then he did something, made some gesture. She wouldn't have known except for Molly's sigh of relief. So she didn't feel too bad when she tied Molly's essence, through the gum she still held, into her shield.

When the coven's magic hit the shield, it was Molly who took the damage. Who died. Molly, her little sister, whose presence she could no longer feel.

Someone, a young man, screamed Molly's coven

name—Wintergreen. And there was a flurry of movement where Moira had last sensed her.

Moira dropped the now-useless bit of gum on the ground.

"Oh, you'll pay for that," breathed her father. "Pay in pain and power until there is nothing left of you."

Someone sent power her way, but it wasn't a concerted spell from the coven, and it slid off her protections without harm. Unlike the fist that struck her in the face, driving her glasses into her nose and knocking her to the ground—her father's fist. She'd recognize the weight of it anywhere.

Unsure of where her enemies were, she stayed where she was, listening. But she didn't hear Tom; he was just suddenly there. And the circle of growing terror that spread around him—of all the emotions possible, it was fear that she could sense most often—told her he was in his lupine form. It must have been impressive.

"Your victim has a brother," she told her father again, knowing he'd hear the smugness in her tone. "And you've made him very angry."

The beast beside her roared. Someone screamed. . . . Even witches are afraid of monsters.

The coven broke. Children most of them, they broke and ran. Molly's death followed by a beast out of their worst nightmares was more than they could face, partially trained, deliberately crippled fodder for her father that they were.

Tom growled, the sound finding a silent echo in her own chest as if he were a bass drum. He moved, a swift, silent predator, and someone who hadn't run died. Tom's brother, she noticed, had fallen entirely silent.

"A werewolf," breathed Kouros. "Oh, now there is a worthy

kill." She felt his terror and knew he'd attack Tom before he took care of her.

The werewolf came to her side, probably to protect her. She reached out with her left hand, intending to spread her own defenses to the wolf—though that would leave them too thin to be very effective—but she hadn't counted on the odd effect he had on her magic. On her.

Her father's spell—a vile thing that would have induced terrible pain and permanently damaged Tom had it hit—connected just after she touched the wolf. And for a moment, maybe a whole breath, nothing happened.

Then she felt every hair under her hand stand to attention, and Tom made an odd sound and power swept through her from him—all the magic Kouros had sent—and it filled her well to overflowing.

And she could see. For the first time since she'd been thirteen, she could see.

She stood up, shedding broken pieces of sunglasses to the ground. The wolf beside her was huge, chocolate-brown, and easily tall enough to leave her hand on his shoulder as she came to her feet. A silvery scar curled around his snarling muzzle. His eyes were yellow brown and cold. A sweeping glance showed her two dead bodies—one burnt, the other savaged—and a very dirty, hairy man tied to a post with his hands behind his back, who could only be Tom's brother Jon.

And her father, looking much younger than she remembered him. No wonder he went for teens to populate his *coven*—he was stealing their youth as well as their magic. A coven should be a meeting of equals, not a feeding trough for a single greedy witch.

She looked at him and saw that he was afraid. He should

be. He'd used all his magic to power his spell—he'd left himself defenseless. And now he was afraid of her.

Just as she had dreamed. She pulled the stone out of her pocket—and it seemed to her that she had all the time in the world to use it to cut her right hand open. Then she pointed it, her bloody hand of power at him.

"*By the blood we share,*" she whispered, and felt the magic gather.

"You'll die, too," Kouros said frantically, as if she didn't know.

"*Blood follows blood.*" Before she spoke the last word, she lifted her other hand from Tom's soft fur that none of this magic should fall to him. And as soon as she did so, she could no longer see. But she wouldn't be blind for long.

TOM STARTED MOVING before her fingers left him, knocking into her with his hip and spoiling her aim. Her magic flooded through him, hitting him instead of the one she'd aimed all that power at. The wolf let it sizzle through his bones and returned it to her, clean.

Pleasant as that was, he didn't let it distract him from his goal. He was moving so fast that the man was still looking at Moira when the wolf landed on him.

*Die,* he thought as he buried his fangs in Kouros's throat, drinking his blood and his death in one delicious mouthful of flesh. This one had moved against the wolf's family, against the wolf's witch. Satisfaction made the meat even sweeter.

"Tom?" Moira sounded lost.

"Tom's fine," answered his brother's rusty voice. He'd talked himself hoarse. "You just sit there until he calms down a little. You all right, lady?"

Tom lifted his head and looked at his witch. She was

huddled on the ground, looking small and lost, her scarred face bared for all the world to see. She looked fragile, but Tom knew better, and Jon would learn.

As the dead man under his claws had learned. Kouros died knowing she would have killed him.

Tom had been willing to give her that kill—but not if it meant her death. So Tom had the double satisfaction of saving her and killing the man. He went back to his meal.

"Tom, stop that," Jon said. "Ick. I know you aren't hungry. Stop it now."

"Is Kouros dead?" His witch sounded shaken up.

"As dead as anyone I've seen," said Jon. "Look, Tom. I appreciate the sentiment, I've wanted to do that any time this last day. But I'd like to get out of here before some of those kids decide to come back while I'm still tied up." He paused. "Your lady needs to get out of here."

Tom hesitated, but Jon was right. He wasn't hungry anymore, and it was time to take his family home.

Patricia Briggs is the author of the number one *New York Times* bestselling Mercedes Thompson series. She lives with seven horses, a dog, three cats, snakes, birds, kids, and a very awesome and tolerant husband in a home that resembles a zoo crossed with a library. The horses live outside.

# Last Call

## Jim Butcher

ALL I WANTED was a quiet beer.

That isn't too much to ask, is it—one contemplative drink at the end of a hard day of professional wizarding? Maybe a steak sandwich to go with it? You wouldn't think so. But somebody (or maybe Somebody) disagreed with me.

McAnnally's pub is a quiet little hole in the wall, like a hundred others in Chicago, in the basement of a large office building. You have to go down a few stairs to get to the door. When you come inside, you're at eye level with the creaky old ceiling fans in the rest of the place, and you have to take a couple of more steps down from the entryway to get to the pub's floor. It's lit mostly by candles. The finish work is all hand-carved, richly polished wood, stained a deeper brown than most would use, and combined with the candles, it feels cozily cavelike.

I opened the door to the place and got hit in the face with something I'd *never* smelled in Mac's pub before—the odor of food being burned.

It should say something about Mac's cooking that my first instinct was to make sure the shield bracelet on my left arm was ready to go as I drew the blasting rod from inside my coat. I took careful steps forward into the pub, blasting rod held up and ready. The usual lighting was dimmed, and only a handful of candles still glimmered.

The regular crowd at Mac's, members of the supernatural community of Chicago, were strewn about like broken dolls. Half a dozen people lay on the floor, limbs sprawled oddly, as if they'd dropped unconscious in the middle of calisthenics. A pair of older guys who were always playing chess at a table in the corner both lay slumped across the table. Pieces were spread everywhere around them, some of them broken, and the old chess clock they used had been smashed to bits. Three young women who had watched too many episodes of *Charmed*, and who always showed up at Mac's together, were unconscious in a pile in the corner, as if they'd been huddled there in terror before they collapsed—but they were splattered with droplets of what looked like blood.

I could see several of the fallen breathing, at least. I waited for a long moment, but nothing jumped at me from the darkness, and I felt no sudden desire to start breaking things and then take a nap.

"Mac?" I called quietly.

Someone grunted.

I hurried over to the bar and found Mac on the floor beside it. He'd been badly beaten. His lips were split and puffy. His nose had been broken. Both his hands were swollen up and purple—defensive wounds, probably. The baseball bat he kept behind the bar was lying next to him, smeared with blood. Probably his own.

"Stars and stones," I breathed. "Mac."

I knelt down next to him, examining him for injuries as best I could. I didn't have any formal medical training, but several years' service in the Wardens in a war with the vampires of the Red Court had shown me more than my fair share of injuries. I didn't like the look of one of the bruises on his head, and he'd broken several fingers, but I didn't think it was anything he wouldn't recover from.

"What happened?" I asked him.

"Went nuts," he slurred. One of his cut lips reopened, and fresh blood appeared. "Violent."

I winced. "No kidding." I grabbed a clean cloth from the stack on the shelf behind the bar and ran cold water over it. I tried to clean some of the mess off his face. "They're all down," I told him as I did. "Alive. It's your place. How do you want to play it?"

Even through as much pain as he was in, Mac took a moment to consider before answering. "Murphy," he said finally.

I'd figured. Calling in the authorities would mean a lot of questions and attention, but it also meant that everyone would get medical treatment sooner. Mac tended to put the customer first. But if he'd wanted to keep it under the radar, I would have understood that, too.

"I'll make the call," I told him.

THE AUTHORITIES SWOOPED down on the place with vigor. It was early in the evening, and we were evidently the first customers for the night shift EMTs.

"Jesus," Sergeant Karrin Murphy said from the doorway, looking around the interior of Mac's place. "What a mess."

"Tell me about it," I said glumly. My stomach was rumbling, and I was thirsty besides, but it just didn't seem right to help myself to any of Mac's stuff while he was busy getting patched up by the ambulance guys.

Murphy blew out a breath. "Well. Brawls in bars aren't exactly uncommon." She came down into the room, removed a flashlight from her jacket pocket, and shone it around. "But maybe you'll tell me what really happened."

"Mac said that his customers went nuts. They started acting erratic and then became violent."

"What, all of them? At the same time?"

"That was the impression he gave me. He wasn't overly coherent."

Murphy frowned and slowly paced the room, sweeping the light back and forth methodically. "You get a look at the customers?"

"There wasn't anything actively affecting them when I got here," I said. "I'm sure of that. They were all unconscious. Minor wounds, looked like they were mostly self-inflicted. I think those girls were the ones to beat Mac."

Murphy winced. "You think he wouldn't defend himself against them?"

"He could have pulled a gun. Instead, he had his bat out. He was probably trying to stop someone from doing something stupid, and it went bad."

"You know what I'm thinking?" Murphy asked. "When something odd happens to everyone in a pub?"

She had stopped at the back corner. Among the remnants of broken chessmen and scattered chairs, the circle of illumination cast by her flashlight had come to rest on a pair of dark brown beer bottles.

"Ugly thought," I said. "Mac's beer, in the service of darkness."

She gave me a level look. Well. As level a look as you *can* give when you're a five-foot blonde with a perky nose, glaring at a gangly wizard most of seven feet tall. "I'm serious, Harry. Could it have been something in the beer? Drugs? A poison? Something from your end of things?"

I leaned on the bar and chewed that thought over for a moment. Oh, sure, technically it could have been any of those. A number of drugs could cause psychotic behavior, though admittedly it might be hard to get that reaction in everyone in the bar at more or less the same time. Poisons were just drugs that happened to kill you, or the reverse. And if those people had been poisoned, they might still be in a lot of danger.

And once you got the magical side of things, any one of a dozen methods could have been used to get to the people through the beer they'd imbibed—but all of them would require someone with access to the beer to pull it off, and Mac made his own brew.

In fact, he bottled it himself.

"It wasn't necessarily the beer," I said.

"You think they all got the same steak sandwich? The same batch of curly fries?" She shook her head. "Come on, Dresden. The food here is good, but that isn't what gets them in the door."

"Mac wouldn't hurt anybody," I said quietly.

"Really?" Murph asked, her voice quiet and steady. "You're sure about that? How well do you really know the man?"

I glanced around the bar, slowly.

"What's his first name, Harry?"

"Dammit, Murph," I sighed. "You can't go around being suspicious of everyone all the time."

"Sure I can." She gave me a faint smile. "It's my job, Harry. I have to look at things dispassionately. It's nothing personal. You know that."

"Yeah," I muttered. "I know that. But I also know what it's like to be dispassionately suspected of something you didn't do. It sucks."

She held up her hands. "Then let's figure out what did happen. I'll go talk to the principals, see if anyone remembers anything. You take a look at the beer."

"Yeah," I said. "Okay."

AFTER BOTTLING IT, Mac transports his beer in wooden boxes like old apple crates, only more heavy-duty. They aren't magical or anything. They're just sturdy as hell, and they stack up neatly. I came through the door of my apartment with a box of samples and braced myself against the impact of Mister, my tomcat, who generally declares a suicide charge on my shins the minute I come through the door. Mister is huge, and most of it is muscle. I rocked at the impact, and the bottles rattled, but I took it in stride. Mouse, my big shaggy dogosaurus, was lying full on his side by the fireplace, napping. He looked up and thumped his tail on the ground once, then went back to sleep.

No work ethic around here at all. But then, he hadn't been cheated out of his well-earned beer. I took the box straight down the stepladder to my lab, calling, "Hi, Molly," as I went down.

My apprentice, Molly, sat at her little desk, working on a pair of potions. She had maybe five square feet of space to work with in my cluttered lab, but she managed to keep the potions clean and neat, and still had room left over for her Latin textbook, her notebook, and a can of Pepsi, the heathen. Molly's hair was kryptonite-green today, with silver tips, and she was wearing cutoff jeans and a tight blue T-shirt with a Superman logo on the front. She was a knockout.

"Hiya, Harry," she said absently.

"Outfit's a little cold for March, isn't it?"

"If it were, you'd be staring at my chest a lot harder," she said, smirking a little. She glanced up, and it bloomed into a full smile. "Hey, beer!"

"You're young and innocent," I said firmly, setting the box down on a shelf. "No beer for you."

"You're living in denial," she replied, and rose to pick up a bottle.

Of course she did. I'd told her not to. I watched her carefully.

The kid's my apprentice, but she's got a knack for the finer aspects of magic. She'd be in real trouble if she had to blast her way out of a situation, but when it comes to the cobweb-fine enchantments, she's a couple of lengths ahead of me and pulling away fast—and I figured that this had to be subtle work.

She frowned almost the second she touched the bottle. "That's . . . odd." She gave me a questioning look, and I gestured at the box. She ran her fingertips over each bottle in turn. "There's energy there. What is it, Harry?"

I had a good idea of what the beer had done to its drinkers—but it just didn't make sense. I wasn't about to tell her that, though. It would be very anti–Obi-Wan of me. "You tell me," I said, smiling slightly.

She narrowed her eyes at me and turned back to her potions, muttering over them for a few moments, and then easing them down to a low simmer. She came back to the bottles and opened one, sniffing at it and frowning some more.

"No taste-testing," I told her. "It isn't pretty."

"I wouldn't think so," she replied in the same tone she'd used while working on her Latin. "It's laced with . . . some kind of contagion focus, I think."

I nodded. She was talking about magical contagion, not the medical kind. A contagion focus was something that formed a link between a smaller amount of its mass after it had been separated from the main body. A practitioner could use it to send magic into the main body, and by extension into all the smaller foci, even if they weren't in the same physical place. It's sort of like planting a transmitter on someone's car so that you can send a missile at it later.

"Can you tell what kind of working it's been set up to support?" I asked her.

She frowned. She had a pretty frown. "Give me a minute."

"Tick tock," I said.

She waved a hand at me without looking up. I folded my arms and waited. I gave her tests like this one all the time—and there was always a time limit. In my experience, the solutions you need the most badly are always time-critical. I'm trying to train the grasshopper for the real world.

Here was one of her first real-world problems, but she didn't have to know that. So long as she thought it was just one more test, she'd tear into it without hesitation. I saw no reason to rattle her confidence.

She muttered to herself. She poured some of the beer out into the beaker and held it up to the light from a specially prepared candle. She scrawled power calculations on a notebook.

And twenty minutes later, she said, "Hah. Tricky, but not tricky enough."

"Oh?" I said.

"No need to be coy, boss," she said. "The contagion looks like a simple compulsion meant to make the victim drink more, but it's really a psychic conduit."

I leaned forward. "Seriously?"

Molly stared blankly at me for a moment. Then she blinked and said, "You didn't *know*?"

"I found the compulsion, but it was masking anything else that had been laid on the beer." I picked up the half-empty bottle and shook my head. "I brought it here because you've got a better touch for this kind of thing than I do. It would have taken me hours to puzzle it out. Good work."

"But . . . you didn't *tell* me this was for real." She shook her head dazedly. "Harry, what if I hadn't found it? What if I'd been wrong?"

"Don't get ahead of yourself, grasshopper," I said, turning for the stairs. "You *still* might be wrong."

THEY'D TAKEN MAC to Stroger, and he looked like hell. I had to lie to the nurse to get in to talk to him, flashing my consultant's ID badge and making like I was working with the Chicago cops on the case.

"Mac," I said, coming to sit down on the chair next to his bed. "How are you feeling?"

He looked at me with the eye that wasn't swollen shut.

"Yeah. They said you wouldn't accept any painkillers."

He moved his head in a slight nod.

I laid out what I'd found. "It was elegant work, Mac. More intricate than anything I've done."

His teeth made noise as they ground together. He understood what two complex interwoven enchantments meant as well as I did—a serious player was involved.

"Find him," Mac growled, the words slurred a little.

"Any idea where I could start?" I asked him.

He was quiet for a moment, then shook his head. "Caine?"

I lifted my eyebrows. "That thug from Night of the Living Brews? He's been around?"

He grunted. "Last night. Closing." He closed his eyes. "Loudmouth."

I stood up and put a hand on his shoulder. "Rest. I'll chat him up."

Mac exhaled slowly, maybe unconscious before I'd gotten done speaking.

I found Murphy down the hall.

"Three of them are awake," she said. "None of them remember anything for several hours before they presumably went to the bar."

I grimaced. "I was afraid of that." I told her what I'd learned.

"A psychic conduit?" Murphy asked. "What's that?"

"It's like any electrical power line," I said. "Except it plugs into your mind—and whoever is on the other end gets to decide what goes in."

Murphy got a little pale. She'd been on the receiving end of a couple of different kinds of psychic assault, and it had left some marks. "So do what you do. Put the whammy on them and let's track them down."

I grimaced and shook my head. "I don't dare," I told her. "All I've got to track with is the beer itself. If I try to use it in a spell, it'll open me up to the conduit. It'll be like I drank the stuff."

Murphy folded her arms. "And if that happens, you won't remember anything you learn anyway."

"Like I said," I told her, "it's high-quality work. But I've got a name."

"A perp?"

"I'm sure he's guilty of something. His name's Caine. He's a con. Big, dumb, violent, and thinks he's a brewer."

She arched an eyebrow. "You got a history with this guy?"

"Ran over him during a case maybe a year ago," I said. "It got ugly. More for him than me. He doesn't like Mac much."

"He's a wizard?"

"Hell's bells, no," I said.

"Then how does he figure in?"

"Let's ask him."

MURPHY MADE SHORT work of running down an address for Herbert Orson Caine, mugger, rapist, and extortionist—a cheap apartment building on the south end of Bucktown.

Murphy knocked at the door, but we didn't get an answer.

"It's a good thing he's a con," she said, reaching for her cell phone. "I can probably get a warrant without too much trouble."

"With what?" I asked her. "Suggestive evidence of the use of black magic?"

"Tampering with drinks at a bar doesn't require the use of magic," Murphy said. "He's a rapist, and he isn't part of the outfit, so he doesn't have an expensive lawyer to raise a stink."

"Howsabout we save the good people of Chicago time and money and just take a look around?"

"Breaking and entering."

"I won't break anything," I promised. "I'll do all the entering, too."

"No," she said.

"But—"

She looked up at me, her jaw set stubbornly. "No, Harry."

I sighed. "These guys aren't playing by the rules."

"We don't know he's involved yet. I'm not cutting corners for someone who might not even be connected."

I was partway into a snarky reply when Caine opened the door from the stairwell and entered the hallway. He spotted us and froze. Then he turned and started walking away.

"Caine!" Murphy called. "Chicago PD!"

He bolted.

Murph and I had both been expecting that, evidently. We both rushed him. He slammed the door open, but I'd been waiting for that, too. I sent out a burst of my will, drawing my right hand in toward my chest as I shouted, "Forzare!"

Invisible force slammed the door shut as Caine began to go through it. It hit him hard enough to bounce him all the way back across the hall, into the wall opposite.

Murphy had better acceleration than I did. She caught up to Caine in time for him to swing one paw at her in a looping punch.

I almost felt sorry for the slob.

Murphy ducked the punch, then came up with all of her weight and the muscle of her legs and body behind her response. She struck the tip of his chin with the heel of her hand, snapping his face straight up.

Caine was brawny, big, and tough. He came back from the blow with a dazed snarl and swatted at Murphy again. Murph caught his arm, tugged him a little one way, a little the other, and using his own arm as a fulcrum, sent him flipping forward and down hard onto the floor. He landed hard enough to make the floorboards shake, and Murphy promptly shifted her grip, twisting one hand into a painful angle, holding his arm out straight, using her leg to pin it into position.

"That would be assault," Murphy said in a sweet voice. "And on a police officer in the course of an investigation, no less."

"Bitch," Caine said. "I'm gonna break your—"

We didn't get to find out what he was going to break, because Murphy shifted her body weight maybe a couple of inches, and he screamed instead.

"Whaddayou want?" Caine demanded. "Lemme go! I didn't do nothin'!"

"Sure you did," I said cheerfully. "You assaulted Sergeant Murphy, here. I saw it with my own eyes."

"You're a two-time loser, Caine," Murphy said. "This will make it number three. By the time you get out, the first thing you'll need to buy will be a new set of teeth."

Caine said a lot of impolite words.

"Wow," I said, coming to stand over him. "That sucks. If only there was some way he could be of help to the community. You know, prove how he isn't a waste of space some other person could be using."

"Screw you," Caine said. "I ain't helping you with nothing."

Murphy leaned into his arm a little again to shut him up. "What happened to the beer at McAnnally's?" she asked in a polite tone.

Caine said even more impolite words.

"I'm pretty sure that wasn't it," Murphy said. "I'm pretty sure you can do better."

"Bite me, cop bitch," Caine muttered.

"Sergeant Bitch," Murphy said. "Have it your way, bonehead. Bet you've got all kinds of fans back at Stateville." But she was frowning when she said it. Thugs like Caine rolled over when they were facing hard time. They didn't risk losing the rest of their adult lives out of simple contrariness—unless they were terrified of the alternative.

Someone or, dare I say it, something had Caine scared.

Well. That table could seat more than one player.

The thug had a little blood coming from the corner of his mouth. He must have bitten his tongue when Murphy hit him.

I pulled a white handkerchief out of my pocket, and in a single swooping motion, stooped down and smeared some blood from Caine's mouth onto it.

"What the hell," he said, or something close to it. "What are you doing?"

"Don't worry about it, Caine," I told him. "It isn't going to be a long-term problem for you."

I took the cloth and walked a few feet away. Then I hunkered down and used a piece of chalk from another pocket to draw a circle around me on the floor.

Caine struggled feebly against Murphy, but she put him down again. "Sit still," she snapped. "I'll pull your shoulder right out of its socket."

"Feel free," I told Murphy. "He isn't going to be around long enough to worry about it." I squinted up at Caine and said, "Beefy, little bit of a gut. Bet you eat a lot of greasy food, huh, Caine?"

"Wh-what?" he said. "What are you doing?"

"Heart attack should look pretty natural," I said. "Murph, get ready to back off once he starts thrashing." I closed the circle and let it sparkle a little as I did. It was a waste of energy—special effects like that almost always are—but it made an impression on Caine.

"Jesus Christ!" Caine said. "Wait!"

"Can't wait," I told him. "Gotta make this go before the blood dries out. Quit being such a baby, Caine. She gave you a chance." I raised my hand over the fresh blood on the cloth. "Let's see now—"

"I can't talk!" Caine yelped. "If I talk, she'll know!"

Murphy gave his arm a little twist. "Who?" she demanded.

"I can't! Jesus, I swear! Dresden, don't, it isn't my fault, they needed bloodstone and I had the only stuff in town that was pure enough! I just wanted to wipe that smile off of that bastard's face!"

I looked up at Caine with a gimlet eye, my teeth bared. "You ain't saying anything that makes me want you to keep on breathing."

"I *can't*," Caine wailed. "She'll *know*!"

I fixed my stare on Caine and raised my hand in a slow, heavily overdramatized gesture. "*Intimidatus dorkus maximus!*" I intoned, making my voice intentionally hollow and harsh, and stressing the long vowels.

"Decker!" Caine screamed. "Decker, he set up the deal!"

I lowered my hand and let my head rock back. "Decker," I said. "That twit."

Murphy watched me, and didn't let go of Caine, though I could tell that she didn't want to keep holding him.

I shook my head at Murphy and said, "Let him scamper, Murph."

She let him go, and Caine fled for the stairs on his hand and knee, sobbing. He staggered out, falling down the first flight, from the sound of it.

I wrinkled up my nose as the smell of urine hit me. "Ah. The aroma of truth."

Murphy rubbed her hands on her jeans as if trying to wipe off something greasy. "Jesus, Harry."

"What?" I said. "You didn't want to break into his place."

"I didn't want you to put a gun to his head, either." She shook her head. "You couldn't really have . . ."

"Killed him?" I asked. I broke the circle and rose. "Yeah. With him right here in sight, yeah. I probably could have."

She shivered. "Jesus Christ."

"I wouldn't," I said. I went to her and put a hand on her arm. "I wouldn't, Karrin. You know that."

She looked up at me, her expression impossible to read. "You put on a really good act, Harry. It would have fooled a lot of people. It looked . . ."

"Natural on me," I said. "Yeah."

She touched my hand briefly with hers. "So, I guess we got something?"

I shook off dark thoughts and nodded. "We've got a name."

BURT DECKER RAN what was arguably the sleaziest of the half a dozen establishments that catered to the magical crowd in Chicago. Left Hand Goods prided itself on providing props and ingredients to the black magic crowd.

Oh, that wasn't so sinister as it sounded. Most of the trendy, self-appointed Death Eater wannabes in Chicago—or any other city, for that matter—didn't have enough talent to strike two rocks together and make sparks, much less hurt anybody. The really dangerous black wizards don't shop at places like Left Hand Goods. You could get everything you needed for most black magic at the freaking grocery store.

But, all the same, plenty of losers with bad intentions thought Left Hand Goods had everything you needed to create your own evil empire—and Burt Decker was happy to make them pay for their illusions.

Me and Murphy stepped in, between the display of socially maladjusted fungi on our right, a tank of newts (PLUCK YOUR OWN *#%$ING EYES, the sign said) on the left, and stepped around the big shelf of quasi-legal drug paraphernalia in front of us.

Decker was a shriveled little toad of a man. He wasn't overweight, but his skin looked too loose from a plump youth combined with a lifetime of too many naps in tanning beds. He was immaculately groomed, and his hair was gorgeous black streaked with dignified silver that was like a Rolls hood ornament on a VW Rabbit. He had beady black eyes with nothing warm behind them, and when he saw me, he licked his lips nervously.

"Hiya, Burt," I said.

There were a few shoppers, none of whom looked terribly appealing. Murphy held up her badge so that everyone could see it and said, "We have some questions."

She might as well have shouted, "Fire!" The store emptied.

Murphy swaggered past a rack of discount porn DVDs, her coat open just enough to reveal the shoulder holster she wore. She picked one up, gave it a look, and tossed it on the floor. "Christ, I hate scum vendors like this."

"Hey!" Burt said. "You break it, you bought it."

"Yeah, right," Murphy said.

I showed him my teeth as I walked up and leaned both my arms on the counter he stood behind. It crowded into his personal space. His cologne was thick enough to stop bullets.

"Burt," I said, "make this simple, okay? Tell me everything you know about Caine."

Decker's eyes went flat, and his entire body became perfectly still. It was reptilian. "Caine?"

I smiled wider. "Big guy, shaggy hair, kind of a slob, with piss running down his leg. He made a deal with a woman for some bloodstone, and you helped."

Murphy had paused at a display of what appeared to be small smoky quartz geodes. The crystals were nearly black, with purple veins running through them, and they were priced a couple of hundred dollars too high.

"I don't talk about my customers," Decker said. "It isn't good for business."

I glanced at Murphy. "Burt. We know you're connected."

She stared at me for a second, and sighed. Then she knocked a geode off the shelf. It shattered on the floor.

Decker winced and started to protest, but it died on his lips.

"You know what isn't good for business, Decker?" I asked. "Having a big guy in a gray cloak hang out in your little Bad Juju-Mart. Your customers start thinking that the Council is paying attention, how much business do you think you'll get?"

Decker stared at me with toad eyes, nothing on his face.

"Oops," Murphy said, and knocked another geode to the floor.

"People are in the hospital, Burt," I said. "Mac's one of them—and he was beaten on ground held neutral by the Unseelie Accords."

Burt bared his teeth. It was a gesture of surprise.

"Yeah," I said. I drew my blasting rod out of my coat and slipped enough of my will into it to make the runes and sigils carved along its length glitter with faint orange light. The smell of woodsmoke curled up from it. "You don't want the heat this is gonna bring down, Burt."

Murphy knocked another geode down and said, "I'm the good cop."

"All right," Burt said. "Jesus, will you lay off? I'll talk, but you ain't gonna like it."

"I don't handle disappointment well, Burt." I tapped the glowing-ember tip of the blasting rod down on his countertop for emphasis. "I really don't."

Burt grimaced at the black spots it left on the countertop. "Skirt comes in asking for bloodstone. But all I got is this crap from South Asscrack. Says she wants the real deal, and she's a bitch about it. I tell her I sold the end of my last shipment to Caine."

"Woman pisses you off," Murphy said, "and you send her to do business with a convicted rapist."

Burt looked at her with toad eyes.

"How'd you know where to find Caine?" I asked.

"He's got a discount card here. Filled out an application."

I glanced from the porn to the drug gear. "Uh-huh. What's he doing with bloodstone?"

"Why should I give a crap?" Burt said. "It's just business."

"How'd she pay?"

"What do I look like, a fucking video camera?"

"You look like an accomplice to black magic, Burt," I said.

"Crap," Burt said, smiling slightly. "I haven't had my hands on anything. I haven't done anything. You can't prove anything."

Murphy stared hard at Decker. Then, quite deliberately, she walked out of the store.

I gave him my sunniest smile. "That's the upside of working with the gray cloaks now, Burt," I said. "I don't need proof. I just need an excuse."

Burt stared hard at me. Then he swallowed, toadlike.

"SHE PAID WITH a Visa," I told Murphy when I came out of the store. "Meditrina Bassarid."

Murphy frowned up at my troubled expression. "What's wrong?"

"You ever see me pay with a credit card?"

"No. I figured no credit company would have you."

"Come on, Murph," I said. "That's just un-American. I don't bother with the things, because that magnetic strip goes bad in a couple of hours around me."

She frowned. "Like everything electronic does. So?"

"So if Ms. Bassarid has Caine scared out of his mind on magic . . . ," I said.

Murphy got it. "Why is she using a credit card?"

"Because she probably isn't human," I said. "Nonhumans can sling power all over the place and not screw up anything if they don't want to. It also explains why she got sent to Caine to get taught a lesson and wound up scaring him to death instead."

Murphy said an impolite word. "But if she's got a credit card, she's in the system."

"To some degree," I said. "How long for you to find something?"

She shrugged. "We'll see. You get a description?"

"Blue-black hair, green eyes, long legs, and great tits," I said.

She eyed me.

"Quoting," I said righteously.

I'm sure she was fighting off a smile. "What are you going to do?"

"Go back to Mac's," I said. "He loaned me his key."

Murphy looked sideways at me. "Did he know he was doing that?"

I put my hand to my chest as if wounded. "Murphy," I said. "He's a friend."

I LIT A bunch of candles with a mutter and a wave of my hand, and stared around Mac's place. Out in the dining area, chaos reigned. Chairs were overturned. Salt from a broken shaker had spread over the floor. None of the chairs were broken, but the framed sign that read ACCORDED NEUTRAL TERRITORY was smashed and lay on the ground near the door.

An interesting detail, that.

Behind the bar, where Mac kept his iceboxes and his wood-burning stove, everything was as tidy as a surgical theater, with the exception of the uncleaned stove and some dishes in the sink. Nothing looked like a clue.

I shook my head and went to the sink. I stared at the dishes. I turned and stared at the empty storage cabinets under the bar, where a couple of boxes of beer still waited. I opened the icebox and stared at the food, and my stomach rumbled. There were some cold cuts. I made a sandwich and stood there munching it, looking around the place, thinking.

I didn't think of anything productive.

I washed the dishes in the sink, scowling and thinking up a veritable thunderstorm. I didn't get much further than a light sprinkle, though, before a thought struck me.

There really wasn't very much beer under the bar.

I finished the dishes, pondering that. Had there been a ton earlier? No. I'd picked up the half-used box and taken it home. The other two boxes were where I'd left them. But Mac usually kept a legion of beer bottles down there.

So why only two now?

I walked down to the far end of the counter, a nagging thought dancing around the back of my mind, where I couldn't see it. Mac kept a small office in the back corner, consisting of a table for his desk, a wooden chair, and a couple of filing cabinets. His food service and liquor permits were on display on the wall above it.

I sat down at the desk and opened filing cabinets. I started going through Mac's records and books. Intrusive as hell, I know, but I had to figure out what was going on before matters got worse.

And that was when it hit me. Matters getting worse. I could see a mortal wizard, motivated by petty spite, greed, or some other mundane motivation, wrecking Mac's bar. People can be amazingly petty. But nonhumans, now—that was a different story.

The fact that this Bassarid chick had a credit card meant she was methodical. I mean, you can't just conjure one out of thin air. She'd taken the time to create an identity for herself. That kind of forethought indicated a scheme, a plan, a goal. Untidying a Chicago bar, neutral ground or not, was not by any means the kind of goal that things from the Nevernever set for themselves when they went undercover into mortal society.

Something bigger was going on, then. Mac's place must have been a side item for Bassarid.

Or maybe a stepping-stone.

Mac was no wizard, but he was savvy. It would take more than cheap tricks to get to his beer with him here, and I was betting that he had worked out more than one way to realize it if someone had intruded on his place when he was gone. So, if someone wanted to get to the beer, they'd need a distraction.

Like maybe Caine.

Caine made a deal with Bassarid, evidently—I assumed he gave her the bloodstone in exchange for being a pain to Mac. So, she ruins Mac's day, gets the bloodstone in exchange, end of story. Nice and neat.

Except that it didn't make a lot of sense. Bloodstone isn't exactly impossible to come by. Why would someone with serious magical juice do a favor for Caine to get some?

Because maybe Caine was a stooge, a distraction for anyone trying to follow Bassarid's trail. What if Bassarid had picked someone who had a history with Mac, so that I could chase after him while she . . . did whatever she planned to do with the rest of Mac's beer?

Wherever the hell that was.

It took me an hour and half to find anything in Mac's files—the first thing was a book. A really old book, bound in undyed leather. It was a journal, apparently, and written in some kind of cipher.

Also interesting, but probably not germane.

The second thing I found was a receipt, for a whole hell of

a lot of money, along with an itemized list of what had been sold—beer, representing all of Mac's various heavenly brews. Someone at Worldclass Limited had paid him an awful lot of money for his current stock.

I got on the phone and called Murphy.

"Who bought the evil beer?" Murphy asked.

"The beer isn't evil. It's a victim. And I don't recognize the name of the company. Worldclass Limited."

Keys clicked in the background as Murphy hit the Internet. "Caterers," Murphy said a moment later. "High end."

I thought of the havoc that might be about to ensue at some wedding or bar mitzvah and shuddered. "Hell's bells," I breathed. "We've got to find out where they went."

"Egad, Holmes," Murphy said in the same tone I would have said "duh."

"Yeah. Sorry. What did you get on Bassarid?"

"Next to nothing," Murphy said. "It'll take me a few more hours to get the information behind her credit card."

"No time," I said. "She isn't worried about the cops. Whoever she is, she planned this whole thing to keep her tracks covered from the likes of me."

"Aren't we full of ourselves?" Murphy grumped. "Call you right back."

She did.

"The caterers aren't available," she said. "They're working the private boxes at the Bulls game."

I RUSHED TO the United Center.

Murphy could have blown the whistle and called in the artillery, but she hadn't. Uniformed cops already at the arena would have been the first to intervene, and if they did, they were likely to cross Bassarid. Whatever she was, she would be more than they could handle. She'd scamper or, worse, one of the cops could get killed. So Murphy and I both rushed to get there and find the bad guy before she could pull the trigger, so to speak, on the Chicago PD.

It was half an hour before the game, and the streets were packed. I parked in front of a hydrant and ran half a mile to the United Center, where thousands of people were packing themselves into the building for the game. I picked up a ticket from a scalper for a ridiculous amount of money on the way, emptying my pockets, and earned about a million glares from Bulls fans as I juked and ducked through the crowd to get through the entrances as quickly as I possibly could.

Once inside, I ran for the lowest level, the bottommost ring of concessions stands and restrooms circling entrances to the arena—the most crowded level, currently—where the entrances to the most expensive ring of private boxes were. I started at the first box I came to, knocking on the locked doors. No one answered at the first several, and at the next the door was opened by a blonde in an expensive business outfit showing a lot of décolletage who had clearly been expecting someone else.

"Who are you?" she stammered.

I flashed her my laminated consultant's ID, too quickly to be seen. "Department of Alcohol, Tobacco, and Firearms, ma'am," I said in my official's voice, which is like my voice only deeper and more pompous. I've heard it from all kinds of government types. "We've had a report of tainted beer. I need to check your bar, see if the bad batch is in there."

"Oh," she said, backing up, her body language immediately cooperative. I pegged her as somebody's receptionist, maybe. "Of course."

I padded into the room and went to the bar, rifling bottles and opening cabinets until I found eleven dark-brown bottles with a simple cap with an *M* stamped into the metal. Mac's mark.

I turned to find the blonde holding out the half-empty bottle number twelve in a shaking hand. Her eyes were a little wide. "Um. Am I in trouble?"

I might be. I took the beer bottle from her, moving gingerly, and set it down with the others. "Have you been feeling, uh, sick or anything?" I asked as I edged toward the door, just in case she came at me with a baseball bat.

She shook her head, breathing more heavily. Her manicured fingernails trailed along the V-neck of her blouse. "I . . . I mean, you know." Her face flushed. "Just looking forward to . . . the game."

"Uh-huh," I said warily.

Her eyes suddenly became warmer and very direct. I don't know what it was exactly, but she was suddenly filled with that energy women have that has nothing to do with magic and everything to do with creating it. The temperature in the room felt like it went up about ten degrees. "Maybe you should examine me, sir."

I suddenly had a very different idea of what Mac had been defending himself from with that baseball bat.

And it had turned ugly on him.

Hell's bells, I thought I knew what we were dealing with.

"Fantastic idea," I told her. "You stay right here and get comfortable. I'm going to grab something sweet. I'll be back in two shakes."

"All right," she cooed. Her suit jacket slid off her shoulders to the floor. "Don't be long."

I smiled at her in what I hoped was a suitably sultry fashion and backed out. Then I shut the door, checked its frame, and focused my will into the palm of my right hand. I directed my attention to one edge of the door and whispered, "*Forzare.*"

Metal squealed as the door bent in its frame. With any luck, it would take a couple of guys with crowbars an hour or two to get it open again—and hopefully Bubbles would pitch over into a stupor before she did herself any harm.

It took me three more doors to find one of the staff of Worldclass Limited—a young man in dark slacks, a white shirt, and a black bow tie, who asked if he could help me.

I flashed the ID again. "We've received a report that a custom microbrew your company purchased for this event has been tainted. Chicago PD is on the way, but meanwhile I need your company to round up the bottles before anyone else gets poisoned drinking them."

The young man frowned. "Isn't it the Bureau?"

"Excuse me?"

"You said Department of Alcohol, Tobacco, and Firearms. It's a Bureau."

Hell's bells, why did I get someone who could think *now*?

"Can I see that ID again?" he asked.

"Look, buddy," I said. "You've gotten a bad batch of beer. If you don't round it up, people are going to get sick. Okay? The cops are on the way, but if people start guzzling it now, it isn't going to do anybody any good."

He frowned at me.

"Better safe than sorry, right?" I asked him.

Evidently, his ability to think did not extend to areas beyond asking stupid questions of well-meaning wizards. “Look, uh, really you should take this up with my boss.”

“Then get me to him,” I said. “Now.”

The caterer might have been uncertain, but he wasn’t slow. We hurried through the growing crowds to one of the workrooms that his company was using as a staging area. A lot of people in white shirts were hurrying all over the place with carts and armloads of everything from crackers to cheese to bottles of wine—and a dozen of Mac’s empty wooden boxes were stacked up to one side of the room.

My guide led me to a harried-looking woman in catering wear, who listened to him impatiently and cut him off halfway through. “I know, I know,” she snapped. “Look, I’ll tell you what I told Sergeant Murphy. A city health inspector is already here, and they’re already checking things out, and I am *not* losing my contract with the arena over some pointless scare.”

“You already talked to Murphy?” I said.

“Maybe five minutes ago. Sent her to the woman from the city, over at midcourt.”

“Tall woman?” I asked, feeling my stomach drop. “Blue-black hair? Uh, sort of busty?”

“Know her, do you?” The head caterer shook her head. “Look, I’m busy.”

“Yeah,” I said. “Thanks.”

I ran back into the corridor and sprinted for the boxes at midcourt, drawing out my blasting rod as I went and hoping I would be in time to do Murphy any good.

A few years ago, I’d given Murphy a key to my apartment, in a sense. It was a small amulet that would let her past the magical wards that defend the place. I hadn't bothered to tell her that the thing had a second purpose—I'd wanted her to have one of my personal possessions, something I could, if necessary, use to find her if I needed to do it. She would have been insulted at the very idea.

A quick stop into the men's room, a chalk circle on the floor, a muttered spell, and I was on her trail. I actually ran past the suite she was in before the spell let me know I had passed her, and I had to backtrack to the door. I debated blowing it off the hinges. There was something to be said for a shock-and-awe entrance.

Of course, most of those things couldn't be said for doing it in the middle of a crowded arena that was growing more crowded by the second. I'd probably shatter the windows at the front of the suite, and that could be dangerous for the people sitting in the stands beneath them. I tried the door, just for the hell of it and—

—it opened.

Well, dammit. I much prefer making a dramatic entrance.

I came in and found a plush-looking room, complete with dark, thick carpeting, leather sofas, a buffet bar, a wet bar, and two women making out on a leather love seat.

They looked up as I shut the door behind me. Murphy's expression was, at best, vague, her eyes hazy, unfocused, the pupils dilated until you could hardly see any blue, and her lips were a little swollen with kissing. She saw me, and a slow and utterly sensuous smile spread over her mouth. "Harry. There you are."

The other woman gave me the same smile with a much more predatory edge. She had shoulder-length hair, so black, it was highlighted with dark, shining blue. Her green-gold eyes were bright and intense, her mouth full. She was dressed in a gray business skirt-suit, with the jacket off and her shirt mostly unbuttoned, if not quite indecent. She was, otherwise, as Burt Decker had described her—statuesque and beautiful.

"So," she said in a throaty, rich voice. "This is Harry Dresden."

"Yes," Murphy said, slurring the word drunkenly. "Harry. And his rod." She let out a giggle.

I mean, my God. She *giggled*.

"I like his looks," the brunette said. "Strong. Intelligent."

"Yeah," Murphy said. "I've wanted him for the longest time." She tittered. "Him and his rod."

I pointed said blasting rod at Meditrina Bassarid. "What have you done to her?"

"I?" the woman said. "Nothing."

Murphy's face flushed. "Yet."

The woman let out a smoky laugh, toying with Murphy's hair. "We're getting to that. I only shared the embrace of the god with her, wizard."

"I was going to kick your ass for that," Murphy said. She looked around, and I noticed that a broken lamp lay on the floor, and the end table it had sat on had been knocked over, evidence of a struggle. "But I feel so *good* now. . . ." Smoldering blue eyes found me. "Harry. Come sit down with us."

"You should," the woman murmured. "We'll have a good time." She produced a bottle of Mac's ale from somewhere. "Come on. Have a drink with us."

All I'd wanted was a beer, for Pete's sake.

But this wasn't what I had in mind. It was just wrong. I told myself very firmly that it was wrong. Even if Karrin managed, somehow, to make her gun's shoulder rig look like lingerie.

Or maybe that was me.

"Meditrina was a Roman goddess of wine," I said instead. "And the bassarids were another name for the handmaidens of Dionysus." I nodded at the beer in her hand and said, "I thought Maenads were wine snobs."

Her mouth spread in a wide, genuine-looking smile, and her teeth were very white. "Any spirit is the spirit of the god, mortal."

"That's what the psychic conduit links them to," I said. "To Dionysus. To the god of revels and ecstatic violence."

"Of course," the Maenad said. "Mortals have forgotten the true power of the god. The time has come to begin reminding them."

"If you're going to muck with the drinks, why not start with the big beer dispensary in the arena? You'd get it to a lot more people that way."

She sneered at me. "Beer, brewed in cauldrons the size of houses by machines and then served cold. It has no soul. It isn't worthy of the name."

"Got it," I said. "You're a beer snob."

She smiled, her gorgeous green eyes on mine. "I needed something real. Something a craftsman took loving pride in creating."

Which actually made sense, from a technical perspective. Magic is about a lot of things, and one of them is emotion. Once you begin to mass-manufacture anything, by the very nature of the process, you lose the sense of personal attachment you might have to something made by hand. For the Maenad's purposes, it would have meant that the mass-produced beer had nothing she could sink her magical teeth into, no foundation to lay her complex compulsion upon.

Mac's beer certainly qualified as being produced with pride—real, personal pride, I mean, not official corporate spokesperson pride.

"Why?" I asked her. "Why do this at all?"

"I am hardly alone in my actions, wizard," she responded. "And it is who I am."

I frowned and tilted my head at her.

"Mortals have forgotten the gods," she said, hints of anger creeping into her tone. "They think the White God drove out the many gods. But they are here. *We* are here. I, too, was worshipped in my day, mortal man."

"Maybe you didn't know this," I said, "but most of us couldn't give a rat's ass. Raining down thunderbolts from on high isn't exclusive territory anymore."

She snarled, her eyes growing even brighter. "Indeed. We withdrew and gave the world into your keeping—and what has become of it? In two thousand years, you've poisoned and raped the mother earth who gave you life. You've cut down the forests, fouled the air, and darkened Apollo's chariot itself with the stench of your smithies."

"And touching off a riot at the Bulls' game is going to make some kind of point?" I demanded.

She smiled, showing sharp canines. "My sisters have been doing football matches for years. We're expanding the franchise." She drank from the bottle, wrapping her lips around it and making sure I noticed. "Moderation. It's disgusting. We should have strangled Aristotle in his crib. Alcoholism—calling the god a *disease*." She bared her teeth at me. "A lesson must be taught."

Murphy shivered, and then her expression turned ugly, her blue eyes focusing on me.

"Show your respect to the god, wizard," the Maenad spat. "Drink. Or I will introduce you to Pentheus and Orpheus."

Greek guys. Both of whom were torn to pieces by Maenads and their mortal female companions in orgies of ecstatic violence.

Murphy was breathing heavily now, sweating, her cheeks flushed, her eyes burning with lust and rage. And she was staring right at me.

Hooboy.

"Make you a counteroffer," I said quietly. "Break off the enchantment on the beer and get out of my town, now, and I won't FedEx you back to the Aegean in a dozen pieces."

"If you will not honor the god in life," Meditrina said, "then you will honor him in *death*." She flung out a hand, and Murphy flew at me with a howl of primal fury.

I ran away.

Don't get me wrong. I've faced a lot of screaming, charging monsters in my day. Granted, not one of them was small and blond and pretty from making out with what might have been a literal goddess. All the same, my options were limited. Murphy obviously wasn't in her right mind. I had my blasting rod ready to go, but I didn't want to kill her. I didn't want to go hand-to-hand with her, either. Murphy was a dedicated martial artist, especially good at grappling, and if it came to a clinch, I wouldn't fare any better than Caine had.

I flung myself back out of the room and into the corridor beyond before Murphy could catch me and twist my arm into some kind of Escher portrait. I heard glass breaking somewhere behind me.

Murphy came out hard on my heels, and I brought my shield bracelet up as I turned, trying to angle it so that it wouldn't hurt her. My shield flashed to blue-silver life as she closed on me, and she bounced off it as if it had been solid steel, stumbling to one side. Meditrina followed her, clutching a broken bottle, the whites of her eyes visible all the way around the bright green, an ecstatic and entirely creepy expression of joy lighting her face. She slashed at me, three quick, graceful motions, and I got out of the way of only one of them. Hot pain seared my chin and my right hand, and my blasting rod went flying off down the corridor, bouncing off people's legs.

I'm not an expert like Murphy, but I've taken some classes, too, and more important, I've been in a bunch of scrapes in my life. In the literal school of hard knocks, you learn the ropes fast, and the lessons go bone-deep. As I reeled from the blow, I turned my momentum into a spin and swept my leg through Meditrina's. Goddess or not, the Maenad didn't weigh half what I did, and her legs went out from under her.

Murphy blindsided me with a kick that lit up my whole rib cage with pain, and had seized an arm before I could fight through it. If it had been my right arm, I'm not sure what might have happened—but she grabbed my left, and I activated my shield bracelet, sheathing it in sheer, kinetic power and forcing her hands away.

I don't care how many aikido lessons you've had, they don't train you for force fields.

I reached out with my will, screamed, "*Forzare!*" and seized a large plastic waste bin with my power. With a flick of my hand, I flung it at Murphy. It struck her hard and knocked her off me. I backpedaled. Meditrina had regained her feet and was coming for me, bottle flickering.

She drove me back into the beer-stand counter across the hall, and I brought up my shield again just as her makeshift weapon came forward. Glass shattered against it, cutting her own hand—always a risk with a bottle. But the force of the blow was sufficient to carry through the shield and slam my back against the counter. I bounced off some guy trying to carry beer in plastic cups and went down soaked in brew.

Murphy jumped on me then, pinning my left arm down as Meditrina started raking at my face with her nails, both of them screaming like banshees.

I had to shut one eye when a sharp fingernail grazed it, but I saw my chance as Meditrina's hands—hot, horribly strong hands, closed over my throat.

I choked out a gasped, "*Forzare!*" and reached out my right hand, snapping a slender chain that held up one end of a sign suspended above the beer stand behind me.

A heavy wooden sign that read, in large cheerful letters, PLEASE DRINK RESPONSIBLY swung down in a ponderous, scything arc and struck Meditrina on the side of the head, hitting her like a giant's fist. Her nails left scarlet lines on my throat as she was torn off me.

Murphy looked up, shocked, and I hauled with all my strength. I had to position her before she took up where Meditrina left off. I felt something wrench and give way as my thumb left its socket, and I howled in pain as the sign swung back, albeit with a lot less momentum, now, and clouted Murphy on the noggin, too.

Then a bunch of people jumped on us and the cops came running.

---

While they were arresting me, I managed to convince the cops that there was something bad in Mac's beer. They got with the caterers and rounded up the whole batch, apparently before more than a handful of people could drink any. There was some wild behavior, but no one else got hurt.

None of which did me any good. After all, I was soaked in Budweiser and had assaulted two attractive women. I went to the drunk tank, which angered me mainly because I'd never gotten my freaking beer. And to add insult to injury, after paying exorbitant rates for a ticket, I hadn't gotten to see the game, either.

There's no freaking justice in this world.

Murphy turned up in the morning to let me out. She had a black eye and a sign-shaped bruise across one cheekbone.

"So let me get this straight," Murphy said. "After we went to Left Hand Goods, we followed the trail to the Bulls game. Then we confronted this Maenad character, there was a struggle, and I got knocked out."

"Yep," I said.

There was really no point in telling it any other way. The nefarious hooch would have destroyed her memory of the evening. The truth would just bother her.

Hell, it bothered me. On more levels than I wanted to think about.

"Well, Bassarid vanished from the hospital," Murphy said. "So she's not around to press charges. And, given that you were working with me on an investigation, and because several people have reported side effects that sound a lot like they were drugged with Rohypnol or something—and because it was you who got the cops to pull the rest of the bottles—I managed to get the felony charges dropped. You're still being cited for drunk and disorderly."

"Yay," I said without enthusiasm.

"Could have been worse," Murphy said. She paused and studied me for a moment. "You look like hell."

"Thanks," I said.

She looked at me seriously. Then she smiled, stood up on her tiptoes, and kissed my cheek. "You're a good man, Harry. Come on. I'll give you a ride home."

I smiled all the way to her car.

Jim Butcher enjoys fencing, martial arts, singing, bad science-fiction movies, and live-action gaming. He lives in Missouri with his wife, son, and a vicious guard dog. You may learn more at www.jim-butcher.com.

# Death Warmed Over

## Rachel Caine

I HATE RAISING the dead on a work night.

My boss Sam Twist knows that, and so it was a surprise when I got the e-mail on a Monday, telling me he would need a full resurrection on Thursday.

"Short turnaround, genius," I muttered. It took days to brew the necessary potions, and I'd have to set aside the entire Thursday from dusk until dawn for the resurrection itself. Not good, because I knew I couldn't exactly blow off Friday. I had meetings at the day job.

Sam, who ran the local booking service for witches, was usually somewhat sympathetic to my day job–night job balancing act, mostly because I was the best resurrection witch he had—not that being the best in the business exactly pays the bills. It was a little like being the best piccolo player in the orchestra—it took skill, and specialty, and not a lot of people could do it, but it didn't exactly present a lot of major money-making opportunities.

Then again, at least resurrections were a fairly steady business. Some of the other types of witches—and we were all very specialized—got a whole lot less. It was a funny thing, but so far as I could tell, there had never been witches who could do what the folklore claimed; those of us who were real worked with potions, not words. We couldn't sling spells and lightning. Our jobs—whatever our particular focus—took time and patience, not to mention a high tolerance for nasty ingredients.

I contemplated Sam's message. If I wanted to, I *could* turn down the assignment—I wasn't hurting for money at the moment. Still. There was something in the terse way he'd phrased it that made me wonder.

So was I taking the job, or not? If I said yes, prep needed to start immediately after work. Part of my mind ran through the things I might need, and matched them against the mental stock list I always kept in my brain. The bowls were clean and ready, I'd put them through the dishwasher and a good ritual scrub with sacred herbs just a week ago. I'd need to put a fresh blessing on the athame. I had most of the other things—rock salt, sulfur, attar of roses, ambergris, and a whole bunch of slimier ingredients. I might be running low on bottled semen, but the truth was, you could always get more of that.

I fidgeted in my chair as I stared at the message. Sam wasn't telling me much—just timing and a dollar amount, which while considerable wasn't enough to pay my mortgage. On their own, my fingers typed my reply: *I might be interested. Who's the client?*

I rarely asked, because most of the time that fell under need-to-know, and I didn't. So long as the client paid Sam, and Sam paid me, we were all good. But this time—this time I felt like it was worth the question.

I went back to my regular work—tonight, that meant straightening out a worksheet the experts in accounting had completely trashed—and was a little surprised when Sam's e-mail came so quickly. Then again, it was a short answer.

*PD.* Police Department.

My hackles went way up. The police didn't part with their money willingly for resurrections. The testimony of the resurrected had been thrown out as inadmissible five years ago, thanks to a Supreme Court decision, and the land-office rush for witches to bring back the dead had dried up just as fast. Some of the richer cities still managed one or two resurrections a year for particularly cold cases, just to generate leads, but I hadn't seen one in Austin for a while.

So if the Thin Blue Line was knocking, something was up, and it was big. Very big.

*Why?* I wrote back, and hit SEND.

It didn't take long to get my answer. Four minutes, to be exact, give or take a few seconds, until my cheery little *you have mail* chime dinged.

*They need a disposable,* he wrote, and this time, I sat all the way back in my chair. And rolled my chair back from the computer. *Tried to talk them out of it. Told them you wouldn't want in. You can pass on it, H.*

In technical terms, a disposable is a long-term resurrection—counterintuitive, but that's police parlance for you. Most resurrections last no more than a few minutes, maybe an hour—you really don't need that much time to do whatever needs to be done. It's mainly finding out the name of their killer, or where they stashed the family silver, or where the bodies are buried if your deceased soul is the one who buried them in the first place. Holding them longer is brutally hard, and gets harder the longer it goes on. When a police department requests a long-term resurrection, it's almost always specific—there's a situation that requires a particular person to resolve, or a particular skill. When the cops ask for a disposable resurrection, well, you know it's going to be bad.

I knew it better than anyone.

I typed my reply back in words as terse as Sam's had been to me. *Bet your ass I'm passing.*

I hit SEND, feeling only a little wistful twinge of regret at all that virtual money disappearing from my future, and began to shut my computer down.

I'd just picked up my purse when my cell phone rang, and I wasn't too surprised when the screen's display told me it was Sam.

"Hey," I said, shouldered my bag, and headed for the elevators. "Don't try to talk me out of it. I don't do disposables. Not anymore."

"I know that," Sam said. He had a deep, smoky voice, the kind that implied a cigarette-and-whiskey lifestyle. I didn't know that for sure; for all I knew, Sam might have lived prim as a preacher. Sam and I didn't exactly hang out; he kept himself to himself, mostly. "Not trying to talk you out of it, H, believe me. I'm glad you turned it down."

"Shut up," said a third voice, male, grim, and completely unfamiliar.

"Who the hell is *that*?" I blurted. "Sam—"

"Detective Daniel Prieto."

"Sam, you *conferenced me*?" He'd never put me on the spot before.

"Hey, they're the cops. I got no choice!"

"Hear me out." Prieto's voice rode right over Sam's. "I'm

told you're the best there is, and I need the best. Besides, you have a prior relationship with the—subject."

My mouth dried up, and I stopped in midstride to lean against the wall. A few coworkers passed me and gave me curious looks; I couldn't imagine what was on my face, but it must have been both alarming and offputting. Nobody stopped. I tried to speak, but nothing was coming out of my mouth.

"Holly? You there?" That was Sam. I could still hear Prieto breathing.

"Yeah," I finally managed to say. "Who?" Not that there was really much of a question. I had a *relationship* with only one dead man. He was the only disposable I'd ever brought back.

And Prieto, right on cue, said, "Andrew Toland."

I felt hot and sick, and I needed to sit down. Never a chair around when you need one. I continued walking, slowly, one shoulder gliding against the wall for balance. "Sam, you can't agree to this. You can't let them do it again. Not to him."

"What can I say? I'm just the dispatcher, H. You don't want to take it on, that's just fine." The words sounded apologetic, but Sam didn't do empathy. None of us did. It didn't serve us well, in this line of work.

Cops had the same problem. "I have to tell you, if you don't agree, we're still bringing him back. It'll just be somebody else running him. You said this Carlotta is next on the list, Mr. Twist? She's the one who recommended this particular guy be brought back, right?"

"*Lottie?*" I blurted it out before I could stop myself. *No. Oh, no.* Carlotta Flores and I went back a long time, and not one minute of it was pleasant. In resurrections, we prided ourselves on detachment, but Lottie took pleasure in the pain that her resurrected souls felt; she *enjoyed* keeping them chained into their flesh. I'd reported her dozens of times to the review board, but there was never any real evidence. Only my own word for what I'd seen.

The dead can't testify.

It was her fondest wish to run a disposable, and it was the very last thing she should ever do. *God, no.* The idea of letting her handle Andrew's resurrection was more than I could take.

Detective Prieto somehow knew that, but then again, I supposed he'd done his homework. He'd probably gotten it from Sam, the chatty bastard.

"That a yes, Miss Caldwell?" Prieto asked. Sam was distinctly silent.

"Yes," I gritted out. "Dammit to hell."

"Right. Let's get to business. City morgue, Thursday at dusk, you know the drill. Come loaded, H." Sam was back to brisk and rough again, his brief moment of empathy blown away like feathers in a hurricane.

"Send me the details." I sounded resigned. I didn't feel resigned. I felt manipulated, defeated, and enraged.

"Will do," Sam said. I heard a click. Detective Prieto had signed off without bothering to say good-bye. "Better you than Lottie, I guess. Though look, if you just don't show up, what're they going to do? Arrest you?"

"They'll let Lottie do it instead. You know I can't let that happen, Sam."

"Kind of guessed, yeah."

"Why *him*? God, Sam—"

"Don't know. Lottie had some kind of chat with Prieto,

next thing I know, he's telling me it's Toland he needs. Maybe Lottie told him about how tough the son of a bitch was. Is."

Maybe Lottie just wanted to yank my chain. Equally possible.

"Holly? Sorry about—"

"Yeah. Whatever. See you." I folded up the phone. I couldn't take any more of Sam's vaguely false apology. He knew my agreement was final. You don't become a witch making false promises. The stakes are far too high.

I must have punched the elevator buttons properly, because next thing I knew I was in the lobby, walking toward the parking garage. I couldn't feel my feet, and wherever my head was, it wasn't a good place. I went to the car on autopilot, got inside, and bent over to rest my aching, sweating forehead on the steering wheel.

My name is Holly Anne Caldwell, and I'm a licensed seventh-generation witch, with a specialty in raising the dead.

And I wished, right at this moment, that I was one of them.

I BURIED MYSELF deep in prep work. It took up most of my nights, and I sleepwalked through my day job until Thursday.

Late Thursday afternoon, I went to raise the dead.

I knew the way to the morgue all too well. I had a parking pass, and the guard at the door knew me by sight. He still checked me against the list and opened up my heavy case to check the contents. All aboveboard, along with my certification papers from the State of Texas. I'd dressed professionally—a nice dark suit, very funeral home–friendly, with sensibly heeled shoes. Moderate makeup. Light perfume.

It helps, because I do run into the odd person who still believes witches come with green faces, cackling, and cauldrons.

The guard hooked me up with a temporary ID badge and escorted me back to the—excuse the phrase—guts of the morgue, which always reminded me of a large-scale industrial kitchen, with all the chrome work surfaces and sharp instruments neatly arrayed on racks. Once there, he checked with the coroner's assistant, then backtracked me to a room that was normally used for family viewings. Nobody had bothered to dress it out for this occasion, so there was a certain creepy sterility to it that unsettled me.

Detective Prieto unsettled me, too. He was about my father's age, stern and possessed of one stony expression as far as I could tell. He didn't like me, and he didn't like what he was doing. He gave me the paperwork, I read and signed, and he checked all my credentials again before leaving the room to stand in the viewing area.

I pulled the sheet back on the corpse, and there, lying pale and still in front of me, was Andrew Toland.

He looked damn good, for having been born in 1843, and especially since he'd died in 1875. By rights, I should have been looking at a skeleton, not a fresh corpse—like last time we'd been through this, another witch had produced a copy from his genetic template. It was known as a homunculus, in the trade. How such things were made was a closely guarded secret, although I knew the body would contain some kind of tissue or bone from the original corpse to hold the link. I wouldn't have known how to begin to conduct that kind of operation, but then again, the witch who'd made the mortal clay couldn't have breathed life into it, either.

Specialists.

I'd been here before, in this very room, with Andrew. One year ago, almost to the day—my first disposable. I'd been nervous, and excited, and thrilled at the prospect of meeting the man who'd made history. I hadn't been prepared, then, for the idea that I would *like* him.

And that I would mourn him when it was time to let go.

I didn't want to do this. It had hurt too much, been too intimate. I wanted to walk away from all of it . . . but if I did, someone else would be standing here within the hour. Someone like Lottie, who would turn something wonderful into something horrible.

I had no choice.

Andrew Toland looked peaceful, frozen at that moment of death. He no longer had the wounds that had killed him; the last witch had repaired that as part of the reconstruction. He was just . . . dead. All I had to do was bring him back.

And once again, I had to wonder: *Why him?* Lottie had wanted him, specifically. It could just have been her one-two punch of hating me and wanting the prestige of running a disposable, but I couldn't believe that. There were easier ways to hurt me, and Andrew Toland was nobody she'd want to mess with. She knew his story, just as I did.

Andrew had lived a hard, interesting life, and he'd earned himself a reputation, in his thirty-two short years, of being one of the toughest men of a rough-and-ready period of American history. A resurrection witch, like me, he'd gone down fighting during one of the worst zombie wars ever conducted in the Southwest. From time to time, a resurrectionist goes bad, and when that happens, the results are massively dangerous. Get three or four of the bad ones together, and you have the makings of an unstoppable army of the dead.

Andrew Toland had gone up against that, and earned himself a broken neck. Then, by prior agreement with his friends, he'd had himself resurrected to fight again.

He'd won. Most of his allies had been taken out, and in the end he'd carried on by himself—a gritty two-week campaign of attrition against the toughest opponents imaginable. And even when his resurrection witch had been killed in the last critical moments, he'd still managed to stay alive long enough to take out the enemy. It had been unheard of then, and it was still without parallel, and in the textbooks apprentices studied, he was an entire chapter all his own.

You just don't get badder-assed than that.

I knew Prieto was watching, and the last thing I needed was to lose my objectivity at a time like this. I put all my feelings away in a lockbox, bent down, and opened Andrew Toland's death-filmed eyes.

I parted his clay-cold lips and poured in the first, massive dose of the potion. It pooled in his mouth, liquid silver, and then I performed the part that nobody else could do.

I kissed him, very gently, on the lips and completed the last step of the preset spell. I felt a line of power spooling out of me, traveling through the dark and connecting, with a jolting snap of power, with the spirit of Andrew Toland.

The last time I'd done this, Andrew's power and strength had overwhelmed me. This time, they felt oddly soothing. Like being folded in warmth and light.

Andrew swallowed, coughed, and blinked. His skin remained pasty white for a few seconds. The cataracts on his eyes faded first, fainter with each blink, and then his skin took on color.

He wasn't back, but he was breathing.

I took his hands and poured more power into him, raw and wild. It was sweaty work, bringing back the dead, and it required me to be vulnerable in ways most witches weren't willing to attempt. I had to touch his soul, and let him touch mine. I had to not just taste death, but to drink it down—accept it as a lover.

He gasped when I made contact, and the shine in his eyes shifted from mere existence to real life. Real consciousness.

I heard the first slow thud of his heartbeat, then the second. Then the rhythm falling into place.

And despite all the drugs cushioning his fall, I saw the agony hit him—I felt it, too, dim but strong, through our link, and had to breathe deeply to control the pain. He didn't scream. Some did, but not Andrew; he hadn't screamed when I'd revived him last year, either. His hands tightened on mine, brutally strong, and I tried not to wince. *It'll pass,* I told myself. *Breathe. Breathe, dammit.*

I was doing fine until he met my eyes, and he whispered, "Holly. Wasn't it finished? Didn't we get him?"

*Holy hell. He remembers.*

For a frozen second I couldn't think what to say, but training came back to me in a rush. *Establish control. Guide the dialogue.*

"Andrew," I said, and my voice was low and gentle and soothing, entirely steady. "Andrew Toland. Do you hear me?"

He nodded. He hadn't blinked since focusing on me.

"I need you to sit up now," I said. "Can you do that?"

He could, and he did. He swung his legs over the edge of

the cold morgue table and came upright, and I stopped him long enough to adjust the sheet over his lap. I wasn't usually so fussy, but Andrew had thrown me off; I couldn't see him as a tool. He was a man, a living, vital *man*.

He hadn't looked away at all from my face. There was something very unusual about him. I'd brought back hundreds of dead, and I couldn't think of a single one who'd begun the process with a question like that. It takes time for the personality to reassert itself, for memories to come clear.

He had been crystal-clear from the moment our souls had touched.

"Holly, you must tell me the truth," Andrew said. "Did we kill that bastard?"

How could he possibly *remember who I was*? I'd had one other soul I'd brought back twice, the CEO of a major corporation who'd forgotten to pass along the passwords to some vital corporate accounts. I'd had to do it twice because the board of directors wanted to be sure they had everything from him, and that man, young and fit as he'd been, hadn't recognized me at all. Hadn't remembered a thing from one resurrection to the next.

"Holly!" His tone was sharp with concern. *He* was concerned. About *me*. I came back from about a thousand miles away and realized that he was frowning, totally focused on me. "Can you hear me?"

I laughed. I couldn't help it. It came out a strained, strangled gasp. "Yes," I managed to say. "I hear you, Andrew. We stopped him."

"Then I expect there's a tale to be told about why I'm back here." He released me from his stare to turn it on the room around us. "Well, this place don't get any prettier."

He remembered that, too? Unbelievable. "How do you feel?"

"Feel?" His gaze came back to me, electric and warm, and his lips curved into a smile. "Alive would say it fine. But I'm not alive, I know that. You've brought me back again. Why?"

I turned away to pick up a stack of clothes from the pile nearby. Hospital scrubs for now, nothing fancy. I handed them to him, and he considered them for a few seconds.

"Clothes," I said. It was unnecessary; he clearly knew what they were, but I was rattled. I was all too aware of Detective Prieto at the viewing window, seeing me lose my cool.

That earned me another fey smile from Andrew. He had a nice face—a little sharp, with a pointed chin. In certain lights, in certain moods, he would look sinister, except for the humor in his eyes. "I know we're well acquainted, but a bit of privacy? . . ."

I turned my back. I heard the faint sound of his bare feet slapping the cold floor as he stood, and the rustle of fabric moving over skin.

He was way, way too fast. Too well adjusted, for any newly revived corpse. He had *continuity*, and that meant he remembered all the trauma of the first resurrection.

"How long?" he asked. "How long have I been away this time?"

I cast a look over my shoulder, and found he was adjusting the fit of the pants on his hips. Except for the slight, indefinable distance in his eyes, he could have been any hospital attendant. He looked completely . . . alive.

"About a year," I said. "Andrew— "

"Feels like yesterday," he said, and looked down at his

hands. He flexed them carefully. "Awful strange, not knowing that."

"We have work for you," I said. I was sticking to my script, even though Andrew had lost his. "I'll help you understand what you need to do. How do you feel?"

"Holly, my sweet, I'm annoyed you're not listening to how I feel." He frowned, and I was right, he could look menacing. "Which shouldn't be true, I think. No corpse revives so quickly as to be annoyed over such minor things." Andrew should know. He'd been a better witch than I ever could be.

"You're no ordinary person," I said. My heart was pounding, my palms were sweating, but I sounded as cool and soothing as any clinical practitioner. "Are you in any pain?"

"No."

"None at all?"

"Miss Holly, I've been in your shoes." His gaze moved to focus on them for a second, smiling. "Never ones so dainty, maybe. But there's no need to treat me like an invalid. I'll let you know when I start feeling it."

I stared at him. He stared back, challenge in those bright blue eyes. He was an average-looking guy in a lot of ways—pleasant features, except for that sharp, aggressive chin; sandy brown hair that had grown into a style that seemed both modern and antique—shaggy, certainly. He had a sharp ridge and twist to his nose, as if he'd broken it early in life.

I tried to get my mind back to business. "If you start feeling anxious or drifting, tell me. I don't know what the police need you for, or how long it will take, but you need to have a dose—"

"Each hour, yes, Miss Holly. I'm the one who wrote up the

damn rules. Police, you say?" That seemed to give him pause for thought. "Why us, again?" *Us,* not just him. Andrew assumed instantly that we were a team.

I didn't want to be a team. It had hurt so much the last time around, I couldn't imagine how bad it would be this time, when I knew him. When I cared.

I opted for neutral topics. "Detective Prieto is waiting to brief us."

Detective Prieto entered the room, and both of us turned to look at him. "Mr. Toland," he said, and nodded stiffly. "I won't say thanks, since I know you didn't really have a choice in coming . . . here." Nice way to avoid the whole death/life conundrum. "But I'm giving you a choice for the job. If you don't want to do it, we'll end this right now."

Andrew had lost his smile. His eyes were narrowed, hard-focused. That was how he looked when he fought, I thought. And yes, he could be intimidating.

"It's no small matter if you picked me," he said. "I slept a hundred and thirty-some-odd years before Miss Holly here brought me back the first time, and I'll allow as how that job was worth the trouble. I expect this one's just as raw."

"Yes," Prieto said. Now that he was face-to-face with the soul he was about to send into torment, possibly horrible death, he seemed deeply uncomfortable. "I need you to help us save lives."

"Didn't expect you brought me back for a pony ride, mister. Fine. I'll do it."

"Andrew," I said quietly. "Hear him out before you agree to anything."

"Don't need to. Like I said, I wouldn't be back here if it wasn't bad."

"All right," Prieto said. "We have a credible terrorist threat against a protected group of individuals here in Austin. Four are already missing, and we've got intel about the next one to be abducted. We think these people are being killed, but we haven't found remains yet."

Andrew studied him for a moment in silence, then said, "I understood little of that, 'cept you have four missing and some dead. I ain't equipped to solve your crimes, so I don't think that's what you need me for, is it?"

"We need you to protect one of the people on the list of potential victims."

"Wait a minute!" I blurted, horrified. The resurrected—even disposables—weren't bodyguards; they were weapons. Point them at a clearly defined objective, and let them go achieve it, no matter what the damage. Disposables didn't have a self-preservation instinct, so they were perfect for sending in on suicide runs.

Bodyguarding was completely different. For one thing, it was likely to be long-term, much longer than a disposable ever lasted. Days. Weeks. Months, even. "Wait a minute," I repeated. My voice was loud enough to ring off the morgue steel. "What the hell? Since when did the resurrected join the force? This is something any cop in Kevlar could do, right?"

Prieto gave me another look. This one was blank and cool. "We've tried that," he said. "Didn't go so well, which is why we decided to go with somebody with nothing to lose, like your friend here. Our intel says the attack's going to come in the next few days. Fact is, when we booked the job in the first place, we were planning to protect a completely different person. While you've been *preparing*, we lost two more of the targets, *and* the teams of cops assigned for protection. So I don't give a shit about your problems, lady. I lost four of my own officers protecting these—people. Least you can do is your job."

"But you can't—"

Andy interrupted me. "Who'd I be protecting?"

Prieto had been waiting for the question, and he seemed to take a special kind of pleasure in saying, "It's her. Holly Anne Caldwell. These fucking freaks are taking out witches."

WE LEFT THE viewing room to go down the hall to a small airless conference room, where Prieto had set up shop for the night. He had folders.

He had a *lot* of folders.

I knew every one of the victims. Shayle Gallagher had been the first—he'd been taken right out of his flower shop (like me, he only moonlighted at the resurrection business), and there had been signs of a vicious struggle. Could have been robbery or a hate crime, so that hadn't raised too many unusual flags at first, especially with no body found.

Two weeks ago, though, Harrison Wright had failed to show up to work at his medical practice, and his multimillion-dollar estate showed signs of the same brutal attack as at Gallagher's store.

Lottie Flores had been the next victim, and she'd disappeared the day after I'd taken the case from Sam.

"We kept it out of the news," Prieto said. "Wasn't easy. Oh, and Sam agreed we shouldn't interrupt you while you were working."

*Sam agreed?* I was going to have a talk with Sam. One involving a punch in the mouth.

"You said there were dead officers," Andy said.

Prieto nodded. "My guys had missed a scheduled check-in. When backup arrived, their car was empty. They were found in the Flores house."

"Why not bring one of them back, find out just what went on?"

Prieto looked grim. "We thought about it, but the families wouldn't sign off, and by then, we were knee-deep in missing resurrection witches. Didn't think we should waste the time trying to convince anybody."

I looked at the photos of the two dead police officers, and felt my stomach twist. They'd been beaten to death. That wasn't easy to do with any cop, but you could at least see how the five-foot-five, petite woman could have been overpowered. Not her partner, six-foot-four and big enough to intimidate pretty much anyone. He looked like he chewed nails as vitamins.

"Neither one got a shot off," Prieto said. "No sign of Flores in the house, but we found blood and the same smash-up indicating a struggle. Blood in the bedroom turned out to be hers."

Lottie's house was neatly kept. Most of the damage was confined to her bedroom—bed pulled sideways, covers wrenched half off, blood smeared on the sheets and floor, leading down the hall. She'd been dragged out.

I hated Lottie. I had good reason; I'd been her apprentice for three resurrections, before I'd transferred to Marvin Jones, my permanent instructor. I'd hated every filthy second of being around Lottie and watching her work. I'd lodged a complaint against her with the Board of Review; nothing had come of it, of course. There weren't so many resurrection witches running around that they could afford to turf one just because she was—let's face it—a psychopath.

Even with all that, it still made me cringe to think about what that had been like . . . and what might still be happening to her.

The next file was even worse, because I had no reason at all to dislike Monica Heitmeyer; she was a nice older lady specializing, like me and Lottie, in resurrections, but she mainly did family gigs, reconciling loved ones. As far as I knew, she'd never done any work with the police. She was in the feel-good business.

Two more dead officers at her house, these two killed in the backyard. One had a snapped neck. The other looked like a sack of raw meat. Someone had used him for punching practice. Monica, like Lottie, was missing, but she'd left behind a lot of blood.

Andrew hadn't said anything. His eyes had gone dark and cold, and whatever he was thinking, he kept it to himself.

"What makes you think I'm next on the list?" I asked.

"Not a hell of a lot of witches in your line of work in Austin," Prieto said. "Most of them are already gone. It's down to you and the other one—"

"Annika," I said. "Annika Berwick." I knew her slightly, not well enough to have much of a feeling for how well she'd handle something like this. Annika was frail, nearly seventy, a sweet old grandmother of a witch who'd informally retired from practice last year. "You're protecting her, right?"

"Sure they are," Andy said softly. His gaze hadn't left Prieto at all. "They leave you open, you're the next target. That the idea, Detective? Holly's your damn stalking horse."

Prieto didn't answer. The truth was that he probably had

strike teams ready to roll, and full surveillance, but he wanted it to look like he wasn't coming anywhere near us.

He wanted everyone to think that we were all on our own.

"Have you talked to Annika?"

Prieto nodded. "She's good."

I didn't know about Annika, but I knew how I felt about it, and *good* didn't exactly ring true. I desperately needed a shower and a gallon of Ben & Jerry's ice cream to deal with this.

All of this explained why the Police Department was willing to spend the exorbitant cost to have Andrew Toland brought back. Resurrection witches were a rare breed, and valuable. Six in a city of more than six hundred thousand; there were fewer in Dallas, only a couple hanging tough against a storm of fundamentalist persecution. Austin remained the home—and refuge—of the weird.

Didn't feel like home right now.

I turned to Andrew. "You don't have to do this," I said. "I can release you. I *should* release you. This isn't your fight, it's mine."

He gave me a look that drilled right into my core. "No, it's not. They were right to bring me into it, Holly. This is how the war starts—put down those who might fight, and do it early. Nobody left to fight when the evil comes calling." His blue eyes took on distance and chill. "I've seen it done."

It had, in fact, been done to him. "It's still not your problem."

"True enough," he said, and there came that slow, warm smile again, breaking my heart. "Still. I think you're my problem."

---

WE DIDN'T SPEAK on the drive back. I heard the jingle of the bottles in my case in the backseat; I'd been watching Andy for any sign that he needed a booster, but he seemed fine. Better than fine, actually. The spell that bound him here also bound us together; I knew I'd feel some sense from him if—when—he began to feel pain, or drift.

So far, nothing. It was like being with anyone. Any living person, that is.

"The last time," Andy said. "I know we got the killer. What about the girl? Did I get her out?"

I shuddered. I couldn't help it, and I couldn't hide it. All of a sudden, the realities of it crashed down on me, and the lockbox of feelings blew open, and I was shaking like a leaf in a storm.

I dimly heard Andy asking me what was wrong, but I couldn't tell him. I pulled the car over into a vacant parking lot, threw it into park, and stumbled out with my arms wrapped around myself for comfort. The warm humid air didn't help. I was coming apart.

I heard Andy's passenger-side door slam, and quick footsteps on the gravel, and then his arms wrapped around me fast and hard. "Hush," he murmured, with his lips against my hair. "Hush, now, Holly. It's not so bad as that."

But it was—oh, it was. His question had opened up Pandora's box, and I couldn't keep any of it under lock and key anymore. "She—she—oh, Andy, I'm sorry—"

"She died," he said, and pushed me back far enough that he could look into my eyes. His were dark, all pupil even under the streetlight. "Feared she would. Couldn't get to her before he cut her. All I could do was try to get her to you before it was too late."

My heart just broke. He remembered, but he didn't *know*. I'd resurrected Andrew last year to deal with a witch out of Chicago who'd been on the run, who'd taken to abducting girls he fancied, killing them, and reviving them over and over for his fun.

Andy had gone in to stop the witch, and save the last girl before it was too late.

He'd accomplished part of it—the witch was dead, and Andy had made damn certain the bastard couldn't come back. The girls he'd enslaved were gone as well.

But that last child, all of sixteen. . . . She'd died in Andy's arms as he used the last of his strength to try to get her to safety. It had felt like it was all for nothing, because of that. It wasn't—the witch wouldn't be hurting anyone else—but it had felt hollow. Horribly empty.

I hadn't realized until just now *why* it had felt so awful. It had been the tragedy of the girl, yes, but it had been *Andy*. Andy's stunning courage.

I'd felt him go, and it had felt like losing someone I loved.

I burst into tears and buried my face in his hospital-style shirt. He smelled sterile, astringent, not living at all, but it didn't matter. He felt *real*.

And I could *not* be in love with a dead man. I just could not. No matter how close we'd gotten before. No matter how good this felt just now.

Andy smoothed my hair with gentle strokes, not speaking. I felt him touch his lips gently to the top of my head.

"I remember, you know," he said at last. "You were there all the time, Holly. You were all that kept me moving, at the last. You were the light."

That only made me cry harder. I was thinking about him

wounded and dying, struggling to save that girl. About how I'd kept him alive, alive, alive through all the pain and agony.

Until I hadn't.

It hadn't been Andy who'd faltered. . . . It had been me. I hadn't been strong enough for him, in the end.

"She was dying before I ever got to her," he said. "And she's peaceful now, Holly. So let it be."

I couldn't stop crying. His hand rubbed my back in slow, gentle circles.

"I don't think you understand what it was like waking up today, seeing you." His fingers touched my chin and tipped it up. "If I need to die for you, I will. But let's not spend the time in tears."

I could feel his heartbeat. See the fast pulse moving under his skin. I could feel our souls touching, intimate in ways that mere living people couldn't achieve, and I understood just how deep this went between us.

I pressed my hand over his heart, feeling the strong, steady pace. "You can't stay with me," I said. My voice, normally so steady, sounded soft and uncertain. "We don't get second chances, Andy."

He smiled. "Sure we do," he said. "What's this, if it ain't a second chance? Or, more proper for me, a third?"

And he kissed me. Warm lips, blood-warm, tasting of the potion that I'd given him. *Toxic*, something in me warned, but I didn't care.

Andy's thumbs stroked my cheekbones, and his big hands seemed so certain about what they were doing.

I was kissing a dead man, and I didn't care a bit. I wanted to keep on kissing him until the sun burned out.

The memory of the harsh, bloodstained photographs Prieto had shown us flashed across my eyes, and I pulled free with a gasp, stepping back.

"What?" he asked. He took my hands, but didn't try to pull me into his arms.

"It's not safe," I said. "We're not safe. We need to get inside."

Andy smiled—a real, full smile. "You think I can't protect you, Holly?"

"I don't want you to have to."

He nodded out into the dark. "Ain't the only one. Prieto sent a couple of fellas on our tail. They're parked over there, watching us."

I shuddered. Somehow, that made it even worse, both that there were eyes on us, and that I was putting Prieto's men at risk just by being such an easy target. "Let's go home."

We got back in the car, and I broke speed limits on the way.

ANDY WAS ALL business when we pulled into the drive. Although he'd never worked as a bodyguard, at least not that I knew of, he made me stay in the car with the motor running and the garage door open as he went into the house and checked it out. I waited tensely, imagining every second that I would feel an echo of *something* through the bond . . . I'd lived through the sickening spiral of his torment and death once already, and I knew what it would feel like.

I nearly screamed when he popped up next to the car and motioned for me to get out. I closed the garage door, shut off the motor, and followed him into the house.

"Locks?" he asked. I turned them, and then set the security

alarm for instant alarm. If any door or window opened, we'd know, and so would the police. My heart was hammering. I thought about Lottie, evidently surprised in her sleep. Monica, taken in the evening as she was getting ready for bed, bathwater gone cold in the tub. "They come at night," I said. "Don't open any doors or windows. The alarm will go off."

"Fancy."

I smiled faintly. "Normal, these days. We live in scary times."

"Ain't nobody ever lived any other time." Andy, not content with the electronic alarm, was roaming around and testing doors and windows, engaging all locks. "You set this magic watchdog when you left today?"

"I didn't know I was being *stalked*."

Andy stopped and looked at me, hands gone still on a windowsill. "They didn't tell you." I shook my head. "Why not?"

"People all that fond of resurrection witches, back in your day?"

That earned me a full crooked grin. "Not enough so you'd blush. Stay here, I'll check the other floor."

I watched him take the stairs, then went to the kitchen and put away the ritual pots I'd washed. I fixed myself a sandwich. Spellcasting took a lot out of me, and despite everything, I was feeling a small, significant drain of energy through the bond with Andy. Needed to keep my strength up, through the magic of carbs and protein.

I was just swallowing the last bite when Andy walked into the kitchen. "Never got to see your house last time," Andy said. He sat down at the kitchen table and looked around. "Big place. Warm. You live here all on your own? What about your family?"

"My parents and my sister live in New England. You going to tell me a woman can't live on her own?"

"I'd never dare," Andy said. " 'Specially not one who holds the keys to life and death. Then again, that's pretty much any woman, so I'll just keep my peace about it. Besides, I don't know your world all that much, 'cept it's about as full of villains as the time I knew. Could be women tell men what's for now, strange as that would seem."

"Andy—"

His blue eyes stopped surveying the granite countertops and focused on me, and *wow*, that packed voltage. "I'm not sorry," he said. "Stupid for a man to fall in love once he's dead, but I've done it, and there it is. But at least you know I'll do everything in my power to keep you alive, Holly Anne."

I couldn't even speak. What do you say to that? A dead man falls in love with you, and there's no chance for a future together. I knew that every minute, every *second* of this was limited. I wanted to take him straight to bed, but I didn't know—I didn't know for certain how that worked. Or even *if* it did. The subject of the sexual performance of dead men had never been included in my apprenticeship—probably deliberately. The potential for abuse of resurrections was huge, and our limits were strict. It was part of why we maintained such emotional distance.

Andy sensed my internal struggle, and he brought out his gentlest smile. It did great things to his face, put a devastating sparkle in his eyes.

I stood up, barely able to feel my legs. "I'm—going to bed. Do you want—?" My throat closed up, and I had to clear it. Embarrassing. "Do you want me to make up the spare bed?"

Andy kept smiling. "No. I ain't sleeping, am I?"

He had a point. Bodyguards didn't, and neither did the dead. I felt flushed and awkward and out of control.

"Okay, then," I said. "Good night."

He nodded, and watched me as I left the kitchen.

A hot shower and a pair of silk pajamas later, I retreated to my soft, lonely bed and tried to sleep. It was getting on toward the wee hours of the morning, but I didn't feel tired. I felt anxious, and achy, and relentlessly squirmy.

I could hear Andy roaming around downstairs. I wondered what he was doing—looking over my bookshelves? Examining my pictures? Getting intimate with me in ways that didn't involve climbing into bed with me?

*Shut up*, I told myself when my brain started to run wild with images. *The man is dead. He's here to do a job, and then he's gone. And that's it.*

Except it wasn't, and Andy had said he loved me, and I *knew* I loved him. No getting around that. Bringing him back a second time—no, for him it was the *third*—had been cruel, and unnecessary, and wrong, and if I'd known what Prieto wanted him for, I'd have said no even at the cost of my own life.

I didn't want Andy dying for me.

I'D DRIFTED OFF into an uneasy half slumber when something woke me up. I felt a tingle inside, and opened my eyes to stare at the ceiling. I knew that feeling, all too well. No chance of sleeping now.

I slipped out of bed, wrapped myself in a silk robe, and went downstairs.

Andy was standing at the windows, looking out. He didn't wait for me to ask. "I'm fine," he said.

"You're not." I'd carried my black case in from the car, and now I flipped it open and reached for the second vial of the stepped dose.

It felt light.

The bottle was empty.

I stared at it in stupefied horror for a few seconds, then dropped it back into the holder and pulled the third. The fourth.

The bottles were *all* empty. I began yanking the rest out to check. *Empty, empty, empty!*

Andy turned at the sound of my labored breathing and the rattle of glass. He frowned. "What?"

"It's not—someone sabotaged my case." *Breathe,* I told myself. *Come on. Think.* The case had been with me, and completely full, at the morgue. All the time? No. I'd set it in the corner of the viewing room, and we'd both gone with Detective Prieto to look over files. The case had been left unattended. "The potions. They're gone."

Andy took a step toward me, then stopped. His blue eyes widened, just a little. "All of it?"

"Everything."

I abandoned the case and raced into the kitchen. I opened the refrigerator.

The four doses I kept on hand for emergencies were gone. I found the bottles in the trash, empty.

"Oh, *Christ,*" I whispered. Andy's hands touched my shoulders, and I felt him behind me, solid and real.

"It's all right," he said. "I don't need it yet."

"It's *not* all right. It takes hours to brew, and—" A terrible thought struck me. I opened the pantry, where I kept all my supplies.

*Gone.* I'd been cleaned out.

I felt a numb horror go through me. "There's nothing. I can't even get the ingredients until tomorrow morning at the earliest, then it takes all day to brew the base—"

"It'll be all right," Andy repeated.

I turned on him, suddenly furious. "It's *not*! Don't you get it? I know you're in pain already! It's going to get worse, Andy, and if I don't let you go—"

His hands closed around my face. "Pain, I can handle. I ain't leaving you alone. They've been here. They were in your house."

"*Who?*"

"Somebody who knows you," he said. "Somebody who knows what you're afraid of."

I was afraid of hurting him. Again.

He smoothed my hair back, and kissed me. It was soft and cool and gentle, but I sensed how much restraint it took for him to keep it that way.

"I can handle this," he said. "I *will*. You believe me, Holly?"

I gulped and nodded convulsively. "Okay."

I didn't, and it wasn't. But he wasn't finished.

"Get dressed and pack a bag," he said. "We're going."

I pulled a suitcase from under my bed and threw a few items in. Then I opened a drawer and took out a pair of pants, a dark shirt, underwear, shoes, and socks: his own clothes, from the last time I'd brought him back. Somehow, I'd never been able to get rid of them. I put them on the bed, and Andy, standing at the door, gave me a long, measuring look that told me he understood why I'd kept them. Why they'd been so close.

He didn't say anything.

"Better change," I said without looking directly at his face.

"Holly—"

"Not now."

As soon as he changed into the clothes, we left.

NO MATTER HOW tough you are, nobody takes pain well when it comes on slow and cold, with nothing to cushion it.

I kept dialing phone numbers, trying to get *somebody* on the phone who could help as we drove. Sam Twist wasn't answering—not his phone, his cell, or his secret emergency number. I tried Annika. No answer there, either. I tried Detective Prieto, but it rang directly to his voice mail.

I thought about calling 911, but what was I going to say? *I have a dead man here who needs his medicine?*

I had no idea what to do. I could feel Andy's pain, black and constant and growing, and I was helpless to prevent it from getting worse.

"Holly?"

I took my eyes off the road for just a second. His lights shone silver, unreal in the dashboard lights.

"Why'd you bring me back?"

Of all the questions I'd expected, that had to be last on the list. I held his stare for a long few seconds, then blinked and focused on the road. "Lottie," I said. "They were going to do it anyway, and they were going to let Lottie—I couldn't let that happen. I thought maybe it would be better for you if it was me, that's all."

"That's all."

"Yes."

"You're a liar. Pretty one, but a liar."

And he was right. I was lying not just to him, but also to myself.

I loved him. I'd grown to love him during that first

resurrection, and I'd lost him, and it had hurt me. Having him back was a painful barbed-wire ball of a miracle, because it contained the seeds of its own destruction.

My hand left the steering wheel and touched his, and his fingers closed warm and strong over mine.

"Where we going?" he asked.

There was only one place, really. The other witches had been abducted, dragged out without warning, which meant that their supplies would have remained intact.

I needed to make him some potion.

Lottie's house was the closest.

"THE COPS," I said. "Are they following us?"

Andrew had shut his eyes—fighting back pain, I could feel it—but he opened them as I turned the car out of the driveway and scanned the street. "Don't see 'em," he said. "Don't mean they ain't around, though. Since we're bait in the trap, they'd like your killer to have room to breathe, seems to me."

I hoped the police would follow us, but I couldn't wait to find out. Time was running out.

On the way, I remembered to call in sick to work—not that keeping my day job was the most important thing in my world, but it was normal life, and I desperately wanted to believe that there would still be a normal life, after today.

The sun was on the rise as we navigated morning rush hour, heading for Lottie's neighborhood. She had a place in an upscale area, one story but sprawling. It was the kind of place that was deserted by day—working families out from seven to seven. The only sign of life along the street was a lawn-service truck in the distance, and a couple of guys on riding lawn mowers.

Lottie's driveway was empty, so I turned in and parked in the back. Yellow police tape fluttered here and there, but they'd finished their work in the yard. An official-looking seal was on the back door, and a newly installed padlock.

I opened the trunk of the car and took out a rusty tire iron, which I handed to Andy. He weighed it in his hand for a moment, then nodded and popped the padlock with a single wrench. He had to stop for a moment and brace himself, and I felt the swirl of darkness between us as the inevitable tide rolled over him.

"Andy," I said. He shook his head.

"Let's just get it done," he said. "This ain't nothing yet."

He was right. It would get a lot worse. That didn't mean it wasn't bad, though, bad enough to drive most men to their knees.

The death-tide was pulling him back. Pulling him away from me.

I ripped open the seal on the door and stepped into Lottie's kitchen.

There were few signs of violence in here—neatly ranked pots and pans, shelves of supplies. I quickly rummaged through them, breathing easier with every single thing I found. Yes, yes, yes . . .

I opened the refrigerator door, and inside saw not just a few bottles, but a gallon jar of swirling silver liquid.

A *gallon jar.*

Andy joined me, alerted by my expression. "Why'd she make so much?" he asked. I shook my head. There was absolutely no reason for Lottie to do a thing like that—the expense was enormous. Unless she'd found an effective way to really store the stuff—no, when I wrestled the gallon jar out of the refrigerator and onto the counter, I could tell that it was at least a week old, probably two. Not bad, but not fresh, either.

In another week, it would be useless. It was a foolish waste. Why the hell did Lottie brew it like this?

"She's been up to something," Andy said. He might have been reading my mind. "Makes you wonder why she wanted me back, don't it?"

I dipped up a cup of the potion, sniffed it again, and tilted it this way and that in the mug. "I don't trust this," I said. "It doesn't feel right, Andy. I just—"

He held up a hand to silence me.

"What?" I whispered.

"I think maybe someone's here," he said.

I sealed up the jar and hefted it. We'd take it with us. It'd have to serve until I could brew my own.

Andy turned his eyes back toward me, and there was something dawning in his expression, something grim and terrible.

He lifted the mug I'd filled and poured it into the sink.

"What are you doing?"

"Somebody's been studying up." Andy didn't bother to keep his voice down. "Used this same trick myself, long ago. Made up a batch of poisoned brew, left it for the revenants to drink when they came looking. Did for quite a few that way, back in the wars."

*Poison.* I looked down at the jar and let it slide out of my hands and back to the counter.

"Come out," Andy said. "You want us dead, you do it barefaced."

"All right," said a smoke-strained, whisky-rough voice from the hall, and a big redheaded man stepped into the light. There was a gun in his hand, pointed not at Andy, but at me. "How's this?"

Sam Twist. *I'm just the dispatcher.* "Sam—" I wet my lips. Andy stepped between me and the gun, and I heard three loud pops in quick succession.

Andy just stood there and took the bullets, shook himself, and said in a voice I didn't even recognize, "You all done, Irish, or you want to reload?"

I slid slowly along the counter, angling for a view of Sam. He was calmly holding the gun at his side.

"No need," he said. "I was just softening you up a little. No question, you're one hell of an opponent. That's why I tried to get Holly to take a pass on bringing you back again."

"Mine," scraped another voice, and the thing that shuffled into view next to Sam . . . if it had been born human, it hadn't stayed that way. Misshapen, malformed as a dropped lump of clay, but roped with muscle. Dead gray eyes. Pointed teeth displayed by lips that had been cut or ripped away. Sam was a big man, and this—creature—topped him by a foot or more. Its shoulders were broader than the doorway.

I remembered the photographs of the cops. Beaten to death. Necks snapped.

Andy had never looked fragile to me until that moment.

If he was worried, or even startled, it didn't show. He bounced lightly on the balls of his feet, eyes fixed on Sam's monster. "Well, ain't you pretty?" he said, cool and quiet. "Your momma must be real proud."

The thing swayed, but didn't move. Its blind-looking gaze strayed from Andy . . . to me.

A low growl started in its throat, a diesel engine running

rough, and I felt Andy's whole body tense. "Get behind me," he said. "Holly, dammit, do that right now."

I did, but not before I got a glimpse at the blood soaking the front of his shirt, and the tattered flesh beneath. Dead men could die, and they could feel pain, and no matter how focused and tough Andy was, he couldn't overcome this monster.

Not alone.

"Who is he?" I whispered. Sam couldn't have brought this creature back, not on his own.

"He was my brother Donal," Sam Twist said. "Before Lottie got hold of him."

He was *Lottie's*. But Lottie was dead. Wasn't she? "She— brought him back?"

"He got knifed in a bar fight," Sam said. "Strongest man I ever knew. I begged her to help, and she did. She brought him back. But I didn't know what she'd *do* with him."

Sam moved over to the side, edging to where he could once again see my face, and line up a clear shot. Andy didn't move. He clearly thought it was better to stand between me and Donal.

"What did she do?" I was acutely aware now of the blood pooling at Andy's feet, of the waves of darkness vibrating the air between us. Death was coming, and coming no matter how hard he pushed against it.

"What does it *look* like she did, you bitch?" Sam spat, and the sudden raw fury in him exploded like nitro. "She *used him*. My own brother. She told me she put him back to sleep, but she didn't. She set him to fighting other dead men like some trained bear, and brought him back, kept dragging him back until there was nothing left. She took *bets*." Sam swallowed hard. "But he remembered. He heard my voice on the phone, and he remembered."

Sam's face was red, distorted with anguish, and his eyes were glittering with tears. I swallowed hard to clear the lump from my throat. "He came to find you," I said. "Oh, Sam, I'm sorry."

He sneered at me. There was no more sanity in his eyes now than in his brother's. "Keep your pity," he said. "I don't want it. I'm putting you down, bitch. I'm putting all of you *down*."

Lottie wasn't dead. Lottie couldn't be dead, if Donal was still alive. Sam had her somewhere, under lock and key, maybe drugged or worse, but still breathing.

She was Donal's only vulnerability.

I was still partly blocked from Sam's view. With my right hand, I dug my cell phone from my pocket, flipped it open, and hit and held the speed dial number I'd assigned to Detective Prieto. I had to hope he'd answer or, at worst, that his voice mail would give him the clues he needed after the fact to put it all together. "You kept Lottie alive," I said. "Right, Sam? To suffer."

"Damn straight," he said. "When I'm done with you, I'll take out Annika, and we can move on to the next town. You have to be stopped, all of you."

"You're using Donal just as much as Lottie did," I said. "Let him go, Sam. God—please, let him *go*!"

"No," he snapped. "Not until every single one of you is dead. Don't move, Holly. I want you to watch what happens next."

He knew. He knew about Andrew; he'd heard how traumatized I was when I'd lost him before.

He wanted me to watch him die again.

---

DONAL WAS FAST, but Andy was faster. Even wounded, he was as lithe as a cat. He dodged Donal's roaring charge, tripped the twisted giant, and bashed Donal's skull hard into the marble counter. I backed away, dodged behind the fighting men, and screamed into the phone, "Prieto, it's Sam Twist, find Lottie, Lottie's the key—"

Donal's hand slapped the phone away from me, and it bounced and broke into scattered pieces against the far wall. A bone snapped in my hand, and I choked back a scream, then another as I felt Andy's torment surge stronger. He was feeling my pain, too.

He'd do anything to stop it, and that was so dangerous.

I needed the gun Sam held.

I settled for grabbing a cleaver from the block next to the stove. Lottie, like all good cooks and witches, kept her tools in order; the cleaver had a wicked fine edge, a silky deadliness that vibrated the air.

I kept Donal between me and Sam as he sought for a clear shot. Andy slipped in his own blood; his strike at Donal's massive throat lost its strength, and Donal's huge gray hands closed on his shoulders.

I felt Andy's arm being wrenched out of its socket. I screamed. He grunted and pulled halfway free, but Donal bunched up a fist and drew back—

I threw myself to the floor and swiped the cleaver through Donal's Achilles' tendons, and he toppled, howling, like a tree. The table collapsed under his impact. Andy squirmed free, panting, and I felt the tide coming faster, deeper, all that darkness swirling and clouding the air between us as he tried to get to me. . . .

Sam fired twice. One shot hit Donal's flailing arm and kicked a fist-sized chunk of flesh out of it. The second shot . . .

The second shot took Andy in the chest as he lunged to cover me.

"No!" I shrieked, and took his weight in my arms as he collapsed against me.

There was no fighting the emptiness that rolled over me now, the call of endless peace, and I felt Andy slipping away.

I felt him find some small, impossible anchor in that tide, and his body shuddered against mine, holding me tight against him. *He can't. He can't make it.* Even the dead had to die.

But Andy refused to go.

He pulled back, and his eyes were liquid silver, the color of the potion I'd dosed him with in the morgue. His skin was as pale as paper. Most of his blood was poured out on the floor, an offering to harsher gods than I could ever worship.

But he *stayed standing*.

He took in a deep breath, and closed his eyes. "Potion," he whispered. "Give it to me."

The jar behind me on the counter.

*Poisoned.*

"No," I said. "No, Andy."

Another shot struck him. I screamed something at Sam, I don't even know what, and he bared his teeth in response. Donal was crawling toward us across the floor. He couldn't stand, but he wouldn't give up. He wanted me dead as much as Sam did.

Andy reached behind me, fumbled the gallon jar of silver liquid, and looked at me with the most heartbreaking plea. "Help," he whispered. I felt the tide roaring in again, stronger this time. He couldn't resist that, not even for me.

I helped him lift the jar.

One swallow.

Two.

Sam's next bullet hit the jar and exploded it into a shower of glass. The potion coated us both and swirled in thick silvery streams in the blood on the floor.

But it worked.

I felt the black surging inside Andy fall away, and the sudden pulsebeat of life took over. For just an instant, his eyes locked with mine, and I saw a promise there.

An acceptance, too.

Donal's huge hand swiped at his feet, but Andy sidestepped and waltzed me with him. He put me gently out of the way, and turned to Sam Twist.

"You got plenty of cause to hate," Andy said. "Your brother's been used hard. But you took it too far, mister. You got no quarrel with Holly."

"She's a witch."

Andy's smile turned wolfish. "So am I, mister. And now you got a quarrel with me."

Sam fired again, and hit Andy. The bullet wounds didn't seem to matter at all; with a bellow of rage, Sam rushed forward, still firing. Andy moved like a bullfighter, avoiding the attack, and swung his arm around Sam's throat from behind. He threw his weight into the motion. Sam's feet slipped in the blood, and his neck snapped with a muffled dry crackle. It happened too fast for me to really take in, and then the life was leaving Sam's blue eyes and his body falling in that utterly empty way that only the dead can fall as Andy let him go.

Donal howled, and it hurt me to hear it. He crawled past

us and cradled Sam's broken body in his massive arms, small as a toy.

I tightened my grip on the cleaver and swallowed hard. As I took a step toward him, Donal looked up at me. I knew he could take me apart.

And I knew he was done fighting.

Andy turned toward me, and our gazes met again.

He'd taken two steps toward me when Lottie's poison took hold. Andy's fearsome strength of will might be able to deny bullet wounds, but this was different. Very different.

His legs folded, and he fell to his side, panting. His pupils grew huge, no longer silver but black, black as the death that was coming for him.

"Next time," he whispered. "You watch yourself, Holly Anne."

I dropped to my knees beside him and put my hand on his forehead as he began to convulse.

I tasted poison on his lips, and I wondered in a black, desolate fury if it would be enough to finish me. It wasn't.

The universe wasn't quite that merciful.

"Miss Caldwell," Detective Prieto said. I raised my head slowly, every muscle aching and hot. Part of it was Lottie's poisonous mixture; the other part was a collection of injuries I hadn't realized I'd accumulated until the heat of battle was past. I was back in the hospital. They'd taken Donal away in a steel prison truck, howling for his dead brother. They'd taken Andy away in a coroner's wagon, along with Sam. I'd screamed about the two of them riding together, but the cops thought I was out of my mind.

Maybe I was.

I looked at Detective Prieto wearily, too exhausted to care about the pity in his eyes. "Did you find her?"

"We did," he said. "She was drugged. Chained up in a room underneath Sam Twist's house."

I nodded. "And the others?"

He just looked at me. Sam hadn't needed the others, of course. He'd needed only Lottie to keep Donal alive.

Perversely, Lottie still lived, like the cockroach surviving nuclear winter. And so did Donal, for all the good it did him.

"You okay?" Prieto asked. It was my turn to stare, and he turned away from what he saw in my expression. "Lottie's down the hall, I hear. They say she'll make a full recovery."

With that, he pushed open the door to the grim little hospital room and left. It hurt too much to stand up, but I did it anyway, and shuffled to follow.

Prieto was getting into the elevator when I emerged, but he caught my eye and jerked his chin down the hall. "Four down," he said.

The doors shut.

Carlotta was a lovely woman with the soul of a pig. I'd always known that, but I'd never really *known*.

I'd never seen the depths. Now I couldn't get out of them. Not without climbing over someone else.

She'd do.

Carlotta was asleep. She looked older than I remembered, with black hair threaded with silver and lines on her face. Could have been someone's mother, someone's grandmother. Asleep, you couldn't see the real person.

Her eyes opened when I dragged a chair up next to her bed—brown, as confused as any soul dragged back from the dark. Except she'd been drugged, not dead, and the softness cleared from her in seconds.

"Holly." She nearly spat my name. "I should have known he'd spare you. Sam always liked *you*."

I didn't answer her. Somewhere, in the coldest part of me, I was seeing the agony of Andy's last moments, and I was realizing how much Lottie would have enjoyed it.

"The others?"

"Dead," I said. My voice sounded soft and distant. "How long have you been doing this?"

"Doing what?"

"Bringing back the dead and fighting them like dogs. For *money*."

Lottie's bitter brown eyes narrowed. "Don't you judge me, you little bitch. We all bring them back for profit." She smiled slowly. "I'm just creative."

The room looked red for a few seconds, and I had trouble controlling my breathing. My hands ached, and realized I'd clenched them into tight, shaking fists.

"Creative," I repeated. "Why'd you ask Prieto for Andy?"

"I knew somebody was stalking us," she said. "If anybody could stop it, Toland would have been the one. Besides—" She was still smiling, and it had a sharp, cutting edge to it. "—he'd have made me a lot of money, after. A *lot* of money."

I shuddered. It was hard to stay in the chair. Hard not to put my hands around her throat and squeeze.

"You're done," I said. "I'm going to make it my personal mission to see you're finished."

"How?" Lottie's laugh broke on the air like ice. "You're a stupid girl. I'm the *victim*. You counting on the Review Board? Better not. With so many resurrection witches gone, they might give me a fine, but they need me. Now more than ever."

She was probably right, at that. Resurrection witches were a rare breed, and she and I were the only ones left working in the city. The Review Board would blame Sam. Lottie would get away with a slap on the wrist.

Lottie would do it again, and I wouldn't be able to stop her. The police wouldn't act. The dead didn't have legal rights.

I stood up. Lottie's dark gaze followed me as I crossed to the door. There was a thumb-lock on the inside, and I flipped it over.

Lottie laughed. "You going to kill me, Holly? You going to spend your life in prison over dead men?"

"No," I said. "Funny thing about comas, Lottie. You can slip back into them without warning. It's really tragic."

A flash of something in her eyes that might have been fear. Her hand reached for the call button.

I got there first.

I held her down. She struggled, and snarled, but when my lips touched hers, it was all over.

I was the best resurrection witch in Austin. One thing about being able to give life to the dead . . . you can take it from the living. It's forbidden, but it can be done.

I didn't take all her life. Just enough.

Just enough to leave her wandering in the dark, screaming, trapped inside her own head. Her body would live, mute and unresponsive, for as long as modern science could maintain it, but Lottie Flores would never, ever bring back the dead again.

Not even herself.

---

ANDY WAS IN the morgue downstairs, and I had to see him. What I'd done to Lottie had hurt me in ways that might never be right again, but somehow seeing his face, even in death, would give me peace.

He was so lovely. And he was at peace, the way I knew he should be.

I kissed him lightly. I didn't have any potion, and I put no spell behind it; it was just a kiss, just the brush of lips.

But the *emotion* behind it—darkness and passion and need, so much need, it seemed to bleed silver from my pores.

Magic.

I felt him reaching for me, in the dark, and I couldn't help but respond. It wasn't my own doing. I wasn't this strong.

I felt the connection snap clean between us, silver and hot, vibrating like a plucked string.

His eyes opened, and he smiled.

"You came back," I murmured.

"'Course I did, Holly," he said. "I'll always come for you."

"I didn't—there's no potion—"

"Don't need it," Andy said. He stirred, and the sheet across his bare chest slipped down, revealing raw bullet holes that were, before my eyes, sealing themselves closed. "Got myself some skills, you know. More than most."

I kissed him again, tasting potions and poisons and my own tears. "How long can you stay?" I asked.

He smiled. "Long as you want me."

Forever.

Rachel Caine is the author of the popular Weather Warden series, with the most recent book, *Gale Force*, released in August 2008. She also writes the *New York Times* bestselling young adult Morganville Vampires series; the fifth installment, *Lord of Misrule*, was released in January 2009, with *Carpe Corpus* following in June 2009. She has another series, Outcast Season, starting in January 2009 with the novel *Undone*. In addition, Rachel has written paranormal romantic suspense for *Silhouette*, including *Devil's Bargain, Devil's Due*, and *Athena Force: Line of Sight* (which won a 2007 *Romantic Times BOOKreviews* Reviewer's Choice award). Visit her Web site: www.rachelcaine.com. Myspace: www.myspace.com/rachelcaine.

# Vegas Odds

Karen Chance

The pounding began at 2:11 A.M. and continued until I hauled my weary ass out of bed. My hand fumbled awkwardly around the nightstand until it finally closed over my gun. I was fuzzy from lack of sleep, but I never left my weapon behind these days. Besides, I was going to need it to shoot whoever was banging on the damn door.

I threw on a robe and stomped downstairs, only to be almost smothered by the huge bouquet of hothouse extravagance that was waiting on the front stoop. "D-delivery?" someone said, about the time I realized that the forest of roses had legs.

"Do you know what time it is?!"

"Uh, a little after nine?" a man's voice said. I belatedly noticed the sunlight cascading over my nonwelcome mat. It was a gift from a sarcastic werewolf and read, MY BITE ACTUALLY *IS* WORSE THAN MY BARK. I'd never been sure if he meant his or mine.

Dammit; my clock must have stopped. And with my

schedule these days, my body was so confused that it hadn't woken me up, either. "Hey," I croaked, like I wasn't still holding a gun on him.

I quickly lowered it, trying to remember how to smile. It didn't seem to help. The overabundant foliage was shaking enough to send a cascade of petals over my doorstep, and a glimpse in the hall boy mirror explained why. My long brown hair was a tangled mess, my eyes were so bloodshot that it was impossible to tell they were gray, and weeks of almost no sleep and constant menace had reduced my smile to something closer to a snarl.

But the delivery guy refused to be deterred by irate, possibly crazed homeowners. "Ms. Accalia de Croissets?" Surprisingly, he didn't mangle the pronunciation of my name.

"Lia," I corrected automatically, reaching to the hall boy for my purse and a tip. I wondered what the right percentage was after pulling a gun on someone. My purse slipped out of my sleep-clumsy grasp and I bent to pick it up—and thereby dodged the spell that tore through my foyer and into my living room.

I had a glimpse of drywall bits cascading over the carpet as the partition between rooms was obliterated; then my gun was up and I was firing. It shredded roses but did nothing to the mage posing as a delivery guy. He had shields, a fact I realized about the time one of my own bullets hit them and ricocheted off, grazing my cheek. So I turned the hall boy over on top of him and ran, cursing my stupidity.

My new job was training recruits to the War Mage Corps, the magical equivalent of the police. Most of my students started out painfully naïve, yet even they wouldn't have answered the door woozy and only half-armed. *I'll probably end up an axiom,* I thought. "Give a demon an edge, and he'll slit your throat with it." "It's amazing how many things a stake through the heart can kill." And "Don't do a Lia; keep your damn weapons with you!" Only mine were on the floor of my bathroom, where I'd dropped them last night before taking a shower.

I could hear the mage thrashing through the mess behind me as I hurled myself at the stairs. I was halfway up when a burst of energy crackled overhead, electrifying my body and making my hair stand on end. The steps in front of me disappeared in a roar of heat and noise.

A splinter the size of a knife stabbed me in the calf as I fell, one leg in the smoking hole, one slipping to the side to wedge itself between banisters. I didn't try to pull free—there wasn't time—just muttered a spell that sent the contents of a bookcase flying down at the mage. Pages fluttered like bird's wings as they soared past my head and slammed into my attacker. They didn't get through his shields, but a few of the larger ones staggered him, and the wildly flapping pages made it impossible for him to see. It bought me a few seconds to rip my bleeding leg free of the hole and hobble the rest of the way up.

The damn splinter had done something nasty to my knee, which was screaming in protest and gave out entirely by the time my foot touched the top step. I dropped to the floor and a spell shimmered and blurred the air overhead. It passed close enough to ruffle my hair on its way to destroy the now-empty bookcase.

Tiny splinters peppered my legs through the thin cotton of my pj's as I threw an impediment spell behind me and started fast-crawling down the corridor. I'd made it a couple of yards before I realized there were no sounds of pursuit. I glanced over my shoulder—because no way had a small diversion like that stopped a war mage—and therefore failed to see the floor in front of me vanish.

The deafening sound of the explosion whipped my head around in time for me to shrink back from the bullets spraying upward through the hole. They ricocheted everywhere in the small space, but I managed to raise my shields before any of them connected. I'd hoped to put that off a little—shields eat power like candy, and my reserves were already low. But my weapons wouldn't do me any good if I didn't live long enough to reach them.

My ears were ringing as I started edging around the gap, trying to balance on the two feet of burnt carpet that remained, when another spell took out even that. The blast was a direct hit, and despite my shields, it was like a punch to the face—stunning, dizzying, knocking my head backwards. I fell a story to land hard on my dining room table, along with a ton of plaster, a couple of ceiling joists and my brand-new chandelier.

The impact knocked the air out of me, which is the only reason I didn't scream. My knee had caught the edge of the table, and of course, it was *that* knee on *that* leg and *oh my God.* Something in the joint thwanged before the pain hit me broadside and the world went weirdly bright for a second.

My slide off the table was more of a fall, my injured leg softening under me. I tried to put some steel into it, to straighten up and find my balance, but the best I could do was a drunken stagger as the room spun around me. I teetered, turned shakily, and barely recoiled in time to avoid the folding door from the hall. It came spinning past my head to crash against the far wall in an explosion of slats.

Imminent death is an excellent cure for dizziness. I threw myself at the kitchen door, planning to make for the back steps and a judicious retreat. But I collided with a fireball spell instead. It bounced off my shields and burst against the kitchen table, flooding the air with the acrid smell of not-found-in-nature materials on fire.

I belatedly realized there was a second assassin in the laundry room. And yet another figure was silhouetted against the frosted glass of the back door, working to get past the wards. So I had at least three dark mages after me, and I still didn't have any weapons.

Well, shit.

The long-standing hostility in the supernatural community between the Silver Circle of light magic users—of which the Corps forms a part—and the Black Circle of dark mages had recently escalated into all-out war. As a result, new recruits to the Corps were being housed at HQ until they acquired enough skills to maybe not get themselves killed. But there wasn't room for everyone, and old hands like me were expected to fend for ourselves. *Which I'm going to start doing any minute now,* I thought, hitting linoleum as the back door blew in.

I looked up to see a werewolf in the doorway holding a couple of fast-food bags. "What the—!" he began, but suddenly the air was full of french fries and gunfire, and the newcomer dived for the floor. I scrambled to reach him, my brain screaming, *Get in front of him, get in front of him, don't let them kill him!* even as he was pulling me backwards into the dubious safe zone between the pantry and the fridge.

"Get down!" I yelled, but the latest spell missed us and hit the ceiling instead, dropping beams and plaster as well as a flood from a waterline. It didn't manage to put out the fire, but it did leave my bathtub teetering on the edge of the abyss.

"Is this a bad time?" Cyrus asked. My boyfriend had plaster in his dark hair and dusting his motorcycle jacket, but his Glock was in his hand and his brown eyes were calm. In fact, he looked more composed than me.

"I don't remember us having a date," I said, dropping my shields for an instant to send a spell at the laundry room door. It exploded inward, and I heard someone yelp. I grinned viciously.

"It's Valentine's Day."

"I hate holidays. Crap always happens to me on holidays." I peered out the window and saw what I'd expected: two shadows fell across the pebbly dirt that passed for a lawn in Vegas, although there was nothing to cast them. Mages under cloaking spells, just waiting for their buddies to flush me out into the open. So not happening, assholes.

Cyrus dragged me under the burning table to avoid a spell from mage number one. He'd taken up a position just outside the dining room door, giving him a good angle on the pantry. "What's going on?" he demanded.

"Delivery guy was an assassin."

"And you fell for that?" He emptied a clip into the mage's shields, forcing him to draw back slightly to conserve power.

"I thought the flowers were from you! I should have known better."

"Are you hinting that I'm unromantic?" He fished a backup 9mm out of his jacket.

"The guys trying to kill me send more flowers than you do."

"I never really pictured you as the flowers-and-candy type."

The bathtub ended the discussion by taking that moment

to kamikaze the kitchen table. The scorched Formica splintered, catching almost none of the tub's momentum before it slammed into my shields, popping them like an overstretched balloon. I had a momentary heart-clench of "Cyrus!" the taste of bile and gunpowder thick in my mouth. But he was okay. Somehow, we both were.

I realized that my shields had lasted for a split second after impact, enough time for him to get a grip on the slick bottom of the tub, keeping it from cracking our heads. That was lucky for more than one reason. A hail of bullets from above and a spell from the side were both deflected by our porcelain-and-steel umbrella.

We crouched near the floor, blind except for a two-inch gap at the bottom. It allowed me to see bullets pelting down like metal raindrops, a cloud of flour sifting into the air, and punctured cans oozing their contents everywhere. So much for the pantry.

I considered our options, and they weren't promising. Going out the back way was to walk into a death trap, but the guy in the dining room had us cut off from the front. I hadn't heard anything more from the mage in the laundry room, but even if he was out of commission—a big if—there was no exit that way.

"I'm open to suggestions," Cyrus said, a little strain creeping into his voice.

I realized why when I brushed against the side of the tub and almost burned myself. The spell had heated the metal like a huge soup pot. "Hold on," I said, resigning myself to trashing yet another portion of my new house. And cast a spell that dissolved the floorboards beneath us.

We landed hard on the concrete floor of my basement.

Cyrus threw off the tub and we rolled to either side barely in time to avoid the spell that crashed down, melting the kitchen tiles we'd brought with us into a gooey puddle. "I need to get to my weapons," I said as he pumped bullets back up the hole.

"And they would be where?"

"In the upstairs bathroom."

"Then why are we down here?!"

"Because levitation isn't in my skill set!" I snapped, running to the tiny basement window set high in one wall. I fumbled with it while Cyrus barricaded the door with an old couch abandoned by the previous homeowner.

"It won't hold," he told me, reloading both guns.

"It won't have to." The rusty lock wouldn't budge, so I borrowed Cyrus's Glock and shot it off. It wasn't like everyone didn't already know where we were.

My shoulders popped out of the window, and I did a quick recon before following them. All I could see from this vantage point was a view of mountains and brush and clear desert sky in one direction, and the sun glinting off a mirror and a curve of chrome in the other. Cyrus's bike, parked in the driveway, just visible around the side of the house. No one was in sight, not that that meant much, but it did beat the alternative.

Then the hushed noise of running feet on gravel sounded for a breath, and unseen hands jerked me the rest of the way out the window. I changed my mind. I much preferred an enemy I could see.

Only I could, a little. There are no true invisibility spells, just ones that redirect the eye or provide camouflage. And neither work at point-blank range. As if to underline my thought, the air flickered around the shape of a fist for an instant, right before it socked me in the jaw.

I reached for a weapon even as my head snapped back, but I'd returned Cyrus's gun, and my clip was empty. So I balled my hand into a fist and managed to get a satisfying punch to what might have been a head or possibly a shoulder. It was hard to tell because, even this close, my attacker was only a vague, indistinct contour—a column of man-shaped water that reflected the scenery around it.

I got another crack to the jaw and a sharp jab to the solar plexus in return. My bum leg gave out, and I fell to my hands and knees, gasping and trying not to throw up. I saw a glimmer of what looked like boots, right before a vicious kick in my ribs sent me stumbling into the house. I hit with a bone-numbing crunch, unable to get my hands up in time to cushion the impact, and bounced off to sprawl on my back. Through the haze of pain and the sound of my own ragged breathing, I heard the scuff of approaching footsteps.

Somehow, I rolled to my knees, lashing out with my good leg as I did so. But I was dizzy and my aim was off, and it failed to connect with anything. And then a numbing spell hit me, reducing my motor skills to zero, and I fell back, hard.

I lay there, aching and jittering, trying to breathe through the pain, and for a moment, I think I grayed out. But it didn't last long, because I noticed when a mage suddenly flickered into view over me. He pointed a gun at my head and our eyes met.

"Jason?" I blinked familiar sandy blond hair, clear green eyes, and a pug, freckled nose into view. "What do you think you're doing?"

"Breaking the curve," he informed me with an incongruous ear-to-ear grin.

He dropped his shields in order to fire, only to have Cyrus's fist turn one cheekbone into mush and send him sailing back several yards. I scrambled drunkenly after him, only half-believing my eyes. "You know this guy?" Cyrus demanded as I knelt beside the limp form.

Jason's cheek had split, showing one pale molar through the red meat of his face, but it was undoubtedly him. He was out cold, but at least he had a pulse, possibly because Cyrus had had a bad angle. "He's one of my students."

Cyrus looked down at the gun still grasped in Jason's fingers. "How bad a teacher are you?" he asked incredulously.

"Not this bad!" I said grimly, as two more indistinct shapes ran for us from the front of the house. I hoped it was the two who had been in the backyard earlier, because otherwise the odds were just getting ridiculous. "Dammit!"

My pulse sped, pumping adrenaline through me as I tried and failed to get my shields back up. Cyrus turned and fired, emptying both his guns to slow them down. The sound of gunfire was deafening, and through the tingling, almost-silence afterwards, I watched his hands jerk the clip out of the Glock, grab another from a pocket, and shove it in. "My last," he told me tersely.

I nodded, having looted Jason for a couple of guns, one of which I handed to Cyrus. Jason wasn't wearing much of a potion collection, and what he did have was standard-issue crap that wouldn't help with industrial-strength shields. But he was carrying half a dozen knives, all of which I sent flying at the approaching figures.

Normally, I wouldn't have been able to control another mage's weapons. They are spelled to respond only to the caster to prevent exactly this sort of thing. But Jason had had problems with the spell to animate them and had asked for my help. We'd had fun layering on the charms, spelling his daggers to find and target enemies on their own and to slice through most shields. Yet the dark-haired girl who rippled into view a moment later batted them away with a gesture.

Amelie had always been good with counterspells, I thought numbly, and sent the garden hose coiling through the air toward her, wrapping her up and throwing her to the ground. "They're all my students," I told Cyrus. "Don't kill them!"

"No problem," he said sarcastically, firing the borrowed gun uselessly into the other mage's shields. It was Colin—a redhead with a talent for finding trouble. Only this time, he seemed to be more intent on causing it. "Think they'll do us the same favor?"

A knife sliced by my ear and embedded itself in the side of the house. "Doubt it," I said. "Run!"

We skirted the house, my head pounding with every beat of my heart, just as Amelie expanded her shields. They snapped the hose like a weak rubber band, and she jumped back to her feet. Colin launched the rest of his arsenal at us and I heard several knives bite into stucco, but most took the corner just fine. I concentrated and finally got a shield of sorts back up before we were impaled by anything, but it wouldn't hold. Especially not when stretched to cover two.

Colin and Amelie followed us into the backyard, silently ordering their weapons to continue the beating. My shields shuddered with every punch. I could measure how long they would last in seconds, and I really doubted I'd get them back up a third time. And when they were gone, so were my options.

Cyrus glanced at me. "Can't you do something?"

"I'm thinking!" It didn't help that Jason's spell was still stuttering along my nerves like a persistent toothache, pounding in my skull, drumming on my bones.

"You're the teacher," he said impatiently. "Surely you have a few surprises you haven't shared with them yet!"

"Yeah. But they're all deadly."

"And that's a problem because?"

"I don't want to kill my students!"

"Too bad they don't share that sentiment. And I'm not dying to keep your graduating class intact! Either deal with this, or I will."

"There has to be an explanation," I said desperately.

"Maybe, but we won't live long enough to hear it if we don't *do* something!"

He had a point. We'd cleared the backyard, avoiding the kitchen door, where flames and black smoke were now billowing skyward, and started up the living room side of the house. Only to find yet another of my students—a lanky African American named Kyle—waiting for us. He added his weapons to the melee, and my shields gave up the ghost. We were officially out of time.

Damn. My insurance agent was going to have a heart attack.

I used the last of my energy to cast a spell that took a chunk out of the living room wall. We stumbled through the opening, and Cyrus pushed the TV cabinet across the breach. We ran for the dining room, and I scrambled onto the table. A ceiling joist had partially come loose, with one end resting on the table while the other remained attached to the second floor. It was as wide as a balance beam and sloped upward at a fairly gentle angle. It wasn't stairs, but it would do. And if anyone was above, they wouldn't be watching a hole in the floor.

"Come on!" I said.

Cyrus pulled my stolen gun from my jeans, keeping a wary eye on the door to the living room. "You first."

I somehow hauled myself to the second floor—or what was left of it—with one leg constantly threatening to buckle under me. "Get up here!" I whispered as he picked up the dining table and wedged it into the door behind him.

"You'll need a distraction or you'll never bunch them up. I'll stay here." I started to argue, but weapons rattled against the other side of the table, shaking the heavy wood, and I decided we didn't have the time. I turned and limped as fast as possible for the bathroom.

It was a mess, with gaping holes in the walls, ceiling and floor. Luckily, my coat hadn't slipped through any of them. It was still lying where I'd dropped it, now water-spotted as well as stiff with dirt, over by the commode.

I edged cautiously around the shallow ridge of cracked tile that was all that remained of the floor. Adrenaline prickled on the surface of my skin, urging me to go faster, *faster*, while my heart hammered in my rib cage and my mouth was metallic with panic. It took every bit of training I had to proceed carefully, to stop my hands from trembling, to *focus*. Since my mother's death, there were a total of two people in the world I really gave a damn about. And one of them was currently facing a group of soon-to-be war mages with an empty gun.

I'd almost made it when a row of tile slithered out from under my feet, cascading down into the mess below. I made a wild grab for the toilet to keep from following and my coat slid toward the edge of the hole. I thought I'd lost it, but it hung on a pipe and I was able to snag it with my toe. I grabbed it just as a rainbow of spells exploded below.

A glance through the missing floor showed me only the wrecked kitchen until Cyrus burst in, his hair on fire from a spell that hadn't missed by much. He barricaded the door with the fridge then looked up when I hissed his name. "Go around—get behind them!" he mouthed, gesturing furiously.

His hands were bleeding for some reason, but he was alive. I nodded and dropped him a gun, then started back as fast as possible. I rooted around in my coat as I ran, grabbing things out of the potion belt I usually wore draped low on my hips. It was weighed down with vials, each in a little leather sheath like bullets in a bandolier. Ironically, I'd been lecturing on potions to this very class just last week.

I really hoped they hadn't been listening.

Most new war mages are all about the flash and glitter of a well-flung spell, with respect for deadly human weapons coming in a close second. They deride potions as old-fashioned and bulky, and half carry them only because they're required to do so. But they are a mainstay of a mage's arsenal precisely for times like this.

The ingredients are chosen not, as norms seem to believe, for their own magical properties, but because they are particularly good at catching and holding magical energy. A potion belt is a sort of extra battery pack for a mage: when we're almost exhausted, the spells we've painstakingly captured in these little vials become a priceless commodity. One that younger mages almost never use to its full potential.

Not that I was ancient at twenty-five, but my father had also been a war mage, and potions were a particular hobby of his. I'd been told a hundred times that a well-made potion might one day save my life. It looked like today was that day.

The hall was an obstacle course of tumbled boards and burnt-edged holes, but I somehow made it back and threw myself at the fallen ceiling beam. I hit with a bone-shattering thump, half-sliding, half-falling into the room—only to have three pairs of eyes swivel toward me. But Cyrus sent a barrage of bullets over the top of the fridge that divided their attention for an instant, buying me time to throw a tiny glass cylinder.

It burst against their shields, starting a firestorm along the edges, popping them one after the other. They hit the floor to avoid the bullets Cyrus was letting fly, making them perfect targets for a second potion—one designed to induce unconsciousness. It shattered against the wall directly in front of them, spreading a soothing purple smoke across their huddled bodies. I nearly fell over in relief when they folded like card tables in a hurricane.

I sagged back against the floor, exhausted and shaking. I couldn't even begin to guess what the hell had just happened. They'd been fine two days ago. What could have gone so wrong in forty-eight hours?

"Hey." I looked up to see Cyrus staring at me over the fridge. "Is that all of them?"

"Probably." If anyone else had been around, they'd missed a perfect opportunity to take me out while I was doing my acrobatic routine in the bathroom.

"Let's make sure," he said dryly, and his head disappeared.

I didn't bother trying to move the fridge, just picked my way back through the remains of the living room—total loss—out the missing chunk of wall and around the house. My leg was killing me, and I stopped to rip open my pj's and check it out. The wound had bled profusely, but the splinter missed any major arteries. Some pieces of it were still in the wound, but I opted against trying to pull them out before a doctor could look at it. Instead, I went to find Jason.

He was still out cold, lying where he'd fallen by the side of the house. I stripped his coat off and hog-tied him with his own belt because I was all out of knockout potions. I gagged him so he couldn't spell anything if he woke up, and hobbled around to the missing kitchen door.

Cyrus had gotten the fire out, although the blackened walls, singed cabinets, and ruined floor were going to require gutting anyway. He stood by the laundry room, but he didn't so much as twitch as I came up behind him. He turned his head slightly toward me when I put a hand on his shoulder, but he didn't move out of the doorway. "What is it?"

He hesitated, blinking a couple of times. At some point, he'd gotten doused. His lashes were clumped into dark spikes and his T-shirt was wet down the back. Physically, he looked better than me, but the skin under the stubble-darkened throat was pale.

"Cyrus?"

He swallowed. "It wasn't your fault," he told me, upping the sick feeling in my stomach by at least a factor of ten.

"Move." I started pushing at him, but budging a full-grown werewolf who doesn't want to go is nothing more than a good workout. "Cyrus! I mean it, let me by!"

He finally stepped aside to reveal a far less chaotic scene than the kitchen. The sun was streaming through the small laundry room window, and dust motes were slowly turning in the air. Maybe it was the poststress endorphins running through me, but all the colors seemed extra sharp: the yellow on the walls that the paint store guy had called butter cream, the blue-

and-white Laura Ashley curtains at the window, and the bright white appliances that were still in one piece. It looked cheerful and almost normal.

Except for the young blond man sprawled against the far wall, his blue eyes wide and gaping, his hands outstretched against the blood-spattered paint.

The lack of sleep, the pain, and the destruction of my house had crippled my brain, because it took me a full three seconds to process what I was seeing. It was Adam, one of the youngest recruits, whose ability with magic far exceeded his seventeen years. He'd just started training, and wasn't set to take the trials for another year.

My hand had dropped to my belt, but it fell away as understanding finally hit. Adam was still on his feet, but only because a section of the laundry room door had embedded itself in the wall through his abdomen, holding him in place like a bug on a pin. The sickeningly sweet smell in the air was blood, which had poured down his body in wide streams to puddle on the floor beneath him.

I felt the muscles in my legs liquefying, my fingers knotting in Cyrus's sleeve to keep from falling. Past the rushing in my ears, I could hear him saying, "Things happen in battle, Lia. You know that."

Things, I thought blankly. Like a random, meaningless death. Like a spell that sent a door flying off its hinges, practically bisecting a young man.

My spell.

MY NEW SUPERVISOR had wavy silver hair, a skeletally thin frame that he hid inside old-fashioned three-piece suits, and a pinched, displeased mouth. He was doing something strange with the last. It took me a minute to realize that he was trying to smile and it wasn't working.

God, I must really look bad if Hargrove was trying to be nice to me.

I was currently in the new Vegas HQ, where the Corps had set up camp after the old headquarters was obliterated in the war. It was a thirteen-thousand-square-foot warehouse on a couple of acres in the vicinity of Nellis Air Force base. The upper level was mainly taken up by administrative offices, training areas, and housing for new recruits. The newly created subterranean sections hid the harder-to-explain stuff, like the interspecies medical facilities, the weapons storage, and the labs.

I'd spent the day there, getting patched up by the doctors and grilled by a series of progressively more senior detectives. It was now 11 P.M., and I was in yet another meeting, this time with my very unhappy boss. "Mage de Croissets!"

I jumped slightly. "Yes, sir."

"Kindly pay attention. I have a seven A.M. meeting tomorrow. I would like to get home before midnight!"

"Yes, sir."

So much for the fatherly bit. I wondered why he'd trotted it out at all. Richard Hargrove was old school, brought out of retirement because of the war, to fill an important desk job and free someone in fighting form for more active duty. He'd made it clear that he didn't like my gender, my service record, or the fact that my mother had been a Were. I'd tried to lie low and stay out of his way, but it hadn't seemed to help.

Of course, it's a little hard to build a relationship with your new boss when you're best known for killing your old one.

He pushed a photograph across the desk at me. "Martina Colafranceschi—that's her birth name. She's going by Ophelia Roberts at the moment."

The woman in the photo was not what I'd have called pretty, but there was something undeniably arresting about her. She was tall, judging by the height of the man standing next to her, with olive skin and short hair gone half-silver. She was well past her prime, but there were traces of beauty in the face—high cheekbones, almond eyes, full lips.

"You're sure she's the one?" It came out remarkably calmly, considering what I'd just learned. I was still in shock, and grateful for it. Because I had an inkling of what I was going to feel when the numbness wore off, and it scared me.

"The trace was ninety percent positive," the man at my elbow said. He was slightly built, almost scrawny, with thinning brown hair and shirtsleeves rolled up around his stringy forearms. They showed off the perpetually pallid skin of someone who does his work inside—in this case, underground.

Benedict Simons was the head technician in the Corps' version of a forensic lab. The magical community long ago gave up on the idea that magic is some mystical, indefinable quantity. There's still a lot we don't understand, but there are some hard-and-fast rules—like the fact that everyone's energy signature is slightly different. No two people cast the same spell in quite the same way. It amounts to a magical fingerprint that allows the caster to be identified in certain circumstances, such as being able to test four people who were still under her spell.

"Ben performed the trace himself—there's no mistake," Hargrove said brusquely.

"And her motive?" I pushed the photo back at him. "I don't know this woman; I've never even heard of her. Why would she go to so much trouble to have me killed?"

"Colafranceschi was one of the founding Assassins."

I frowned. "If she was an assassin, why didn't she just do the job herself?"

"Not *an* assassin," he said impatiently. "One of *the* Assassins. They were a group of hit men—and women—who styled themselves after a sect of eleventh-century Islamic extremists. The modern-day Assassins were wiped out twelve years ago. The mage who led the investigation and the final raid was Guillame de Croissets."

I blinked. "My father."

"Exactly."

"Okay." I rubbed my eyes and tried to ignore the throbbing headache that had been building all day. "I see why this woman might target his daughter. But why in such a convoluted way?"

"Because Colafranceschi specializes in weaving illusions. Perhaps she liked the irony of destroying you using one of our own spells."

And that hurt worse than anything—the idea that Adam had died attempting to impress me. He and the other students had attacked me while under a carefully crafted illusion. It was officially known as the Trials, although the local slang term was "Vegas Odds," because you had about as much chance of beating it as you did of hitting a million-dollar jackpot. Of course, that was kind of the point—this was one game you weren't supposed to win.

Students were led to believe that the Trials would give

them a chance to demonstrate the skills they'd acquired by the end of basic training. In fact, it was a test of character. The specifics of the test varied from person to person, because each instructor designed and supervised their own. But they all had one thing in common: a no-holds-barred fight where your friends all died around you and you were left with the decision to either finish the allotted task and die, or save yourself and fail.

If you chose the latter, no matter how good your performance otherwise, you washed out. And if you chose the former, you found out how you faced death by actually doing it. The test was brutal but necessary. If a dark mage covertly entered the program, he or she wouldn't learn anything new in basic training. But the apprenticeship phase was much more advanced, and no one liked the idea of someone picking up the latest magical breakthroughs only to turn them on us.

Adam had been a year or more away from the Trials, but someone had spelled him and the other four to believe that they were undergoing it now and that their mission was to assassinate me. Of course, had they really been in the Trials, they would have been closely supervised, with someone in the illusion along with them to guide it and chart their progress. Nothing they experienced would have actually taken place—not my death, not their own. As it was, the Trials had wreaked the usual havoc, but this time, everything had been very real indeed.

"If the Assassins *are* reforming, it could explain the unusually high number of losses we've sustained in recent months," Hargrove was saying. "More than two dozen mages have been killed in suspicious circumstances, to the point that we started an investigation into a possible leak in the department. But it found nothing—possibly because there was nothing to find."

"The Assassins usually worked for profit alone," Simons added. "But in our case . . . it is conceivable that they bear enough of a grudge to forgo that in favor of revenge."

"And picking off our operatives would ensure that we were stretched too thin by the war to come after them," Hargrove added. "Now, I want to know everything that happened today—every detail—and don't tell me it's already in the reports."

I didn't bother arguing. It was too late and we were all too tired. Besides, if there was anything in what had happened that might help catch Colafranceschi, I wanted it as much as they did.

I sat there for another hour, recounting yet again a detailed description of the attack. It was starting to sound like a catalog of personal failures: caught half-asleep with inadequate weapons—check; let them get past the front door and thereby through the wards—check; unable to capture them without leaving one dead on the ground—check. It was hard to see how I could have screwed things up any worse.

Hargrove obviously agreed. By the time I finished, his mouth was even tighter than before and his shrewd blue eyes were slits. "Fortunately, there is a way to redeem your error," he told me sourly. "Colafranceschi has been located. She has a loft downtown in a converted office building." He gave me the address, and I had to admit, it was impressive work for the time they'd had.

"How did you get this so quickly?"

"We turned young Markham loose a few hours ago. He led us right to her."

"What?" I was certain I'd heard wrong. "You sent Jason *back* to that creature?"

"He remains under her spell," Hargrove said impatiently. "They all do."

"So you decided to use him as bait?!"

He flushed puce. "Better that than young Adam's fate," he hissed.

And that was enough to send me over the brink into anger so intense that I couldn't speak, couldn't even *splutter*, because all the fury—at Hargrove for being such a cold-hearted bastard, at the Assassins for existing, at the fucking universe for not letting me pause for *one second* before muttering that spell—was choking me, cutting off my breath.

"Illusions that deep are notoriously difficult for another mage to dissolve without damage to the mind in thrall," Simons said, glancing back and forth between the two of us. He looked a little spooked. "We . . . we tried, of course, but without her cooperation, I'm afraid there isn't much hope. Lifting the spell would likely shred their minds along with the illusion."

"That doesn't justify sending him back! Jason failed her. Do you really think she's going to keep him alive?"

"No," he said quietly. "But if the spell is not lifted soon, they'll all die. They will continue to attempt to carry out her last command to the exclusion of everything else. They won't eat unless fed intravenously, or sleep unless sedated or do anything except to search for you."

"Then we'll make them believe I'm dead," I said a little unsteadily. "We could fake—"

"Yes, but then they would be like robots on standby, waiting for the next order. Which would never come. A zombie, in effect, for life."

I had a sudden visual, and it was horrible. I strongly

suspected that they'd prefer Jason's fate—whatever it was—to a future as drooling vegetables or comatose druggies. For that matter, so would I.

"If you want to help your students," Hargrove said, "I suggest you use the opportunity to remove this creature from my territory."

"We could call upon our own assassins, of course," Simons offered. "But you have one great advantage over them—your Were blood leaves you impervious to illusions. Her greatest weapon will be useless against you."

"Unless you would prefer someone else to clean up your mess," Hargrove said silkily.

"No, *sir*," I snapped. Hargrove was a *dick*, but he was a dick with a point. Adam's death was my fault, and if I didn't get this bitch soon, the others faced something even worse. I was suddenly, fiercely glad that this assignment was mine.

"Then you're dismissed."

I pushed through the front entrance a few minutes later, practically blinded by tears and guilt and rage, and nearly leapt out of my skin when I came right up against the solid wall of Cyrus's body. His hands shot out to grip my sides, and I flinched. He pushed my shirt up, revealing the purpling bruise that covered half my left side, and sucked a hot breath between his teeth. "Christ."

"The docs checked me out; it looks worse than it is. What are you doing here?"

"Availing myself of some free medical. Like I told the guys at the house—if the Corps can mess me up, it can damn well fix me up."

"You're hurt?" I didn't give him time to reply, just turned his arms over and pushed up his sleeves. The red gashes he'd sustained from fending off a knife attack while I ran for weapons had already faded, with only a few white scars and irregular patches of skin remaining. But some of the deepest lines were still puckered, with a faint ridge of flesh running down his right forearm. Another bisected his left palm, like the seam on a glove.

"I'm sorry." I hugged myself, staring at the signs of what friendship with me had cost him. It made me remember the way I'd felt when I'd seen him dive for the kitchen floor, unsure whether he'd been hit, like my insides were tumbling out onto the linoleum. The scars would probably fade completely in another day, Were metabolism being what it was. But if he'd been a little slower . . .

Cyrus stared at me for a moment, then tugged me into a loose hug. I closed my eyes and went, arms still wrapped around myself. His mouth brushed my ear. "I've had worse from a hunt," he said. And then, even more softly, "You scared the shit out of me." And then we were hugging so tight that his leather jacket creaked.

"Where are you staying?" he asked after a moment.

I blinked. Because, yeah, going home wasn't an option. Even if the house had been habitable, I couldn't go back there with a dark witch on my tail.

"I hadn't really gotten that far yet."

"Then it's settled. You're coming with me."

Cyrus's bike, a black-and-silver Harley-Davidson, was propped against one side of the building. It was where I usually kept mine, too, since no one had gotten around to marking out parking places yet. Cyrus threw a leg over, I climbed on back, and we took off, ignoring the scowls of the guards at the front gate. I laid my cheek against his back and enjoyed the feeling of freedom, the cool night air unbelievable heady after a day spent inside suffocating hallways and concrete-gray offices.

"You want pizza?" he yelled back a few minutes later.

"Only if I get to pick the toppings."

"Deal."

We made a pit stop at a late-night diner that still had a crowd, then headed to the motel that Cyrus currently called home. His room was clean, if not particularly large, and there was a noisy but functioning air conditioner. He shrugged out of his jacket, leaving him in a black T-shirt and jeans, and carefully checked his guns before putting them within arm's reach on the nightstand. He finally allowed himself to relax, kicking off his boots and stretching out on the bedspread.

I borrowed a shirt and took a much-needed shower. I'd restocked my potions supplies and ammunition at HQ, but the only clothes in my locker had been a rangy old pair of socks. Luckily, a T-shirt is a T-shirt, and Cyrus's looked fine on me. Plus the long tail almost covered the bloodstains on my jeans.

We didn't have a table, so we'd put the pizza in the middle of the bed after laying down some towels to catch the grease. I hadn't eaten all day, and suddenly I was starving. The pie was soggy in the middle and half cold and tasted wonderful. I did damage to my half, then rolled onto my back and stared at the watermarked ceiling tiles. Classy.

I let my body start to relax, and it was a mistake. I'd been running on adrenaline and the instinct drilled into me during training that let me push through pain and exhaustion and fear by walling off my emotions until it was safe to deal with them. That detachment had started to crack when Hargrove told me the recruits had been targeted because they were mine. That, essentially, I'd killed Adam twice, because if someone else had been his trainer, he wouldn't have been there in the first place. And now it felt like the two halves of my rib cage were being slowly squeezed together by some invisible vise.

The gentleness of hands on my face was no comfort; it rattled me, made my body burn and my stomach clench. Cyrus leaned down and kissed me, so slowly and thoroughly that I felt like I was sinking into the mattress. His teeth were smooth, the edges catching sharp against the thin skin behind my ear, his hands big and rough, sliding down my sides. It threatened to break something in me, just the warmth of him. I squeezed my eyes shut, biting my bottom lip hard to keep the insane, embarrassing sounds I could feel building behind my teeth where they belonged.

"Stop blaming yourself," he said softly.

"There's nothing wrong with blaming myself when it's my fault," I snapped, rolling away from him. I didn't want to feel better; I didn't deserve to feel better. Not yet.

He lay back, hands behind his head. "Are you going to tell me what happened?"

I almost said no, but bit it back. I'd desperately wanted company—his company—but it would have been better to find a bolt-hole somewhere else. I'd never been sure if it was a Were thing or a macho thing or just something he did to drive me crazy, but Cyrus had a protective streak a mile wide. And like most Weres, he seriously underestimated magic.

I'd tried to explain that, yeah, Weres were faster, stronger, and had senses far more acute than any humans—even magical ones. But none of that made a damn bit of difference when facing a well-trained magic user. Cyrus's hardheadedness on that subject was going to get him killed someday. I'd just prefer it wasn't this one.

But Weres could smell a lie, so I had to give him something. I settled on a version of the truth, leaving out the part about the Assassins and the vengeful witch. I didn't want him deciding to go after Colafranchesi himself.

"You're saying that someone in the Corps wants you dead?" he demanded when I finished.

"I'm not universally popular, but I don't think it's gotten that far yet."

"But who else would know about the spell?"

Someone who had made a lifelong study of illusions, I didn't say. "I'm sure the investigators are working on that."

Cyrus didn't look satisfied. "If this test is so important, how come I've never heard of it?"

"It isn't a popular topic of conversation," I said dryly. "No one is allowed to give the recruits any hints, and most people who've passed are happy to forget the experience."

Cyrus cocked an eyebrow at me. "How did you do?"

"I didn't," I said, trying to keep an edge out of my voice. "My Were blood made me difficult to influence. If Dad hadn't been with the Corps, that probably would have ended my career right there. But he called in some favors." I guess no one had really thought that Guillame de Croisset's daughter was likely to be a dark mage plant. Or if they did, they weren't about to say it to his face.

For the first time, I wondered if it might have been better if they had.

Everyone always assumed that Dad was pulling strings for me, that I would never have found a mentor or made it through training or gotten my first promotion on my own. In fact, he'd done it only the one time, and only because he considered it partly his fault that I was facing that particular hurdle. Dad had taught me to be tough, self-reliant, and competent. Only the Corps had never given me the chance.

I'd tried overcompensating for a while, taking the hardest assignments, working the longest hours, but nothing erased the stain of my mother's blood. Somewhere along the line, I'd decided that undercompensating was a lot easier. It didn't get me any more promotions, but nothing was likely to do that. Nor did it make me any more popular among my peers, who had transitioned smoothly from resenting me for showing them up to resenting me for slacking off. But at least it left me with more free time.

"They just let you skip it?" Cyrus asked, breaking into my thoughts.

"Not exactly. My trainer sent me on a three-week hike through a Louisiana swamp instead." My only companions had been a bad map to the finish line, an occasional alligator, and a horde of mosquitoes the size of my thumb. But the trainees I talked to afterwards thought I'd gotten the better deal.

"I still don't get why anyone would target you," Cyrus said, circling back around to the main point. "Why not order a hit on the head of the Circle? Or at least the head of the local branch?"

An unpleasant rolling sensation bloomed in my gut. It might have been the pizza, but I didn't think so. Because I'd just had a flash of Adam, sprawled helplessly against the wall; only this time, he was wearing Cyrus's face.

"Why not me?" I countered, swilling the last of the now-lukewarm beer.

"Out of all the possibilities? Don't you think it's a little—?"

"I've been in the news lately," I reminded him.

After Hargrove's predecessor turned dark and tried to take out the Were Council, I'd been forced to shoot him. Unfortunately, Gil and I were known to have had problems—to the point that he'd been agitating for my dismissal before he ended up dead by my hand. I'd been cleared of wrongdoing by the Circle's investigation, but that hadn't stopped the media speculation. For the first time, I was glad of it.

"I'm still going to have the clan post a guard," Cyrus said stubbornly. "It may not be necessary, but I'll feel—"

"A guard on who?"

His eyes narrowed. We were so close, I could see the tiny lines that framed them, graven by years of laughter and squinting against the sun. Only he wasn't laughing now. "On you."

I just stared at him. I hadn't even anticipated that, and I should have. I'd ostensibly joined Arnou, Cyrus's clan, a few months ago, after playing a part in saving the life of the leader's daughter. Not that a half-Were who had steadfastly refused the change could ever really be a part of any clan. But after my mother's family tried to force me to change, I'd needed protection and Sebastian had provided it. It was the Were way to return a favor in kind, and by adopting me into Arnou, he'd ensured that no other clan could touch me.

But having them stick up for me now would be a disaster. If the Assassins even suspected that Arnou was helping me, they'd become the next target. Way to repay them for taking me in.

"I don't need protection, Cyrus," I told him forcefully. "And I don't think the clan would appreciate you dragging them into this."

He frowned. "What is that supposed to mean?"

A surge of frustration zinged along my nerves, making my muscles bunch and jump even lying completely still. "Exactly what I said! I don't expect trouble, but if anything happens, I'll deal with it. Alone."

"You don't seem to understand what belonging to a clan means," he said slowly. "You don't go it alone—ever."

"You know damn well I'm no more part of Arnou than I was of Lobizon," I said angrily. And suddenly, I didn't want to be there, didn't want to wait until morning, wanted to beat the living shit out of something *now*.

I started to get up, but Cyrus rolled on top of me, pinning me in place. And for the first time, he looked angry. "Oh, forgive me. Because I was under the impression that Sebastian threw three representatives of Lobizon out of court just last week, for daring to threaten the life of our newest clan member!"

I stared up at him, my heart feeling like someone was squeezing it in a fist. "He shouldn't have done that. I'm not—"

"Not what?"

"Not worth it!" I threw him off and started for the door, only to find that he'd gotten there first.

He grabbed my arm and I hesitated, not sure if I planned to push him away or hit him, and he drew me in before I could decide. I could smell the vaguely spicy scent of him, feel the warmth of his body, and in a flash, something sparked between us. We were kissing, almost biting, as we shoved against each other. A series of sensations slammed into me: a warm hand at the back of my neck, a broad chest pushing me against the door, a hot mouth on mine, a rough tongue stroking in.

We stumbled toward the bed, fighting for dominance,

until we hit the side of the mattress. We stood there, vibrating, bodies hard against each other, for a long moment. Then Cyrus seemed to come to himself, to remember who he was with—the little half human who might break if you looked at her wrong—and his touch softened. His hand ghosted over my face, followed my hairline, and drifted down my temple to trace the line of my jaw. Then strong hands were pushing up my shirt, sliding tenderly up my rib cage, thumbing a nipple, making me shiver.

But not with desire.

He was being too damn *gentle,* and I didn't deserve that, didn't want it, not *now*. I shoved him down onto the bed, sending the pizza box flying, and crawled between his thighs. He stared up at me, startled and hungry, and something in my chest tightened. I wanted to—god, I didn't even know.

I yanked his T-shirt up until it caught on his arms and face, covering everything above the rough-bearded skin of his Adam's apple. Grasping the material firmly, I twisted it a couple of times, preventing him from easily freeing his raised arms. "That's my favorite shirt," he complained, but his voice was rough and his chest was rising and falling rapidly.

I didn't answer, and the makeshift blindfold stayed in place. He started to say something else, but I kissed him again, this time through the thin cotton, and he groaned and opened his mouth. "Leave it," I murmured.

He stayed tense for a moment longer before letting his body relax, trusting me. It was a bit of a balancing act to hold on to the shirt with one hand and unbutton his jeans with the other, but I managed it. They were heavy, so in case he wrecked the bike he didn't get too much asphalt embedded in his flesh, and difficult to budge so I didn't bother pulling them off. Just pushed them down and took him in.

He inhaled sharply, and the muscles of his thighs flexed hard beneath me. I shut my eyes, concentrating on the feel of his pulse beating against my tongue. He'd hardened before I reached the tip and started letting out soft desperate-sounding noises from behind the makeshift gag. They were sweet and damn near addictive, but not nearly frantic enough. They did nothing to ease the furious thing inside me.

He was holding back, like always. The guy could tear a house down with his bare hands, but he never showed me any sign of it. He was always so cautious when we were together, so conscious of the difference between us, so afraid he might hurt me that he never left a single bruise.

It felt like judgment, just another way I was inadequate. Not Were enough for him, not human enough for the Corps. Angry tears sprang to my eyes, and I wiped them away, livid. I wanted to teach him to lose control, to want something so badly, he forgot to be careful, to want *me*. But that wasn't going to happen.

I scrambled up on numb, shaky legs, Adam's face wavering in front of me. Yet another way I'd failed, and suddenly I could barely breathe. I felt almost hysterical, like I was going to shatter into pieces if something didn't break soon.

"Lia . . ." Cyrus had felt the bed move when I rose, but I pulled up the bottom of the T-shirt and pressed my mouth to his, smothering any questions he might ask. For a moment, the world contracted to his body under my hands, the rough-slick feel of his tongue in my mouth. I finished him off with my hand, my face pressed into the skin just below his jaw, until he came with a noise that sounded like pain.

"I'm sorry," I told him, reaching into my bag.

"For what?" he panted, sprawled bonelessly on the bed.

I dropped a quick kiss on his mouth, which was surprisingly soft, even edged with late-evening beard bristle. "For this," I said, and with a swift uppercut, knocked him out.

I'd have much preferred to use a potion, but Weres are really resistant. Of course, they are to socks to the jaw, too, meaning that I had maybe a minute before Cyrus came around. My hands shook slightly as I fitted magical restraints around his wrists, binding them to the frame of the bed. It wouldn't hold him for long, but I needed only moments to get away.

He was going to be pissed when he woke up, but better that than dead.

The Corps had assassins who were given special training for assignments like these. But as Simons had noted, none would be impervious to a powerful illusion. Unlike Jason, they would probably recognize it and try to disperse it, but in the meantime, they would be vulnerable. And while illusions wouldn't bother or probably even register on Cyrus and his wolves, other magic certainly would.

I was the only one who had a chance of surviving both. So this was my fight. If Cyrus brought in the wolves, someone would bleed and maybe die because I'd waited for help I wasn't supposed to need. And I really thought enough innocent people had died because of me today.

I TOUCHED THE door and felt a tingle at the back of my neck. It told me that the outer edges of my body's energy field had brushed up against something they didn't like. I hadn't tripped the ward yet, but it was already ruffled and it wouldn't take much more. I withdrew my hand and it calmed down, but I was left with the impression that the heavy old door was glowering at me.

Served me right for trying the front entrance. I looked around, but the building that housed Colafranceschi's loft was well-warded, with every other entrance just as impenetrable. But the place had four stories and a lot of windows, and wards like that were expensive. I was betting that the ones guarding the upper floors weren't so high-end.

The building next door was almost as tall and was close enough to make doing a Spider-Man impression at least feasible. And as a bonus, it was open to the public, containing a very loud bar on the first floor. I decided I needed a drink.

It was not a slick tourist trap. My sleeve stuck to the sticky bar top, there was a tear in the pleather cover of my stool, and the place looked like its last cleaning had been about the time Dean Martin signed the faded photo behind the bar. But Jim Beam would probably kill any germs on the glasses, so I ordered a double.

Simons was a little overconfident about my ability to shrug off illusions. Mother's blood helped, but I was half human, too, and therefore not entirely immune. Powerful illusions could still play games with me, assuming I was clearheaded enough. Luckily, alcohol seriously messes up concentration, sense perception, and memory, all of which are needed for a good illusion to work.

It's impossible for any mage to fake the thousands of bits of sensory info needed to make even a simple false impression seem real. The trick to getting someone to mistake a fantasy for reality was to plant a few powerful suggestions, then let the person's own imagination take over. It worked surprisingly well, unless said imagination was too preoccupied with its own pink elephants to notice yours.

I tossed back the whiskey about the time a shaft of angry, bloodred light stabbed into the bar. A glance toward the street showed me a couple of large guys in biker gear headed in the door and, when they moved toward a table, an equally tall woman behind them. A woman with familiar almond-shaped eyes and close-cropped silver hair.

My choking fit won me a condescending look from the bartender and a disinterested glance from the woman. Then she did a double take, her eyes widened, and she threw out a hand. A wave of disorientation hit me—so sharp, it was almost a physical pain; then the guys who had come in ahead of her drew a couple of SIG 552s out from under their table and started blasting everything in sight.

I hit the dirty floor, wondering how the hell they'd smuggled two commando subcarbines in without my seeing them, while the mirror over the bar detonated in a storm of gunfire that rained glass over everything. It took me a second to notice that the people at the other tables not only hadn't ducked for cover, but were staring at me like I'd lost my mind. I shook my head, blinked a couple of times, and looked up to find the bartender scowling at me.

"I'm cutting you off," he said while the scene in front of me shattered and re-formed—like the mirror that wasn't broken and the guns that didn't exist, except for the one in my hand.

*Shit!*

I scrambled to my feet and ran into the street, but she was gone. A map charm showed me seven people within a block radius, and only one of them was alone and heading away at a fast clip. I took off in pursuit, hoping I'd guessed correctly, and in less than a minute caught a glimpse of her trying to spell open the lock on a shop's door.

Why she didn't head home, where she had not only powerful wards but presumably a host of newly minted Assassins as well, I didn't know. Maybe she assumed I'd have backup, although considering how powerful that off-the-cuff illusion had been, I was really glad I didn't. Someone that good might be able to convince my allies that I was the enemy, at least long enough for me to get dead.

That kind of power warranted caution, so I hit her with a locator spell in case I lost her again. She felt it, of course, and went dark and furious, giving up on the door in favor of throwing something back at me. A disorienting sphere exploded onto the concrete as I leapt behind a mailbox, but my shields were up and absorbed the shock before it could send me into a dead faint.

I looked up in time to see her image wink out of existence. I kept my eyes on the spot where she'd disappeared, since cloaking spells don't tend to cover movement very well. I'd probably be able to pick her out as soon as she made a break for it, unless she did so very slowly.

My leg was throbbing again, but I scuttled across the street pretty fast anyway, not knowing what other nasty surprises she might be carrying. My shields weren't even close to 100 percent at the moment, and there were things that would get past them. I headed for a Dumpster near her last position, wanting to be as close as possible when I fired. She was an assassin, not a war mage, so her shields likely wouldn't hold up for long.

Assuming I could find her.

And assuming she didn't take me out first.

Another spell hit the ground when I was almost there, this time a disruptor with the punch of about twenty human grenades. It picked me up and threw me into the side of the nearest building. If I hadn't been shielded, I'd have broken every bone in my body when I landed. As it was, I bounced off bricks, slammed into concrete, and rolled back to my feet in time to see a vague ripple streak into a side street. Dammit!

I followed, gun up, and activated the tattoo on my left arm. It was a small horned owl that Father had given me when I joined the Corps. I didn't use it unless absolutely necessary, because, while it fed partially off the world's natural energy like a talisman, it also drained my own reserves somewhat. But in this case, I thought it might be worth the power loss.

Immediately, my vision grew ultrasharp and clear, better than I could see in daylight. And like the predator on my arm, I was also more prone to notice any flicker of movement now. Not that there appeared to be any.

Everything was suddenly deathly quiet, as though I was wearing sound-muffling headphones from the shooting range. An icy shimmer of fear flashed up my spine, and for a moment I thought seriously about casting a cloaking spell on myself. I was supposed to be the hunter, not the prey, but for some reason it didn't feel that way. But I had only so much energy to go around, and those spells use a lot. I decided against it.

I'd always prided myself on my sixth sense. Like an itch at the back of my brain, it fills my head with wary alertness. I was usually almost glad when the moment finally came and things went bad.

I wasn't feeling so much that way right now.

To my surprise, I made it to the corner without incident. For about the hundredth time, I wished I'd inherited at least some of my mother's ultrasharp senses, but no such luck. And to human ears, nothing moved along the whole street, nothing breathed.

Then a door opened and a couple came out, the man obviously inebriated, the woman amused. The corner of my eye caught a shadow running down the side of the buildings, using the couple's laughter as a distraction, and I took off after it. As soon as I did, the streetlights began flickering overhead and a chorus of mad growls echoed down the street. The couple glanced at me as I ran past, but they didn't turn to see what might be chasing me.

Another illusion, then.

I picked up speed, and so did the harsh panting on my heels. I told myself that the sounds were imaginary, but my nerves weren't buying it. I put my head down and ran faster, ignoring my leg, which had stopped throbbing and started screaming.

My focus narrowed to the thin tug of the spell, ignoring outside distractions, until a stream of bullets smashed into my shields. For a moment, I didn't know if they were real or not, until one took out a streetlight overhead. I lunged into an alley for cover, the faint smell of electrical smoke drifting down around me. Nothing else entered, yet the snarls were still right behind me. That settled it—they weren't real, just illusions designed to herd me into a trap. A trap that the four mages running down the street had just sprung.

There was no point in subtlety—they knew where I was. And

the longer we played around, the more time Colafranceschi would have to get away. And that wasn't in the game plan.

The mages had guns up, not shields, making it clear that they didn't intend to talk before blowing me away. My own shields wouldn't hold for long against four opponents, not as drained as they already were. So I threw a vial onto the concrete that sent a dense white cloud boiling up around us and dropped my defenses, too.

My tattoo allowed me to see through the smoke, but it looked like my attackers didn't have that advantage. One slammed full speed into the metal side of a trash can, and another pulled up right before he hit a wall, tripping over the first guy in the process. But the third and fourth mages were a little savvier, and one of them must have had a tattoo to increase hearing, because he stepped around the corner and fired straight at me.

The bullets went over my head because I had gone into a crouch as soon as the fog hid me. I fired at point-blank range, my bullets biting deep into his chest even as I turned, shoved the barrel underneath his buddy's chin, and pulled the trigger. He jerked violently and went down. I went with him to avoid the splatter of bullets from one of their friends, who had recovered enough to zero in on the direction of my shots.

I shoved the mage to the side once we hit concrete and rolled across the alley, crawling through the trash from the mangled can toward the entrance. Mage number two passed me in the process, firing as he moved in. I could have taken him, but I didn't know where his friend was. I opted to go for the street instead, exiting the alley carefully, looking for mage number one. And found him pressed flat against the brick wall outside, waiting for me.

He grabbed me before I could shoot, and this one knew how to use his body, wrapping his legs around mine and twisting my gun arm nearly to the breaking point. Not to mention that he wasn't above hair-pulling, which considering his crew cut gave him a really unfair advantage. He somehow got behind me, his hand closing over my wrists as he snarled a spell into my ear. And the world went white behind my eyes.

I fought blindly, tuning out the pain of my overtaxed muscles and slamming him back against the wall behind us. The force of the blow made him grunt, but he didn't let go, or call off the swarm of enchanted knives that were buzzing about, scraping bricks as they tried to zero in on me. He didn't have to kill me, I realized, as the searing pain of a blade tore through my shoulder. All he had to do was keep me immobilized long enough for his weapons to hunt me down.

I sent my own arsenal into the air, hoping it would hold them off for a few seconds, and heard the clash of steel on steel as I twisted my gun enough to fire. It only hit him in the arm, but he yelled and jerked back, bashing his own head against the brick. His hold loosened and I tore out of his grasp, spinning to fire into his still-open mouth.

My feet were clumsy as I staggered away, gritting my teeth on a scream, blood welling up between my fingers as they clutched my shredded shoulder. I hadn't heard anything from mage number two, which probably meant he was sneaking up on me, but he wasn't my problem—the witch was. I felt around with my senses, and surprisingly, the tug of the locator spell was very nearby; she must have wanted to watch her boys take me apart. I got a fix on her position and started to run.

I didn't get far. I'd taken maybe half a dozen steps when my feet became clumsy, like I was trying to walk through molasses. It's just another damn illusion, I told my body, but it didn't seem to be listening. There was a low-level buzz of energy vibrating through the air, plucking at my awareness, and suddenly a giant face appeared in the air above me, peering down like the Great and Powerful Oz.

"Impressive," Colafranceschi said as I struggled against my legs' stubborn belief that they were dragging hundred-pound weights. "How much are you being paid?"

*Not nearly enough*, I thought, forcing myself to concentrate on the fire escape two buildings down. My eyes told me that there was no one there, but the spell said differently. "Why do you want to know?"

"Because whatever it is, I'll double it," she offered. "I could use someone like you. Good help is hard to find, as you must have noticed."

"Doesn't sound like you're mourning your men too much," I noted, trying to concentrate on the conversation while also listening for approaching footsteps and keeping a read on the locator charm.

"Four against one are good odds; they should have killed you," the projection said, shrugging a misty shoulder.

"Not much of an epitaph," I gritted out, barely keeping the strain out of my voice as blood gushed down my arm. I ignored it because I couldn't afford the magic loss it would take to staunch it. I'd passed the first building, but going forward was getting harder with every step. What had felt like molasses was starting to resemble half-set glue. "But I guess your business isn't so much about compassion, huh?"

"In my business, you don't meet too many people who deserve it," she said wryly.

And for a moment, that stopped me, freezing my feet as her spell hadn't, a rage flooding my veins. "Did Adam deserve it?" I spat. "Did Jason?"

"Who?" she asked, just as somebody dived at me out of the night.

I'd reloaded, but I didn't bother firing. I tossed a vial instead, one that shattered against the mage's shields in a cloud of blue flames, evaporating them like smoke before engulfing the man himself. He fell to the ground, writhing as they ate into him, and was dead before he could scream.

That particular potion was one of Dad's more spectacular inventions. And while it wouldn't have been so effective against a war mage's shields, this guy hadn't been one. It was gruesome enough to snap Colafranceschi's concentration and allow me to cover the last few yards before she could get off the fire escape. I threw her to the ground and straddled her, gun under her chin before she could blink.

"One chance. Where's Jason? And if he's dead, so are you." I forced the barrel into her skin hard enough to bruise.

"I don't know who you're talking about!" she said, eyes huge. "I don't know a Jason."

And that infuriated me even more, that she hadn't even known the names of the men she'd used, of the lives she'd destroyed in pursuit of her revenge. I grabbed her up and dragged her back to the spot where the mage's body had already been reduced to cinders. "You sent him to kill me less than twenty-four hours ago. Ring any bells?"

"No!" She was crying and her nose was running and she looked like she was about to pass out. Some superassassin.

I deliberately stepped into the middle of what had been the mage's body. It collapsed with an inaudible sound, causing black particles to billow up around us. "How about now?"

"I swear I don't know what you're talking about!" she shrieked, then choked on part of her former colleague. "Please, let me pay you—anything you want. I have a big payday tomorrow—"

"Who were you planning to kill?" I demanded, wondering who was next in line.

She looked confused again. "No one. One of my marks—one of the men I'm blackmailing—has until then to pay me. And when he does, I could give you—"

"A blackmailer *and* an assassin. You do stay busy, don't you?" I took another vial out of my belt and held it in front of her eyes. "Tell me where Jason is, or you're going to die the same way as your friend here."

Her eyes fixed with horror on the tiny tube. It wasn't more of Dad's special dose—I was all out—but she didn't have to know that. "I don't know what you're talking about," she whispered, licking trembling lips, her eyes never leaving the vial. "I swear I don't know anyone by that name."

And something in her face made me pause. Because I'd been around enough fear to recognize it when I saw it. And terrified people seldom made good liars.

"There's a phone in my right coat pocket," I said abruptly.

Her eyes switched to me. "What?"

"A phone. Get it out. And be careful. If you make any sudden movements or any movements at all that I don't like, that's it. The same goes for trying an illusion."

She nodded and opened my coat slowly, carefully extracting my cell phone. She held it out to me, but I shook my head. "Hit speed dial one."

It took her three tries to get it right, because her hands were shaking. By the time she managed it, I was starting to feel a little light-headed myself from the blood loss. But then Dad's voice was on the phone.

"Who the hell is this?"

"Your loving daughter."

"Do you know what time it is?"

"Yeah. Do you know what Martina Colafranceschi looks like?"

That made him pause for half a second. "Yes. Why?"

"Later. Just tell me."

Dad hadn't been a war mage for over sixty years without being able to respond quickly in a crisis, which the strain in my voice told him this was. "Short, dark, busty—"

"Short?" I repeated, eyeing the tall, slim woman in front of me.

"Maybe five foot two. She was Ferretti's mistress for years, and he had a type: petite and *extremely dangerous*."

I noticed the inflection, but didn't need the warning. "I'll be sure to keep that in mind if I ever meet her," I said evenly. "Bye, Dad."

The woman cut the connection on my signal. "Who are you?" I demanded.

"O-Ophelia Roberts."

"And you're a blackmailer."

"Yes."

"And those men?"

"My bodyguards. One of the challenges of blackmailing powerful people is staying alive long enough to collect."

"Yeah. I guess so." I was putting the clues together, and not liking the picture they made. She'd run when she saw me not because she recognized me, but because I was a war mage reaching for a weapon. And she hadn't gone back home, because she wasn't a cool-headed assassin, but a panicked blackmailer. Which meant she wasn't the one I was after.

"Are you telling me this was all a mistake?" she asked shakily, openly crying now. "I thought you'd been sent by one of my clients who had decided not to pay!"

I looked numbly down at the ashes dusting away over the concrete, now being splattered with my blood. "I think I was."

IT WAS ALMOST 5 A.M. by the time I made it back to HQ. The halls were as silent as they ever got, empty except for an occasional early riser and piles of unpacked crates. The medical facilities were still staffed, but I didn't stop by. I'd done an emergency patch-up job on the way here. My shoulder felt like it might need surgery, but at least the bleeding had stopped. Anything else could wait.

Like everything else, the labs were still in the process of getting organized, with half-finished electrical wiring poking out of the walls and stacks of files and paper everywhere. A ward wove itself around my fingertips, its dainty tendrils like threads of fine silk as I opened the door to Simons's office. I pushed past it, setting off the alarm and bringing him running from the back.

"Oh, it's you," he said, his face relaxing. "Did you get her?"

"You waited here all night to ask me that?" I let my finger trail through the dust on a packing crate. "Such devotion to duty."

"We've all been working extra hours lately," he said, tensing up again slightly.

"That's what I like to see—someone looking on the bright side. Our guys are getting ambushed left and right, but hey, at least there's overtime."

"That's not what I—"

"It's a good thing we've stepped up recruitment. Assuming most of them pass the Trials, we'll have replacements soon. Speaking of which, how did you do?"

"What?"

"The Trials. How did you do?"

Simons looked a little squirrely suddenly. "I—I did fine. Obviously. Or I wouldn't be here. What does this have to do with—?"

"I bet you did. Just as I would have if I'd taken them. Because the spell doesn't work on us half Weres, does it?"

"I'm no such—"

"Then you won't mind taking a blood test, will you?" I asked innocently. "There are doctors right down the hall and lab facilities onsite. We can have the results in minutes."

He closed his eyes. "She talked."

"Oh, yeah. Roberts told me all about how she used her ability with illusions to help you fool the docs who did your physicals. They put you down as one hundred percent human, allowing you to infiltrate the Corps. You're the one who's been sending reports to your dark mage allies about our every move."

"They aren't my allies," he said, opening his eyes to glare at me. "They pay through the nose for everything I give them."

"So you're in it for profit?"

"What else?" he asked viciously. "Not all of us had famous fathers to pull strings in our behalf! If I'd applied to the Corps as I was, how far do you think I'd have gotten?"

"But you did get in," I pointed out. "You've been here over a decade. You're head of a department! Why turn now?"

"Don't be naïve," he sneered. "I've been feeding the dark information for years! It's only recently that the price has sky-rocketed. Thanks to the war, I've made enough to retire on—pleasantly—in the last six months."

I smiled. "Glad to hear it. If only I had a little nest egg like that, I might think twice about turning you in."

"Is that what this is about? Ophelia puts the squeeze on me, and now you think you'll try it?" He looked almost indignant, like how dare I do something so dishonorable. Under other circumstances, it would have been funny.

"Why not? You know my reputation. I'm not a fan of hard work, and war is turning out to be very hard indeed."

The sneer on his face became a little more pronounced, but his shoulders relaxed slightly. "Aren't you afraid? The last person who blackmailed me—"

"Ended up dead, yes. But only because I killed her for you. Which I don't get, by the way. You're a war mage. Why not just do it yourself?"

He looked irritated. "I'm a lab tech! I went through basic training a decade ago and wasn't much good at it then. I didn't know if my skills would be enough. She warded her apartment and acquired protection."

"So? It was nothing your dark mage buddies couldn't have handled."

"I told you—they aren't my 'buddies.' And you can't trust people like that. Some of them might have decided to kill her and take over where she left off."

"So you sent me instead."

"I needed someone with the ability to shrug off illusions and the necessary combat skills. It was a short list."

"You sent my own students to attack me, knowing they'd fail, that I might have to kill one or more of them—" I cut myself off before my voice got away from me. I'd always had more trouble controlling it than my face.

"To give you a motive to go after her, yes. I have no idea what happened to the real Colafranceschi, but if she's still alive, she's probably hiding under an alias. All I did was substitute a photo of Roberts in her file and fake the tests to make it seem that she had originated the Trial spell instead of me."

"So I'd kill her for you."

"Yes." He looked perplexed. Why talk to her first? It's one thing I didn't expect—"

"Because she had Jason—or so I assumed. I've been racking up a lot of black marks lately and figured getting him back would erase most of them. Out of curiosity, where is he?"

Simons ignored the question. "I should have thought of that, shouldn't I?" he asked fretfully. "But I've been run ragged with the demands of the war and trying to do intelligence gathering on the side and then that bitch showing up with her ridiculous demands . . . I couldn't be expected to think of everything."

"Guess not. So where is he?"

Simons shot me a suspicious look. "Why do you care?"

"I told you: I'm curious."

Something in my face must have finally slipped, because his eyes widened. "You're not here to shake me down, are you?"

Fuck it. I hadn't really thought this was going to work. I drew my gun and pointed it at him. "Where?"

And then had to duck to avoid the curse he threw in my direction. It hit the metal shelving behind me like a hammer blow, knocking it over and sending a bunch of still-full packing containers tumbling down on top of me. One of them crashed into my skull and another hit my wounded shoulder, opening it up again and spraying the floor in front of me with red droplets.

I scrambled to my feet, slid on my own blood and went down again, before finally getting enough traction to follow him into the next office. There was no one in sight. Dammit! He'd already disappeared through the door to the hallway.

I started after him, but there was a violent hammering in my chest and the room started spinning. And then I was grabbed from behind and dragged out the door. The hallway wasn't so quiet anymore. Half a dozen mages blocked the way to the stairs, and three more loitered near the one elevator that had so far been installed. Simons headed for it anyway, but drew up at the sound of his boss's voice.

"Ben! You bloody fool!"

Simons whirled, taking me with him, in time to see Hargrove walking down the corridor toward us. He looked as pulled together as always, not a hair out of place, not a wrinkle on his snappy charcoal suit. He even had a little yellow pocket hankie standing to attention over his left breast.

Simons jerked us back against the wall, holding me in front of him like a shield, making my brain slosh up against the back of my skull. I bit back a groan—I really hadn't needed that. "Tell them to get out of the way or I'll kill her," he said, looking wildly at the mages surrounding us.

For some reason, Hargrove was looking at me instead of his onetime colleague. "You never took the Trials, did you, Accalia?" he asked thoughtfully.

"I'm not joking!" Simons screamed, shoving a gun into my ribs.

Hargrove ignored him. "I always wondered. How would you have chosen?"

If I'd had a hand free, I swear I'd have flipped him off. I knew what he was asking, and for a moment I tried to think of appropriate last words, but they kept tripping over the edges of my tongue, falling away into oblivion. "Oh, fuck it!" I finally said. "Just kill him already!"

I slammed an elbow back into Simons's gut and tried to wrench myself free, but he held on. There was a series of explosions and something slammed into my side, quickly followed by searing pain. The room spun wildly and he dropped me, sliding down the wall to a seated position, leaving a wide smear of red on the unpainted concrete. I staggered a few feet, but my leg gave way and I fell, my head bouncing off the floor when I hit.

And then nothing.

I WOKE UP in a hospital bed under cold fluorescent lights. The division's leading physician was bending over me, his usual scowl firmly in place. It deepened when he noticed that my eyes were open. "Trust you to wake up early," he muttered.

I had just enough time to think, *Oh, I guess I'm alive*, before every nerve ending in my side exploded. I screamed and thrashed, sending him staggering back into the wall. And wow, was that a mistake.

Sedgewick has a reputation for being brusque, unsympathetic, impatient, and mean. But that's for patients who haven't almost knocked him out. I not only had to endure having my bandage changed more perfunctorily than normal, but was treated to a tongue lashing as well. No extra charge.

He finally finished torturing me and left, only to be replaced by an unsmiling Hargrove. I wasn't alive, I decided. I'd died and gone to Hell.

Hargrove settled himself primly on a hard metal seat. "His bedside manner compares unfavorably with Torquemada's, doesn't it?" he asked.

I blinked at him. Obviously, I was hallucinating. Because it sounded like Hargrove had made a funny.

When I just stared at him, he sighed and pinched the bridge of his nose. "I have a meeting in fifteen minutes, so I'll make this quick. You're to receive a commendation for your actions yesterday. It will go in your file whenever I get caught up enough to write it."

"Yesterday?" The edges of my vision were doing this weird butterfly thing. I blinked, but it didn't help much.

"You've been out of it for more than twenty-four hours."

I absorbed that for a moment. "Why aren't I dead?"

"Because you were shot literally yards from our main medical facilities and you're half Were," he said tersely.

"So I take it Simons is—?"

"Dead, yes. And before you can ask, Jason is fine. Simons instructed him to lead us to the Roberts woman and then to elude capture and double back to his apartment. We found him there last night."

"He's okay." I couldn't quite believe it. Hargrove had wanted to send in a team to deal with his traitorous subordinate, but I'd insisted on going myself. I was the only war mage with a reputation bad enough that Simons might believe I could be bought off, giving me a chance to talk to him before he panicked. I'd been almost certain that he wouldn't have risked keeping Jason alive, but I'd had to know. I guess he'd been telling the truth about his busy schedule lately.

"All four recruits have made full recoveries, at least physically," Hargrove informed me. "I believe they are somewhat concerned about what effect attempting to murder their instructor will have on their grades. I trust you will exploit that fear to the fullest."

"I'm still an instructor?"

He cocked an eyebrow at me. "Why wouldn't you be?"

"I—Adam—"

"Was murdered, yes, but not by you."

"It doesn't feel that way," I said softly.

"Nonetheless, that was the case. Rather than becoming maudlin, you should perhaps try to focus on the fact that you saved four lives, as well as helped us to identify the mole who has been leaking our battle plans. We knew it had to be someone in a key position, but we were looking at combat personnel, not laboratory technicians. But as one of our forensic specialists, Simons was often privy to sensitive information."

"Yeah. I was hoping it wasn't you. Killing two bosses in less than a year might have looked bad."

Hargrove didn't dignify that with a response. One of his assistants ran into the room, looking frantic, and he sighed. "Get some sleep," he ordered, and left.

I'd planned on staying awake and maybe prying a few more specifics out of the orderlies, but my body had a different idea. I woke up what felt like only a few minutes later, but it must have been longer because a florist shop had exploded in my room. There had to be thirty bouquets, most of them roses. The place was so stuffed that it took me a moment to notice Cyrus, asleep on the chair.

He was curled up in a dark bundle under a blanket, a tuft of hair sticking out the top, and I couldn't stop the smile that spread over my face. I hated finding things like that charming, but when it was Cyrus I couldn't seem to help it. I tugged slightly at the blanket and it slipped enough for me to see his face. My grin faded.

He looked like shit. There was several days' worth of scraggly brown beard on his cheeks, dark circles under the fan of his eyelashes and he was pale underneath his tan. He was snoring, a low, almost soothing rumble, like distant thunder.

I spied a half-eaten box of chocolates beside him with my name on the card, and my stomach rumbled. Halfway through the caramels, he woke up and sat there for a minute, blinking at me. "I could have them bring breakfast, if you're up for it," he finally said.

I shrugged. "This is good."

"It's not very nutritious."

"It has nuts." I gave him the hairy eyeball. "You finally bring me candy and you eat all the creams."

"You hate creams."

"Only those nasty coconut—" I had to break off because his mouth was on mine and he was kissing me, hard and thorough, like he never ever wanted to stop.

"How could you do that?" he demanded sometime later,

voice low and urgent. His hands encircled my upper arms, but he used only the lightest pressure, like he was afraid I would break. This time it didn't make me angry, because for once I thought he might be right.

"The doc said I'll be fine. It's not as bad as it looks."

Cyrus wasn't buying it this time. "You have a concussion, a knife wound in your shoulder, and a bullet in your ribs! If you hadn't twisted at the last minute, he'd have shot you through the heart!"

I sighed. I should have known Sedgewick would talk. Bastard. "But he didn't. I'm fine—or I will be."

"Until the next time you tie me up and go after a group of crazed mercenaries on your own!"

"It was one woman, and she wasn't—"

"You didn't know that!" Cyrus said with his best *you infuriate me* glare. "When I woke up in those damn restraints and realized you might be off getting killed and I couldn't do shit about it—"

"It's my job." But while that was true, it wasn't the point, and we both knew it. "And you're . . . I couldn't risk you," I added awkwardly.

"Run that by me again?"

"You have to understand. . . ." I trailed off, watching emotions chase themselves across his face: worry, fear, and then something a lot more desperate. It was obvious that he *didn't* understand. "You're not dispensable," I finally said. "You're one of only two indispensable people in my life. You have to know that."

"Then make sure I'm *in* your life," he said, sounding strangled. "No more lies, no more leaving me behind."

"If you agree to stop treating me with kid gloves."

"When do I do that?"

"All the time! You act like you think I'm breakable!"

"Give me one example!"

"Every time we . . ." I glanced at the thin partition posing as a door and decided not to risk it. "You know."

He looked blank for a minute, and then incredulous. "This is *not* about our sex life!"

"Not so loud!" I hissed. "And yes, it is. Because if you're almost too afraid to touch me, what reason do I have to believe you wouldn't take a bullet for me?"

"Because I'm not *stupid*?"

"I'm being serious."

"So am I!"

"You mean you *wouldn't* jump in front of a bullet for me?"

"With your shields? I'd be more likely to jump behind you!"

"Then why aren't you . . . more intense . . . when we're together?"

He groaned. "Because I was trying to give you what you wanted!"

"Why would you think—?"

"What part of your life *isn't* intense, Lia?" he demanded. "You're kicked around, beaten up, stabbed, shot, and almost spelled to death on a regular basis! I thought you might want something a little different from me." His hands left my arms to explore my shoulders, my neck, my cheek. "I thought you might have had enough of the bad kind of intense—" A hand dropped to my breast and I sucked in a breath. "—that you might want this kind for a change. The good kind."

I pressed my face against his sleep-warm neck. "Okay, then," I whispered. Suddenly, this was feeling pretty damn intense, too.

Cyrus pulled my mouth to his, and his hands came up to clutch my face and for a moment, everything lurched—my stomach, the room, the world. And then I was kissing him back greedily. His fingers tightened on the back of my neck, drawing me close, and his mouth tasted like chocolate and dark promise and every holiday I'd never enjoyed until now.

"All right. That's enough!" I looked up to see three grinning orderlies and a glowering Sedgewick. "I said five minutes, not five hours," he snapped.

"She was asleep most of the time," Cyrus protested.

"As she should be. She needs to recover."

"He's not bothering me," I said.

"I could tell. Out!"

Cyrus grinned down at me. "Read the card," he mouthed, and left.

I waited until the room was clear, then pulled the heart-shaped box over and slipped the card out from under the bright red bow. It had one line: *Next time, you get tied up.*

I grinned and ate my chocolate. I was looking forward to it.

Karen Chance grew up in Orlando, Florida, the home of make-believe, which probably explains a lot. She has since resided in France, Great Britain, Hong Kong, and New Orleans, mostly goofing off but occasionally teaching history. She is currently back in Florida courtesy of Katrina, where she continues writing while dodging hurricanes (and occasionally drinking a few). Her Cassandra Palmer novels (*Touch the Dark*, *Claimed by Shadow*, *Embrace the Night*, and *Curse the Dawn*) are *USA Today* and *New York Times* bestsellers, and a new series begins with the novel *Midnight's Daughter* (October 2008). Check out KarenChance.com for excerpts, trailers, contests, and more.

# Hecate's Golden Eye

P. N. Elrod

## Chicago, June 1937

Hanging around this alley gave me the creeps because it looked exactly like the one where I'd seen a man gunned down in front of me. That had been shortly before my own murder.

The man in front of me tonight was my partner, Charles Escott, who was unaware of my thoughts while we waited for his client to show. I didn't like the meeting place, but the client had insisted, and Escott had to earn a living. At least he'd invited me along to watch his back. Too often he ignored risks and bulled ahead on his own, which was damned annoying when it wasn't scaring the hell out of me.

The air was muggy to the point of settling down in your lungs and forgetting to pay rent. I had no need to breathe regularly anymore, but still found the heaviness uncomfortable in this hot, windless place. A car cruised by, briefly visible in the alley opening. The faint wash of light from its headlamps allowed Escott to see my face.

"Stop worrying, old man," he said, speaking quietly, knowing I could hear. "Miss Weaver just wants to be careful."

That would be Miss Mabel Weaver, his prospective client, who was late. She'd made the appointment hours ago when the sun was up and I lay dreamless and, for all other purposes, dead in the basement under Escott's kitchen.

Yeah, dead. I'm undead now, the way Bram Stoker defined it, but don't ask me to turn into a bat. He got that wrong, among other things.

I moved closer so Escott could hear. "Careful? Wanting to meet you in a dark alley is nuts."

"Less so than wanting to meet you."

He had a point, but Miss Weaver didn't know I was a vampire, so it didn't count. "Charles, this has to be a setup. Someone with a grudge paid some pippin to get you here. They figured you wouldn't be suspicious if a dame called asking for help."

"I considered that, but there were notes of hope, anger, frustration, and desperation in her voice that are difficult to convincingly feign. . . . I think I know when someone is lying or not."

He was uncannily good at reading people, even when there was a telephone in between. I could trust his judgment; it was this damned alley that put my back hairs up. Just like the other place, it had stinking trash barrels, a scrawny cat nosing through the garbage, and sludgy water tricking down the middle.

This one didn't have a body in it yet, but my mind's eye could provide.

"I have my waistcoat on," Escott added, meaning his bulletproof vest. His business occasionally required dealing with all sorts of unsavory characters—I was considered by a select few to be one of them—so I was grateful he'd bothered. How he could stand the extra weight of those metal plates in this heat was a mystery, though.

"You think you need it?"

He gave a small shrug, fingers twitching once toward the pocket where he kept his cigarettes. That told me he had some nerves after all. A smoke would have calmed him, but it was also a distraction. For a meeting with an unknown client in a dark alley he'd keep himself focused.

We glanced up at the sound of thunder rumbling a long, slow warning. I couldn't smell the rain yet, but change was in the sky. It would get worse before it got better. Storms coming down off the lake from Canada were like that.

"Crap," I said.

He grunted agreement. "If she doesn't appear before—"

We jumped when the door in the building on my left abruptly opened, filling the alley with the noise and brightness of a busy kitchen. A large man in a sweat-stained undershirt banged out with two buckets of leavings. The scrawny cat went alert and darted toward him with an impatient *meow*, tail up. This was a regular event. Escott must have come to a similar conclusion, but he relaxed only slightly.

The stink of cooked food fought against the rotting stuff in the garbage cans a few yards away. Fresh or foul, unless it was blood, all food smelled sickening to me. Coffee was the one exception; I'd yet to figure out why.

The big man dumped the buckets' contents more or less accurately into a trash barrel and tossed a large scrap of something to the eager cat, who seized it and ran off. The man fit one bucket inside the other, giving Escott and me a hard once-over.

We had no legitimate reason to be here, and I looked suspicious. Escott was respectably dressed, but I was in my sneaking-around clothes, everything black and cheap, because sneaking around can be rough work. The man would be within his rights to tell us to clear out or dump us into the barrel with the leavings—he had the size for it.

"You waitin' for someone?" he finally asked.

It was Escott's turn to take the difficult questions. I made sure the guy didn't have a gun or friends with guns.

"I'm from the Escott Agency, waiting for a Miss Weaver. Is she an acquaintance of yours?"

He gave no answer, going back into the kitchen. A second later, a tall, sturdily built woman hastily emerged.

She was too big-boned to be fashionable, but there was grace in her simple blue dress. A matching hat teetered on her head, barely held in place by several hatpins stuck in at various angles. The hat was an oddball thing with a brim that was supposed to sweep down to cover one eye, but now askew, as though she'd pushed it out of the way and then forgotten. She had a small purse, but no gloves. My girlfriend never left her flat without them.

"Miss Weaver?" Escott stepped forward into the spill of light.

"Yes, but not here," she whispered. She shut the door, moved toward him, and promptly skidded on something in the sudden dark. I caught her before she could fall. She gave a gasp of surprise. I can move fast when necessary, and this alley murk was like daylight to me. I decided to be kind and not tell her what she'd slipped in. Maybe that cat would come back later and eat it.

"Sorry," I said, letting go when she got her balance.

"Mr. Escott?" She squinted at me, uncertain because my

partner and I have nearly identical builds, tall and lean. Our faces are very different, and I look about a decade younger even though I'm not.

"The skinny bird with the English accent and banker's suit is who you want. I'm just here for the grouse hunt."

Escott shot me a *pipe down* look. "I am Charles Escott. This ill-mannered fellow is my associate, Jack Fleming."

I tipped my hat.

"Mabel Weaver," she said, and ladylike, extended a hand to let us take turns shaking her fingers. She had dusty red-brown hair, a long, narrow, humped nose in a long face, and a lot of freckles no amount of makeup could conquer.

"May I inquire—?" began Escott.

"We have to be quick and not attract attention," she said, glancing toward the kitchen door. Her strong husky voice sounded unused to whispering. "The owner's an old friend and let me sneak out the back."

"Toward what purpose?"

"I'm ostensibly having dinner with my boyfriend and his parents. They're my alibi—no one else should know about any of this. I'll tell you why if you take the job."

"Which is? . . ."

"I heard about you through Mrs. Holguin. She said you pick locks, recover things, and can keep quiet. She said I could trust you."

Escott does everything a private detective does, except divorce work, calling himself a private agent instead. It's a fine point, allowing him to bend the law when it's in the interests of his client. He'd found it profitable.

"Mrs. Holguin's assessment is accurate. How may I assist you?"

"I need you to recover something my cousin Agnes stole from me. She's my first cousin on my late mother's side. We've never liked each other, but this time she's gone too far."

"What was taken?"

"This . . ."

Miss Weaver wore a long necklace with a heavy pendant dangling from it. She held it up. Escott struck a match to see. Set in the pendant's ornate center was an oval-cut yellow stone the size of a big lima bean.

She pointed at the stone just as the match went out. "This is *supposed* to be a nearly flawless intense yellow diamond. That color is rare, and one this size is *really* rare. Sometime in the last week my cousin Agnes got into my *locked* room and switched them. She had a copy made of this pendant, a good one—that's real white gold, but around a piece of colored glass. She thinks I'm too stupid to notice the difference."

"You want to recover the original?"

"And substitute this one, but I'll handle that part. I happen to know she *is* too stupid to know the difference. When I get the real one back I'll put it in a safety deposit box so she can't steal it again, but it has to be done tonight. Can you help me?"

"Before I undertake such an errand I need proof of your ownership of the diamond."

She gave a flabbergasted stare, mouth hanging wide. "Isn't my word good enough?"

"Miss Weaver, please understand that for all I know, you—"

I put a hand on his arm before he could finish. Accusing a client of being a thief using us to do her dirty work was a good way to get slapped. She looked solid enough and angry enough to pack quite a wallop.

Another, louder rumble of thunder rolled over our little piece of Chicago. A stray gust of cool air made a half-assed effort to clear the alley stink, but failed and died in misery.

"Tell us a little more," I suggested.

For a second it was even money whether Miss Weaver would turn heel back into the kitchen or give Escott a shiner, but she settled down. "All right—just *pretend* you believe me. The diamond is called Hecate's Golden Eye. It's been in my family for generations, passed down from mother to daughter. There's no provenance for *that*."

"What about insurance? Is your name on a policy?"

"There is none, and before you say so, yes, that's stupid, but I can't afford the premium. The family used to have money, but it's gone. I work in a department store, and it's been enough until now because I lived in the family home, then Grandma Bawks died and left the house to Agnes, so I've had to start paying rent."

"Your cousin charges you rent?"

"With a big simpering smile. One of these days I'll rearrange her teeth. I'm moving out. I'd rather live in a Hooverville shack than under the same roof with her and that smirking gigolo she married."

"Could you put events in their order of occurrence?" Escott asked.

"Yes, of course. I know all this, but you don't. Hecate's Eye belonged to Grandma Bawks—my late mother's mother—and in her will left it to me. Agnes got the house. It's a big house, but the Eye could buy a dozen of them."

"It's that valuable?"

"And then some, but Grandma Bawks knew I would always keep the gem and someday pass it down to my daughter. She couldn't trust Agnes to do that. Hecate's Eye has been in our family for generations; it's always brought good luck to those who respect it."

"Interesting name," I said.

"It's for the one flaw in the stone. It looks like a tiny eye staring at you from the golden depths."

"Hecate, traditionally the queen of witches," Escott murmured. "Does this diamond have a curse?"

"Yes. It does."

For all that Escott's own friend and partner was a vampire, he had a streak of skepticism about other supernatural shenanigans. He'd also apparently forgotten that the customer is always right. "Really, now . . ."

She put her fists on her hips, ready for a challenge. Most women fall all over themselves once they hear Escott's English accent, but she seemed immune. "There are stories I could tell, but suffice it to say that any man who touches the Eye dies."

Her absolute conviction left him nonplussed for a moment. I enjoyed it.

"That's why I have to be along, to protect you from the curse."

"Keep going, Miss Weaver," I said in an encouraging tone. She favored me with a brief smile. It didn't make her pretty, but she was interesting.

"Grandma Bawks passed on two weeks ago. Before she went, she gave me the pendant. She put it into my hand and gave her blessing the way it's been done for who knows how long. I'm not the eldest granddaughter, but she said the stone wanted to be with me, not Agnes."

"Agnes didn't agree with that?"

"Hardly, but she wouldn't say anything while Grandma was alive or she'd have been cut from the will. Agnes got the Bawks house and most everything in it; I got a little money, some mementos, and Hecate's Eye, but that's more than enough for me. My cousin wanted everything, so she stole the Eye. I had it well-hidden in a locked room, but somehow she found it."

"Being female, your cousin is exempt from the curse?"

"She doesn't believe in it, neither does that rat she married, but if he so much as breathes on it, he'll find out for sure. Her being female might not matter: Grandma gave it to me. The stone will know something's wrong."

"Curses aside, these are tough times," I said. "A rock like that could buy a lot of money for you."

"That's how Agnes thinks. She's never had a job, and her husband's too lazy to work. She's selling the stone to live off the proceeds. It would never occur to her to try earning a living."

I liked Miss Weaver's indignation.

"I don't want the *money*, I want my grandmother's gift back." She looked at Escott. "You can go through the history of the family at the library, look up old wills wherever they keep those things, and I can show you Grandma Bawks's will and her diary, and it will all confirm what I've just told you, but there's no *time*. Agnes is selling the stone tonight to a private collector, then it's gone forever. I *must* switch it before he arrives. Will you help me?"

Escott glanced my way, though he couldn't have seen much more than my shape in the dark. I knew what he wanted, though.

*Damnation*.

"I believe her," I said, hoping to get out of things.

"Best to be absolutely certain, though."

He was right. Neither of us needed to be involved in a jewel theft, though my instincts were with Miss Weaver being on the up and up. She'd gotten truly angry having her word questioned. Honest people are like that.

"Miss Weaver? Over here a moment," I said, moving toward the kitchen door. Might as well get it over with.

"What for?"

"A private word." I opened the door just enough to provide some light to work with. She had to be able to see me.

"Will you do this or not?" she demanded.

I looked her hard in the eyes, concentrating. "Miss Weaver, I need you to listen to me very carefully. . . ."

I'd not smelled booze on her breath. This is difficult to do when they're drunk or even just tipsy. Or insane. Fortunately, she was neither and went under fast and easy. That was fine with me; hypnotizing people gave me a headache, and lately it had been worsening. Even now it felt like a noose encircling my skull, drawing tight.

Escott stepped in close. "Miss Weaver, are you the rightful owner of Hecate's Eye?"

"Yes." Her voice was strangely softened. Her eyes were her best feature, nearly the same color as her hair, a darker red brown. At the moment they were dead looking. I hated that.

The rope twisted tighter.

"Did your cousin Agnes steal it from you?"

"Yes."

He glanced my way again, questioning. It was up to me. He'd need my help and not just to watch his back.

"Count me in," I said. I wanted to see what a cursed jewel looked like.

He nodded and turned to our new client. "You may trust us, Miss Weaver." It was both acceptance and an instruction.

"All right," she agreed, almost sounding normal.

I quietly shut the door. The darkness crowded close around us. She'd wake on her own shortly. My head hurt. I think it had to do with guilt. The more guilt, the sharper the pain. I didn't like doing that to people, but especially to women. I have my reasons.

Miss Weaver would not recall the interlude. Just as well. She might have popped me one, and I'd have deserved it.

Escott was satisfied we weren't being duped into committing a criminal act—not much of one, anyway. When Miss Weaver woke, they shook hands, clinching the deal.

Stealing back a stolen item was nothing new to him. The work was no great mental challenge, but paid his bills. This would be a legal cakewalk. Agnes the thief wouldn't dare report it to the cops, especially since Miss Weaver's boyfriend and his family would swear she was with them all evening, wearing the heirloom pendant.

The cat shot out of the dark, lancing between us for the street. I shoved our client behind Escott and rushed the other way, pulling my gun from its shoulder holster. Yeah, I'm a vampire, but Chicago is a tough town . . . and I have bad memories concerning alleys.

A man crouching behind the garbage barrels slowly stood, hands out and down, his hat clutched in one of them. He had an egg-shaped balding head, thick arching black eyebrows, and plenty of teeth showing in his smile. "Easy, there, friend. No need to get bothered. Me an' Charlie over there are old acquaintances. You just be askin' him."

An Irish accent combined with a sardonic tone. I didn't

turn to check on Escott; he'd moved next to me and had his own gun out, a cannon disguised as a Webley. A small flashlight was in his other hand, the beam on the man's face.

"Riordan," my partner said. "What the devil are you doing here?"

"That would be tellin'. We two bein' in the same line, I'm sure you understand I have to maintain a bit of hush about me business." He spoke fast with a glint in his eye, as though daring the world to call him a liar, even if it was true.

Escott held his gun steady. "Following Miss Weaver, are you? Working for Cousin Agnes?"

Riordan didn't blink, just kept grinning. "Now is that civilized, asking a man questions he can't answer while tryin' to blind him? Not to mention threatenin' him with no less than two deadly weapons. I ask you now, is it?" When he got no reply, he looked my way, squinting against the light in his eyes. "So you're the mystery fellow who's been keepin' this lad out of the red. Pleased to meet you. Shamus Riordan, me name is me game, spell it the same." He put a hand out.

I took my cue from Escott and kept him covered.

Miss Weaver came cautiously forward. "Is that true? Agnes hired that man to follow me?"

"Circumstances favor it," said Escott. He looked tense and—rare for him—unsure of himself.

Riordan raised his hat. "Pleased to meet you, Miss. We appear to be at a partin' of the ways, so if you don't mind I'll be takin' me leave."

"Jack . . ."

I'd seen this coming, even if I wasn't clear on the why behind Escott's caution. Gun holstered, I stepped forward to grab Riordan and pin his arms, but he bolted an instant ahead of me. He dragged a garbage can down to block my path, but I had enough speed when I jumped it to land square on his back and tackle him. That should have finished him, but he twisted like a snake, hammering short, powerful blows under my ribs with one hand, while his other covered my face, pushing me away, his fingers curled for eye-gouging.

Before that happened I vanished.

I'm good at it. It drains me, but damnation, it's the second best thing about my change from living to undead. The first best has to do with my girlfriend, but I'll talk about that some other time.

My abrupt absence didn't faze Riordan; he scrambled up and sprinted, but by then I'd re-formed in front of him and landed a solid fist to his gut that almost stopped him cold. Struggling for air, he staggered and stubbornly kept going, but I swung him face-first against a brick wall and hauled his arms back just short of dislocation. I was fresh for more fight. Vanishing heals me: no bruises in my middle. Even my headache was gone.

Escott caught up, our client in his wake.

"What do we do with him?" I asked. Let him go and he'd phone Cousin Agnes.

"I suggest a refreshing nap."

Escott held the light; I turned Riordan around and made myself calm. I couldn't let myself get emotional. It adds an extra pressure to things that can permanently damage a mind.

Riordan was gasping, his face red under the sweat, but his brown eyes were alert and suspicious, his forearms raised to ward off a physical attack. I fixed my gaze hard on him and told him to listen to me, just as I'd done with Miss Weaver.

Only nothing happened.

The noose went tight around my head from the effort, but Riordan stayed conscious. His breath told me he was sober, leaving one alternative.

"Charles . . . he's crazy."

Riordan grinned. "We Irish . . . are a mad race . . . or so I'm told," he puffed out. "What concern . . . is it t'you?"

Escott snorted. "I'm not surprised. He still wants a nap."

"No problem," I said, and popped Riordan one the old-fashioned way. His eyes rolled up, and he slithered down the bricks as his legs gave out.

Miss Weaver gaped. "My God, did you kill him?"

"Not yet." I hauled him up over one shoulder like a sack of grain. He was heavy, all of it muscle. "Let's find his car."

Escott knew the vehicle—a battered black Ford—got the keys from Riordan's pocket, and opened the trunk. It was full of junk, but there was just room enough to stuff him in.

"He'll suffocate in this heat," she said.

She had a point. I found a tire iron in the junk and used the prying end to punch half a dozen air holes into the trunk lid before slamming it shut. They looked like bullet holes but larger.

"He can get help in the morning if he yells loud enough," I said, trying for a reassuring smile. The businesses along this street behind the restaurant were closed. There was little chance of a stray pedestrian passing by, especially with a storm looming.

"Who *is* he?" Miss Weaver asked, voicing my own question.

"No one important," Escott said. He took the tire iron from me, dropping it and the car keys on the front seat of the Ford. "He fancies himself to be a private investigator, but his methods are sloppy and his personal ethics questionable. If you offered him a dollar more than your cousin's payment, he would cheerfully switch sides until such time as he could solicit her for a counteroffer."

I'd talk to Escott later about Riordan. The way he grabbed the crowbar while glaring at the car trunk told me that it was just as well there was a locked steel barrier between them.

ESCOTT DROVE US to Bawks House; Miss Weaver—Mabel now, she insisted—sat next to him. I had the backseat to myself, slumping low in case she noticed I wasn't reflecting in the rearview mirror.

She fussed with her hat, trying to secure it better. She was cheerful, almost relaxed, and made a point of turning around to beam at me now and then as we talked. Escott had instructed her to trust us. With her, trust must also include liking a person. She acted as though we were all old friends. I'd have been uncomfortable, but she'd forget it in a few weeks.

We had the windows down on his Nash; the hot air blowing in was viscous as tar. Through breaks in the buildings we saw restless clouds thickening, making plans. Lightning defined their shifting forms for an instant, thunder grumbled, and they went dark until the next flash. We headed north, right into it.

Escott gently plied questions under the guise of conversation.

Since discovering the fake gem, Mabel had been careful not to give anything away to her cousin, otherwise the real diamond would evaporate to a safer hiding place. For the present, it was still in the house, cached in a shoe in her cousin's bedroom closet.

"How did you find that out?" he asked.

"Agnes is always eavesdropping on the extensions, but

until now I had no reason to do the same to her. She thinks I'm too goody-goody. Well, I started listening, too, and got an earful on everything."

"You must have had opportunity to switch pendants prior to this."

"No, I have not. One or the other of them is always home, they keep their bedroom door locked, and I don't have a key. I'm sorry I couldn't give you more time, but only this morning did I learn about the collector coming tonight. Agnes's husband found him. Agnes married *him* just a few months ago. He saw the big house, met our sick grandmother, and assumed he'd be coming into big money soon enough. Agnes didn't set him straight. She and Clive were made for each other: both sly, greedy Philistines."

Escott came subtly alert. "Is he English? That's not a common first name in America."

"Clive Latshaw's no more English than I'm Greta Garbo. He puts on a good show, though. He'll high-hat anyone if he thinks he can get away with it. He even charmed Grandma, but not enough so she'd change her will."

"Who is this private collector?"

"I didn't get a name, but they're meeting at Bawks House at ten. We'll be able to sneak in with no trouble. Agnes and Clive are always in the parlor with the radio on. She won't go up for the Eye unless she sees the money."

"This is very uncertain, if they should catch us—"

"Then I came home early from dinner, and you're my invited guests. If we're caught, I'll be embarrassed, but I'm getting my property back. If it was me facing just Agnes I'd be fine, but Clive would step in, and he can be mean. I can't fight them both."

"Your gentleman friend did not put himself forward as a protector?"

"Bartie's a good egg but no Jack Dempsey. Clive won't try anything with you there, but if we're careful, we can be in and out, and they'll never know a thing. I just wish I could see Agnes's face when she tries to palm off a piece of glass as a diamond."

A reviving gust of cooler air hit my face. "What about this curse?"

Mabel was thoughtful. "I know it sounds silly, but I've always believed it. Grandma told stories, lots of them, about what happened whenever someone tried to take Hecate's Eye away from its . . . well, Grandma called herself and the other women before her its guardians."

"It kills people?"

"Men. It kills men. The Eye has always brought bad luck to them and good luck to women, but I don't want to trust that too much."

"How so?"

"If Agnes sells it, I think something terrible will happen to her. I don't like her, but she's family. I have a duty to try to protect her from herself."

The storm hit just as we made the turn to Bawks House, and even I couldn't see much of the joint through the heavy gray sheets of rain. It was big, and a single vivid lightning flash made it look haunted.

Mabel directed Escott to a branching in the drive that went around to the rear. He cut the headlamps, and we had to trust to luck that more lightning wouldn't suddenly reveal us to anyone watching from the house.

She pointed toward a porte cochère serving the back door.

Escott glided under its shelter, parking next to a snappy-looking Buick coupe, which was parked pointing outward. The rain drumming on our roof ceased. We'd put the windows up to keep out the water and rolled them down again to let in the air.

"Feels like winter," said Mabel in a more normal tone, sounding pleased.

"Whose vehicle?" Escott asked.

"Clive's. He never uses the garage. Likes to leave quick when he has someplace to go."

"Aren't we a bit obvious here?"

"They'll stay in the parlor so they can watch for their big buyer."

"I'm curious about this providentially wealthy collector of rare gems—how would Clive Latshaw find such a person?"

"He must have asked around. Maybe he went to a jewelry store."

"What about his background?"

She shrugged. "He said he was from New England—but his accent says Detroit. We must get moving. For all I know, Agnes might have brought the Eye down early, and all this effort will be wasted."

I cleared my throat. "Say she did. We can still get it."

Mabel gave me a sideways look. "What do you mean?"

"Nothing violent, but I can have a talk with them, make them see reason."

"If it's nothing violent, why mention it?"

"My associate has a very persuasive and calming manner even with the most obstreperous of types," Escott explained.

"You always talk like that?"

"Like what?"

She waved a hand. "All right, but let's try my way first. I'll get the door open and you two follow. And be *quiet*."

On the drive over, she'd given us her plan of attack, which was to sneak upstairs, have Escott pick the bedroom lock, and I'd keep lookout.

Of course, I had my own way into the room that involved vanishing and sieving under the door, but Mabel Weaver didn't need to witness it. This was her party; let her have her fun.

She left the car, carefully not slamming the door. Escott and I did the same, following her through the back entry into a sizable mudroom. I had no need of an invitation to cross the threshold. Bram Stoker, go jump in a lake.

Mabel took her shoes off and gestured for us to do likewise.

Escott leaned close to whisper. "We're shod in gum-soled shoes, Miss Weaver."

"Really? I thought that was just in the movi—" She clapped a hand over her mouth, apparently remembering her own order about silence.

The mudroom opened to a dim kitchen, also large. There were dinner leavings forgotten on the table in the dining room on our left. The parlor was the next room over, visible through an open door; a comedy show played on the radio.

In silence, Mabel led us to a plain hall with stairs going up. The house had been built for a large family with a lot of servants, all long gone and moved on. It seemed a shame to have it wasted on two thieves, but I was just the hired help and not entitled to an opinion about the wisdom of Grandma Bawks's bequest.

There were walls between us and the parlor, but I heard

Rochester making a comment to Jack Benny and getting a huge laugh despite static from the storm affecting reception. The noise would mask our own movements, and just as well—the old wooden stairs squeaked.

We took them slow. Mabel would stop and listen, anxious, then move up a few more steps. She finally made the landing, and then padded down the hall on tiptoe. Escott kept up with her, not quite so silent as I, but damned close. He had the small flashlight in one hand, but enough ambient glow from an uncurtained window allowed them to navigate. The lightning flashes were getting more frequent, the thunder insistently louder. Mother Nature wanted to let everyone know who was in charge tonight.

Mabel stopped before a door and pointed. Escott gave her the flashlight and dropped to one knee, reaching for his inside coat pocket. He drew out his lockpick case, opened it, and went to work.

I eased toward a second staircase that curved down to the entry foyer. White marble, lofty columns, paneled walls—nice place, but I couldn't see myself ever living in anything this fancy. Maybe Grandma Bawks hadn't done Agnes any favors. The property taxes would be steep, and with a husband who was allergic to work . . . I suddenly wanted a look at those two.

It was easy to build a mental picture of them from Mabel's talk, but I knew better than to trust such things. The parlor was temptingly close, just off the entry to judge by the radio volume.

Escott performed his magic, listening and feeling his way as he attacked the lock. With the thunder and rain, it was taking longer than usual. Mabel held the flashlight, her fingers covering most of the beam, letting just enough escape so Escott could work. Neither noticed when I vanished.

Escott would know I'd be reconnoitering and not worry, but he'd have a tough time convincing Mabel to do the same. What the hell, he could use the practice.

Formless, I drifted downstairs, hugging the wall for orientation. When I ran out of wall, I bumbled toward the radio noise. When invisible, I can't see and my hearing's muffled, but I've no shins to crack. I flowed gently along, working around, and sometimes under, furniture until I was in the parlor next to the radio.

It crossed my mind that this would be a perfect night to suddenly go solid and yell *boo*, but I restrained myself.

A quick circuit gave me a sense of where various obstacles like chairs were located, as well as where Agnes and Clive had roosted. She sat close to the radio; he stood by a wall.

Pushing away, I found what I hoped was the opposite wall and forced myself to go high until I hovered against the ceiling.

I hate heights, but most people don't look up. If luck was with me, Clive and Agnes would be doing what I did myself: watching the radio. The thing isn't a movie screen, but you get into the habit of staring at the glowing dial as though it's a face.

Slowly I took on solidity and got some of my sight back, though the view was faded and foggy. The more solid, the better my vision, but the more weight. If I didn't hold to a semitransparent state, I'd drop like a brick.

Agnes flipped through a picture magazine, her head down. She had dark hair and looked more lightly built than Mabel.

Clive was at a window, holding the curtain to one side. Maybe he liked storms, but my money was on the gem collector's arrival being the object of his interest. He was a square-looking specimen, clear featured, nothing unpleasant about him.

They were not the shifty-eyed, snarling crooks with pinched and ugly mugs my mental picture had conjured. They were as ordinary as could be, enough so I doubted Mabel's assessment.

An important message interrupted Jack Benny's show. Before the announcer could make his point over the increasing static, Agnes shut the sound down.

"He won't arrive faster for you watching," she said, flipping a magazine page.

Clive grunted. "I'm sure I saw a car turn in."

"If it did, then it went out again. We're near the end of the lane. They use the drive for that all the time. It's too early, anyway."

"What if that was Mabel coming back?"

"She'd be inside by now, and we'd have heard her big feet clomping up the stairs. I'll be glad when she goes."

"Taking her rent money with her."

Agnes looked up. "You're a funny one. The money we're making tonight and you're worried about her five-and-dime rent?"

"The deal's not a sure thing, I've told you a hundred times."

"Then why's he coming over if not to buy? Once he sees the diamond, he'll want it."

"Don't be too confident about that."

She slapped the magazine shut. "And you don't be too anxious to sell or he won't make a good offer. I know what the thing's worth, and if he isn't up for that, then you'll just have to find another man."

"Listen, crazy collectors who don't ask questions aren't falling out of trees. I had to hustle to find this one."

"But it's not like we're in a hurry. Mabel's not caught on yet, and she never will."

He chuckled. "Did you see her going out?"

"You know I did. I nearly broke something trying not to laugh. The way she was sweeping around like some queen in the crown jewels, the big snob. One of these days I'm going to tell her about this."

There was a white flash from the window, and thunder boomed like a cannon a bare second after. Agnes yelped, Clive jumped, the lights flickered, and I vanished altogether. It startled me, too. Just as well—people tend to look up when that happens.

"Come away from the window before you get electrocuted," Agnes said, shaken.

"It's right over us. Did you feel that? Shook the whole house."

"I'll get a candle before we blow a fuse."

She passed under me, using the doorway into the dining room. She fumbled around and returned.

"That's better," she said some moments later. "Makes it cozy. Want a drink?"

"Not until this is over."

"Then I'll wait, too."

"What are you doing?"

"Grandma was always gabbing on about the good old days and how it looked by candlelight. I want to see."

"Put it up."

"The yellow goes away in this light. The old bat was right. It looks like a real diamond now—come see."

"No thanks."

"Don't tell me you believe that crock about the curse."

"You were just telling me not to be too anxious. What's Taylor going to think when he walks in and sees you waving that thing around like a Cracker Jack prize?"

"That maybe I have some sentimental attachment to it and will be reluctant to sell. I'll make sure he hears my heart breaking."

"Go easy on the Sarah Bernhardt act—this isn't his first time. He'll know if you're trying to—"

I missed the rest, being too busy finding and shooting back up the stairs. I moved along the hall, bumping into someone who gave a sudden shiver. Escott once compared the kind of cold I inflict in this form to that feeling you get when someone waltzes on your grave.

"Problem?" Escott whispered, evidently recognizing the chill.

I hung back, not knowing where Mabel might be.

"Miss Weaver isn't here."

I resumed form and weight. Gravity's always an odd shock, like climbing out of a swimming pool after a long float.

The door he'd been working on was open. I looked in. The flashlight was on the floor. Its beam took in Mabel, who was on her knees by a closet going through dozens of pairs of women's shoes. They have only two feet, why is it dames need so many things to put them in?

Mabel stopped when she heard my *psst.* She hastily got up.

"We're skunked," I whispered. "Agnes has the rock with her. You want to try the next plan?"

She scowled. "You'll never talk her out of it. No matter what, there's going to be a fight."

"Jack has a winning way with people," Escott assured. "This won't take long. We can wait in the car."

"Oh, this I've got to see."

"No." I was decisive. "You two clear out."

"But—"

"I promise not to break anything. Hand over the fake. I'll trade them."

"But if you touch the real one . . . the curse—I can't." She was absolutely serious.

"Please." I put a little pressure on. Since she'd been under so recently, it didn't take much. If the real diamond killed men, it was too late for me.

Reluctantly, Mabel slipped the pendant off its chain. "You're sure?"

I jerked my head toward the scattered shoes. "Put those back so she won't know."

While she made repairs, I turned to Escott. "You hear of any gem collectors named Taylor?"

He shook his head. When it came to various criminals working in Chicago and points east and south, he was an encyclopedia. Honest citizens held little interest for him.

Mabel came out, easing the door shut; Escott locked it again. We took the back stairs down. The vulnerable spot on our exit was the dining room door, still wide open with a view through to the parlor. Anyone looking our way would see us passing.

I put an eye around the edge. The coast was clear. A quick gesture, and Escott and Mabel slipped by, heading for the mudroom. Thunder covered the sounds they made.

The coast was still clear, so I ducked into the dining room, staying solid and sneaking up on the parlor door.

Standing behind it, I could peer through the crack on the hinge side.

Agnes was in her chair with the magazine; Clive was back staring out the window.

If they'd split up, the job would be easy. I could hypnotize them one at a time into a nap. Both at once would necessarily be violent. I'd have to physically restrain one while working my evil eye whammy on the other. Not impossible, but it's noisy, exasperating, and never goes smoothly.

My best bet was to draw one of them from the room long enough to get to the other. A couple spoons from the uncleared dinner table would do. I'd toss them at the marble in the foyer. Clive was already up and more or less pointing in the right direction. . . .

The doorbell rang.

"It's him," said Clive, excited.

*Crap*. I didn't want to have to take out three of them.

"Didn't you see him drive up?" Agnes asked.

"It's like Niagara out there. You can't see anything."

She put the magazine to one side, stood, smoothed her dress, and sat down again, ankles crossed, hands in her lap they way they teach girls to do in finishing schools. She had a little black box in one hand, not hard to guess what was in it. "When this is done I want a real honeymoon," she said with a spark in her eyes. She was as tall as Mabel, but finer-boned and more aristocratic in features.

"You got it, baby!" He hurried to the foyer.

I had my chance. He'd be busy with the guest, finding a place for his hat and umbrella. I'd have the moment I needed to steal in and put her out.

Only Agnes did something odd, and that made me hesitate. While looking toward the foyer with the box in her left hand, her right hand left her lap briefly, brushing against a pocket on her dress. It was swiftly and deftly done. She'd checked to make sure something was where it was supposed to be.

*What's in your pocket, Mrs. Latshaw?*

Then my opportunity was gone. Clive led the buyer in and introduced William D. Taylor (the Fourth) to his wife. I guess they make eccentric collectors in all types and sizes, but this one looked as average as Clive. Taylor wore a nice suit, a stuffy expression behind his wire-rimmed glasses, and had a briefcase.

Pleasantries were exchanged about the terrible weather. Mr. Taylor apologized and was forgiven for arriving early.

"You'll pardon if I'm in a rush, Mrs. Latshaw, but I've a train to New York to catch. The sooner I make a decision on this stone, the sooner I may leave. This dismal rain . . ."

"I understand."

"Excellent. I came prepared." He produced a jeweler's loupe. "Mr. Latshaw, may I trouble you to move a lamp to this table?"

When the lamp was in place, Agnes stepped forward.

"This is my family's prize heirloom: Hecate's Golden Eye," she said with a well-calculated dose of hushed respect as she opened the box.

Taylor accepted the box, held it under the lamp's light, peered at the contents, and set it down on the table. He pulled on a pair of white gloves, and only then picked up the pendant. I wondered if they'd be enough to protect him from the curse.

He screwed the loupe in one eye and spent several minutes examining the gem.

Clive and Agnes exchanged worried looks, but resumed their poker-playing faces when Taylor grunted.

"The genuine thing. Superb clarity for its size. I can see that legendary flaw quite clearly. A perfect eye with pupil and even lashes. Extraordinary."

"My dear grandmother often mentioned it. She loved the piece very much."

"No doubt. I'm sure you would rather keep it in the family."

Clive worked hard to hide his alarm. "You're not interested?"

"I am, sir, but cannot offer you much for it. I collect with the intent of appreciation of value as well as for a gem's unique beauty. Without provenance—you were clear this diamond has none beyond private family records which, forgive me, can be forged—I cannot easily resell it in the future for as much profit as I would like."

"You could to another private collector."

"Humph. That would be that so-and-so Abercrombie. I'd never give him the satisfaction. I'm glad he's moved to Switzerland or he might have gotten wind of this first. I'm sorry, but I can offer you only so much and no more. You may take it or leave it as you choose."

Then he said a number that made my jaw drop.

The Latshaws failed to hide their gleeful satisfaction.

Clive recovered first. "My wife and I assure you that we would be very pleased for Hecate's Eye to become part of the Taylor collection."

"Very good." They shook hands.

"A check will suffice, and once it clears you may take possession."

"Mr. Latshaw, my train won't wait for the banks to open, but I am prepared to conclude this transaction now."

He put the briefcase on the table and opened it to reveal a respectable load of wrapped banknotes. The Latshaws were appropriately impressed. My jaw kept swinging. I'd seen bigger stacks of cash, but only in gangster-controlled gambling clubs. I drew breath for a silent whistle and could actually smell the ink.

"How can you carry all that?" Agnes asked. "What if you're robbed?"

"I can take care of myself, ma'am." Taylor opened his suit coat just enough to give her a glimpse of his shoulder rig and whatever gun it held. "If Mr. Latshaw would count the money and sign a receipt, I'll be off to catch my train."

Clive counted, and Agnes poured sherry into three stemmed glasses, making small talk with Taylor. Alone on the table was the open black box with the Eye still in it.

Even across the room I could tell it was a real gem. The glass imitation in my pocket was a vulgar peasant compared with the elegant royalty over there. Simply lying on its white silk padding, the stone glowed like molten gold. It took light and set it on fire. When I shifted, futilely trying to move closer for a better view—I swear it—the thing winked at me.

*That* was eerie. The longer I stared, the less I liked it. The damned thing was just a chunk of crystallized carbon in an unexpected color with a fancy name, and for some reason, people had decided it was worth something. They killed and died for such shiny baubles. Insane.

Despite that, I wouldn't have minded having a few locked up in the safe at home.

Just not this one.

Hecate's Eye twinkled goldly at me, and I fought down a shiver.

Clive finished his count and closed the briefcase. Taylor said he could keep it along with the cash.

Taylor picked up the Eye and peered through his loupe. Wise of him. He'd been distracted by Agnes; Clive could have slipped a fake in.

"It is beautiful," Taylor said. "I've seen its equal only at the British Museum, and that one had two inclusions, but neither like this simulacrum."

They made a toast, and everyone looked pleased. Agnes gently took the pendant from Taylor—to have one last look at her darling grandmother's pride and joy, she said.

"I shall miss you," she said, holding the stone to the light, gravely wistful.

Clive and Taylor exchanged glances, two men in silent agreement about the frail sentiment of the fair sex, shaking their heads and smiling. By the time they turned back, Agnes had made the switch.

She'd practiced; she was so fast, I almost missed it. She put *a* pendant in the box and closed the lid, handing it to Taylor. The real stone was still in her palm so far as I could tell. While the men shook hands, she slipped it into her dress pocket.

Slick, but foolish. Sooner or later, Taylor would take another gander at his toy and call the cops. How could she think she'd get away with it?

Someone eased up behind me, and I did not trust it to be Escott checking to see what was taking so long.

I ducked and twisted in time to avoid the full force of the crooked end of a tire iron on my skull. It smashed into my left shoulder square on the bone joint. Most of the time a regular person hasn't got the strength to damage me, but the application of raw kinetic force on a single spot with an unbreakable tool—something's going to give. I heard it do just that with a sickening, meaty pop and dimly knew that it hurt, but was too busy to register how much. I spun the rest of the way around to face Riordan. He was ready and punched the iron hard into my gut. It had a hell of a lot more force than a bare fist. I doubled over.

Not needing to breathe, I wasn't yet on the mat, and I lunged forward to tackle him. He danced back and almost made it, but collided violently into the dining table, tumbling it and himself over with a satisfyingly noisy crash. A woman screamed.

My left arm was completely useless and hanging. I grabbed at Riordan with my right, but he didn't stop, cracking the tire iron smartly on the back of my hand. I heard bones snap, but again felt no pain, which meant serious, crippling damage. Before he caught me another one—dammit, he was *fast*—I got a fist in his belly. It was a lighter tap than I wanted, since I was forced to use my right. No pain—things were moving too quick.

Riordan *did* have to breathe, and slowed just enough that I had time to stun him silly with an open-handed slap on the side of his head. Again, not my full muscle behind it, but it got the job done so well that I wanted to scream as my shattered bones ground against one another under the skin.

The starch left him, but he fought it, his eyes going in and out of focus. I grabbed the iron. It took effort to pry from his grip, and I had to drop it immediately as my fingers gave up working. Everything came to roaring, agonizing life. One arm dead, the other much too alive, I needed to vanish so I could heal.

"*Hands up!*"

William D. Taylor (the Fourth) had me covered with an efficient-looking semiauto. A .32 or .38, it gave the impression of being field artillery from my angle on the floor.

I froze. I *hate* getting shot. It hurts like hell, I lose precious blood, and the bullets go right through to hit anything and anyone with the bad luck to be behind me. I also tend to involuntarily vanish. With the damage I already had, I'd not be able to stop the process.

Couldn't risk it in front of this bunch. None of them needed to know that much about me. In the spirit of cooperation, I tried to raise my one moving arm. Pain blazed down it like an electric shock. I gasped and hunched over it, suddenly queasy. My left arm wasn't responding at all; a major nerve or something was gone, couldn't feel it except as a heavy dragging weight. I smelled blood where the skin was broken on my shoulder, but the black shirt hid it.

Clive Latshaw, the outraged man of the house, demanded to know who I was and what I was doing there.

Not having a good answer for either, I told him to call the cops.

Their reaction was interesting. When trespassers demolish your house, most folk are eager to turn them in.

This trio hesitated with an exchange of uncomfortable glances.

Taylor spoke first. "I *have* to be on that train tonight. It's vital to my business."

Clive slowly nodded. "Of course. I can take care of this. We don't need the police."

Not too strangely, given the switch she'd pulled and the fact that she'd stolen the gem in the first place, Agnes did not utter a single reasonable objection to this extraordinary statement. Instead, she glared at the wreckage that happens to a nice room when two grown men try to kill each other in it.

"Who *are* they?" she asked, somehow taking me and Riordan in at the same time.

She'd shown no recognition at all for him, but then neither had Clive. They were both competent enough liars. Were they in on it together or separately? Did she have a reason not to tell her husband about hiring a man, or had Clive retained him and not shared with her?

Visible through the parlor curtains, lightning flashed bright. Thunder boomed, shaking the whole house again. We all jumped a little under flickering lights.

Her hand was in her pocket, nervously touching Hecate's Golden Eye, and I wondered briefly about the curse. This weather had me spooked.

I'd only *looked* at the damned thing and had a bushel basket of bad luck dropped on me. Had I been normal, I'd be maimed for life.

I needed to vanish; a few seconds out of their sight would be enough. My best option was to hypnotize them into a nap on their feet, but attempting to take all three at once while they were on guard was bound to fail. I was too distracted by pain, which was getting worse.

*Get them separated.*

"Call the cops," I said, looking at Clive, willing him to listen. If just one of them left, I had a chance. "I'm a burglar and this is another burglar. We came here to steal everything, and we should be jailed."

Riordan roused himself enough to mutter, "Y'daft b'sturd."

He was soaked through from the storm. He might have entered the house from some other door than the one in the mudroom, but it wasn't likely. Worry for Escott and Mabel stabbed through me, breaking my concentration. If he'd gotten the drop on them . . .

Riordan won his struggle back to consciousness and dragged himself to a sitting position. "Jesus, Mary, an' Joseph, for a skinny git, you know how to scrap."

"Where are they?" I snarled.

"If you're meanin' the Holy Family, take yourself to a church, they'll be glad to inform you. If it's Charlie an' his new sweetheart, you'll find them tight as sardines in the boot of his car."

Clive looked ready to choke. "*Quiet!*"

As if to punctuate him, thunder boomed over the house, rattling everything and everyone.

Riordan squinted up at him. "Friends in high places, have ye?" With a groan, he found his unsteady feet.

Agnes instinctively retreated behind her husband. "Clive . . ."

"Stay right there," Taylor ordered, reminding us he was armed.

"I'm no burglar, missus, not t'worry." Riordan looked at me. "Don't kid yourself, mate, I had a great pleasure in bustin' you up, but it happens I'm here on me own business."

"What business?" Taylor's aim was steady. A man used to firearms.

Riordan rubbed the side of his head. "Me ears are ringing, but I've no time for that phone. It's you"—he looked at Clive Latshaw—"I want a word with."

Clive had a good poker-playing face, but not good enough. Riordan was the last person he wanted here, that was plain.

"Clive—do you know that man?" Agnes stared at him.

"Indeed he does, missus. Pleased to meet you. Shamus Riordan, me name is me game, spell it the same. Pardon me manners, but I've had a bad night. I want a word with your mister about me payment."

"Who *is* he?"

Clive did his best. "He's a man I hired to follow Mabel. It's nothing important." He was desperate for her to take the hint. Mention of Mabel could bring out that she was the real owner of the Eye. Taylor might not care, but then again, he might.

"An' paid well for it," Riordan added. "Very well indeed from a man with holes in his shoes. Polish on top, holes on the bottoms, an' I'll not mention too loudly the shockin' state of your heels. You had work for me, that's all I care about. But I began wonderin' how you got hold of so much lovely money, when it was clear you were in such need for yourself—"

Clive told him to shut up. I had to read his lips; the thunder drowned him out.

Despite the agony, I started to laugh, getting a collective glare from them. Perversely, I enjoyed the moment. It happens when the adrenaline's running and certain oddities suddenly make sense.

"Would you let us in on the hilarity?" Riordan asked.

"You already got the joke." I let the laughter run down. Continuing was too painful.

"I don't consider it t'be all that amusin'."

He wouldn't. No one would. It was hard to read Taylor's

eyes behind those wire glasses. My guess was that I'd said too much already. We were in dangerous waters.

Riordan started to speak, but I caught his eye and gave a fast wink, hoping the others would miss it and that he'd take the warning. If I got shot, I'd vanish. Riordan would bleed out and die.

He gave a snort of contempt, muttered about "bloody Yankee Doodles," and subsided, turning away. Good man.

Another exchange of looks between Taylor and Clive. I pretended not to see, but Agnes had picked up on things. She backed off to watch them both, her eyes sharp and suspicious.

Clive took charge, speaking slowly, his voice thick. "Mr. Taylor, as this has nothing to do with you, I think you should leave. If you would give me the loan of your gun, I can take care of this situation. I'll return it later; I have your address."

Thinking it over, Taylor finally nodded, but didn't move right away. He blinked several times and rubbed his eyes. Clive extended a hand sideways toward him, but there was an unusual sluggishness to the action.

"I have . . . your address," he repeated.

Taylor made no reply.

Agnes stepped forward and took the gun from Taylor's hand. Neither of the men protested; their faces had gone slack in what to me was a too-familiar dead-eyed stare. She rounded on me and Riordan, scowling.

"What am I going to do with you two?" she wanted to know.

One to one, the odds were in my favor. I pushed away the pain and concentrated on her.

But there was still some bad luck left in the barrel. Another lightning flash edged the curtains with white fire for a breathless moment. Thunder boomed seemingly right over the house. The lights failed.

*Skunked again, dammit.* At least when it came to hypnosis. But if the power stayed off long enough . . .

The parlor candle was far enough away to leave the dining room sufficiently dark. I went out like the lights, and for a few precious seconds the gray nothingness swept me from the weight and pain of physical burdens. It was a little bit of heaven, tempting me to linger. Alas, no.

When I came back, my arms worked just fine again; I was also right behind Agnes, grabbing for her gun. Taylor and Clive continued to stand in their tracks, oblivious as a couple of store-window mannequins. I caught of glimpse of a gleeful Riordan grinning like a maniac in the face of all the impossibilities taking place.

Agnes put up a hell of a fight, screaming, clawing, hissing, kicking, and not letting go of the gun, not giving an inch as we danced around. With a ferocious twist, she broke free and fired at me, the gun's roar matching the thunder for sheer eardrum-breaking sound.

At less than ten feet she missed, but you can do that if you're excited and don't know how to shoot.

However, even an excited, inexperienced shooter can get lucky. Time to leave.

I retreated in haste to the dining room. Riordan, no fool, was just ahead, scrambling toward the kitchen.

She fired again, screaming something abusive. We dashed toward the mudroom, jamming shoulders in the doorway, fighting to be the first out. Riordan slipped sideways and won, slamming through the back door into the rain with me at his heels.

He took off down the drive, presumably to reclaim his car. We should have tied and gagged him. He was too good an escape artist.

He looked back once, teeth white in the darkness. "Till the next round!" he yelled, then sprinted away.

Escott's Nash was still there, the keys and his Webley on the front seat. Mabel and Escott were indeed inside the trunk, to tell by the muffled shouts and thumping, but they could wait.

I got the car started, shifted gears, and shot out from under the porte cochère. Rain once more pounded the roof with brutal force, but the heavy fall and general darkness would obscure the vehicle from Agnes, hopefully throwing off her aim. I didn't stop to look.

When I judged the distance to be far enough, I cut the motor, vanished, and beelined my invisible way back to the house. Wind buffeted me, and the rain was a startling unpleasantness. I usually get that kind of quivering discomfort when sieving through solid walls. When it stopped, I made the reasonable assumption I was under shelter.

With great caution, I took on just enough solidity to get my bearings. Clive's flashy coupe was in front of me. I let myself float up into a dim corner to watch.

In the few moments since Riordan and I escaped, Agnes had been busy.

Wearing hat and gloves, she emerged from the back door, the leather case with the money in one hand, a travel suitcase in the other. She tossed them into the passenger side of Clive's coupe and hopped in herself. She was laughing, a free and easy sound of pure delight and triumph.

I half expected a fateful bolt of lightning to strike just then, but nothing happened. The storm seemed to be letting up.

Agnes revved the motor, shifted gears, and roared off into the rain.

ESCOTT HAD PAST experience at being locked in car trunks, so he was more sanguine about it than our client. That, or maybe he'd enjoyed being stuffed into a small space with a healthy young woman on top of him. I'd kept a straight face when I'd let them out, though they were rather badly rumpled.

Mabel was livid and ready to strangle Riordan, but I explained he was long gone. I had a lot of explaining to do, but first had her give me the location of the fuse box so I could get the lights working.

She was none too pleased at the state of the dining room, appalled and aghast at the sight of Clive and Taylor literally asleep on their feet, and furious with me on general principles. She visibly fumed as I eased each man flat on the floor. They were breathing okay, hearts pumping steadily, so they didn't seem to be in any immediate danger.

"Some kind of curare?" Escott ventured, studying them with his own brand of cold-blooded curiosity. "If so, they might well be aware of everything we're saying."

I shrugged. "Just don't touch the sherry. It might be a good idea to empty all the open bottles into the drain. Agnes could have left a booby trap behind."

Mabel was ready to explode. "*What* happened?"

I sat down because I was damned tired. Before dawn, rain or no, I'd have to stop at the Stockyards and have a long drink.

With the promise of fresh beef blood in my near future, I told them everything that happened, including Riordan's badly timed interruption and the fight, leaving out the part about my injuries. I'd tell Escott later. He'd need to know just how violent his acquaintance had gotten.

"You let her *go*?" Mabel's throaty voice rose.

I held up a hand. "She didn't get away with anything."

"Only with Hecate's Eye and all that money. She'll never come back."

I took the pendant—the real one—from my pocket and held it out to her.

Mabel gaped, then reached for it, fingers shaking. "You switched them!"

"Said I would. It took long enough, what with Agnes fighting me every inch of the way."

"You mustn't touch it. My God, put it down before something horrible happens."

I put it into her hand and told her how I'd played pickpocket during the tussle. Agnes must have thought I was some kind of masher since I'd had to keep my hands moving. No wonder she'd shot at me.

"She still got away with the payment—Taylor will set the police on her."

"No, he won't. He brought a case full of funny money to buy the gem. It's as counterfeit as the pendant he got. Agnes had two fakes made. Maybe the jeweler cut her a deal for making two."

That took them both a moment to digest. I used the pause to take the little box from Taylor's coat pocket and spilled *his* fake pendant onto the table.

"But how did you know about the money?" Escott asked. "You couldn't have gotten a close look at it."

"It was the smell. Ever smell uncirculated cash straight from the bank? Nothing like that fresh ink, only this was just too fresh. It was strong enough that I picked up on it in the next room, but its importance didn't click until Riordan showed up wanting to talk with Clive. When he hired Riordan to follow Mabel, he paid with counterfeit bills."

"How did *he* get them?" she asked. "Oh—oh, it couldn't be."

"It could. He and Taylor are partners, working a long confidence game. Clive the gigolo marries an heiress with expectations. I wouldn't be surprised if he's left a number of wives in his wake."

"A bigamist?" Mabel stared at him as though he were an exotic zoo specimen.

"It's likely. Marriage is a tool of the trade. I bet this time the deal wasn't as sweet as he'd hoped. Agnes got the house, but it was worthless to him. A family heirloom like a rare diamond was much better. He probably put a few words in her ear about how unfair it was that you got it, unless it was her idea to start with. When the time was right, he called in Taylor to pose as a wealthy gem collector. The hard part for them was probably finding really good counterfeit cash. The printer should have let it dry longer."

More gaping from Mabel; then she began to hoot with laughter. There was no love lost between her and her cousin. That Agnes had married a confidence man and possible bigamist bothered Mabel not at all. Tears ran down her face, and she had to blow her nose.

When she got her breath, I continued. "Neither of them knew that Agnes had her own angle, which was to drug them, switch the gems, and drive off with both brass rings. Clive would wake in the morning with no wife and no cash. Maybe Taylor would crash his car in the rain or not, but . . ." I let it hang.

That sobered Mabel up. "I can't believe she'd have gone that far."

"She might have planned to delay him long enough for the mickey she slipped to put them out. Riordan interrupted when he tried to crack my skull open."

"You're sure you're not hurt?"

"It'll take more than a crazy Irishman with a stick to do that." I turned to Escott. "You're going to tell me more about him, right?"

He looked pained. "Not just now."

"I suppose I'll have to call the police," said Mabel about the supine mannequins on the parlor floor.

"Don't worry about it. I've a friend who will want to meet these jokers."

My friend was a gang boss of no small influence who owed me a favor or three. Northside Gordy would be very interested in hearing Taylor and Clive's life stories and why they were operating in his city without his permission, thus denying him his cut of their deal. If they were lucky, he might let them go with most of their body parts intact.

"Poor Agnes." Mabel snickered. "When she starts spending that fake money . . ."

"She could go to jail," Escott completed for her.

"It'd serve her right, but I better let the police know that she stole a car."

Mabel put Hecate's Eye in its little box and went to the kitchen to make the call.

Escott and I looked at the gem, neither of us disposed to get closer.

A last bit of lightning from the fading storm played hob once more with the house lights. They flickered, leaving the one candle to take up the slack for an instant before brightening again.

"Did you see that?" I asked. "Tell me you saw that."

"Trick of the light, old man, nothing more." But Escott looked strangely pale. "It absolutely did *not* wink at us."

P. N. Elrod has sold more than twenty novels, at least as many short stories, scripted comic books, and edited several collections, including *My Big Fat Supernatural Honeymoon.* She's best known for her Vampire Files series, featuring undead gumshoe Jack Fleming, and would write books more quickly but for being hampered by an incurable chocolate addiction.

More about her toothy titles may be found at www.vampwriter.com.

# Bacon

## Charlaine Harris

Dahlia Lynley-Chivers looked good in black; in fact, she looked great—and normally that was extremely important to her. But tonight she wasn't thinking about herself or about the picture she made sitting alone at the elaborately laid table in the upscale restaurant. Seeleys' tablecloths might have been designed to set her looks off: the undercloth was black like her hair; the overcloth was snowy white like her skin.

Dahlia had been dead for a very long time.

Though she was sitting motionless, her back perfectly straight, Dahlia was conscious of the passing of time. The witch was late. Under any other circumstances, she would have left Seeleys and found something more amusing to do than wait for a human: but she'd gone to considerable trouble to arrange this meeting, and she wouldn't give up so easily.

Clifford Seeley, who'd arranged to wait tables at his dad's restaurant this evening, put a glass of TrueBlood in front of

Dahlia with a theatrical flourish. "Something to sip on while you wait, madam," he said formally. Then he whispered, "I haven't worked here since I was twenty. Am I doing okay?"

Dahlia didn't exactly smile. She wasn't in the mood. But her face looked a bit less stony as she looked up at the tall young werewolf, and she inclined her head an infinitesimal degree. She liked Clifford, had since the moment she'd met him at her friend Taffy's wedding reception. Taffy, like Dahlia, had married into the Swiftfoot pack.

Taffy's husband Don was the packleader. Dahlia's husband was dead.

"Heads up," said Clifford suddenly, and swooped off to check his other tables. Dahlia saw the headwaiter gliding toward her, a young woman stumbling along behind him. Dahlia's attention sharpened. Since on their dullest day vampires had senses at least five times more acute than those of humans, this meant Dahlia might as well have been walking right next to the newcomer. The woman was plump, tousled, and breathing heavily, and she didn't seem to know how to walk on high heels. Dahlia, who wore stilettos on every possible occasion, let her nostrils flare in contempt, though she made sure to repress any expression well before the young woman reached her chair. That took longer than it should have, since Dahlia's guest was not Ms. Fitness.

When the newcomer was seated, considerable fuss ensued until she found a place for her purse, yanked at the shoulder of her dress, tossed her head so her long red hair would hang behind her shoulders, and asked the headwaiter for some water. (He replied, "I'll send your waiter, Clifford, right over," in a rather stiff voice.)

"I'm so sorry I'm late, Mrs. Swiftfoot. I caught the wrong bus, and after that, everything else seemed to go wrong," the young woman said.

Dahlia studied her silently. Making people squirm was something Dahlia did very well. "You are the Circe, the witch?" Dahlia said finally, in her frostiest voice. But her tone was not as cutting as she could make it. Dahlia had gone to too much trouble setting up the meeting to go overboard with the hostility.

"Yes, oh, yes, I didn't introduce myself!" The young witch giggled, tossed her head again. "I'm not the original Circe, of course. That was my—well, my many-times great-grandmother. But I'm the direct descendant, yes."

"And you are a trained witch?"

"Oh, yes, I went to school and everything." The Circe wore glasses, and she blinked anxiously at the tiny vampire across the table. "I graduated with honors."

"I was under the impression that witches were taught by their predecessors," Dahlia said. "I understood that the knowledge was passed along by word of mouth, and in the family grimoire. There's no—Hogwarts in your past, I presume?" The reference to Harry Potter was a real stretch for Dahlia, who tracked current culture with some effort. Dahlia had ventured the mild pleasantry to put the panting young woman at ease, but Dahlia was not terribly adept at mild or pleasant.

The Circe recoiled. "No," she snapped. "And I'll thank you not to refer to those books again. Everyone thinks we're cute now, and we've lost a lot of the respect we used to be accorded."

"Some would say that any publicity is good publicity,"

Dahlia said, curious about this unexpected sign of temper. No one had snapped at Dahlia in, oh, five decades. She'd caught an unexpected glimpse of the darker thing that lived inside the untidy young creature sitting across the table.

"If one more person asks me where my owl is, or how to get to Gringotts, I'll turn them into a . . ."

"Pig?" Dahlia suggested.

The Circe glared at her. "That was my ancestor's thing, not mine," she said.

Interesting. "Let's start again, from the beginning," Dahlia said. "Please don't call me Mrs. Swiftfoot. Swiftfoot was my husband's pack name. I've broken my connection with his pack."

Clifford, setting the witch's glass of water before her and supplying both of them with menus (though Dahlia didn't need one, of course), winked at Dahlia with his face carefully turned away from the Circe.

The Circe took several deep breaths in a visible effort to calm herself. "What shall I call you?" She smiled at her hostess, tossed the red hair again.

"You may call me Dahlia," the vampire said. "Do you have a human name?"

"Yes. Kathy Aenidis."

"Kathy?" Dahlia might have been saying "dead mouse."

"Yes," the young woman said defiantly. "I had to have one name that was easy to spell."

Dahlia raised her black brows. She'd never in her life done anything because it would be easy for humans. She'd changed her own original name, which was hardly pronounceable by modern tongues, to keep some protective coloration. That had been eighty years ago. "And you make your living by the practice of sorcery?" Dahlia asked in a gentle voice.

"Actually, a girl can't make a living at full-time sorcery anymore," Kathy said with a brave smile. "Not with so many of the supernaturals trying to do things the official, human way. The only sorcerer who's gone public is in Chicago, and I hear he's struggling. I'm a schoolteacher."

"You teach human children." There was no expression at all in Dahlia's voice.

Kathy nodded happily. "Oh, yes, third grade. They're so cute! It's an ideal age, I think, because they're all well past being potty-trained and they know their basic socialization skills; standing in line, waiting their turn to speak, sharing . . ."

"Potty-trained," Dahlia said, turning even whiter, if that were possible. Dahlia reflected that she herself had never learned any socialization skills, if Kathy Aenidis's list was complete.

The witch babbled on, while Dahlia considered the possibility that she'd made a huge mistake. Could her information be at fault? This woman was a blathering fool. Dahlia was tempted to get up and walk out, leaving the witch sitting at the table. But her sheriff, Cedric, and her one remaining friend in her husband's pack, Clifford, had worked hard to make this appointment for Dahlia, and she decided she should at least see this meeting through to the next step.

"But here I am, chattering away," Kathy said, just when Dahlia was thinking she might lean across the table and break Kathy's arm. The witch beamed at Dahlia. "You asked me here because you thought I might be able to do something for you. Can I ask in what way? The original Circe, the founder of the line, never got to meet a vampire, though I'm assuming there were vampires back then. I'm so excited to meet you, and I hope I can help you. And of course I can always use extra money!"

Dahlia was relieved to be getting to the point. It had been a long time since she'd dealt with a breather (however different a human a witch might be) with herself cast in the role of supplicant, and it wasn't easy. "I am a widow."

"Really?" Kathy looked startled.

Dahlia began to suspect Kathy was a better actress than she appeared. "Can you not see I am wearing black? Total, unrelieved black?"

"Yes, but . . . don't vampires like to wear black anyway? And it's very low-cut," Kathy said.

Dahlia's eyes flashed red for a second. "Do you expect me to look like a frump because my husband died?" Her voice was so cold, there were icicles hanging from every word.

"No," Kathy said hastily. "Oh, no, of course not. Black is always appropriate." She appeared to fumble around for a change of topic. "Excuse me for asking, but what happened to Mr. Swiftfoot?"

"He was murdered," Dahlia said with no expression at all.

"Oh, my Gods! I'm so sorry! Did you want to contact his spirit? Because I don't do that kind of work, but I do know a very good medium. She's the real deal. If she can't connect with him, no one can." Kathy's eyes blinked earnestly behind the lenses of her glasses.

Dahlia worked hard to suppress her instant reaction, which was to spit on Kathy. Or spit her. Either one would relieve her anger. Since Todd's death, she'd had a hard time keeping control of her emotions. Temper control had never been her best thing, anyway. But now was not the time to break discipline. She had a goal, a plan.

"No, I don't want to contact Todd," Dahlia said, her voice very hushed and smooth. "What would be the point of that? He can't come back. I went to the trouble of finding you because I want to punish those who killed him."

"Ah." Kathy sat back in her chair and smiled. And though nothing obvious about her had changed, she looked quite different from the messy, bumbling schoolteacher who'd followed the headwaiter to the table. Suddenly, Dahlia was convinced she was on the right track. Cedric and Clifford had been right. This Circe was the right witch. "Now, that's much more doable," Kathy continued. "What did you have in mind?"

"I want them all dead. That's what I have in mind."

"Oh, dear."

Clifford popped out of nowhere to take Kathy's order and to bring Dahlia another wineglass full of TrueBlood. Dahlia stared at it resentfully. It looked real, it tasted real—but there was no substitute for blood straight from the source. Nights like this, she just wanted to grab someone and chomp. Her fangs ran out at the thought.

"Would you tell me how his death came about?" Kathy asked very respectfully.

Dahlia had to wait for a moment to get her fangs under control. She looked at the witch with great attention, but now Kathy didn't seem to be uneasy at all. "Here in Rhodes," Dahlia said, "there are two main werewolf packs, as you may know. The Swiftfoot pack is fairly large, thirty or forty strong, and its members live mostly in the humbler neighborhoods of the older part of the city. Swiftfoot pack members tend to be manual laborers or low-level professionals: motorcyclists, cops, city workers of all kinds. My husband Todd was a Swiftfoot, of course. We have . . . had been married a year."

Though the legislation was being debated in the House, it was not yet legal for vampires to marry humans, and since werewolves had not yet revealed themselves to the populace at large the way the vamps had, they were counted as human. Dahlia and Todd's marriage hadn't been legal any more than Don's and Taffy's, but Dahlia didn't care for human law.

"I understand," Kathy murmured.

Dahlia was skeptical about that, but she continued, "The other pack is the Ripper pack from the western suburbs. The Ripper pack is growing in numbers. It's composed mostly of professionals—dentists, nurses, architects. Psychologists. Schoolteachers," Dahlia added, her upper lip curling in a snarl that would have done credit to any Were.

"I understand," Kathy said again. "Different social strata, but they're all the same animal under the skin, right?" She spread her hands in an all-inclusive gesture.

Dahlia could see the telltale signs of someone who'd taken counseling courses: the wise nod, the intent eye focus, the effort to draw the talk out more. Dahlia shuddered, very delicately. But she needed this woman, and she laced her fingers together so her little fists wouldn't bury themselves in the witch's abdomen. Dahlia waited while Clifford placed Kathy's salad in front of her. Behind the witch's back, he gave her a questioning look, and she nodded. After making sure Kathy had everything she needed, he wheeled off to the kitchen to make a phone call.

"The Rippers opposed two of the Swiftfoot pack marrying vampires," Dahlia said. "They feared such marriages would pull them into the spotlight before they were ready to be seen." Her mouth folded in a tight line. "Quite disregarding the fact that the wolves have been considering that very course of action. They'd been talking it to death, months before I'd even met Todd."

"So you feel partially responsible for what happened to your husband," Kathy said, stabbing into her salad with her fork, her voice as full of sympathy as a beehive is of honey. Yep, counseling courses.

"On the contrary," Dahlia said in a truly chilling voice. "I blame the Rippers entirely and completely, and I want their heads on a platter."

Kathy jumped, but then she concentrated on her plate for a few minutes to give Dahlia some composure time. Kathy was exhibiting a bit more intelligence than Dahlia had given her credit for possessing. "How many Rippers do you estimate there are?" Kathy asked when a glance informed her that Dahlia was no longer rigid with fury.

"That would be over fifty. My friend Taffy has counted them when the Ripper and Swiftfoot packs hold their rare joint pack meetings. She's a vampire, like me. She's very good at evading attention. Taffy's married to Don Swiftfoot, the packleader."

"What is the attitude of the Swiftfoot pack to Todd's death?"

"According to their standards, it was a legal death."

"Legal?"

"Yes, so they decided. Werewolves," Dahlia said in a tone of deepest disgust. She'd lost her self-control, but closed her eyes, took a moment, regained her hold on herself. She'd known this would be a delicate interview; she hadn't realized quite how difficult she'd find it. "My husband was the best of them, and they will not avenge his death. But I will. Will you help me?" Her glowing eyes skewered the witch across the table—this witch who taught little children, this Circe whose ancestor had turned visitors to her island home into pigs because she'd damn well felt like it.

"The figure we discussed over the phone . . ."

"Stands," Dahlia said, nodding solemnly, sure now she'd been talking to the right person.

"I'll consider it. It sounds risky," Kathy said. "My many-times great-grandmother was all about vengeance, especially against men. I'm partial to men when they're only as tall as my waist and have trouble tying their shoes." She laughed, and took off her glasses to polish them on her napkin. "Then, I figure I have a chance to set them straight. By the time they're grown up, it's too late."

That was the Circe's party line, Dahlia could tell by the ease with which Kathy spouted the words. Dahlia had been a very successful predator for more years than she could count, and a successful predator knows her prey. She thought Kathy wasn't exactly being honest. She thought Kathy liked men very much. "So it's true about the pigs?" Dahlia asked.

"Yes, absolutely." Kathy smiled proudly. "The original Circe fed Odysseus's men drugs, which made them hallucinate they were pigs, but since then we've learned how to do it better."

Clifford removed the salad plate and told Kathy that her steak would be ready in just a moment. Kathy waved a hand at him rather than looking at Clifford directly.

"Was Odysseus really so good in bed?" Dahlia asked. She'd heard it personally from a vampire who'd lived on a neighboring island, but it was always interesting to hear stories from an inside source. "Circe kept him for a year . . . the legend says." Actually, "the legend" was Dahlia's buddy Thalia, who was even older than Dahlia. Thalia, during her nighttime hunting, had come across Odysseus a time or two.

"Not only entertaining, but . . ." Kathy held her hands apart about nine inches, glanced at Dahlia to make sure she'd registered the gesture, then made an incomplete circle with her thumb and pointer finger to indicate girth. Dahlia's eyes widened. She was genuinely impressed. "And he knew how to use it," the witch said. "That's what she said in her spellbook."

Clifford placed the steak and baked potato in front of the Circe as if they had been ambrosia made by the gods. From the price on the menu, they might as well have been. He inquired discreetly if Kathy needed anything else, and upon hearing she was fine, he left.

"You say the original Circe left a record." Dahlia looked approving. "The grimoire you spoke of. Is that the same thing as a spellbook?"

"Yes, it is. And it's also a record of a witch's life and deeds. All hereditary witch lines keep one, though of course, ours is several books now," Kathy said proudly. "If you don't mind me changing the subject, and maybe getting into something painful, how did your husband's death come about?"

Dahlia wanted to end the meeting right there, on the spot, at that moment. But she had to show the woman she trusted her. Dahlia braced herself and said, "Todd was second in command of the Swiftfoot pack. Whoever wanted to become packmaster had to go through Todd first. Of course, you wouldn't know this, but the Swiftfoot pack hangs out at the Full Moon Bar."

Kathy, who was chewing steadily, nodded to show she'd absorbed that information.

"A wolf from the Ripper pack came to the Full Moon one night when Todd and Don were both there. There was no open enmity between the two packs up until then, so this wasn't so very unusual. According to a friend of mine, Todd was surprised when the Were challenged Todd after they'd had a couple of beers together. I believe that the wolf put something in Todd's beer."

Kathy lay down her fork and stared over at Dahlia. She looked horrified.

"Todd fought, but Don said he staggered a couple of times and seemed to have trouble focusing. Eventually, it became clear that Todd couldn't win. But he wouldn't concede. Don told Taffy that Todd didn't even seem to know where he was. And after a time, the Ripper dealt the killing blow."

"Don couldn't stop it?"

Dahlia looked down at her hands to keep her face private. "He kept urging Todd to say the right words of surrender, and Todd wouldn't or couldn't. Since he didn't speak, Bart Ripper was technically within his rights to kill him."

Kathy looked rather ill. "I'm so sorry. I'm gathering that you weren't there?" she said, her voice faltering.

"No. I didn't like to spend evenings at the Full Moon. I'm not very popular with most of the pack." Dahlia shrugged with supreme indifference.

"Was your friend Taffy there?"

"No, though Taffy is far more popular with the Weres than I." Dahlia's lack of worry about this was apparent. "But she's very concerned. Now her husband has a Ripper second, who'll certainly challenge him at the next full moon in two nights, or the one after that. Who knows what tricks Bart has in store?"

Kathy seemed to relax a bit. "Okay, I got the picture now," she said with a reassuring half smile. "Have you figured out a way to do this, and what you want done?"

"Yes, I have," Dahlia said. "Are you willing?"

"I'm enthusiastic about trying," Kathy said, though she didn't sound enthusiastic. "But, of course . . . I'm doing this as a professional. When we agreed on a price, I didn't realize there would be up to fifty people to take care of; and let me tell you, schoolteachers are always short of money. . . ."

So for the next five minutes, they revisited the topic of price.

DAHLIA'S FRIEND TAFFY was waiting at the vampire nest. In the city of Rhodes, the largest vampire nest was owned by the sheriff, or local vampire leader, a rather lazy and indolent vamp named Cedric, who had excellent connections. Dahlia and Taffy had both lived in the nest before their marriages, and Dahlia had returned to live in her former room after Todd's death.

At this hour of the night, the rest of the resident vampires were out amusing themselves. The big mansion seemed pleasantly empty.

"What was the Circe like?" Taffy asked. Her blond hair was piled up high on her head, and she wore the slut clothes Don favored—leather pants that fit like a glove, and a red halter top studded with silver circles. Her earrings were ancient Sumerian, though, and Dahlia smiled when she noticed them. Taffy hadn't totally gone over to the dark side.

Dahlia described her meeting with Kathy Aenidis . . . in detail. "We need to find out if she's really as good as she says she is," Dahlia said. "No matter how many stories Cedric has heard about her, there's nothing like firsthand evidence. So we'll need to ask a breather. I think Clifford wouldn't mind doing some more research for us."

Taffy swatted her friend on the shoulder. "Dahlia, you know that's just rude! Can't you say 'human'? Clifford's already brought us the tape from the bar. No one's seen it but us."

"Clifford seems pleased to help. He was very fond of Todd," Dahlia said. "I think he actually enjoyed an evening at his old job. He said he was making sure the Circe didn't poison me at the restaurant. I don't think she ever realized that I knew more than I told her."

"If it hadn't been for the tape, we would never have known what happened."

"My Todd was poisoned. And I believe Kathy Aenidis prepared that poison. My research shows she's probably the only witch in Rhodes with the knowledge to make a potion that would cause Todd to do what Don described."

"The tape clearly shows Bart putting something into Todd's beer," Taffy said.

"I think we know the truth now," Dahlia said. Her pretty face was hard and unyielding as a rock. "But we need to ask Clifford to visit us. I want to be absolutely sure she's the one we need. Cedric did some wonderful research, and to my mind she gave herself away, but I have to be certain she understood what she was doing." The two vampires looked at each other. Though outwardly so different, they'd shared a nest for years, and they understood each other very well.

Clifford was there within the hour. Though visibly uneasy

at being in a vampire nest, he did his best to be jaunty and nonchalant. Dahlia thought he might be more relaxed in her own small room on the bedroom floor, and the young Were did seem to find Dahlia's personal domain more homey.

Clifford had been an invaluable accomplice, and Dahlia was already worried about how she could reward him for his service. Though he said he was helping because he'd been devoted to the older Todd, Dahlia knew very well that Clifford also found Todd's widow intriguing and attractive.

He'd come to Dahlia after Todd's death when he'd reviewed the security tapes of the events at Full Moon Bar the night Todd died. Clifford, who was in training to become pack shaman, was in charge of all the security tapes at all the Swiftfoot businesses in Rhodes, and he attended film classes at Rhodes University whenever he could fit them in to his shaman training schedule. Like most of the Swiftfoot males, he was tall and had light brown hair. Though he hadn't grown into his full strength, he was formidable enough to humans.

"Dahlia," he said, and bent to kiss her on the cheek.

Dahlia hugged him, taking care to be gentle. It was so easy to break their bones.

Clifford was blissfully unaware of her restraint. He turned from Dahlia to Taffy. "Wife of my packmaster," he saluted her formally. He bowed his head, and Taffy sniffed his neck, as she was supposed to do. She rolled her eyes at Dahlia while Clifford couldn't see her. Then Taffy gave the young Were a little lick, and he straightened. "What do you beautiful ladies want me to do for you?" He spoke to both of them, but his gaze was on Dahlia.

"We need you to film a third-grade classroom," Taffy said.

"We need to know if there's anything suspicious, or simply different, about the way the teacher treats the children. The teacher will be the young woman you saw tonight in the restaurant. Just in case, we need some leverage."

Clifford flinched. "You think she's, like, abusing the kids or something?"

"Oh, probably not," Dahlia said. Clifford didn't seem reassured. "Let me warn you, Clifford, you must have a story to tell, and it has to be a good one, a credible one. This woman is a witch and she can do awful things to men, if her predecessor is any example to go by."

Clifford brightened. "Hey, I'm a shaman and a Were," he said proudly. "If she's a woman—and I know that she is—I can charm her out of her pants."

The two vampires raised their brows, clearly skeptical.

"Well, maybe it wouldn't work on you ladies," Clifford conceded. "But a witch? Piece o' cake."

The two vampires exchanged glances. It was true that many young Weres possessed a lot of physical charm. And if their suspicions were correct, the witch had already proved susceptible to that particular brand of charm. They looked at Clifford, and they nodded simultaneously.

THE NEXT NIGHT, Clifford rang the mansion doorbell just after the sun had gone down. Taffy, who'd been waiting anxiously since the second she'd risen, gaped up at the young man. He now had grayish-white horns sprouting from his forehead. They were about half the size of a longhorn bull's, and they were sharp-pointed. Dahlia, who'd heard Clifford's voice and come to greet him, put her hand over her mouth.

"Piece of cake," Taffy said. She turned away because she was trying not to laugh. Even Dahlia's lips curved in a quick smile. She preceded Taffy and the Were down the hall to her room. "Please sit down, Clifford," she said, trying to make her voice as level as ever. "You seem to have acquired a burden." They passed a yawning male vamp on their way, and his mouth fell open when he took in Clifford's new head decorations.

The young Were was trying hard not to look as chagrined as he must have felt. "Well, okay, stuff happened. I filmed in several classrooms," Clifford began, but had to stop and rearrange himself in the chair. The unaccustomed weight of the horns put him off balance unless he sat absolutely straight. "So that part was okay. The school seemed happy that the university film class was making a short feature about children. But after I filmed Kathy's kids, I hung around while they were on the playground, trying to make a pass at her. I got her address and phone number, so she went along with it, up to a point. But when she realized I was a Were, and she figured out I knew what she was, she felt free to show her real nature. I pushed a little too hard with the sexual innuendo, maybe." Clifford shrugged, and his horns wobbled. He had to reach up to grab his head to make it balance. "She twiddled around with her fingers and said a few words in some language I didn't know. I felt okay at first, but by the time I got home, the horns had started growing."

The two vampires stared at the young Were without saying a word. Then they burst into laughter, and he glared at them while they rocked back and forth.

"Well, we know she's the real deal now," Taffy said to Dahlia.

"Yes. Let's watch Clifford's film."

"You'll find it interesting," Clifford said, though he wouldn't elaborate. Payback for the laughter, of course. He passed Dahlia a disc.

Dahlia had a television and a DVD player in her room, and it was the work of a second to start Clifford's morning project. In a moment they were watching Kathy Aenidis's third-grade class. The children all looked well scrubbed and neat, which was a surprise to Dahlia, who had kept up with the progress of modern education through the newer vampires.

Taffy said, "They look so tidy."

"Yeah, the kids in her room did look better than the kids in the adjoining rooms," Clifford agreed. "Shoelaces tied, clothes clean, shirts tucked in. But you'll understand why in a minute."

Kathy Aenidis, also known as the Circe, passed through the rows of desk doing her teacher thing. Her red hair was coming out of its low ponytail, and her glasses were sliding down her nose. Her long skirt came down almost to the socks and Birkenstocks on her feet.

Dahlia shuddered, and Taffy said, "Ewwww."

While the camera followed the young teacher around her classroom, Kathy patted, corrected, encouraged, and chided. But all the while, her fingers were moving unobtrusively by her side.

"I see," said Dahlia.

"See what? Aha!" said Taffy a moment later. "There, you see? She's spelling them as she goes."

"Their test scores are significantly higher," Clifford said as his hands shot up yet again to still his wobbling head. "The principal told me so. The whole staff thinks Miss Kathy is the greatest thing since sliced bread."

"She's definitely got another side," Dahlia murmured, her

eyes fixed on the image of the plump and sweet Circe, whose fingers flickered constantly as she taught the children arithmetic. "I'll give her this. The teaching job is good cover. Who would believe a word anyone spoke against her?"

"Oh, we would," Taffy said. Taffy took things literally.

"I sure as hell would," Clifford said. "Ladies, what am I gonna do about these horns? If I go to my instructor, he'll laugh his ass off and make it a dinner story for years. And I haven't had enough experience to attempt anything like this myself. I might vanish my whole head. These horns are throwing my skull off balance! What do you think? Ideas, please."

"Cut them off?" Dahlia suggested.

Clifford flinched. "Don't even say that as a joke," he said.

"They actually look good on you," Dahlia said, eyeing Clifford with some appreciation. She felt better than she had since Todd's death. She'd enlisted the services of exactly the right witch, and she was going to have her vengeance. As for her glimpse into the morals of the Circe, Dahlia wasn't overly concerned. After this job was done, she wasn't planning on having dealings with the witch again.

Taffy wasn't so distracted by dreams of the future as Dahlia. "Come on, Clifford," she said. "We'll go see the Ancient Pythoness. She'll fix you up."

"If she's in her right mind today," Dahlia said quietly while Clifford was busy pulling on his coat and opening his umbrella, the only thing that would halfway conceal his horns.

"I called the Depository," Taffy whispered back. The Depository was the vampire headquarters for Rhodes, the place where all the secret ceremonial things were kept—and anything or anyone that the vampires wanted to hide or imprison. The Ancient Pythoness, who'd been turned when she was a very old woman, was one of the artifacts who needed to be hidden, for her own good. She was still quite a seer and quite a witch, but her powers were erratic and poorly controlled. Making a magical person a vampire had been a bad idea.

"While you're there," Dahlia said, struck by a sudden thought, "ask her if she can see where the current Circe hides her grimoires."

"They really keep books? Full of spells and stuff?"

"Yes, they do. The current Circe said as much."

"Oh," Taffy said. "Well, that's very interesting. Are you thinking we could steal them and hold them for ransom? And she wouldn't be able to use the spells, because we'd have them."

Dahlia tried not to look as exasperated as she felt. "No, Taff, that's not what I was thinking. Just find out from the AP, and we'll plan from there."

Dahlia had thought of a final polish to her plan.

TAFFY REPORTED THAT Clifford had had a great time with the Ancient Pythoness, who was in a chipper mood and propositioned him several times. Clifford easily dodged the AP's salacious suggestions, charmed her with his health and youth and budding shaman abilities—and his horns—and in the end, obtained everything he'd been told to ask for.

He reported back the next night, happily rid of his unwanted head decorations, to tell Dahlia and Taffy that he'd located the meeting place of the Ripper pack. Dahlia wouldn't have been surprised if they'd convened in a Starbucks, but it was even worse; they met in a gym called the Fitness Firm.

Taffy made gagging sounds.

"What?" Clifford asked. It was the night before the full

moon, and he was antsy and tense. "It looked like a great gym. Boy, those Rippers got some good-looking women, let me tell you!" He let out a happy yip, then looked sideways at Dahlia, embarrassed. "Hey, you'll never believe who I saw in there with the Rippers, looking really not-so-great in yoga pants!"

"Oh," Dahlia said, "I think I can guess."

"Why'd you want to know where the Circe's spellbooks are hidden?"

"Because we need one."

"But they're going to be protected by all kinds of magic," Clifford said.

"Yes, it is. But the magic will be geared to live people."

"How can you be sure?" The young Were was doubtful, and Taffy was clearly anxious.

"The original Circe never met a vampire," Dahlia said. "Her descendant told me so. It stands to reason that the spells to safeguard the grimoires do not protect them from the dead."

"You're willing to risk it," Taffy said. "And I have to thank you, sister, because I'm too frightened." She looked ashamed. "But I know my husband is the one in danger, and whatever else you tell me to do, I'll do it well. You've never let me down."

Dahlia did not mind one bit that Taffy had failings. She herself was simply more self-sufficient and ruthless. "Was Bart there?" Dahlia asked Clifford.

"Oh, yeah. He's our second in command, so he's supposed to hang with us since he's a Swiftfoot now. But no, there he was with his old pack acting large and in charge. I saw him doing imitations of our pack members. I mean, I could recognize them, he was so good. The Rippers were laughing their asses off."

"How could you see that?" Dahlia said. "We told you not to risk getting close."

"The gym is a big glass cube," Clifford said reasonably. "It's the second floor of an office building, and the Fitness Firm is a very highfalutin gym. Between nine and ten every night, it's open only to select parties. That's when the Rippers go."

"Well, how very obliging of them," Dahlia said, and Taffy began laughing.

"Do you have any idea where the Circe is now?" Taffy asked Clifford when she'd calmed down.

"She's out with her boyfriend," Clifford said. "They're at the movies. You want I should delay them on their way home?"

"Yes, please," Dahlia said.

She left twenty minutes later, dressed head to toe in a very becoming facsimile of Kate Beckinsale's skintight outfit in *Underworld*. Dahlia could tell Clifford's mouth was watering when she strode into the darkness. It perked her up no end.

The Circe had a little house on a cul-de-sac in a bland suburb of Rhodes. As camouflage, it was perfect, and the taxes would be reasonable, too. Dahlia could appreciate the choice, which definitely looked more Kathy Aenidis, Schoolteacher, than Circe, Dread Sorceress.

Kathy's defenses were formidable, but the Ancient Pythoness had supplied Clifford with a charm, and it seemed to work for a vampire as well as it would have for a werewolf. Dahlia was still uncertain if Kathy would have thought about defending her family records from a dead creature, but at least Dahlia had managed to cross the deck to the back door without being turned into a lizard or impaled on a sliver of bamboo. Dahlia crept close to the door and listened intently. A cat was meowing inside. Whether it was sounding a warning, like some kind of feline burglar alarm, or simply talking to itself, Dahlia couldn't tell. She was not a pet person.

Just before she was about to pick the lock, Dahlia had second thoughts. Second thoughts were rare for her, and she listened to them when she had them. The door was simply too obvious, too likely to be booby-trapped. In one smooth leap, Dahlia made it up onto the roof. She moved lightly across the shingles, noting that Kathy Aenidis needed to get a roofing crew in pretty soon. To avoid the loose shingles, she lifted herself off the roof and flew to the chimney. Pulling away the screen designed to keep out birds and bugs, Dahlia peered down into the heart of the house. The flue was open, and she could see light. Ooooh, Miss Scary Witch left a night-light on. Dahlia dropped a piece of shingle down the aperture. The piece of shingle exploded in a puff of bright light.

Okay, so the chimney was protected. If the magic would explode a chimney tile, it would certainly deal with Dahlia, too. Time to regroup.

Dahlia floated down to the grass and circled the house. The backyard was fenced in, and Dahlia felt less conspicuous there, so after one circuit she found herself sitting on a large wooden bench in the middle of the Circe's herb garden. The bench was probably also storage for garden tools; she was sitting on the lid, not a true seat, as she stared at the back wall of the house. With her excellent night vision, she watched bugs enjoying the spring garden. Bugs had short, short lives, especially if they encountered a bug zapper, like the one she saw hanging on Kathy Aenidis's deck. One flash, and they were gone.

One flash.

In a jiffy she was back up on the roof, looking down into the chimney. She had another piece of tile in her hand, and she tossed it down. Ha! No flash! The Circe's alarm didn't automatically reset. It needed to be charged up again, now that it had gone off.

Dahlia looked at the dimly lit brick and had another rare moment's misgiving. But then she squared her shoulders and plunged into the chimney, twisting her flesh and bones with a fluidity even a shapeshifter might envy. By the time she landed in the fireplace—she was grateful that the house-proud Kathy had cleaned it out after the last fire of winter—she was battered and her black leather suit was scuffed and scraped far beyond its previous pristine smartness.

Dahlia crouched in the semidarkness, listening and looking with all her senses on alert. The only thing living in the house was the cat, whose mewing had gotten quite aggravating. Dahlia emerged from the fireplace and straightened gratefully into her normal shape and size. A clock ticked, the cat kept making noise, and somewhere a faucet dripped. She waited for five minutes, and no other sound intruded.

First, silencing the cat. Dahlia found the animal caged in the basement. Dahlia had taken the precaution of bringing down the box of hard cat food she'd seen in the kitchen, and she poured some into the bowl which protruded out from the cage. The food slid into the inner portion of the bowl, and the cat began eating immediately. It had water in a bottle suspended from the side of the cage. At least the animal was temporarily quiet.

The Ancient Pythoness had told Clifford that the grimoires were "sealed in a dark place under the light spell."

"Thanks, oh wrinkled one," Dahlia said out loud, and the cat paused its eating for a moment to take a look at her. "That means absolutely nothing," said Dahlia, and began to search the house's dark places. There were a few in the basement—closets and the like. Upstairs, in the very flowery living room and the gleaming little dining room, no dark places after she'd looked under the couch. Dahlia was a good searcher, and very swift and sure, and it didn't take her long to go over the house in detail, including the two bedrooms and the attic, which contained only (empty) luggage.

Dahlia stood in the middle of the bedroom and pondered. She couldn't rest her soot-stained bottom on the high bed; it was covered with a flounced white spread. Dahlia was not surprised it had a matching canopy. All the bedroom furniture was painted white and gold. The bathroom was pink, with red roses stenciled around the ceiling. Dahlia hated the decor with a passion. The only illicit thing she'd found had been a wood box of sex toys pushed discreetly under the ruffled bed. She'd tapped the floors for hidden compartments, checked for pockets in the walls, thumped the stairs, and opened the suitcases. Grimoires had to be bulky. Though Kathy had a computer, she wouldn't have committed the grimoires' contents to such a hackable machine.

Admitting defeat, Dahlia prepared to wriggle up through the chimney. As she braced herself to dislocate her shoulder, she muttered, "Charon's balls! Where could the damn thing be?"

The cat began meowing down in the cellar.

Dahlia cursed in a several ancient languages and stomped

down the stairs again. It was the work of a second to weaken the clasp on the cage so it would appear the cat had butted against it once too often. Then Dahlia opened the wire door and the animal leaped out.

"Come on, then," Dahlia said, and went back upstairs to the chimney piece. Before she began working her way up the narrow opening, she held out her arms and the cat leaped into them. The added burden made the upward trip even more difficult, but when Dahlia set her mind to something, she generally succeeded.

After some painful minutes, she was again in the garden, again sitting on the wooden box, this time with the cat leaning against her legs and purring. Again, she stared at the house. Dahlia was beginning to feeling a bit discouraged. There was no garden shed, no garage.

The cat stretched up to begin sharpening its claws on the hinged wooden lid. It howled. Dahlia glared down at the animal—and then she got the message.

In a flash, Dahlia had leaped off and raised the lid, felt a shift in the atmosphere that indicated the presence of magic, and tossed out trowels and saws to find books wrapped in heavy plastic. They were bound in different ways, in different materials. But one was clearly the most ancient. Dahlia hugged it to herself for a moment of triumph. Then she reloaded the garden tools in the box. I only hope she doesn't need it tonight, Dahlia thought, and gripping the book and the cat to her body, she rose into the sky. Under the black leather of her jumpsuit, her arms were feeling curiously itchy. She wondered if there'd been bugs in the wooden box, bugs with a fondness for dead flesh. Or perhaps she was allergic to cats? She snorted. Vampires didn't have allergies.

---

That night Kathy's boyfriend's car had two flat tires when he and Kathy emerged from the cinema. He was burly and strapping, a dark man with enough chest hair to stuff a mattress. When he saw the tires, he cursed fluently and called AAA. Kathy took the opportunity to practice an inflation spell, but it didn't work well enough to get the car out of the parking lot and into the street.

Clifford watched from a restaurant across the busy street while the two waited for the AAA truck, which was forty minutes in arriving. When the truck pulled in, the young shaman called Dahlia, who had consented to carry a cell phone that night just for the occasion.

"They'll be out of here in thirty minutes," he said. "You through?"

"Yes, I'm out of the house and I have it with me," she said, though her voice sounded funny to Clifford. He thought he heard a cat mew in the background.

"Well, see you tomorrow," he said.

"Yes," Dahlia said, and clicked END. She couldn't concentrate on flying anymore, so she walked through the streets carrying a large and ancient book swathed in plastic and followed by a black cat. As if that weren't conspicuous enough (very dusty tiny woman carrying huge whopping book through the night), Dahlia had another problem. She was clinging to every bit of available shadow for a very good reason. Her arms were covered with vines that had erupted from her skin.

Some magic did work on dead flesh. It had been a spell of light, just as the Ancient Pythoness had predicted. Light meant growing things. A garden meant vines; vines that itched.

The rest of the night was extremely painful. After she had crept into Taffy's room and frightened Taffy in the middle of having a weepy phone conversation with Don, Dahlia had conscripted her friend for surgery duty. It took an hour and more, but finally Taffy finished shearing off the vines at skin level. Dahlia was so battered by that time that Taffy gave Dahlia a drink from her own wrist. Even Cedric, who wandered into Taffy's room in search of diversion, was surprised enough to donate some healing blood to his nest child.

Once Dahlia had quit cursing, and after the open cuts began healing, she opened the spell book and began to translate, slowly and painfully. There were advantages to being extremely old and to having friends who even more ancient.

"We'll be ready tomorrow night, right?" Taffy asked anxiously. "I don't want Bart to challenge Don. He'll use some trickery to defeat him."

"We'll take care of it," Dahlia said. "My husband is dead, but we'll save yours." Truthfully, though Dahlia loved Taffy, she didn't give a rat's ass about Don. Her goal was vengeance, just as she'd told the Circe. She was just aiming that vengeance in a different direction, and she planned on doling it out in different amounts.

CLIFFORD WAS RELUCTANT to stay with the two vampires the next night, to Dahlia's exasperated amazement. He'd kept surveillance on the Fitness Factory off and on since his shaman class let out earlier in the afternoon, and when full dark fell, he'd rendezvoused with Dahlia and Taffy.

They'd already performed one errand together, the three of them, and Dahlia was carrying a big sack over her shoulder. It snorted, from time to time, in a sleepy way.

But when they hurried back toward the gym, Dahlia heard Clifford whimper as he looked up at the sky. It was the moon night. From the corner of her eye, she caught him almost twitching with anxiety to be away, to have his run with the rest of the Swiftfoot pack, even though its new second in command would have to be included with the pack tonight.

Dahlia remembered Todd's erratic behavior on moon nights, and she felt some sympathy for her partner in crime. But Dahlia figured magic might need to be cast by a live person; she was worried that her essential deadness would pervert the effects of the spells. Clifford, though he hadn't completed his training, was as close to a witch as she could get on short notice, so she ruthlessly exerted her charm, along with a little bullying, to ensure his help for just a little longer. She had a three-pronged plan that would punish all the wrongdoers with the correct degree of severity. Once she had made sure that earlier that afternoon Clifford had told Don exactly how Bart had been able to defeat Todd, she and Taffy herded the young Were along with them.

"You'll get to go run, very soon," Taffy reassured him. "We just need one more little thing, and then you're off to join the others."

The Rippers had been gathering since the evening began, most of them stopping at the Fitness Firm when they got off work. Clifford told Dahlia and Taffy, "I think they're going to change in their gym. Then they can just slip out into the park when it gets dark enough." A large city park was less than a block away.

The Rippers had thought their procedure through, but tonight, Dahlia had developed other plans for the pack.

When the three decided the pack had completely assembled, they waited ten more minutes to be sure. Then Dahlia and Taffy drew specific patterns in chalk all the way around the building. They had studied the pattern and they were steady and swift, but it was still quite a job. When they finished, Dahlia glanced at Clifford's watch, which conveniently lit up. "They'll be changing any minute," she said. "We have to proceed."

"Did you check to see no one else was in the building?" Clifford asked in a whisper.

Dahlia looked a bit surprised. "No," she said. She shrugged. "Whoever's there must take his chances along with the Rippers."

Clifford huffed a little over this, but Dahlia fixed him with her glowing green eyes and he subsided. Dahlia could tell the young Were was not so enchanted with her as he had been; he undoubtedly thought he understood a little better now why his elders in the pack avoided the undead.

But Clifford had promised he'd help tonight, and he would complete his task. Unless Dahlia's observational skills were faulty, and she didn't think they were, the young Were was also a little excited by the prospect of the special hunt later on.

The three stood across the street in a recessed doorway, watching the Ripper pack in their very own gym. Suddenly, the lights in the gym went out. Clifford almost howled. He knew the Weres inside were changing into their other forms, and he longed to change, too.

"Just a few more minutes, young Were," Dahlia said, gripping his arm with a force that recalled Clifford to his duties.

"Now's the time to use the grimoire." Clifford had been studying it most of the day. The words he had to repeat seemed to hurt his throat when he spoke them, but Clifford persevered. When the last word had clicked the spell into place, he heard a dismal howl float through the air. It was faint because it issued from the glass-walled second story of the building across from them. A chorus of other howls followed in its wake.

Dahlia and Taffy smiled at each other.

Taffy, and then Dahlia, embraced Clifford.

"Thank you, friend," Taffy said. "We owe you."

Dahlia gave him a cold kiss on the cheek, having to stretch up on her toes to deliver it. "I won't forget what you've done for Todd these past few days. Now, go enjoy your moon time."

Clifford didn't need telling twice. In a flash, he was bounding down the street to find his pack, who ran out by the reservoir. He could hardly wait. The Swiftfoot pack was going to have a special hunt tonight, though the chosen prey didn't know it yet. He'd be told soon enough.

The pack would give Bart a head start, because that was only sporting. The packmembers had been democratic about it; they'd voted on whether or not to accept a cheater as their second in command. Unfortunately for Bart, who hadn't been invited to the pre-change meeting, the vote against him had been unanimous.

THE PUBLIC DOOR into the building lobby was still open, and Dahlia and Taffy entered as silently as snowflakes. They took the stairs up to the gym, just in case any Weres were trying to slink down. They found one confused female, and they herded her back into the large open room to join the others.

"We need more light," Taffy said, and found the switch. She could see wonderfully well without any help. The moon's radiance was flowing through all the glass walls. But she wanted to view the whole picture, and then she wanted to take a few. She'd brought her Nokia camera along.

They were all hairless, all the wolves. They were embarrassed and horrified and naked and bare, because they retained just enough of their human selves to understand their condition. Taffy laughed until she felt sick, and even Dahlia had a broad smile.

A few of the large wolves growled at the two vampires, but most of them seemed to be completely demoralized by their own state. They whined and paced while Taffy took pictures.

"What do you think this is?" Dahlia said conversationally, holding the big sack out. She supported it without effort, though she was a very small woman and the sack was very full and heavy.

The yellow wolf eyes focused on the bag and the sensitive wolf noses sniffed the air. All the wolves rose to their feet. Just then, whatever was inside woke up, and gave a big questioning snuffle. Then there was a terrified oink as the creature smelled the wolves.

The Ripper pack began to growl in anticipation.

Taffy turned off the light, just in case someone walked by in the street below. "Ah, yes, you know that smell," she said coaxingly. "You may be hairless, but you're still wolves."

"This is your lucky night," Dahlia said, turning over the sack and dumping a very fat sow onto the gym floor.

In a squeal that sounded very like Kathy Aenidis's voice, the pig tried to tell the Rippers that she was a valued friend of the pack, that she was beloved girlfriend to their packmember

Bart. If she could have spoken, she would have reminded the wolves of all the spells she'd cast for them, all the potions she'd brewed—including one that had caused Todd Swiftfoot to become confused and weak and dead.

But tonight the Rippers were wolves, and they'd been humiliated enough to make them on edge and impatient, and they were hungry.

"I've brought you something," Dahlia said. "Look! Bacon!"

Charlaine Harris is the author of the light-hearted Aurora Teagarden books as well as the edgier Lily Bard series and the very popular Harper Connelly and Sookie Stackhouse books. The latter are being read in twenty countries and are now a series on HBO called *True Blood*. Find out more at www.charlaineharris.com.

# Signatures of the Dead

## Faith Hunter

It was nap time, and it wasn't often that I could get both children to sleep a full hour—the same full hour, that is. I stepped back and ran my hands over the healing and protection spells that enveloped my babies, Angelina and Evan Jr. The complex incantations were getting a bit frayed around the edges, and I drew on Mother Earth and the forest on the mountainside out back to restore them. Not much power, not enough to endanger the ecosystem that was still being restored there. Just a bit. Just enough.

Few witches or sorcerers survive into puberty, and so I spend a lot of time making sure my babies are okay. I come from a long line of witches. Not the kind in pointy black hats with a cauldron in the front yard, and not the kind like the *Bewitched* television show that once tried to capitalize on our reclusive species. Witches aren't human, though we can breed true with humans, making little witches about 50 percent of the time. Unfortunately, witch babies have a poor survival rate, especially the males, most dying before they reach the age of twenty, from various cancers. The ones who live through puberty, however, tend to live into their early hundreds.

The day each of my babies were conceived, I prayed and worked the same incantations Mama had used on her children, power-weavings, to make sure my babies were protected. Mama had better-than-average survival rate on her witches. For me, so far, so good. I said a little prayer over them and left the room.

Back in the kitchen, Paul Braxton—Brax to his friends, Detective or Sir to the bad guys he chased—Jane Yellowrock, and Evan were still sitting at the table, the photographs scattered all around. Crime scene photos of the McCarley house. And the McCarleys. It wasn't pretty. The photos didn't belong in my warm, safe home. They didn't belong anywhere.

Evan and I were having trouble with them, with the blood and the butchery. Of course, nothing fazed Jane. And, after years of dealing with crime in New York City, little fazed Brax, though it had been half a decade since he'd seen anything so gruesome, not since he "retired" to the Appalachian mountains and went to work for the local sheriff.

I met Evan's gray eyes, seeing the steely anger there. My husband was easygoing, slow to anger, and full of peace, but the photos of the five McCarleys had triggered something in him, a slow-burning pitiless rage. He was feeling impotent, useless, and he wanted to smash things. The boxing bag in the garage would get a pummeling tonight, after the kids went to bed for the last time. I offered him a wan smile and went to the Aga stove; I poured fresh coffee for the men and tea for Jane and me. She had brought a new variety, a first flush Darjeeling, and it was wonderful with my homemade bread and peach butter.

"Kids okay?" Brax asked, amusement in his tone.

I retook my seat and used the tip of a finger to push the photos away. I was pretty transparent, I guess, having to check on the babies after seeing the dead McCarleys. "They're fine. Still sleeping. Still . . . safe." Which made me feel all kinds of guilty to have my babies safe, while the entire McCarley family had been butchered. Drunk dry. Partly eaten.

"You finished thinking about it?" he asked. "Because I need an answer. If I'm going after them, I need to know, for sure, what they are. And if they're vamps, then I need to know how many there are and where they're sleeping in the daytime. And I'll need protection. I can pay."

I sighed and sipped my tea, added a spoonful of raw sugar, stirred and sipped again. He was trying to yank my chain, make my natural guilt and our friendship work to his favor, and making him wait was my only reverse power play. Having to use it ticked me off. I put the cup down with a soft china clink. "You know I won't charge you for the protection spells, Brax."

"I don't want Molly going into that house," Evan said. He brushed crumbs from his reddish, graying beard and leaned across the table, holding my eyes. "You know it'll hurt you."

I'm an earth witch, from a long family of witches, and our gifts are herbs and growing things, healing bodies, restoring balance to nature. I'm a little unusual for earth witches, in that I can sense dead things, which is why Brax was urging me to go to the McCarley house. To tell him for sure if dead things, like vamps, had killed the family. How they died. He could wait for forensics, but that might take weeks. I was faster. And I could give him numbers to go on, too, how many vamps were in the blood-family, if they were healthy, or as healthy as dead things ever got. And, maybe, which direction they had gone at dawn, so he could guess where the vamps slept by day.

But once there, I would sense the horror, the fear that the violent deaths had left imprinted on the walls, floor, ceilings, furniture of the house. I took a breath to say no. "I'll go," I said instead. Evan pressed his lips together tight, holding in whatever he would say to me later, privately. "If I don't go, and another family is killed, I'll be a lot worse," I said to him. "And that would be partly my fault. Besides, some of that reward money would buy us a new car."

"You don't have to carry the weight of the world on your shoulders, Moll," he said, his voice a deep, rumbling bass. "And we can get the money in other ways." Not many people know that Evan is a sorcerer, not even Brax. We wanted it that way, as protection for our family. If it was known that Evan carried the rare gene on his X chromosome, the gene that made witches, and that we had produced children who both carried the gene, we'd likely disappear into some government-controlled testing program. "Moll. Think about this," he begged. But I could see in his gentle brown eyes that he knew my mind was already made up.

"I'll go." I looked at Jane. "Will you go with me?" She nodded once, the beads in her black braids clicking with the motion. To Brax, I said, "When do you want us there?"

THE McCARLEY HOUSE was on Dogwood, up the hill overlooking the town of Spruce Pine, North Carolina, not that far, as the crow flies, from my house, which is outside the city limits, on the other side of the hill. The McCarley home was older, with a 1950s feel to it, and from the outside, it would have been hard to tell that anything bad had happened. The tiny brick house itself with its elvish, high-peaked roof, green trim, and well-kept lawn looked fine. But the crime scene tape was a dead giveaway.

I was still sitting in the car, staring at the house, trying to center myself for what I was about to do. It took time to become settled, to pull the energies of my gift around me, to create a skein of power that would heighten my senses.

Brax, dressed in a white plastic coat and shoe covers, was standing on the front porch, his hands in the coat pockets, his body at an angle, head down, not looking at anything. The set of his shoulders said he didn't want to go back inside, but he would, over and over again, until he found the killers.

Jane was standing by the car, patient, bike helmet in her hands, riding leathers unzipped, copper-skinned face turned to the sun for its meager warmth on this early fall day. Jane Yellowrock was full Cherokee, and was much more than she seemed. Like most witches, like Evan who was still in the witch-closet, Jane had secrets that she guarded closely. I was pretty sure I was the only one who knew any of them, and I didn't flatter myself that I knew them all. Yet, even though she kept things hidden, I needed her special abilities and gifts to augment my own on this death-search.

I closed my eyes and concentrated on my breathing, huffing in and out, my lips in an O. My body and my gift came alive, tingling in hands and feet as my oxygen level rose. I pulled the gift of power around me like a cloak, protection and sensing at my fingertips.

When I was ready, I opened the door of the unmarked car and stepped out onto the drive, my eyes slightly slit. At times like this, when I'm about to read the dead, I experience everything so clearly, the sun on my shoulders, the breeze like a wisp of pressure on my face, the feel of the earth beneath my feet, grounding me, the smell of late-blooming flowers. The scent of old blood. But I don't like to open my eyes. The physical world is too intense. Too distracting.

Jane took my hand in her gloved one and placed it on her leather-covered wrist. My fingers wrapped around it for guidance and we walked to the house, the plastic shoe covers and plastic coat given to me by Brax making little shushing sounds as I walked. I ducked under the crime scene tape Jane held for me. Her cowboy boots and plastic shoe covers crunched and shushed on the gravel drive beside me. We climbed the concrete steps, four of them, to the small front porch. I heard Brax turn the key in the lock. The smell of old blood, feces, and pain whooshed out with the heated air trapped in the closed-up home.

Immediately I could sense the dead humans. Five of them had lived in this house—two parents, three children—with a dog and a cat. All dead. My earth gift, so much a thing of life, recoiled, closed up within me, like a flower gathering its petals back into an unopened bloom. Eyes still closed, I stepped inside.

The horror that was saturated into the walls, into the carpet, stung me, pricked me, like a swarm of bees, seeking my death. The air reeked when I sucked in a breath. Dizziness overtook me and I put out my other hand. Jane caught and steadied me, her leather gloves protecting me from skin-to-skin contact that would have pulled me back, away from the death in the house. After a moment, I nodded that I was okay and she released me, though I still didn't open my eyes. I didn't want to see. A buzz of fear and horror filled my head.

I stood in the center of a small room, the walls pressing in on me. Eyes still closed, I saw the death energies, pointed, and said, "They came in through this door. One, two, three, four, five, six, seven of them. Fast."

I felt the urgency of their movements, faster than any human. Pain gripped my belly and I pressed my arms into it, trying to assuage an ache of hunger deeper than I had ever known. "So hungry," I murmured. The pain grew, swelling inside me. The imperative to eat. Drink. The craving for blood.

I turned to my left before I was overcome. "Two females took the man. He was surprised, startled, trying to stand. They attacked his throat. Started drinking. He died there."

I turned more to my right, still pointing, and said, "A child died there. Older. Maybe ten. A boy."

I touched my throat. It wanted to close up, to constrict at the feel of teeth, long canines, biting into me. The boy's fear and shock were so intense, they robbed me of any kind of action. When I spoke, the words were harsh, whispered. "One, a female, took the boy. The other four, all males, moved into the house." The hunger grew, and with it the anger. And terror. Mind-numbing, thought-stealing terror. The boy's death struggles increased. The smell of blood and death and fear choked. "Both died within minutes."

I pointed again and Jane led me. The carpet squished under my feet. I knew it was blood, even with my eyes closed. I gagged and Jane stopped, letting me breathe, as well as I could in this death-house, letting me find my balance, my sense of place on the earth. When I nodded again, she led me forward. I could tell I was in a kitchen by the cooking smells that underlay the blood. I pointed into a shadowy place. "A woman was brought down there. Two of them . . ." I flinched at what I saw. Pulled my hand from Jane's and crossed my arms over me, hugging myself. Rocking back and forth.

"They took her together. One drank while the other . . . the other . . . And then they switched places. They laughed. I can hear her crying. It took . . . a long . . . long time." I blundered away, bumping into Jane. She led me out, helping me to get away. But it only got worse.

I pointed in the direction I needed to go. My footsteps echoed on a wood floor. Then carpets. "Two little girls. Little . . . Oh, God in heaven. They . . ." I took a breath that shuddered painfully in my throat. Tears leaked down my cheeks, burning. "They raped them, too. Two males. And they drank them dry." I opened my eyes, seeing twin beds, bare frames, the mattresses and sheets gone, surely taken by the crime scene crew. Blood had spattered up one wall in the shape of a small body. To the sides, the wall was smeared, like the figure of angel wings a child might make in the snow, but made of blood.

Gorge rose in my throat. "Get me out of here," I whispered. I turned away, my arms windmilling for the door. I tripped over something. Fell forward, into Brax. His face inches from mine. I was shaking, quivering like a seizure. Out of control. "Now! Get me out of here! *Now!*" I shouted. But it was only a whisper.

Jane picked me up and hoisted me over her shoulder. Outside. Into the sun.

I came to myself, came awake, lying in the yard, the warm smell of leather and Jane all around. I touched her jacket and opened my eyes. She was sitting on the ground beside me, one knee up, the other stretched out, one arm on bent knee, the other bracing her. She was wearing a short-sleeved tee in the cool air. She smiled her strange humorless smile, one side of her mouth curling.

"You feeling better?" She was a woman of few words.

"I think so. Thank you for carrying me out."

"You might want to wait on the thanks. I dropped you, putting you down. Not far, but you might have a bruise or two."

I chuckled, feeling stiffness in my ribs. "I forgive you. Where's Brax? I need to tell him what I found."

Jane slanted her eyes to the side, and I swiveled my head to see the cop walking from his car. He wasn't a big man, standing five feet nine inches, but he was solid, and fit. I liked Brax. He was a good cop, even if he did take me into some awful places to read the dead. To repay me, he did what he could to protect my family from the witch-haters in the area. There were always a few in any town, even in easygoing Spruce Pine. He dropped a knee on the ground beside me and grunted. It might have been the word "Well?"

"Seven of them," I said. "Four men, three women, all young rogues. One family, one bloodline. The sire is male. He's maybe a decade old. Maybe to the point where he would have been sane, had he been in the care of a master-vamp. The others are younger. All crazy."

For the first years of their lives, vampires are little more than beasts. According to the gossip mags, a good sire kept his newbie rogues chained in the basement during the first decade or so of undead-life, until they gained some sanity. Most experts thought that young rogues were likely the source of werewolf legends and the folklore of vampires as bloody killers. Rogues were mindless, carnal, blood-drinking machines, whether they were brand-new vampires or very old ones who had succumbed to the vampire version of dementia.

If a rogue had escaped his master and survived for a decade on his own, and had regained some of his mental functions, then he would be a very dangerous adversary. A vampire with the moral compass of a rogue, the cunning of a predator, and the reasoning abilities of a psychotic killer. I huddled under Jane's jacket at the thought.

"Are you up to walking around the house?" Brax asked. "I need an idea which way they went." He looked at his watch. I looked at the sun. We were about four hours from sundown. Four hours before the blood-family would rise again and go looking for food and fun.

I sat up and Jane stood, extended her hand. She pulled me up and I offered her jacket back. "Keep it," she said, so I snuggled it around my shoulders, the scent of Jane rising around me like a warm animal. She followed as I circled the house, keeping between Brax and me, and I wondered what had come between the two while I was unconscious. Whatever it was, it crackled in the air, hostile, antagonistic. Jane didn't like cops, and she tended to say whatever was on her mind, no matter how insulting, offensive, rude, or blunt it might be.

I stopped suddenly, feeling the chill of death under my feet. I was on the side of the house, and I had just crossed over the rogues' trail. They had come and gone this way. I looked at the front door. It was undamaged, so that meant they had been invited in or that the door had been unlocked. I didn't know if the old myth about vamps not being able to enter a house uninvited was true or not, but the door hadn't been knocked down.

I followed the path around the house and to the back of the grassy lot. There was a playset with a slide, swings, a teeter-totter and monkey bars. I walked to it and stood there, seeing what the dead had done. They had played here. After they killed the children and parents, they had come by here, in the gray predawn, and played on the swings. "Have your crime people dusted this?"

"The swing set?" Brax said, surprised.

I nodded and moved on, into the edge of the woods. There was no trail. Just woods, deep and thick with rhododendrons, green leaves and sinuous limbs and straighter tree trunks blocking the way, a canopy of oak and maple arching overhead. I looked up, into the trees, still green, untouched as yet by the fresh chill in the air. I bent down and spotted an animal trail, the ground faintly marked with a narrow, bare path about three inches wide. There was a mostly clear area about two feet high, branches to the side. Some were broken off. A bit of cloth hung on one broken branch. "They came through here," I said. Brax knelt beside me. I pointed. "See that? I think it's from the shirt the blood-master was wearing."

"I'll bring the dogs. Get them started on the trail," he said, standing. "Thank you, Molly. I know this was hard on you."

I looked at Jane. She inclined her head slightly, agreeing. The dogs might get through the brush and brambles, but no dog handler was going to be able to make it. Jane, however . . . Jane might be able to do something with this. But she would need a blood scent to follow. I thought about the house. No way could I go back in there, not even to hunt for a smear of vampire blood or other body fluid. But the bit of cloth stuck in the underbrush might have blood on it. If Jane could get to it before Brax did . . . I looked from Jane to the scrap of cloth and back again, a question in my eyes. She smiled that humorless half smile and inclined her head again. Message sent and received.

I stood and faced the house. "I want to walk around the house," I said to Brax. "And you might want to call the crime scene back. When the vampires played on the swings, they had the family pets. The dog was still alive for part of it." I registered Brax's grimace as I walked away. He followed. Jane didn't. I began to describe the crime scene to him, little things he could use to track the vamps. Things he could use in court, not that the vamps would ever make it to a courtroom. They would have to be staked and beheaded where he found them. But it kept Brax occupied, entering notes into his wireless notebook, so Jane could retrieve the scrap of cloth and, hopefully, the vampires' scent.

Jane was waiting in the drive when I finished describing what I had sensed and "seen" in the house to Brax, her long legs straddling her small used Yamaha. I had never seen her drive a car. She was a motorbike girl, and lusted after a classic Harley, which she had promised to buy for herself when she got the money. She tilted her head to me, and I knew she had the cloth and the scent. Brax, who caught the exchange, looked quizzically between us, but when neither of us explained, he shrugged and opened the car door for me.

THE VAMPIRE ATTACK made the regional news, and I spent the rest of the day hiding from the TV. I played with the kids, fed them supper, made a few batches of dried herbal mixtures to sell in my sisters' herb shop in town, and counted my blessings, trying to get the images of the McCarleys' horror and pain out of my mind. I knew I'd not sleep well tonight. Sometimes not even an earth witch can defeat the power of evil over dreams.

Just after dusk, with a cold front blowing through and the temperature dropping, Jane rode up on her bike and parked it. Carrying my digital video camera, I met her in the front garden, and without speaking, we walked together to the backyard and the boulder-piled herb garden beside my gardening house and the playhouse. Jane dropped ten pounds of raw steak on the ground while I set up my camera and tripod. She handed me the scrap of cloth retrieved from the woods. It was stiff with blood, and I was sure it wasn't all the vampires'.

Unashamedly, Jane stripped, while I looked away, giving her the privacy I would have wanted had it been me taking off my clothes. Anyone who happened to look this way with a telescope, as I had no neighbors close by, would surely think the witch and friend were going sky-clad for a ceremony, but I wasn't a Wiccan or a goddess worshipper, and I didn't dance around naked. Especially in the unseasonable cold.

When she was ready, her travel pack strapped around her neck, along with the gold nugget necklace she never removed, Jane climbed to the top of the rock garden, avoiding my herbs with careful footsteps, and sat. She was holding a fetish necklace in her hands, made from teeth, claws, and bones.

She looked at me, standing shivering in the falling light. "Can your camera record this dark?" When I nodded, my teeth chattering, she said, "Okay. I'll do my thing. You try to get it on film, and then you can drive me over. You got a blanket in the backseat in case we get stopped?" I nodded again and she grinned, not the half smile I usually got from her, but a real grin, full of happiness. We had talked about me filming her, so she could see what happened from the outside, but this was the first time we had actually tried. I was intensely curious about the procedure.

"It'll take about ten minutes," she said, "for me to get mentally ready. When I finish, don't be standing between me and the steaks, okay?" When I nodded again, she laughed, a low, smooth sound that made me think of whiskey and woodsmoke. "What's the matter?" she said. "Cat got your tongue?"

I laughed with her then, for several reasons, only one of which was that Jane's rare laugh was contagious. I said, "Good luck." She inclined her head, blew out a breath, and went silent. Nearly ten minutes later, even in the night that had fallen around us, I could tell that something odd was happening. I hit the record button on the camera and watched as gray light gathered around my friend.

If clouds were made of light instead of water vapor, they would look like this, all sparkly silver, thrust through with motes of blackness that danced and whorled. It coalesced, thickened, and eddied around her. Beautiful. And then Jane . . . shifted. Changed. Her body seemed to bend and flow like water, or like hot wax, a viscous, glutinous liquid, full of gray light. The bones beneath her flesh popped and cracked. She grunted, as if with pain. Her breathing changed. The light grew brighter, the dark motes darker.

Both began to dissipate.

On the top of the boulders where Jane had been sat a mountain lion, its eyes golden, with human-shaped pupils. Puma concolor, the big cat of the western hemisphere sat in my garden, looking me over, Jane's travel pack around her neck making a strange lump on her back. The cat was darker than I remembered, tawny on back, shoulders, and hips, pelt darkening down her legs, around her face and ears. The tail, long and stubby, was dark at the tip. She huffed a breath. I saw teeth.

My shivers worsened, even though I knew this was Jane. Or had been Jane. She had assured me, not long ago, that she still had vestiges of her own personality even in cat form and wouldn't eat me. Easy to say when the big cat isn't around. Then she yawned, snorted, and stood to her four feet. Incredibly graceful, long sinews and muscles pulling, she leaped to the ground and approached the raw steaks she had dumped earlier. She sniffed, and made a sound that was distinctly disgusted.

I tittered, and the cat looked at me. I mean, she *looked* at me. I froze. A moment later, she lay down on the ground and started to eat the cold, dead meat. Even in the dark, I could see her teeth biting, tearing.

I had missed some footage and rotated the camera to the eating cat. I also grabbed her fetish necklace and her clothes, stuffing them in a tote for later.

Thirty minutes later, after she had cleaned the blood off her paws and jaws with her tongue, I dismantled the tripod and drove to the McCarley home. Jane—or her cat—lay under a blanket on the backseat. Once there, I opened the doors and shut them behind us.

There was more crime scene tape up at the murder scene, but the place was once again deserted. Silent, my flashlight lighting the way for me, Jane in front, in the dark, we walked around the house to the woods' edge.

I cut off the flash to save her night vision, and held out the scrap of bloody cloth to the cat. She sniffed. Opened her mouth and sucked air in with a coughing, gagging, scree of sound. I jumped back, and I could have sworn Jane laughed, an amused hack. I broke out into a fear-sweat that instantly chilled in the cold breeze. "Not funny," I said. "What the heck was that?"

Jane padded over and sat in front of me, her front paws crossed like a Southern belle, ears pricked high, mouth closed, nostrils fluttering in the dark, waiting. Patient as ever. When I figured out that she wasn't going to eat me, and feeling distinctly dense, I held out the bit of cloth. Again, she opened her mouth and sucked air, and I realized she was scenting through her mouth. Learning it. When she was done, which felt like forever, she looked up at me and hacked again. Her laugh, for certain. She turned and padded into the woods. I switched on my flash and hurried back to my car. It was the kids' bedtime. I needed to be home.

IT WAS 4 A.M. when the phone rang. Evan grunted, a bear-snort. I swear, the man could sleep through a train wreck or a tornado. I rolled and picked up the phone. Before I could say hello, Jane said, "I got it. Come get me. I'm freezing and starving. Don't forget the food."

"Where are you?" I asked. She told me, and I said, "Okay. Half an hour."

Jane swore and hung up. She had warned me about her mouth when she was hungry. I poked my hubby, and when he swore, too, I said, "I'm heading out to the old Partman Place to pick up Jane. I'll be back by dawn." He grunted again and I slid from the bed, dressed, and grabbed the huge bowl of oatmeal, sugar, and milk from the fridge. Jane had assured me she needed food after she shifted back, and didn't care what it was or what temp it was. I hoped she remembered that when I gave it to her. Cold oatmeal was nasty.

Half an hour later, I reached the old Partman Place, an early-nineteenth-century homestead and later a mine, the homestead sold and deserted when the gemstones were discovered and the mine closed down in the 1950s, when the gems ran out. It was grown over by fifty-year-old trees, and the drive was gravel, with Jane standing hunched in the middle. Human, wearing the lightweight clothes she carried in the travel pouch along with the cell phone and a few vamp-killing supplies.

I popped the doors and she climbed in, her long black hair like a veil around her, her thin clothes covering a shivering body, pimpled with cold. "Food," she said, her voice hoarse. I passed the bowl of oatmeal and a serving spoon to her. She tossed the top of the bowl into the floorboards and dug in. I watched her eat from the corner of my eye as I drove. She didn't bother to chew, just shoveled the cold oatmeal in like she was starving. She looked thinner than usual, though Jane was never much more than skin, bone, and muscle—like her big cat form, I thought. Criminy. Witches I can handle. But what Jane was? Maybe not so much. I hadn't even known shape changers or skinwalkers even existed. No one did.

Bowl empty, she pulled her leather coat from the tote I had brought, snuggled under it, and lay back in her seat, cradling the empty bowl. She closed her eyes, looking exhausted. "That was not fun," she said, the words so soft, I had to strain to hear. "Those vamps are fast. Faster than Beast."

"Beast?"

"My cat," she said. She laughed, the sound forlorn, lost, almost sad. "My big hunting cat. Who had to chase the scent back to their lair. Up and down mountains and through creeks and across the river. I had to soak in the river to throw off the heat. Beast isn't built for long-distance running." She sighed and adjusted the heating vents to blow onto her. "The vamps covered five miles from the McCarleys' place in less than an hour yesterday morning. It took me more than four hours to follow them back through the underbrush and another two to isolate the opening. I should have shifted into a faster cat, though Beast would have been ticked off.

"You found their lair?" I couldn't keep the excitement out of my voice. "On the Partman Place?"

"Yeah. Sort of." She rolled her head to face me in the dark, her golden eyes glowing and forbidding. "They're living in the mine. They've been there for a long time. They were gone by the time I found it. They were famished when they left the lair. I could smell their hunger. I think they'll kill again tonight. Probably have killed again tonight."

I tightened my hands on the steering wheel and had to force myself to relax.

"Molly? The lair is only a mile from your house as the vamp runs. And witches smell different from humans."

A spike of fear raced through me. Followed by a mental image of a vampire leaning over Angelina's bed. I squeezed the wheel so tight, it made a soft sound of protest.

"You need to mount a defensive perimeter around your house," Jane said. "You and Evan. You hear? Something magical that'll scare off anything that moves, or freeze the blood of anything dead. Something like that. You make sure the kids are safe." She turned her head aside, to look out at the night. Jane loved my kids. She had never said so, but I could see it in her eyes when she watched them. I drove on, chilled to the bone by fear and the early winter.

---

JANE WAS TOO tired to make it back to her apartment, and so she spent the day sleeping on the cot in the back room of the shop. Seven Sassy Sisters' Herb Shop and Café, owned and run by my family, had a booming business, both locally and on the Internet, selling herbal mixtures and teas by bulk and by the ounce, the shop itself serving teas, specialty coffees, brunch and lunch daily, and dinner on weekends. It was mostly vegetarian fare, whipped up by my older sister, water witch, professor, and three-star chef, Evangelina Everhart. My sister Carmen Miranda Everhart Newton, an air witch, newly married and pregnant, ran the register and took care of ordering supplies. Two other witch sisters, twins Boadacia and Elizabeth, ran the herb store, while our wholly human sisters, Regan and Amelia, were waitstaff. I'm really Molly Meagan Everhart Trueblood. Names with moxie run in my family. Without a single question about why this seemingly human needed a place to crash, my sisters let Jane sleep off the night run.

While my sisters worked around the cot and ran the business without me, I went driving. To the Partman Place. With Brax.

"You found this how?" he asked, sitting in the passenger seat. I was driving so I could pretend that I was in control, not that Brax cared who was in charge so long as the rogue vampires were brought down. "The dogs got squirrelly twenty feet into the underbrush and refused to go on. It doesn't make any sense, Molly. I never saw dogs go so nuts. They freaked out. So I gotta ask how you know where they sleep." Detective Paul Braxton was antsy. Worried. Scared. There had been no new reported deaths in the area, yet I had just told him the vamps had gone hunting last night.

There were some benefits to being a witch-out-of-the-closet. I let my lips curl up knowingly. "I had a feeling at the McCarleys' yesterday, but I didn't think it would work. I devised a spell to track the rogue vampires. At dusk, I went to the McCarleys' and set it free. And it worked. I was able to pinpoint their lair."

"How? I never heard of such a thing. No one has. I asked on NCIC this morning after you called." At my raised brows he said, "NCIC is the National Crime Information Center, run by the FBI, a computerized index and database of criminal justice information."

"A database?" Crap. I hit the brakes, hard. Throwing us both against the seat belts. The wheels squealed, popped, and groaned as the antilock braking system went into play. Brax cussed as we came to a rocking halt. I spun in the seat to face him. "If you made me part of that system, then you've used me for the last time, you no-good piece of—"

"Molly!" He held both hands palms out, still rocking in the seat. "No! I did not enter you into the system. We have an agreement. I wouldn't breach it."

"Then tell me what you did," I said, my voice low and threatening. "Because if you took away the privacy of my family and babies, I'll curse you to hell and back, and damn the consequences." I gathered my power to me, pulling from the earth and the forest and even the fish living in the nearby river, ecosystems be hanged. This man was endangering my babies.

Brax swallowed in the sudden silence of the old Volvo, as if he could feel the power I was drawing in. I could smell his fear, hear it in his fast breath, over the sounds of nearby traffic. "NCIC is just a database," he said. "I just input a series of questions. About witches. And how they work. And—"

"Witches are in the FBI's data bank?" I hit the steering wheel with both fists as the thought sank in. "Why?"

"Because there are witch criminals in the U.S. Sorcerers who do blood magic. Witches who do dark magic. Witches are part of the database, now and forever."

"Son of witch on a switch," I swore, cursing long and viciously, helpless anger in the tones, the syllables flowing and rich. Switching to the old language for impact, not that it had helped. Curses had a way of falling back on the curser rather than hurting the cursed.

I beat the steering wheel in impotent fury. I was a witch, for pity's sake. And I couldn't protect my own kind. Rage banging around me like a wrecking ball, I hit the steering wheel one last time and threw my old Volvo into drive. Fuming, silent, I drove to the Partman Place.

The entrance, once meant for mining machinery and trucks, was still drivable, though the asphalt was crazed and broken, grass growing in the cracks. The drive wound around a hillock and was lost from view. Beyond it, signs of mining that were hidden from the road became more obvious. Trees were young and scraggly, the ground was scraped to bedrock, and rusted iron junk littered the site. An old car sat on busted tires, windows, hood, and doors long gone. The office of the mining site was an old WWII Quonset hut, the door hanging free to reveal the dark interior.

Though strip mining had been the primary means of getting to the gems, tunnels had gone into the side of the mountain. The entry to the mine was boarded over with two-by-tens, but some were missing, and it was clear that the opening had been well used.

Brax rubbed his mouth, looking over the place, not meeting

my eyes. Finally, he said, "I would never cause you or yours trouble, Molly Trueblood. I do my best to protect you from problems, harassment, or unwanted attention from law enforcement, federal NCIC or otherwise."

"Except you," I accused, annoyed that he had apologized before I blew off my mad.

He smiled behind his hand. "Except me. And maybe one day you'll trust me enough to tell me the truth about this so-called tracking spell you used to find this place. I'm going to check out the area. Stay here. If I don't come back, that disproves the myth that vamps sleep in the daylight. You get your pal, Jane, to stake my ass if I come back undead."

"Your heart," I said grumpily. "If you actually have one. Heart, not your ass."

He made a little chortling laugh and picked up the flashlight he had brought. "Ten minutes. Half an hour max. I'll be back."

"Better be fangless."

FORTY-TWO MINUTES LATER, Brax reappeared, dust all over his hair and suit. He clicked the flash off and strode to the car, got in with a wave of death-tainted air, and said, "Drive." I drove.

His shoulders slumped and he seemed to relax as we turned off on the secondary road and headed back to town, rubbing his hand over his head in a habitual gesture. Dust filtered off him into the air of the car, making motes that caught the late-afternoon sun. I rolled the windows down to let out the stink on him. We were nearly back to my house when he spoke again.

"I survived. They either didn't hear me or they were asleep. No myths busted today." When I didn't reply he went on. "They've been bringing people back to the mine for a while. Indigents, transients. Truant kids. There were remains scattered everywhere. Like the McCarleys, most were partially eaten." He stared out the windshield, seeing the scene he had left behind, not the bright, sunny day. "I'll have to get the city and county to compile a list of missing people."

A long moment later he said. "We have to go after them. Today. Before they need to feed again."

"Why not just seal them up in the mine till tomorrow after dawn," I said, turning into my driveway, steering carefully around the tricycle and set of child-sized bongos left there. "Go in fresh, with enough weaponry and men to overpower them. The vamps would be weak, hungry, and apt to make mistakes."

"Good Golly, Miss Molly," he said, his face transforming with a grin at the chance to use the old lyrics. I rolled my eyes. "We could, couldn't we? Where was my brain?"

"Thinking about dead kids," I said softly as I pulled to a stop. "I, on the other hand, had forty-two minutes to do nothing but think. All you need is a set of plans for the mine to make sure you seal over all the entrances. Set a guard with crosses and stakes at each one. That way you go in on your terms, not theirs."

"I think I love you."

"Stop with the lyrics. Go make police plans."

UNFORTUNATELY, THE VAMPS got out that night, through an entrance not on the owner's maps. They killed four of the police guarding other entrances. And then they went hunting. This time, they struck close to home. Just after dawn, Brax woke me, standing at the front door, his face full of misery. Carmen Miranda Everhart Newton, air witch, newly married and pregnant, and her husband, had been attacked in their home. Tommy Newton was dead. My little sister was missing and presumed dead.

The attention of the national media had been snared, and more news vans rolled into town, one setting up in the parking lot of the shop. Paralyzed by fear, my sisters closed everything down and gathered at my house to discuss options, to grieve, and to make halfhearted funeral plans.

I spent the day and the early evening hugging my children, watching TV news about the "vampire crisis," and devising offensive and defensive charms, making paper airplanes out of spells that didn't work and flying them across the room, to the delight of my babies and my four human nieces and nephews. I had to come up with something. Something that would offer protection to the person who went underground to avenge my sister.

Jane sat to the side, her cowboy boots, jeans, and T-shirt contrasting with the peasant tops, patchwork skirts, and hemp sandals worn by my sisters and me. She didn't say much, just drank tea and ate whatever was offered. Near dusk, she came to me and said softly, "I need a ride. To the mine."

I looked at her, grief holding my mouth shut, making it hard to breathe.

"I need some steak, or a roast. You have one frozen in the freezer in the garage. I looked. You thaw it in the microwave, leave your car door open. I shift out back, get in, and hunker down. You make an excuse, drive me to the mine, and get back with a gallon of milk or something."

"Why?" I asked. "I don't understand."

Her eyes glowing a tawny yellow, Jane looked like a predator, ready to hunt. Excited by the thought. "I don't smell like a human. The older one won't be expecting me. I can go in, find where they're hiding, see if your sister is alive, and get back. Then we can make a plan."

Hope spiked in me like heated steel. "Why would the vampires keep her alive?" I asked. "And why would you go in there?"

"I told you. Witches smell different from humans. You smell, I don't know, powerful. If he's trying to build a blood-family, and if he has some ability to reason, the new blood-master might hold on to her. To try to turn her. It's worth a shot." Jane grinned, her beast rising in her. Bits of gray light hovered, dancing on her skin. "Besides. The governor and the vamp council of North Carolina just upped the bounty on the rogues to forty thou a head. I can use a quarter mil. And if you come up with a way to keep me safe down there, when I go in to hunt them down, I'll share. You said you need to replace that rattletrap you drive."

I put a hand to my mouth, holding in the sob that accompanied my sudden, hopeful tears. Unable to speak, I nodded. Jane went to get a roast.

I SLEPT UNEASILY, waiting, hearing every creak, crack, and bump in the night. If we smelled differently from humans, would the vampires come after my family? My other sisters? Just after dawn, the phone rang. "Come and get me," Jane said, her voice both excited and exhausted. "Carmen's still alive."

I called my sisters on my cell as I drove and told them to get over to my house fast. We had work to do. When I got back with Jane, my kitchen had three witch sisters in it, each trying to brew coffee and tea, fry eggs, cook grits and oatmeal. Evan was glowering in the corner, his hair standing up in tousles, reading the newspaper on e-mail and feeding Little Evan.

Jane pushed her way in, ignoring the babble of questions, and took the pot of oatmeal right off the stove, dumping in sugar and milk and digging in. She ate ten cups of hot oatmeal, two cups of sugar, and a quart of milk. It was the most oatmeal I had ever seen anyone eat in my life. Her belly bulged like a basketball. Then she took paper and pen and drew a map of the mine, talking. "No one'll be going into the mine today. Count on it. The vamps killed four of the men watching the entrances, and the governor won't justify sending anyone in until the national guard gets here. Carmen is alive, here." She drew an X. "Along with two teenage girls. The rogue master's name is Adam and he has his faculties, enough to see to the feeding and care of his family, enough to make more scions. But if he dies, then the girls in his captivity are just another dinner to the rogues. So I have to take him down last. I need something like an immobility spell, or glue spell. But first, I need something to get me in close."

"Obfuscation spell," I said.

"No one's succeeded with that one in over five hundred years," Evangelina said, ever the skeptic.

"Maybe that's because *we* never tried," Boadacia said.

Elizabeth looked at her twin, challenge sparkling in her eyes. "Let's."

"But according to the histories, a witch has to be present to initialize it and to keep it running. No human can do it," Evangelina said.

"I'll go in with her," Evan said.

My sisters turned to him. The sudden silence was deafening. Little Evan took that moment to bang on his high chair and shout, "Milk, milk, milk, milk!"

"It would have to be an earth witch," Evangelina said slowly. "You're an air sorcerer. You can't make it work, either." As one, they all turned to look at me. I was the only earth witch in the group.

"No," Evan said. "No way."

"Yes," I said. "It's the only way."

AT FOUR IN the afternoon, my sisters and Evan and I were standing in front of the mine. Jane was geared up in her vamp-hunting gear: a chain-mail collar, leather pants, metal-studded leather coat over a chain vest, a huge gun with an open stock, like a *Star Wars* shotgun. Silvered knives were strapped to her thighs, in her boots, along her forearms; studs in her gloves; two handguns were holstered at her waist, under her coat; her long hair was braided and tied down. A dozen crosses hung around her neck. Stakes were twisted in her hair like hairsticks.

I was wearing jeans, sweaters, and Evangelina's faux leather coat. As vegetarians, my sisters didn't own leather, and I couldn't afford it. I carried twelve stakes, extra flashlight, medical supplies, ammunition, and five charms: two healing charms, one walking-away charm, one empowerment, and one obfuscation.

Evan was similarly dressed, refusing to be left behind, loaded down with talismans, charms, battery-powered lights, a machete, and a twenty-pound mallet, suitable for bashing in heads. It wouldn't kill a vampire, but it would incapacitate one long enough to stake it and take its head. We were ready to go in when Brax drove up, got out, and sauntered over. He was dressed in SWAT team gear and guns. "What? You think

I'd let civilians go after the rogues alone? Not gonna happen, people."

We hadn't told Brax. I glared at Evan, who shrugged, unapologetic.

"What are you carrying?" Jane asked. When he told her, she shook her head and handed him a box of ammunition. "Hand-packed, silver-fléchette rounds, loaded for vamp. They can't heal from it. A direct heart shot will take them out."

"Sweet," Brax said, removing his ammunition from a shotgun and reloading as he looked us over. "So we got an earth witch, her husband, a vamp hunter, and me. Lock and load, people." Satisfied, he pushed in front and led the way. Once inside, we walked four abreast as my sisters set up a command center at the entrance. Behind us I could hear the three witches chanting protective incantations while Regan and Amelia began to pray.

We passed parts of several bodies. My earth gift recoiled, closing up. There were too many dead. I had hoped to be able to sense the presence of the rogue vampires, but with my gift so overloaded, I doubted I'd be of much help at all. The smell of rancid meat and rotting blood was beyond horrible. Charnel house effluvia. I stopped looking after the first limb—part of a young woman's leg.

Except for the stench and the body parts, the first hundred yards was easy. After that, things went to hell in a handbasket.

We heard singing, a childhood melody. "Starlight, star fright, first star . . . No. Starlight blood fight . . . No. I don' 'member. I don' 'member—" The voice stopped, the cutoff sharp as a knife. "People," she whispered, the word echoing in the mine. "Blood . . ."

And she was on us. Face caught in the flashlight. A ravening animal. Flashing fangs. Bloodred eyes centered with blacker-than-night pupils. Nails like black claws. She took down Evan with one swipe. I screamed. Blood splattered. His flashlight fell. Its beam rocking in shadows. One glimpse of a body. Leaping. Flying. Landed on Jane. Inhumanly fast. Jane rolled into the dark.

I lost them in the swinging light. Found Evan by falling on him. Hot blood pulsed into my hand. I pressed on the wound, guided by earth magic. I called on Mother Earth for healing. Moments later, Jane knelt beside me, breathing hard, smelling foul. She steadied the light. Evan was still alive, fighting to breathe, my hands covered with his blood. His skin was pasty. The wound was across his right shoulder, had sliced his jugular, and he had lost a lot of blood, though my healing had clotted over the wound.

I pressed one of the healing amulets my sisters had made over the wound, chanting in the old tongue. "*Cneasaigh, cneasaigh a bháis báite in fhuil*," over and over. Gaelic for, "Heal, heal, blood-soaked death."

Minutes later, I felt Evan take a full breath. Felt his heartbeat steady under my hands. In the uncertain light, my tears splashed on his face. He opened his eyes and looked up at me. His beard was brighter than usual, tangled with his blood. He held my gaze, telling me so much in that one look. He loved me. Trusted me. Knew I was going on without him. Promised to live. Promised to take care of our children if I didn't make it back. Demanded I live and come back to him. I sobbed with relief. Buried my face in his healing neck and cried.

---

WE CARRIED EVAN back to the entrance, where my sisters called for an ambulance. As soon as he was stable, the three of us redistributed the supplies and headed back in to the mine. I saw the severed head of the rogue in the shadows. Jane's first forty-thousand-dollar trophy.

We had done one useful thing. We had rewritten the history books. We had proved that vampires could move around in the daylight so long as they were in complete absence of the sun. That meant we would have to fight rather than just stake and run. Lucky us.

There were six vampires left and three of us. By now, the remaining ones were surely alerted to our presence. Not good odds.

We were deeply underground when the next attack took place. Jane must have smelled them coming, because she shouted, "Ten o'clock! Two of them." Her gun boomed. Brax's spat flames as it fired. Two vampires fell. Jane dispatched them with a knife shaped like a small sword. While she sawed, and I looked away, she murmured, "Three down, four to go," over and over, like a rich miser counting his gold.

We moved on. Down a level, deeper into the mountain. Jane led the way now, ignoring some branching tunnels, taking others, assuring us she knew where we were and where Carmen was. Like me, she ignored Brax's questions about how.

Just after we passed a cross-tunnel, two vampires came at us from behind, a flanking maneuver. I never heard them. In front of me, Jane whirled. I dropped to the tunnel floor, cowering. She fired. The muzzle flash blinded me. More gunshots sounded, echoing. Brax yelled, the sound full of pain.

Jane stepped over me, straddling me in the dark, her boots lit by a wildly tottering light. I snatched it and turned it on

Brax. He knelt nearby, blood at his throat. A vampire lay at his knees, a stake through her chest. My ears were ringing, blasted by the concussion of firepower. In the light, I saw Jane hand a bandage to Brax and pull one of her knives. Her shadow on the mine wall raised up the knife and brought it down, beheading the rogues; my hearing began to come back; the chopping sounded soggy.

She left the heads. "For pickup on the way out. The odds just turned in our favor."

I couldn't look at the heads. I had been no help at all. I was the weak link in the trio. I squared my shoulders and fingered the charms I carried. I was supposed to hold them until Jane said to activate them. It would be soon.

We moved on down the widening tunnel. Jane touched my arm in the dark. I jumped. She tapped my hand and mouthed, "Charm one. Now."

Clumsy, I pulled the charm, activated it, and tossed it to the left. The sound of footsteps echoed, as if we were still moving, but down a side tunnel. Then I activated the second charm, the one my sisters and I had worked on all day. The obfuscation charm. It was the closest thing in all of our histories to an invisibility spell, and no witch had perfected it in hundreds of years.

Following the directions I had memorized, I drew in the image of the rock floor and walls, and cloaked it around us. I nodded to Jane. She cut off the light. Moments later, she moved forward slowly, Brax at her side. I followed, one hand on each shoulder. The one on Brax's shoulder was sticky with blood. He was still bleeding. Vampires can smell blood. The obfuscation spell wasn't intended to block scents.

A faint light appeared ahead, growing brighter as we moved

and the tunnel opened out. We stopped. The space before us was a juncture from which five tunnels branched. Centered, was a table with a lantern, several chairs, and cots. Carmen was lying on one, cradling her belly, her eyes open and darting. Two teenaged girls were on another cot, huddling together, eyes wide and fearful. No vampires were in the room.

We moved quietly to Carmen and I bent over her. I slammed my hand over her mouth. She bucked, squealing. "Carmen. It's Molly," I whispered. She stopped fighting. Raised a hand and touched mine. She nodded. I removed my hand.

She whispered, "They went that way."

"Come on. Tell the others to come. But be quiet."

Moving awkwardly, Carmen rolled off the cot and stood. She motioned to the two girls. "Come on. Come with me." When both girls refused, my baby sister waddled over, slapped them both resoundingly, gripped each by an arm, and hauled them up. "I said, come with me. It wasn't a damn invitation."

The girls followed her, holding their jaws and watching Carmen fearfully. Pride blossomed in me. I adjusted the obfuscation spell, drawing in more of the cave walls and floor. Wrapped the spell around the three new bodies. The girls suddenly could see us. One screamed.

"So much for stealth," Jane said. "Move it!" She shoved the two girls and me toward the tunnel out. Stumbling, we raced to the dark. I switched on the flashlight, put it in Carmen's hands. Pulled the last two charms. The empowerment charm was meant to take strength from a winning opponent and give it to a losing, dying one. It could be used only in clear life-and-death situations. The other was my last healing charm.

We made the first turn, feet slapping the stone, gasping. Something crashed into us. A girl and Jane went down with the vampire. Tangled limbs. The vampire somersaulted. Taking Jane with him. Crouching. He held her in front of him. Jane's head in one hand. Twisting it up and back. His fangs extended fully. He sank fangs and claws into Jane's throat, above her mail collar. Ripping. The collar hit the ground.

Brax shouted. "Run!" He picked up the fallen girl and shoved her down the tunnel. The last vamp landed on his back. Brax went down. Rolling. Blood spurting. Shadows like monsters on the far wall.

In the wavering light, Jane's throat gushed blood. Pumping bright.

Carmen and I backed against the mine wall. I was frozen, indecisive. Whom to save? I didn't know for sure who was winning or losing. I didn't know what would happen if I activated the empowerment charm. I pulled the extra flashlight and switched it on.

Brax rolled. Into the light. Eyes wild. The vampire rolled with him. Eating his throat. Brax was dying. I activated the empowerment charm. Tossed it.

It landed. Brax's breath gargled. The vampire fell. Brax rose over him, stake in hand. Brought the stake down. Missed his heart.

I pointed. "Run. That way." Carmen ran, her flashlight bouncing. I set down the last light, pulled stakes from my pockets. Rushed the vampire. Stabbed down with all my might. One sharpened stake ripped through his clothes. Into his flesh. I stabbed again. Blood splashed up, crimson and slick. I fumbled two more stakes.

Brax, beside me, took them. Rolled the vampire into the light. Raised his arms high. Rammed them into the rogue's chest.

Blood gushed. Brax fell over it. Silent. So silent. Neither moved.

I activated the healing amulet. Looked over my shoulder. At Jane.

The vampire was behind her. Her throat was mostly gone. Blood was everywhere. Spine bones were visible in the raw meat of her throat.

Yet, even without a trachea, she was growling. Face shifting. Gray light danced. Her hands, clawed and tawny, reached back. Dug into the skull of the vampire. Whipped him forward. Over her. He slammed into the rock floor. Bounced limply.

Sobbing, I grabbed Brax's shoulder. Pulled him over. Dropped the charm on his chest.

Jane leaped onto the vampire. Ripped out his throat. Tore into his stomach. Slashed clothes and flesh. Blood spurted. She shifted. Gray light. Black motes. And her cat screamed.

I watched as her beast tore the vampire apart. Screaming with rage.

WE MADE IT to the mine entrance, Carmen and the girls running ahead, into the arms of my sisters. Evangelina raised a hand to me, framed by pale light, and pulled the girls outside, leaving the entrance empty, dawn pouring in. I didn't know how the night had passed, where the time had disappeared. But I stopped there, inside the mine with Jane, looking out, into the day. In the urgency of finding the girls and getting them all back to safety, we hadn't spoken about the fight.

Now, she touched her throat. Hitched Brax higher. He hadn't made it. Jane had carried him out, his blood seeping all over her, through the rents in her clothes made by fighting vampires and by Jane herself, as she shifted inside them. "Is he," she asked, her damaged voice raspy as stone, "dead because you used the last healing charm on me?" She swallowed, the movement of poorly healed muscles audible. "Is that why you're crying?"

Guilt lanced through me. Tears, falling for the last hour, burned my face. "No," I whispered. "I used it on Brax. But he was too far gone for a healing charm."

"And me?" The sound was pained, the words hurting her throat.

"I trusted in your beast to heal you."

She nodded, staring into the dawn. "You did the right thing." Again she hitched Brax higher. Whispery-voiced, she continued. "I got seven heads to pick up and turn in"—she slanted her eyes at me—"and we got a cool quarter mil waiting. Come on. Day's wasting." Jane Yellowrock walked into the sunlight, her tawny eyes still glowing.

And I walked beside her.

Faith Hunter has written three urban fantasy novels in the Rogue Mage series, about stone-mage Thorn St. Croix, and collaborated on a role-playing game by the same name. *Skinwalker,* based on the character Jane Yellowrock, introduced in this story, will be released in July 2009 from ROC. Being totally schizoid, she has also written numerous mysteries and thrillers under her pen name, Gwen Hunter. She lives with her husband and two long-haired yappy dogs, works full-time in a hospital lab, and writes two books a year. She would write faster but discovered that occasionally she needs sleep. You can find out more about her at www.faithhunter.net or www.gwenhunter.com.

# Ginger

## Caitlin Kittredge

### A Nocturne City Story

I'M NOT BRAVE. Ask anyone. *Sunny Swann? Oh yeah, she's a complete wuss. Scared of her own shadow.*

When I was ten, my cousin Luna convinced me that if I fell asleep, Freddy Krueger was going to come into my room and behead all my dolls. When I inevitably *did* sleep, she sneaked around taking all their heads and putting them into bed with me.

At least the two of us get along better now. Hell hath no fury like a ten-year-old with headless dolls.

Luna's always been the brave one. Older. Taller. Tougher. She ran away to Nocturne City from our going-nowhere hometown, and I followed. She got tangled up with some bad blood witches, and I helped her. She's the troublemaker. I'm dependable.

And a wuss. It was why I sat in the very back of the courtroom while Luna was on the stand. I didn't really want to be noticed. If our grandmother saw me here, she'd go ballistic, and I had to live with the woman. I'm a peacekeeper. Grandma and Luna don't get along, to the extreme. You do the math.

The defense attorney had a hundred-dollar haircut and a suit that hid the fact that he was fat, except from the back. His pants were straining their seams as he strode to and fro in front of the stand.

"You admit that you broke into Seamus O'Halloran's office, Detective?"

Luna gave him that look, the one that says, *You'd be tasty. I think I'll eat you.* She's a werewolf. It happens. "No, sir."

"No?" He looked shocked, eyes bugging out, round upper body shooting forward. "How is that possible, Detective?"

"I had a key."

"And you obtained this key how?"

"I found it in my Lucky Charms."

Snickers erupted from the first two rows of benches. Luna had some friends in the Nocturne City PD, even now, with the whole werewolf scandal.

The judged banged her gavel. "Settle down. I *will* clear this courtroom."

"Your Honor, would you please instruct the witness to answer truthfully, and remind her what the penalty is for perjury?"

"Quit grandstanding, Mr. Fisk, and move your questioning along. Detective Wilder isn't here to help you make your case."

Fisk blushed, and the judge folded her arms and dared him to contradict her. Luna smirked at the defense before she leaned into the mic and said, oh so sweetly, "Shall I elaborate, sir?"

Fisk went from a schoolgirl blush to tomato. "I'm done with this witness," he said tightly.

"Detective Wilder, you can step down," said the judge. The prosecutor stood up. He was younger and slimmer than Fisk, his suit didn't fit, and he was cute. That, at least, was some small reward for sitting on this rock-hard bench all afternoon while Luna waited to testify.

"Your Honor, could we request a recess before the next witness? My cocounsel and I need to go over our questions one last time."

"Lack of planning on your part is not my problem, Mr. Procter," said the judge. She looked like a less cuddly version of Kathy Bates. "But fortunately for you, I could use a cup of coffee. Thirty-minute recess." The gavel came down, and chatter erupted.

Luna slumped into the seat next to mine. "I swear to the gods, I was about one step from vaulting the rail and nailing that smarmy bastard right in the gonads." This was a standard greeting from Luna, so I nodded.

"Think he'll get Trotter off?" Gordon Trotter was the CFO of the O'Halloran Group, and he was on the hook for securities fraud and a bunch of other shenanigans that made my eyes glaze over. Seamus O'Halloran, the CEO, wasn't next to him. Seamus O'Halloran was dead.

Luna snorted. "Oh, yeah. O'Halloran was one smart bastard, and what he couldn't do with dummy corporations and stock fraud, he magicked into being. There isn't one shred of evidence to tie any of them to the shit the O'Halloran Group was pulling. Flunkies will go down and Trotter will get a deal."

"You make it sound so certain." I looked at the back of Trotter's head, at the defense table. His bald spot was sweating under the TV lights that sprang to life as soon as the judge called a recess.

"Cuz, when you've seen as many scumbags as I have make deals and go on their merry way, you get a certain amount of cynicism."

I was going to answer and tell her if cynicism was booze, she'd be a third-stage alcoholic, but the sense of someone else's magick slammed into me like a truck and stole my words.

Witches aren't rare, especially in Nocturne City, but I'm used to being the only one in a given room. Whipping my head around, I saw a court clerk lugging an attaché case, winding through the milling spectators toward the defense table. His magick flowed behind him, bright and hot as a forest fire. Somehow, I got the feeling he wasn't delivering a brief.

"Luna," I said, standing up. She followed my eyes.

"What?"

"You have your gun?"

She patted her hip under her vintage Valentino jacket. "Glock. Don't leave home without it."

"Good. You may have to use it in a second."

Leaving her sputtering, I shoved past the people at the end of my row and into the aisle.

I felt the working rise as the clerk—overweight, white, glasses, no one you'd expect to be anything special—closed in on Fisk and Trotter. He was muttering something over and over. "*Vengeance est mei.*"

He dropped the case, papers scattering like doves. His hand came up, the black glass caster in it catching the light as he raised it over his head. Trotter stared at the clerk, wide-eyed as the man screamed, "*Vengeance est mei!*"

His working struck. I felt the ambient magick in the room rush toward his caster, and felt myself stick to the spot like I was Superglue Girl. I'd seen the result of offensive magick before—burning cars, twisted bodies, the black aftershocks in the aether that happen only when someone uses their craft to cause someone else a messy death.

Luna gave a shout, a few steps behind me. She was moving. She had her gun out.

She wouldn't be fast enough, even with were-speed.

My hand twitched down to my coat pocket, where I kept my own caster. Wood, for purity. Silver-edged, for strength. Before I really knew what had happened, it was out, thrust in front of me, at the second witch.

"Bright lady bind the circle and protect all those within," I whispered, yanking magick into the caster and funneling it into a circle around Fisk and Trotter.

The witch turned, blinking at me from behind thick glasses. "Bitch," he said in disbelief. "You can't stop me!"

"Put it down or you get two between your beady little eyes!" Luna bellowed next to my ear. Her gun looked big as a house.

He started to laugh. "I will be the exalted one. I'll be the master!" His working rose, strengthened. I could feel the spectral flames licking my face, begging to be called into this world.

"Bright lady bind the circle, and protect all those within!" I said, frantic. It came out jumbled through my panic-numbed lips. *Brightladybindthecircle* . . .

I pushed. He shoved. I felt my circle snap into place, a bubble of light magick over the defense table, barely holding under the onslaught of the second witch. He went red in the face, sweat dripping off him.

"In Persephone's . . . name . . . ," he ground out. He was strong. Not trained, but strong as an ox. I was trained, terrified, and losing ground with my protection circle. I wondered which one of us would explode first.

The two magicks manifested as we put more and more power into them, my circle wavering gently, like a soap bubble, and his explosive spell charring the floor of the courtroom. Blood leaked from my nose, spattering my shoe and the wood in front of me.

The witch grinned into my bloody face. "I win."

*Pop. Pop pop.* The clerk screamed as his leg and shoulder erupted in three red fountains. His caster fell and went skittering under the prosecution's table.

His working snapped, all the power running out like a drain as his concentration broke.

I held my circle. Held it with every ounce of me. Feedback screamed in my head, the warning that I was pulling down too much power, burning out my circuits . . .

"Sunny."

I gasped, and looked to Luna, who was holding her Glock down at her side. She put her hand on my shoulder. "It's okay. You can stop now."

She peeled the caster out of my hands. The silver had burned my palms. Luna winced at the injury, and holstered her weapon, putting her hands over mine. "You did good, kid."

Trotter and Fisk were looking at me like I had three heads. As I came back to myself, I saw the entire courtroom was gawking with them. Luna laughed, low down in her stomach.

"Hey. For once, they're not all staring at me."

---

THE CLERK, WHOSE name turned out to be Joe Abrams, got taken away to Nocturne Memorial, and Trotter and Fisk went to Luna's precinct, the Twenty-fourth. She let me ride with her without comment.

I couldn't stop shaking. "If my circle hadn't held, everyone in that room would have died," I said out loud as we mounted the steps.

"But it did," Luna said. "I gotta take statements. You can wait at my desk, okay?"

I sank into her creaky swivel chair and pressed my hands over my face. *Everyone could have died, and it'd be all my fault.* This is why I'm not heroic. It's too damn taxing.

Luna's phone rang, and kept ringing, and eventually a detective at the next desk glared at me. "You gonna answer that or serenade us all day?"

I sighed and picked it up. "Luna Wilder's desk."

"That was quite a display today, Miss Swann." The voice was high, cultured, like a dapper butler from an old movie.

I blinked at the phone. "Excuse me?"

"This *is* Rhoda Sunflower Swann, of 213 Battery Cliff Road, yes?"

Damn it, I really hated when people figured out my full name. It was embarrassing. "Who is this?"

"A party most overcome by your skills, Miss Swann."

"Uh . . . you can just call me Sunny."

"As you wish. Sunny, you are wasting your talents. If you wish to remedy that, I am authorized to extend an invitation to meet with our little group and see if you find it more to your liking."

"That's really nice of you, but I don't—"

The prissy voice cut me off. "Eighty-nine Old Nocturne Way, at seven P.M. this evening. Be there, or we will consider you an uninterested party and have no further contact." A pause. "But I do hope you come, Miss Swann."

The connection cut off. I put the phone back slowly and looked all around Luna's squad room. She'd warned me about police pranks, but no one was looking at me with any amount of curiosity.

"Sunny. You okay?"

I jumped, rolling my chair over Troy McAllister's foot. He yelped and started hopping around.

"Oh, gods," I cried, jumping up. "I'm so sorry, Lieutenant."

"I told you," he gritted, clutching his mangled loafer. "Call me Troy."

"Right. Yes. Dear gods. I'm so clumsy. . . ."

Troy slumped into the seat I'd just vacated, and took off his shoe and sock. His big toe was turning purple. I clapped a hand over my mouth, hoping it would hide the mortified shade of red on my face. "I'll get ice."

"Forget it." Troy waved a hand. "It beats a poke in the eye with a stick. Now. What's the matter with you? Usually it's your cousin who's causing me bodily harm."

"I got a weird phone call," I said, hoping that I didn't sound insane to Troy's ears. "Someone who heard what happened in court."

Troy narrowed his eyes. "Oh yeah? Tell me details."

Having him turn the full force of his gaze on me was like being trapped in oncoming headlights. Luna had told me stories about Mac, but this was different. I'd always thought of him as nice, slightly scattered, overworked. Right now, he was glaring at me with his ocean-colored eyes like he could look into my soul.

"It was just . . . It was silly," I murmured, looking at my feet. "They said they saw what happened in court today, and, um. Wanted me to meet them."

Troy stood up and put his shoe back on, then grabbed me by the elbow. "Come with me." We walked—well, he walked and I got dragged—into one of the interrogation rooms.

LUNA WAS IN there, filling out paperwork along with a woman I didn't recognize. She was very polished. If I were catty, I might even go to *plastic*, but I'm not. Red hair with perfect highlights, even under fluorescents. Green eyes, suit to match, an emerald set in silver at her throat and black high heels that could kill somebody, like Oddjob's bowler could lop off heads.

"Sunny, this is ASA Nielsen," Mac said. "She's the state's attorney working the federal case against the O'Halloran group. Nielsen, I think you should hear what just happened to Sunny."

She turned those high-powered cat eyes on me. I looked at my feet and murmured out the story of the strange call. Nielsen tapped a finger against her chin, a studied gesture.

"And after the state's trial, Trotter belongs to us," she said. "We want to thank you for your timely action today, Ms. Swann. Trotter can't fulfill his deal with us if he's dead."

Luna mouthed *Told you* at her paperwork.

"Unfortunately," Nielsen went on, "this isn't an isolated incident. Trotter has been moved to ad-sec at Los Altos after two attempts on his life."

"Advanced security," Mac whispered. "Where the snitches live."

"And there's this." Nielsen produced a digital recorder and hit playback.

"This is a warning," a solemn voice ground out. "If Mr. Trotter continues to divulge secrets of the craft to those not of the blood, there will be consequences. Grave ones. Deliver my message. We want him to know death is coming."

"Spooky," Luna commented. "Mac, I'm gonna go file my shooting report to Internal Affairs. Copy on your desk?"

"Stay for a minute," he urged, and ushered me into a chair.

"Considering the sudden interest in you, Ms. Swann . . ." Nielsen smiled at me. I felt a little bit like a mouse looking at a cobra. "We were hoping you could enlighten us as to the nature of this message."

"Well . . ." I was very hot. The room was hot. They were all staring at me. Did I have sweat marks? Or worse, blood on my shirt? I'd been awfully close to Abrams when Luna shot him. . . .

"Sunny's strictly white-magick," Luna said. "She doesn't know anything. Why don't you ask Trotter?"

"Trotter was a minion in the witchcraft aspect of all this," said Nielsen. "He's told us what he knows. Doesn't look like she's of any more use. Sorry to waste your time, Mac."

"Seamus O'Halloran was the most powerful caster witch on the Pacific Coast," I blurted. Now I was hot for entirely different reasons. I was used to Luna dismissing me, but ASA Barbie? Uh-uh.

"We're all aware of that," she snipped coolly. I suddenly understood why Luna was angry at her job 90 percent of the time.

"He's dead now," I pressed, "and obviously, it's created a power vacuum. Trotter is the last power player in O'Halloran's little coven. You get rid of him and you pave the way for a new witch to take on O'Halloran's position, and that comes with a lot of perks. Influence, money, sacrificial rites . . ."

"I thought caster witches didn't sacrifice," Luna reminded me.

"It's for *dramatic effect.*" I gritted at her, flushing. Nielsen was regarding me like we were playing poker and she'd just learned my tell.

"Well, then, Ms. Swann. We think you should go to this meeting."

I blinked at her stupidly. Luna was out of her seat. We said "What?" at the same time, with different levels of *You've gotta be kidding me.*

"No offense, ASA, but there's no *we* about this. Sunny isn't a police officer, and she's not used to this sort of magick," said Mac. "I won't authorize it."

"Oh, yes. If you want bombs and death threats to continue to be a part of your precinct, be my guest," Nielsen purred. "Or maybe you want to actually stop witches committing crimes, in which case, Ms. Swann is our only in."

"Well, she's not doing it," Luna snarled, and I saw the gold creep into her eyes. The were was always there, watching from under my cousin's skin. "Sunny's not built for this. Forget it."

"Since when do you give orders?" Nielsen asked.

"Since you want to get my cousin involved in something that's way over her head!"

"Excuse me!" I hissed at Luna. She blinked, and her eyes were their usual gray. "Would you step outside with me, please?" My tone must have conveyed my mighty annoyance, because she nodded meekly and we went into the hall.

"Will you stop doing that?" I demanded. Luna spread her hands, a gesture that hadn't changed since my mother, her aunt Delia, had found pot in her bookbag.

"What?"

"Acting like I'm some frail thing that needs protecting! Maybe I *want* to do this."

"Sunny, undercover work is dangerous. Hell, *I* wouldn't do this, and I'm *trained*."

"You're not a witch," I said plainly. "They'd probably pull your skin off in the first five minutes."

"Charming. You're still not doing it." She crossed her arms. I glared.

"I hate to tell you this, Luna, but it's not up to you. If someone is willing to kill to be on top of the caster witch circuit, do you have any idea what will ripple out? Bad magick in this city is already thicker than coke dealers, and you're willing to exacerbate that when we can stop it?"

She grumbled. "You don't even know that the call came from the same people."

"What's that you detectives get? Hunches. Yeah . . . one of those. Who *else* would be watching that courtroom to make sure Abrams blew it up?"

"Sunny, you don't *get* it—"

"No, Luna, I do." I got into her personal space, because I knew it irritated her. "You hate the idea that I can do something you can't, because you need to be the one on top. But I *want* to do this and I think I'm *going* to."

"Fine. Fine!" Luna snarled, and then threw up her hands. "Go to it. But when it all goes horribly wrong, don't come crying to me." She started to walk back to her desk. "And watch out for Nielsen. She smells off."

"Helpful," I commented. "I'm so glad we had this little talk."

My cousin flipped me the bird and walked away. I wish I could say that's unusual for our family, but I'd be a liar.

FIVE HOURS LATER, I sat sweating miserably in one of Luna's vintage cocktail dresses (both too long and too loose for me, who'd gotten the petite end of the gene pool; Luna got the Wonder Woman end) inside an unmarked squad car while Troy and Luna both threw advice at me from the front seat.

"Don't act nervous."

"Don't touch your wire."

"Don't go wandering around."

"Don't act suspicious of anything they might do or say."

I held up my hands to stop the duet. "I get it. Keep the wire on and don't be a spaz, right?"

"Pretty much," said Luna. She handed me a pin. "Camera in there. Your earpiece is your transmitter. Don't lose either of them—department budget is bad enough as it is."

I pinned on the camera and Luna fiddled with it to activate the lens and transmitter. Troy raised his radio.

"Tech van, this is McAllister. You receiving?"

"Ten-four, LT. You sure do look pretty."

Troy looked me up and down. "Nice work, Luna. She looks innocent."

"That's because she is," Luna said. "And if anything happens in there to change that, it's your ass, Mac."

"Hey," he said. "This was all Nielsen's idea. Go cry to her."

"I'm leaving the car now," I informed them. "Enjoy your banter."

"Sun." Luna caught me by the wrist. "Be careful."

I gave her what I hoped was a reassuring smile. One that did not telegraph the eels currently warring with the butterflies in my stomach, or the fact that my heart was throbbing like I was in the middle of a cardiac incident.

Then I turned, and walked across Old Nocturne Way toward number 89.

It was a brick foursquare, circular drive filled with shiny cars with names like Boxer and Stinger and other aggressive nouns. I climbed the tall set of stone steps and rang the bell.

A goon answered. I can only describe him as such, because he looked like he'd arrived via a Mafioso convention. Shaved head, shoulders wide enough to plug an industrial pipe, mean little eyes and hands that reached out to stop me from stepping over the threshold.

"Name?" He had a clipboard.

"Uh . . . Sunny Swann. Rhoda."

"Which is it, sweet cheeks?"

Fantastic, Sunny, this is off to a smashing start what with him thinking you're a gate-crasher. Luna's voice erupted in my ear, and I jumped a mile.

"Get it together, Sunflower."

The goon cocked his head. "Something wrong?"

"Uh . . ." Think, dammit. What would Luna say? *Go piss up a rope, cueball.* Okay, that's not helpful at all. Get someone else in your head. . . .

"Just the fact that you can't seem to find my name on that list," I snapped, drawing my spine straight as if my grandmother were there.

Cueball rolled his eyes, obviously disgusted with the vagaries of the rich. "Swann, you said?" He ran a blunt finger down the lines of type. "Here you are. Sorry for the confusion, miss."

"Yes, well." I flounced by him and into the entryway, my borrowed heels clacking on the parquet floor. A chandelier swooped above me. Walls covered in mural scenes of Greek myths surrounded, dryads and satyrs cavorting along the plaster.

"It's a bit much, isn't it?"

I spun around and almost fell off my heels.

The woman laughed. She was tall and golden—skin, hair, jewelry and even the silk pantsuit she wore. "It was my father's house. Never got around to taking a wrecking ball to the old pile, but it suits for parties like this."

"I . . ."

"You must be Rhoda. Come into the salon—everyone's here."

"I . . . thanks. Are you the one who called me?"

She laughed again, and damn if it didn't sound like honey pouring. "No, that would be Bentley, my second. He handles all of my administrative affairs."

We stepped into a salon, glass looking down the slope toward Siren Bay, a view many climbers in Nocturne City would die for. Goldie waved a hand. "Oh, Bentley? Come here, dear. There's someone I'm dying to introduce you to."

"Bright lady," said Luna in my ear, "what is this? *Dallas*?"

"Shut. Up," I hissed, trying not to move my lips. "You're gonna blow my cover."

Bentley scurried across the room, dodging penguin-suited waiters carrying trays of champagne and nibbles. "Yes, Mrs. Hanover?"

"Dear boy, this is Rhoda Swann. You remember—from the courthouse? That was a terrible upset, wasn't it?" She didn't sound like she thought it was terrible. More like it was terrible Abrams hadn't managed to blow something up.

Bentley shook my hand and left sweat behind. I couldn't even wipe it on the dress—Luna would kill me. "Hello."

"Hi. Yeah, I just did what anyone would do. That guy was . . . well . . . crazy."

"Not what *anyone* would do," Mrs. Hanover corrected me. "But what a brilliant witch would do. You know, my dear, you rather remind me of myself."

Ew. I was so not this old bat thirty years ago—or maybe forty, judging by how tight her face was.

"Get her talking about Trotter," Troy murmured in my ear.

I smiled at Mrs. Hanover. "When did you start practicing?"

"More years ago than I admit in mixed company," she hooted. Bentley was still standing by us like Gollum in Armani. "Go refresh my drink," she admonished, waving a highball glass at him. "And get one for Miss Swann while you're at it."

Bentley bobbed his head and hurried off.

"He's a gem," Mrs. Hanover sighed. "Gayer than a treeful of Mardi Gras monkeys, but oh!—so efficient, and trustworthy."

I craned my neck for any escape excuse—fire, apocalypse, the sudden appearance of Brad Pitt—but no one looked at me. I was trapped with Hanover. Swell.

She made conversation about her charity work with the city for another five minutes before someone stepped in. "Martha, shame on you. You're keeping this gorgeous woman all to yourself. That's not considerate to your guests, not at all."

I blinked at the prosecutor from the courtroom. He smiled back at me. His tuxedo fit much better than his suit.

"Oh. Hello."

"Hello yourself," he said, reaching out a hand weighed down by a gold watch.

"Where the hell did he get that?" Luna muttered.

"The same place you got that knockoff bag," Troy said. They started to argue. I reached up and palmed the earpiece, dropping it into my purse. They'd get sound back when they could behave.

"Matthew David Procter," said the prosecutor, gripping my hand. His palm was warm. "I never got a chance to thank you."

He was blond, tall, blue eyes, and a strong jaw. Throw a star-spangled headpiece on him, and he could be Captain America. I swallowed. "For what?"

"For saving us all from being a courtroom-sized extra-crispy meal," he said. "You dropped Abrams like you'd done that before."

"No," I stammered. "Never. Just lucky." Men talking to me, other than to ask "You want fries with that?" doesn't happen a whole lot. Luna had guys buzzing around like bees on a flower. I was more like a plastic bouquet.

Matthew laughed. "Could have fooled me."

"I'll leave you two alone," Martha cooed, swooping across the room to ensnare more hapless victims into conversations about polo and tea luncheons. Poor bastards.

"She's harmless," said Matthew, following my look. "Just a little overbearing."

"Are you a witch?" Whoa, look at you go, Sunflower. Way to blurt.

Matthew laughed, little crinkles forming at the corners of his eyes. They gave him a tinge of authority that kept him from seeming like a frat boy. "No, I'm not. Just a good citizen who's not afraid of a little magick."

"Ah. Well, good. Do you know much about this . . . whatever it is?"

"For that, you'd have to ask Martha or someone else in the coven," he said. *Coven?* Covens went out with putting people in the stocks.

"Maybe I should," I said, squaring my shoulders. "I like to know what I'm getting into."

Matthew clasped my hand as music started burbling from speakers hidden around the perimeter of the room. It was slow, big-band sound doing "As Time Goes By." Good thing I was here instead of Luna. Her sense of cool would be irrevocably dented.

"You know what I think? I think you're way too serious for a pretty girl at a party. Dance?"

Before I could say *No, I have the coordination of a drunken fruit bat,* he spun me around like the Tilt-A-Whirl at the Las Rojas boardwalk. Crap, I really was going to fall off these shoes. Maybe he'd catch me. . . .

*Oh, get a grip, Swann.* I gasped and grabbed on to Matthew's shoulders as he dipped me again. From my upside-down vantage point, I saw a flash of red hair disappear into the tall doors at the far end of the room. A couple swung by me, and the door slipped shut.

"You're fine," Matthew said. "I've got you."

"I need to use the ladies' room," I said, disentangling myself from his strong, heroic grasp. "And then I'd like to talk about why I was invited here."

"I'll tell Martha," he said. "But do hurry back. I'm going to look awfully silly if you run off."

"I'll do my best," I said, and walked to the doors, managing to keep my footing in the devil shoes. I didn't actually need to pee. This whole subterfuge thing was easier than it looked.

I slipped inside, following the person I'd seen. "Hello?"

A door creaked and slammed far ahead. The house was dark and dusty, away from the party. The walls were dark-paneled and red-painted, portraits glaring sternly at me from lighted alcoves. Martha Hanover had some really unattractive ancestors.

"Hello?" I whispered, my steps silent on the carpet. I dug out my earpiece and stuck it back in. Only static fizzed. "Fantastic," I muttered. Suddenly, I didn't feel so fearless. Having a badass were in your head will do wonders for your confidence.

I walked the length of the hall, checking doors as I went. Bedrooms, an office, a laundry closet. No dead bodies or anything. It was quiet, and the quiet spooked me. The house felt like it was holding its breath, waiting for the explosion.

The hall ended at a plain door, paint chipped off, locked. I rattled it, and checked behind me, the shadows closing in. I reached into my purse and rubbed my caster. It pricked my fingers. There *was* ambient magick here, although who was using it was anyone's guess. I hadn't pegged another witch besides Martha and Bentley since I walked in.

I passed over the caster for my wallet, and pulled out my debit card. Luna had lost the keys to our first apartment often enough that she'd finally taught me to jimmy locks. I hadn't paid much attention during the lessons—I had better things to do than hone my criminal skills—but it was a simple bolt, and after five minutes of fiddling and cursing, I had a chewed-up card and an open door.

Which led down a set of slick cement stairs into a black basement.

"This," I said to the dark, "just gets better and better."

I don't smoke, and I don't carry a light, but feeling around the wall got me a switch, and an arthritic bulb flickered on at the bottom of the steps. It buzzed and dimmed, casting pulsating shadows over the stairs and the murky dark beyond.

*Okay, Sunny. You can leave, go back to the car, and make Luna go down into the basement, whereupon she will never let you forget this. Or, you can go down into the basement like every horror movie ever, and die in some gruesome manner with your dignity intact.*

I took option two. I may be a wuss, but I have my pride.

Shoes in hand, I descended the stairs. In another part of the basement, I heard a gate rattle and muffled laughter. I swore that if the end of this road was a skanky cross-dresser with a poodle, demanding that I put the lotion in the basket, I was going to strangle my cousin.

I made it about ten steps across the cellar, bare except for a few shrouded pieces of furniture, when the light went out with a shower of sparks. I yelped and dashed ahead, blindly. Another light came on, much farther away than the size of the house would suggest. I felt my way along the wall, texture changing from plaster to brick under my fingers. Water squelched between my toes. I was in a tunnel. A tunnel of evil, no doubt. But at least there was light at the end.

No way I was going back to that basement. I walked on.

---

A LONG, STICKY time later, I hit the other end of the tunnel. An old wooden door was propped closed and illuminated by a spitting lightbulb.

I stopped and listened again. The murmur of voices that had freaked me out in the basement was closer.

Hand on the door, I felt for magick. Nothing, just the same curious dead sensation. That was starting to freak me a lot more than feeling Abrams's raw, tainted power had. It's like when you're in the woods and all the birds stop, and you know the Blair Witch is going to burst out of the trees and eat your organs.

The door opened with only a whisper, and I stepped into a bricked-over rotunda with an earthen floor, the smell of urine and too many bodies making me gag.

"Hello?" I coughed, clapping my free hand over my nose and mouth. The room was mostly in shadow, and I caught a gleam of metal bars in the corners my eyesight couldn't penetrate.

The whisper was quiet, but it almost made me jump out of my skin all the same. A child's voice, harsh with fear. "Help us. . . ."

It was at times like this that I really wished I smoked. A lighter would have solved the whole blindness problem in a heartbeat. "Who's there?" I hissed.

"We're locked up," the voice said plaintively. "Let us out."

*Oh, holy crap*, I whispered to myself. This was either going to be really sick or really bad. Either way, I wasn't going to end the night without a trauma moment.

The kid—or whatever it was—started to cry. "I wanna go home!"

"O-okay," I stuttered, taking a step toward the shadows. "Let's just think about this for a minute."

As soon as my foot touched the earth in the center of the round room, I felt it. Magick grabbed me like thorns in a briar patch, got under my skin, and wouldn't let go.

Pain exploded behind my eyes, and my legs turned into rubbery spaghetti, dropping me in the dirt without ceremony. I retched as the binding wrapped around me, tighter and tighter, until I had the illusion it was squeezing out my air.

The lights came on, not that I could see anything, and footsteps came toward me, not that I could pick out how many over the amount I was screaming.

"Stop that," a voice ordered me crossly. "No one can hear you."

Hands dragged me into the shadow, the magick following me, holding me in place and stamping out anything I might have been able to pull down myself. As a final insult, the hands wrenched my purse away, taking my caster with it.

Luna's purse. Luna's dress, muddy. She was going to kill me, if whoever had caught me in their binding didn't get to the job first.

I thought about that, and I started to cry in earnest, not from pain but from a pure cold fear that ate at me from the inside.

When I woke up, the binding was still on me, sticky on the skin like mostly dried blood.

I felt around a little bit for magick, but it was dead to me. Okay, so this one was going to be a wits-only sort of deal. Fantastic.

The lights were on, at least. Across the round space under

the earth, a metal table held a bank of CCTV monitors and a keyboard. A surgical table sat in the center of a casting circle with padded restraints, like they use on mental patients. And all around the perimeter of the room were cages. Old rusted iron bars and fat padlocks. The cages, I could see most clearly.

I was in one.

AFTER I GOT done freaking out, yelling and rattling the bars with the little strength I had left, I curled in the corner and put my forehead on my knees. Luna would come for me. My radio and camera had to be dead this far underground, and she and Mac would storm the place, find the tunnel, and get me back. I just had to wait. Wait, and not go crazy.

I was able to convince myself of that for maybe an hour. Then I started hitting the bars again. "Let me out! I'm a fucking human being! What's the matter with you people!"

"They never answer." The papery voice came from across the room. The figure in the cage was small—maybe ten or eleven at the most. I squinted and saw that most of the other cages were occupied by kids, some barely out of training pants and some almost teenagers. They were all dirty, skinny, and scared as I was.

"Who are they?"

The little girl who had talked to me shrank back. "We call her Ginger. She gets upset if you say her real name."

I grabbed the bars to steady my hands, which were shaking so hard, they vibrated. "What's *your* name?"

She lifted a shoulder. "We don't have names down here."

"I'm Sunny. You must have had one before you were . . . here."

After a minute she bit her lip and whispered, "Madison."

"Hi, Madison. I'm going to get you all out of here, all right?" *How* was the part that didn't exactly work yet. It was a Luna thing to promise—crazy and risky and grandiose. I didn't even know if I could still use magick. There was a chance the binding had burned me out, killed my ability to use magick for good. My guts lurched.

I couldn't think like that. I had to get us out of here. I was the grown-up. The wussy, freaking-out grown-up.

"When is Ginger coming back?" I asked Madison. She shook her head.

"Soon. I don't like it when she's here. You gotta be quiet or else she gets mean."

"Great," I sighed. "She sounds like a real princess."

The door to the tunnel banged open. "I'm no princess," ASA Nielsen said. "What I am is the boss."

To say I was gobsmacked would be like saying Luna gets sort of cranky on the full moon. I stared at the woman, in what I'm sure was a comical gape-jawed fashion.

"Nice to see you again, Sunny," she said, tilting her head to the side. Her copper hair caught the light and turned molten. I bet she dyed it. That bitch.

"You . . . what . . ." I was not the most eloquent captive, just then.

"Yes, I am a witch. No, I don't intend to let you go. Yes, I had Bentley call you and no, your cousin with the body-hair problem won't be coming to your rescue. That about cover everything your little brain was trying to put out?" She pulled up a CCTV picture, and there I was, at the party, gossiping and laughing with a martini glass in my hands.

I hit the bars and drew blood from my knuckles. I had

never been so angry. "You took my blood for that glamour! You had to!"

"Not only that," said Nielsen, "but your microphone and camera are broadcasting a loopback signal. No one knows anything at all is wrong."

"Blood witch bitch," I hissed. Nielsen blinked.

"Oh, please. Bentley is the blood. I'm a caster, like you. Pure."

"That makes this whole locking-me-in-a-cage thing *so* much easier to take. Not to mention you torturing these kids. What the *Hex* is the matter with you people? Why are you doing this?"

"We'll talk more in the morning," said Nielsen. "In the meantime . . . say good night, children."

"Good night," they chorused miserably. Nielsen smiled like she'd just won Mother of the Year.

"And to you, Ms. Swann . . . don't try anything stupid."

I slumped. Luna *had* to come. But until that moment, I was the default mastermind of our escape.

The lights went off again, and I immediately tried every stupid thing I could think of. There were no weak spots in the bars, and the floor was clay, so I couldn't dig my way out. The door was locked with a padlock, so no more picking, even if I had my purse still.

I was stuck down here, with a psychotic caster witch and a bunch of kidnapped children.

That did it. I started to cry. Muffling my sobs into my hands, but shaking like I was convulsing. Fat, panicked tears rolled down my face.

"Sunny?" Madison whispered.

I sniffed. "I'm fine."

"You stop crying after the first few nights," she said. "But it's okay if you want to. I did."

Oh, gods. Here I was being cheered up by an abducted, abused ten-year-old. I was some big hero.

"Madison?" I said, gripping the bars and letting the cold metal flow calm through me.

"Yeah?"

"Get some rest. Tomorrow, we're getting out of here."

I DIDN'T SLEEP. I went over and over what had happened in my head. Nielsen tried to kill Trotter. She was a caster witch, trying to fill the void left by the O'Halloran clan. She was damn powerful, ruthless, and completely off her rocker.

None of this explained why she'd snatched me. Was I the last piece of some puzzle I hadn't gotten a look at? Would I be treated to a Bondian monologue about how soon Nielsen would rule *zee vurld*?

The lights snapped on, and I heard the far-off basement door of the Hanover mansion rolling back. Nielsen and Bentley came in, Bentley swinging a pair of prison shackles from his right hand.

"If you think you're putting those on me, you're in for a surprise," I told him. He smiled at me and adjusted his glasses.

"I've tasted your blood, Rhoda. Do you really want to take such an aggressive tone with me? Just think what I could do to all of the blood still in you."

I backed down. He was right, the bastard. No one raised practicing witchcraft picks a fight with a blood witch if they can help it. They're nasty and mean and don't need a caster to pull magick down to them. Fortunately, they also have a much higher death rate. Casting black magick spells in blood tends to go down the "horrible accident" road. Go figure.

Nielsen walked the perimeter of the room, pointing to children every so often. Bentley followed her and unlocked their cages with a fat ring of keys. The kids were docile to a man, lining up in the center of the floor. Neilsen paused when she hit my cage.

"Are you going to play nice, Ms. Swann?"

I glared up at her. She was wearing a summer-green linen suit today, and her hair was done up in a chignon. How dare she look so good when I'd spent the night in a freaking cage?

"Ms. Swann?" she prompted. "Are we going to cooperate?"

"Don't bet on it," I snapped. Hex me, I was starting to sound like my cousin.

Nielsen sighed. "Bentley, put the chains on her."

He was a lot stronger than he looked, and manhandled me out of the cell and into shackles before I could uncramp my muscles enough to even think about trying to fight. My magick still buzzed like a busy signal when I tried to pull it.

Nielsen stroked her necklace. "Neither of us can call workings as long as this stays on. I'd hate to see some hamfisted escape attempt. It would be beneath someone with your talents." She smiled and licked her lips. "And also, Bentley would flay your skin off one inch at a time."

With that charming pronouncement, she turned and strode to a door in the far wall. It closely matched the brick, and Nielsen opened it with a few charm words.

Bentley shoved me. "Move."

"You're a nasty little man," I said. "And I'm getting pretty tempted to give your nasty little groin a kick."

"Blood," he reminded me, and then leaned over and licked up the side of my neck. "Ohhh. Fresh is so much better than scattered all over a courtroom."

I shied away, my stomach jigging violently. Nielsen clapped her hands. "Bentley! I hardly think Ms. Swann is your type. Get her moving. I'll get the children."

We frog-marched into the next room, another low round hump under the earth, bricked over and slimy with mold and plant growth. "Where are we?" I demanded.

"China tunnels," Bentley said. When I looked blank he heaved a sigh. "Sailors get shanghaied? For ships in port? They took them through here. It lets out at the harbor. After that, it was girls and bootlegging until the Hex Riots closed the old sewer system down. Now it's just us down here, and a few ghosts."

He pulled a switch to an overhead lamp, and I let out a yelp.

Matthew's body lay on the floor.

I shied away from it, quivering, and Bentley laughed. "Don't act so scared. That's just the original. The improved model is alive and well. You met him at the party last night."

"I . . . I did?" The prosecutor's body was bloated from the damp, and a fine spray of mold had crept from the corners of his nose and mouth. A congealed red-black gash in his neck spoke to his last moments at Bentley's hands.

"You did," Nielsen agreed. "And I must say, he was quite taken with you."

"He's got three more days, maximum," Bentley reminded

her in a bored tone. "And that blood in the rotter there isn't going to be any good for a new spell."

Nielsen strolled across the room like she was on a runway and kicked at the body with the toe of her Jimmy Choo. "Hm. You're right. Fortunately, I think I can convince Judge Battleaxe to declare a mistrial. What with the bombing and all. Matthew won't have to show up in public much longer. And then a car crash, I think. Tragic, nothing drunken or debauched. A fire to destroy all the exterior spell markings."

"Oh, dear gods!" I exclaimed, my voice bouncing off the bricks. "You're replacing people with your glamour constructs! That's disgusting!"

"The shoe drops," said Nielsen. "We like to keep them alive, but Matthew here was untenable. He gave Bentley quite a fight."

Leaving me to chew over that, Nielsen went to an intercom box on the wall and snapped, "Get down here. We're all waiting on you."

Bentley herded the children around the perimeter of the room, and then jerked my shackles, bringing me to the center. I looked down at the black paint traveling over the floor. I was in the center of an enormous working circle.

Terrific.

An ancient pulley-operated elevator groaned to a stop, and three of the vapid socialites I recognized from the party last night—tonight? I had lost all sense of time underground—stepped out, clad in plain white cotton pants and tunics, with bare feet. It was all very Jonestown. I hoped the Kool-Aid was cold.

"Bentley." Nielsen snapped her fingers, and her little toady scurried forward with three vials of blood.

"What on the Hexed black earth are you planning?" I asked Nielsen. She wagged her finger at me.

"Now, now, Miss Swann. I know better than to spell and tell."

"Oh, you are too cute. I might vomit," I muttered. Bentley shoved me to my knees in the center of the circle.

Nielsen carefully lifted the emerald off her neck and set it to one side. I felt the magick in the room spike—Bentley's tainted blood-fueled power, Nielsen's hard, glittering brand of caster magick, and the children, every one of them, bright as candle flames in the dark. The three puppets waiting patiently at the edge of the paint ring had a few echoes, nothing special—just enough to hold down a charm or two.

Neilsen pulled a sleek ivory caster from her pocket and held it, turning it concentrically in her fingers. She started to pull down power and it lay over me like a wet wool blanket, hard to breathe, musty with the edge of deceit in her workings.

"I see the future," she said. "I see what *should* be. Do you see?"

"We do," the three at the edge returned. Nielsen cracked an eye.

"Children, what do we say to Ginger?"

"We see for you," they chorused unevenly. Their concentration sharpened, poured into her power well. Those poor kids. One of them swayed and fainted. Bentley scurried over and slapped him awake.

Nielsen unstoppered the blood vials and dipped her finger into each one, smearing it down her face. "I take the power to shape the world to what I see," she said. "I take it *now.*"

One by one, the three witches came forward and let Nielsen anoint their heads. The air around them shimmered as the glamour fought with reality, bruise-purple. I shivered. Blood and caster magick should never combine like this. It was filthy.

"Gets you going, doesn't it?" Bentley hissed. "Imagine what I did with your blood, Glinda."

"Go Hex yourself," I hissed back at him.

The witches groaned and cried out as the glamour took hold, and their bodies changed. One grew tall and bulging like Fisk, the defense attorney, one turned into a prison guard in a uniform, and one turned into Trotter.

Nielsen stepped back, lowering her caster and surveying her work. "You'll do." She passed the guard a keycard. "That will get you into the ad-sec wing at Los Altos. Make sure to keep your face out of the cameras."

"Yes, ma'am," said the witch in a high female voice. Nielsen sighed, and I felt her power spike again. The glamours cemented, all the little details sliding into place—bags under the eyes, messy hair, suits missing a cuff button.

Nielsen was good. Too bad she was such a bitch.

She turned back to me. "We'll just freshen you up, Miss Swann, and then we'll be done here."

Whether or not *Done here* ended with me lying next to poor Matthew, she didn't give away. I decided that I couldn't let her get to that point. Bentley produced a knife, sliding the blade open and locking it. "You were tough, I want you to know," Nielsen said. "Not only looking right, but smelling right. You and that stupid mangy cousin of yours."

"Gee, I'm so glad I provided a challenge for you," I said, shying from Bentley's blade. "My biggest ambition in life, you know." I was going to have one shot at this, while the magick was up and I had to make it count. Fortunately, I needed only a little, hardly enough for an ego case like Nielsen to notice.

I pulled the magick down to me, feeling it spiral from my forehead down to my fingers. I shut my eyes and thought about locks. Bentley grabbed my wrist and exposed the underside, the veins, and I felt the swoop of air as the knife came down.

Locks. Open. My locks. How I wished I'd paid more attention to Luna. . . .

*Focus. The pin, the tumbler, the latch.* The magick found the mechanisms of the handcuffs, struggled in amongst them—gods, I wished I had the kind of memory Luna did for details—and formed my magick into a key.

The shackles snapped open and I let go, twisting in Bentley's grip and bringing my other fist around to whack him right below the belt buckle. It wasn't the kick I'd wanted, but it would do.

He let go of me, air singing out of him. The knife dropped. Nielsen reached for her necklace instead of her magick. I wasn't about to tell her that if she'd just pulled down more power, she could have dropped me. She was stronger and a hell of a lot more skilled.

I let her grab for the spell-jammer instead. I was too busy running.

UP THE ELEVATOR, the pulleys groaning as I hit the lever and set them free, down a maze of hallways through the Hanover house, and out onto the street.

Bluish morning, the sun not quite up yet. Cars and delivery vans poking through the street. I ran into the middle of the road and flapped my arms like a lunatic, attracting the attention of the nearest van driver. "You okay, sweetie?" he called.

"No!" I shrieked. "I need the police!"

The delivery guy lent me his cell phone and I called the precinct, getting Rick, the desk sergeant and then Lieutenant McAllister.

"Mac," I said. "Mac, we need help . . . there are kids . . . they're in cages. . . ." I managed to spit out the whole story. I don't know how long it was before Mac and a bunch of squad cars and ambulances and other official vehicles showed up. . . . I sat down on the curb and drifted, shock finally crashing over me. I'd almost died. I'd come within a handspan of it. But I wasn't—I was here, exhausted and dirty in a dress that was too big for me.

A pair of feet in combat boots came to an abrupt halt in front of me. "Sunny?" Luna choked, dropping her paper cup of coffee onto the pavement.

"Luna!" There was chaos around us, officers carrying out the children, more of them searching the house, radios and sirens filling up the morning like electric birdcalls. Madison looked at me as a paramedic carried her to his ambulance, but she was too weak to do more than stare.

I needed to forget about the night under the ground, the dull hopelessness on the kids' faces. I went to hug my cousin, and then froze.

I was standing a few feet behind her.

Trying to describe seeing yourself staring back at is like trying to describe a visit to Willy Wonka's factory—nothing you say will ever do the moment justice.

"Luna," I heard myself say urgently. "Who's that?"

"You bitch!" I launched myself at her. "You glamour-wearing bitch!"

Luna held us apart as fake-me cowered and I spat invective that I had learned from Luna but never had the occasion to use.

"I don't know what's going on!" Fake-Sunny cried, cowering.

"Luna, it's a blood witch glamour!" I screamed. "She's not me!"

"Everybody shut the hell up!" Luna bellowed. She leaned over to me, back to the fake Sunny, and took a deep sniff. Her eyes widened, gold creeping in around the edges. "You need a shower, Sun," she whispered to me. "But I'll take it over the stinky perfume you came back with."

"I've been in a freaking cage all night," I muttered. "Give me a break."

"What the *fuck* is that thing I've been having coffee with down at the precinct?"

"A witch using my blood."

I was prepared for Luna to turn around and beat seven kinds of hell out of the fake me, but I wasn't prepared for Not-Sunny to grab Luna's sidearm out of holster and aim it. At us.

"Nobody move!" he/she ordered. Luna shook her head, rubbing her temples.

"This is the weirdest gods-damned morning I've ever had."

"We're all going to get in the car and drive out of here nice and calm," said Not-Sunny, "and nobody is going to be hurt."

"Oh, dude, *somebody* is hurting for this," Luna assured it. "The therapy alone is going to take months."

A shadow loomed up behind Not-Sunny, from around the corner of an ambulance but I kept my eyes on it.

"Get real," I snapped, to keep her . . . its? . . . whatever, eyes on me. "You're in the middle of a damn police raid. Where are we gonna go?"

Troy materialized, holding a portable fire extinguisher. He said, "Excuse me."

Not-Sunny spun, and he whammed her across the temple with the metal cylinder.

Luna let out a breath. "Took you long enough, Mac."

I stood over the glamour, looking at my slack face. "How'd you know that wasn't me, Mac?"

"Maybe because you'd never go insane and grab my gun?" Luna snorted. "You're way too mild."

Troy put his hand on my shoulder. "Sunny wouldn't need a gun. She's too stylish for that." He winked at me, and then called the paramedics over. "Treat her and cuff her. Make sure she goes to the prison ward at the hospital."

Luna sat me on the hood of her car and got me a water bottle, although I think we both wished it was a glass of scotch. "So Nielsen stole your blood from the courthouse, made that thing look like you and sent her back here, while entrapping you and using a bunch of kidnapped kids to raise her power for . . . what?" She shook her head. "You damn witches never make a lick of sense. Why does she have such a hard-on for you?"

"They turned into Trotter, his attorney, and a prison guard," I recited. I was tired of telling the story, and remembering the sick, twisted-up magick that Nielsen commanded. And remembering how useless I'd been. I curled my fists in my lap. "Maybe . . . after the courthouse . . . they wanted me out of the way." It couldn't be because I was a real threat. I was nothing next to Nielsen's skill. It galled me.

"At least now we know how every witch trying to replace O'Halloran is getting picked off," Luna muttered. "ASA Batshit has access to all of his case files and known associates. Soon there won't *be* any competition. Just her."

My head snapped up. "Luna." I had it, the flash and the tumbling of dominoes that comes when everything that's been whirling around your brain suddenly clicks together. It was sort of a rush. Also, sort of nauseating.

Luna blinked at me. "What? You look like you just swallowed a marble."

"If there's just *her*, she won't have a hope of cementing control over the city," I rushed. "Nobody even knows she's a witch. She hides it with this big green emerald thing."

"How very Indiana Jones," Luna said dryly. I waved her quiet and went on.

"But if she gets *Trotter* on board, then she has a mouthpiece," I cried. "He's the last of the O'Halloran circle."

"He'd never do it," said Luna. "And anyway, he's going to prison."

Her face lost color as she arrived at the same station as my train of thought. "Hex me."

"Trotter wouldn't do it, but the glamour would," I said. "And thanks to that explosion-happy idiot in court, Nielsen will get a mistrial."

"She'd have to pop the real Trotter." Luna's finger drummed against her desk. "Prison guard, you said?"

"Yes . . . ," I started, but she was already in the car. I followed her, and we fishtailed onto the street and the freeway in the direction of the Los Altos federal prison.

WE DROVE NORTHWEST through sunrise, and into morning, Luna in grim silence, me in a slightly panicked one. My stomach twisted. What could I do against Nielsen? She'd wipe the floor with me.

Los Altos is a clump of gray at the top of gray cliffs with the blue Pacific washing the bottom. Bolted to the bedrock, it has a reputation of being nearly escape-proof. That is, if you weren't being set upon by a couple of witches bent on your death.

The guard at the outside wall didn't want to let me in, but Luna snarled at him until he relented.

We ran through a maze of industrial-lit hallways until we came to the ad-sec block. Luna fetched up against the desk, panting. "You got a Nathan Trotter in custody?"

"Yeah," said the guard, "but you're going to have to wait your turn, Detective. He's meeting with the state's attorney."

Luna hit the desk. "Shit."

"Open the door," I said. "It's an emergency."

The guard yawned. She looked like she was waiting to get her nails done. "Give me one good reason."

"The state's attorney is a witch bent on taking over Nocturne City and instigating a new reign of magickal warfare. She's here to kill Trotter and replace him with a bespelled blood witch. Oh, and she locked me in a cage."

The guard blinked. She looked to Luna, "An emergency, you said?"

"Lady, just open the gods-damn door!" I bellowed, making both Luna and the guard jump.

"Okay, fine," she grumbled, buzzing us in. Luna jerked her sidearm out of holster, shoved it at the guard, and stormed through the gate. "Nocturne City cops," the guard said under her breath, the way you'd say *Donkey-licking bondage freaks.*

Luna ran ahead of me down the hall to the visitor's room. Through the wire-mesh door, we could see Bentley and Nielsen sitting with Trotter, who was pushed as far back against the wall as he could get.

The guard outside the door was familiar. "He's the glamour," I gasped at Luna. She locked on to the guy like a Titan missile.

The guard turned his head, had enough time to say "What?" and went down like a sack full of nails. Luna shook her fist out, knuckle bones popping back into place.

"What was that?" Nielsen said from behind the door.

Bentley stuck his head out. Luna wrapped her hands around his throat before he could say or see anything other than her face. "Lock *my* cousin in a cage?" she growled, and then threw him back into the visitor's room, where he bounced off the table and into the wall with a *clang.*

Nielsen stood up, reaching for her necklace clasp. Bentley drew his knife and Luna grabbed for it, the two of them wrestling. Trotter looked at the four of us, eyes wide.

"Don't," I said to Nielsen.

Her lips curved up. "Don't what, Sunny? Don't kill you? Don't take out one of the few witches who could be a problem to me while I have such a perfect chance?"

"Don't kill him," I said, pointing at Trotter. Nielsen moved her hands away from the clasp of her necklace.

"You know, considering how tricky you are when your magick is up, I think we'll do this the old-fashioned way." She picked up Bentley's knife from where Luna had beaten it out of his hand and advanced on Trotter.

I froze, watching the scene play out in my mind. Blood spatter, Trotter twitching in his cuffs, the glamour coming to take his place . . .

Nielsen put the knife to Trotter's throat. "Do something!" he screamed at me.

I've been in exactly two fights in my life: with Joey Grant, an odious boy who threw my sandwich into the sandbox in first grade, and Mary-Anne Price, the girl in middle school who started calling me "Blood-freak." She was a lot bigger than me, and she won. I got a black eye and would have gotten worse if Luna hadn't pulled her off me and broken her nose.

Luna and Bentley were still fighting, he powered by blood and she by rage. I was on my own.

This sucked.

I had no magick, and all I could hear was my heart beating. Nielsen pulled Trotter's hair back and put the knife to his throat. And she *smiled* at me, like she knew I had no hope of winning.

Something inside me snapped. I lunged for Nielsen and caught her around the waist, knocking her away from Trotter. She fought me off, long manicured nails scratching for my face, and I balled up my fist and hit her, right in the eye.

"Ow!" Nielsen shrieked. "That *hurt*!"

My fist twinged and there was blood on my knuckles. Luna made that look so easy.

I grabbed Nielsen's necklace and pulled. "That's the idea."

The cord snapped, and I felt the magick flood back over the room. I'd let Nielsen's power free, but my magick came back to me, hot and white with the adrenaline in my blood. I looked at Trotter. "Do you want to die?"

"No!" he yelled.

"Then you better help me," I ordered, and reached for my caster.

Nielsen's power came up at the same time, and it was like standing under a thirty-foot wave. I threw up a shield, a wall of pure energy, and I felt Trotter's join me. He wasn't very strong, but he had precise control.

Nielsen laughed. "This is great. You really think you're going to hold me off until what? The cavalry comes? ASA Nielsen can make you all look like a bunch of crooked cops and crazy witches, and Ginger will make sure that if that doesn't work, your bodies will never be identified."

She pushed again, and I staggered, feeling blood come from my nose. Nielsen was laughing. Trotter and Luna were screaming at me, but I couldn't hear them.

Nielsen could beat me. She could beat me easily and she knew it. I gasped, going to one knee, and let my shield crack, just a little.

"Gods!" Trotter yelped. "What's going on?"

I watched Nielsen through my lashes as she closed on me. "She's weak, is what," Nielsen said. "And you're next. Ginger can't be stopped."

I gathered my magick to me, in a tight, hot ball of shield. I was going to get only one shot at this.

"Ginger is going to kill you, Sunny Swann," Nielsen singsonged. "How do you feel about that?"

I met her eyes. "Bitch, please. We all know that's not your natural color."

My magick flew from my caster, singing through the air and spreading like a battering ram, catching Nielsen's burgeoning shield. It threw her backwards into the wall, smoke coming off her caster and her hands. I kept pushing her until there was nothing left and I fell on the floor, for real.

The next thing I remember is seeing Luna standing over me, blood running from her cut lip, grinning.

THE PRISON DOCTOR patched us up and declared us fit to leave. Luna radioed for someone to collect Nielsen and Bentley, who looked like he'd been slammed repeatedly into the grille of a Mack truck, and the U.S. Marshals to move Trotter to a different prison. He barely looked at me as we went by his holding cell, and I sniffed, "You're welcome."

"You did good, Sun," Luna said when she came over to the car. I was sitting on the hood, letting the sun warm me. I ached all over from the fight with Nielsen, and my head buzzed as my drained reservoir of power echoed inside.

"I learned from you," I said. Luna waved it off.

"No. You've got a lot of spine, kid. You should let it out more often."

"Luna?" I said, sliding off the hood and opening the passenger door. "It's been fun, foiling a magick conspiracy and all, but if you *ever* hear me suggest that I should do something like this again, do me a favor?"

She dug in the glove compartment for a pair of sunglasses. "What?"

"Shoot me before I can say yes."

"Fair enough."

I settled back against the seat and shut my eyes. "I did pretty much kick ass, though, didn't I?"

Luna laughed as she started the motor and pulled onto the highway. "You want some tights to go with that cape and cowl?"

"Oh, Hex you."

"Hey, I'm just saying . . ."

I let her talk while we drove back toward my real life, mundane and magickal only in ways that didn't hurt. I wasn't going to start running around protecting the weak, but the small warm thought grew in my mind that I'd used my magick down and dirty, gotten into a fight, and felt the euphoria of life-or-death.

And I gotta admit, I kind of liked it.

Caitlin Kittredge is the author of the Nocturne City series, featuring werewolf detective Luna Wilder, and the Black London series, featuring mage Jack Winter. She lives in Olympia, Washington, with two pushy cats, and wears a lot of black, thus fulfilling two writer clichés at once. She maintains a popular blog about writing, films, and life at www.caitlinkittredge.com.

# Dark Sins

Jenna Maclaine

## Venice, 1818

My body hit the wooden floor with a loud thud. I'm not sure if it was the fall that knocked my breath from my chest, or the naked man who landed on top of me. Either way, I was left lying on the cold floor, blinking up at the ceiling, and trying to drag some air back into my lungs. I don't *have to* breathe, you understand, but it's one of those human quirks, like a love for whiskey and chocolate, that being dead just doesn't change. You see, I'm a vampire.

"And a very bad witch," I muttered, trying to push Michael's body off of mine.

He groaned and rolled to one side. "You are not a bad witch, love. But I think you might have dislocated my knee that time."

I gave him an arch look. "Where the hell are our clothes?" I asked.

We both sat up and looked back at the bed. Sure enough, there were our clothes, lying on the sheets as if our bodies had simply vanished from them. Which they had.

"Oh, damn," I spat. "We were supposed to end up naked in the bed, and the clothes were supposed to end up on the floor!"

Michael smiled at me indulgently, his blue eyes twinkling. "Yes, dear, I know. You're getting better, though. We were just a few feet away this time."

I growled in frustration as he stood, scooped me up, and tossed me on the bed. He started at my right ankle and began slowly kissing his way up the inside of my leg.

"I am a bad witch," I said. "I've spent the last three summers in Inverness with my aunt Maggie, who hates me, and the best we've accomplished is to give me enough control over my magic so that things don't blow up or burst into flames anymore. Even Maggie thinks I'm a bad witch. And possibly evil."

"She doesn't hate you, darling. She's just afraid of what you are, and I think she's also a bit jealous."

"Of me? For the love of the Goddess, why? She's got more magic in her little finger than I could even think about calling."

He stopped kissing the side of my knee and looked up at me. In the candlelight, his cheekbones stood out in sharp relief, making his beautiful face look more than a little dangerous.

"Not more magic," he said, "and not better magic. I've seen your magic, Cin, and your aunt cannot even come close to it. She's just better at working with what she has than you are. Be patient, love. You'll find your way. I believe in you."

I smiled and reached down, pushing a lock of dark blond hair off his forehead. "But what if I never figure it out, Michael?" I asked softly. "I have all this power, I can feel it inside me, but I just can't seem to get it to work the way it's supposed to. My spells are a disaster and only work a fraction of the time. The rest of the time I have to be careful that I don't accidentally . . ."

"Turn someone into a weasel?" he asked.

And, yes, I had done that once. I groaned and flopped down against the pillows.

"Cin, sweetheart, love of my undead life," Michael said as he trailed kisses up the inside of my thigh, "it's only been three years. You're the first witch anyone's ever heard of who's been turned into a vampire and still kept her powers. We have eternity ahead of us. Have some patience, and it will come to you."

I snorted. "You know very well that I'm the least patient person—"

"Are you going to talk the entire way through this?" he asked as his breath caressed the most intimate part of me. I shivered as his mouth hovered there, almost touching but not quite, and everything I was about to say went clean out of my head. "Because I have more interesting things you can do with your mouth, *mo ghraidh*."

I giggled and raised my arms over my head, grasping the headboard, stretching my body across the decadent satin sheets to display my curves and valleys to their best advantage. "Oh, no," I replied with a wicked grin, "I'm finished. Please continue."

He lowered his head, and I heard the wood under my fingers crack as I called his name.

Sometimes I have premonitions. It's a gift I inherited from my father, as I inherited my magic from my mother. What I feel is never a solid knowledge of what's to come, but a nebulous feeling of unease that something is wrong, or about to be. It happens sporadically enough that I know that just because I don't feel that I'm in danger, it doesn't mean I'm not. On the other hand, whenever I *do* feel it, I know without a doubt not to ignore it.

I woke with Michael's body curled against my back, his right arm slung over me. I blinked several times, wondering what had pulled me from my sleep, and then I felt it. My stomach dropped, as if I'd just fallen from a great height, and chills broke out along my skin. I threw the covers off and jumped from the bed. I checked the lock on the door, then starting tossing clothes at Michael.

"Michael, get up. Something's wrong," I said, and threw his boots at him.

"What is it?" he asked.

"I don't know," I replied, "it's only a feeling, but I'll be damned if I'm going to get caught naked in bed by a bunch of vampire slayers. I have no wish to repeat what happened in Austria last year. Fighting naked is just awkward."

I struggled into the leather riding breeches I'd had on last night. Getting into them was not easy, but the only things I'd unpacked thus far were dresses. I would rather not fight in a dress if I had a choice in the matter. Actually, I would rather not be fighting at all. Michael and I, along with our companions Devlin and Justine, spent most of our undead lives hunting and executing rogue vampires but this trip to Venice was supposed to be a holiday. As a human, I had always wanted to see the city and it was one of the places Michael had promised to take me when he'd turned me into a vampire three years ago.

Pushing down all thoughts of romantic gondola rides, I

pulled my boots on. I had just reached for my dagger when the first blow hit the apartment's door. I winced and hoped that Devlin and Justine had heard the crash from their rooms down the hall. If it came to a fight, I certainly wanted our friends at our backs. Michael grabbed his claymore and stalked from the bedroom, wearing nothing but his pants and boots. I hastily pulled his shirt on over my head, tucked the dagger into the waistband of my breeches, and followed him.

The third blow cracked the frame, and the door swung drunkenly in on one hinge. Five men and two women swarmed into the room. I choked on the smell of sulfur and blood. Witches, then. Ones who practiced dark magic. Michael glanced at me, and then pulled the great claymore from its scabbard. A tall man, apparently the leader, stepped forward. The wizard wore dark clothes and a black cloak. He might have been handsome, even with his slightly receding hairline and a nose that was too large for his face, if it hadn't been for the fact that evil and dark dealings radiated from him like heat from the sun. The tip of Michael's claymore came to rest at the man's throat.

"*Cosa volete?*" Michael asked. "What do you want?"

Despite this invasion, Michael would be reluctant to run the man through. The Dark Council and the High King himself frowned on vampires killing humans, and the wizard had not offered us violence. Yet.

The man never spoke. He simply raised his right hand to his mouth, palm up, and blew across his palm. A cloud of pink powder swirled into the air and, before I could shout a warning, Michael's sword clattered to the floor and he collapsed beside it. I rushed forward, falling to my knees next to him. I turned

Michael's face to me, and brushed his hair away, running my fingers over his lips, across his sculpted cheekbones, over his dark brows. I knew he wasn't dead. Without whatever magic animated a vampire he would be nothing more than a seventy-year-old corpse, dust and bone in my fingers. He was alive, but he wasn't breathing. I knew he didn't have to, but in the three years we'd been together I had never seen him not breathe, even in his sleep. Whatever the wizard had dosed him with had put him so far under that there was no consciousness left.

I glared up at the man, fear squeezing my heart. "What have you done, wizard?"

The man smiled, and it was not a nice smile. I lunged for Michael's sword and had just wrapped my fingers around the hilt when the wizard's companions fell on me like a pack of wolves. Fingers dug into me from all directions as I rose to my feet. The four men had taken hold of my arms and one of the women had grabbed me around the waist. The other woman had attached herself to my legs, trying to pull me back down. I threw my weight backward and the women fell to the floor in a tangle of skirts and limbs. Pulling my sword arm in front of me, I forced the two men holding my right arm to stumble forward and I brought my knee up into one man's groin. He released his grip on me, falling to his knees in a howl of agony. I jerked my arm from the other one's grasp and slammed my elbow into his nose. Swinging Michael's claymore in a wide arc toward the other men, I smiled as they released their hold on me.

"*Codardi!*" one of the women shrieked as the men stumbled back in fear.

She stood, with her steel-gray hair disheveled around her face and a maniacal look in her eyes, and raised her hands toward me. My Italian wasn't good enough to follow what she was saying, but the slow, deliberate cadence of her voice certainly made it sound like a spell. I was not about to give her the opportunity to finish it. I called up my own magic, feeling it build within me, and hoped that just this once it would do as I bid it.

I held my left hand out in front of me and a surge of power hit the woman with the force of a battering ram, sending her flying across the room. Hearing movement behind me I whirled around, magic in one hand and the great claymore in the other, just in time for the wizard to hit me squarely in the face with a handful of his pink powder.

The look of satisfaction on his hawkish features was the last thing I saw before the world went black.

THE DRONING HUM of voices pulled me back into consciousness and I found a stone floor, cold and damp, under my cheek. Groaning, I rolled onto my back and pushed my dark red hair from my face. What had I been doing? What time was it? What day? I blinked, and stared up at the ceiling. There seemed to be a netting of black lace above me. That wasn't right. I frowned, trying to get my bearings through the fog that clouded my head and dragged at my body.

And then it all came rushing back.

I sat up so quickly that the room spun and I had to brace my hands on the floor and close my eyes to keep from blacking out. When I finally opened them again, I found myself in a large rectangular stone chamber. Torches and numerous large candelabra, such as you would find in a church sanctuary, illuminated the windowless room and cast flickering shadows over the wizard's black-robed coven, gathered at one end of the hall.

A quick assessment of my surroundings revealed that the only way out was the heavy wooden door behind me. It was a massive thing studded with iron bolts and flanked by two cloaked and hooded figures. The one to the left of the door raised her head as I struggled to my feet. The witch with the steel-gray hair glared at me, her eyes blazing with hatred, but the monotonous repetition of the spell the two of them were chanting never wavered. I braced myself for the impact of their magic but when nothing happened the tension in my body eased slightly and I allowed myself to turn my back to them and survey the rest of the room more closely. What I saw made my stomach tighten in fear.

Against the wall to my left was a heavily carved stone altar, perhaps four feet high and ten feet long. Laid out of top of it was Devlin, the leader of our group, looking much the same as Michael had back at the palazzo. He looked as though he was asleep, but I could detect no rise and fall of his chest, no movement of any kind from him. He was a huge man, well over six feet tall, and every inch of him was thickly muscled. His massive chest was bare, but he still wore breeches and boots.

I turned to my right to see Justine, his consort and my dearest friend, laid out on a similar altar against the opposite wall. She was stark naked. Justine was a former courtesan, and a very practical Frenchwoman. Unlike Devlin, she would have gone for her weapons before her clothing. At least our attackers had given her some semblance of dignity by draping her long, silver-blonde hair over her bare breasts. It still made me angry to see her there like that, naked and helpless. She was Justine, the Devil's Justice, and she deserved better than that.

I swung around to face the phalanx of robed figures at the far end of the chamber. There were ten of them, all garbed in black robes with hoods raised to hide their faces. They chanted in low voices, perhaps in Latin, in perfect unison with the other two witches behind me. Some were women and some were men, but the man I was searching for exuded so much evil that I could have easily found him in a crowd of a hundred, let alone ten. The wizard stepped forward and pushed his hood back to reveal his blond hair, graying at the temples, and his cold, dark eyes.

"Where is Michael?" I demanded in English, hoping he would understand.

I was frightened and angry, and the smattering of Italian I knew had deserted me. There were undoubtedly other questions I should have asked, but this was the most important one. Michael was my world; without him, nothing else mattered.

The man looked a bit surprised and then stepped aside, waving a hand to the other robed figures who parted to reveal yet another stone altar. There was blood on this one, but it was old blood, human blood. None of it belonged to the man who was laid out on top of it.

"Michael," I whispered, and surged forward.

Too late I remembered the strange black netting. I hit it with the full force of my body, and it popped and sizzled as it burned me. I staggered back, one singed hand reaching up to touch my face. The wizard laughed. It was a ward, and a particularly nasty one at that. I called up my magic, summoned it from that place where it lives deep inside me, and pushed it out through my hands, visualizing it moving through my body and into the ward. The netting wavered, like cobwebs in a breeze, but held fast. I tried again, hoping that I had weakened it. The steady hum of the coven's voices grew louder as I gathered all the magic I could call and threw it at the ward. Whatever spell they were chanting strengthened the binding and my magic bounced off the barrier and flew back at me, hit me squarely in the chest and knocked me to the floor.

"They said you were a powerful witch, and yet you cannot break a simple ward," the wizard observed, and I was surprised to realize that he was English. Then again, Venice was lousy with Englishmen these days. I rose unsteadily to my feet as he stalked around the ward, which surrounded me in a ten-foot circle and arched above my head as though someone had hung a net woven of darkness over me. "I thought perhaps you would make a useful addition to my coven, vampire, but even the most inexperienced of my followers knows the spells to break a ward. I must say, you are a disappointment."

I glared at him. It was close enough to the truth, but I wouldn't let him see that he'd hurt my pride, even a little bit.

"I'll kill you for this, wizard," I spat.

He leaned in close to the ward, his dark eyes mocking me with cool disdain. "You can threaten me all you want, vampire, but nothing on this earthly plane frightens me, especially not an inept witch caught in my web."

I smiled. "Oh, you'll fear me before this is over. I promise you, you'll die screaming for my mercy."

Sometimes bravado is all you have.

His arrogance faltered just a bit, and then he recovered and inclined his head, returning my smile. "We shall see, vampire. We shall see."

"What do you want?" I asked. "Who are you?"

"My name is Edmund Gage, and what I want is vengeance."

As I watched him circle the ward, I tried to recall ever having seen the man before, let alone having done anything to him that would require this level of retribution.

"I don't believe I've ever wronged you, Mr. Gage," I stated.

"Oh, not you, vampire, not you. It's that bastard Marco I'll have my vengeance on."

Marco was the Regent of Venice, the local master vampire. I'd met him when we'd arrived in town, since it was proper protocol to present ourselves at the local court whenever we entered a new city.

"If you seek to harm Marco through us, then you've chosen the wrong vampires, wizard. We do not belong to him."

He shrugged. "You will do for my purposes all the same."

"Do you have any idea who we are?" I asked.

He inclined his head again. "You are The Righteous—judge, jury, and executioner in the world of the vampires."

He was correct. We constantly traveled throughout Western Europe, and it was our duty to deal with anything the local Wardens couldn't handle. We had no allegiance to Marco, though, or to any Regent. Unfortunately that also meant that with all four of us trapped here, it was unlikely anyone would notice we were missing for quite some time.

"If you know so much about us, Gage, then you should know that we do not belong to Marco. We are the High King's subjects alone, and if you kill any of us, you will bring down his wrath upon you. Trust me when I tell you that you really do not want that."

I'd never met the High King, but we were his, and I hoped that I was right about him avenging our deaths.

"Ah, but it must be you, my dear. A witch for a witch—that is what I require. Marco took something precious from me, and it will shame him that I took you in his city."

"A witch for a witch," I repeated. "What are you talking about?"

Gage came within an inch of the ward. If I could have breached it, I could have snapped his neck before he had time to draw a breath.

"He took my daughter from me," he said, each word filled with pain and barely contained rage. "She would have been the greatest of us all, and he bespelled her, defiled her, and turned her into a bloodsucking leech."

Marco's consort . . . Sara? Now that I thought about it, she did look a bit like Gage, the same blonde hair, the same dark eyes. She must have inherited her mother's nose. She was a pretty little thing, not at all someone I would take for a practitioner of the dark arts, and she was completely in love with Marco and he with her. And there was not a bit of magic left in her. It seemed I truly was the only witch whose powers had survived the turning.

"Sara is your daughter?" I asked.

"Do not!" he yelled, and then his voice dropped to nothing more than a sibilant hiss. "You are not fit to say her name."

I shook my head. "Marco may have bespelled her, Gage, she may have even been bespelled when he turned her, but once she was turned, he lost all power over her. Vampire tricks do not work on other vampires. She has complete free will. I saw her not a fortnight ago, and she was happy. If she's under any spell, it's only that of a woman in love."

"You speak in twisted lies," he spat.

"It's no lie. They are in love, and she is his consort. Her magic is gone though, Gage," I said softly. "Let her go. Let *us* go. Vengeance will not bring your daughter, or her power, back to you."

"No," he said flatly. "Marco will pay for what he did. He will pay, Cin Craven. He took from me, and I will take The Righteous from under his nose. It is not enough, not nearly enough, but it will do for a start. Your friends are merely here for my amusement. There are some devious spells I can spin with the blood of a vampire, you know. You, however, you will be mine."

"Not in your wildest dreams," I assured him.

"Oh, no, dear—in reality. You will get hungry eventually, and then you will drink of my blood and I will bind you to me, as I have bound my other followers."

I laughed. "I'll die before your tainted blood ever passes my lips, Gage."

He smiled. "That's fine with me, too."

I TRIED, TRULY I did. Long after Gage had gone, I looked for holes in the warding, any spot where there might be a weakness in the magic that held it together. I tested it until my hands were raw and bloody with burns. The thing that frustrated me the most was that I knew Aunt Maggie had a book specifically on spells to break wards. When I closed my eyes, I could see the damned thing on the shelf in her rented flat in Inverness, its brown leather-bound spine mocking me. If I'd been a better student, then maybe I'd have remembered something about what was *in* the book but, as Maggie had often said of me, I concentrate about as well as a puppy. And now that one, tiny character flaw was going to get us all killed.

Two of Gage's followers were in the chamber with me at all times. Apparently the chanting had to be continued for the spells to hold, because they rotated in turns every few hours. I tried talking to them. I tried begging, pleading, bribery. The only response I received from any of them was when one spat at me and hissed, "I hope the master kills you slowly, you bloodsucking whore."

I stopped trying after that. There's no reasoning with zealots.

The sound of the door opening brought me unsteadily to my feet. Gage stalked in with an ornate golden cup in his hands. I could smell fresh blood from across the room, and my stomach churned. I had no idea how long we'd been his prisoners, but I hadn't fed since the night before we were taken—and I was hungry.

"I have something for you, vampire," he said. "Something I think you want badly by now."

He walked up to the ward. Here was my chance. If he wanted me to drink, he would have to break the warding. I watched in fascination as the warding melted for him, and his hand and the cup passed through the small hole. It wasn't as much as I'd hoped for, but it would do. If I couldn't get out, then I would pull him through the ward to me. I lunged for him and nearly made it, too. I had been so intent on what the one hand was doing that I didn't notice that he'd conjured a ball of pure magic in the other. The magic hit me when I was a bare inch away from him. The force of it slammed me into the far side of the ward, searing the skin on my back through the fabric of Michael's shirt.

The man was smart. There was no way he could have thrown that blast in *reaction* to my movements. I was a vampire and, whatever his unnatural magical talents, he was still human. I could move faster than his eyes could track. No, he'd thrown his magic at me at the same instant he'd passed his hand through the ward. As I slowly picked my battered body off the floor, he set the cup on the ground and then stepped back.

"Drink," he said.

I walked to the cup slowly, never taking my eyes off him. I picked it up and passed it under my nose. It was human, but I didn't want to drink it. I knew it was his.

"It's your blood, isn't it?" I asked.

"Yes, and it's filled with my power. Drink it and join me, Cin Craven, and I will let you live."

I drew back to throw the cup in his face.

"Before you do that," Gage said, staying my hand, "think of what I can offer you. Think of the power, Miss Craven, what it would feel like to bend all that magic inside you to your will. I can make you the witch you were born to be."

"A practitioner of the dark arts was not what I was born to be, Gage."

He laughed. "You are a vampire. You live in darkness. Now let that darkness live in you. I can make you more powerful than any white witch could dream of being. Let me make you what you were meant to be."

I saw the utter conviction of what he was saying shining in his eyes, and for the smallest moment I was tempted. I glanced at the cup of blood. What would it feel like to have utter control over the magic I possessed? I looked back at Gage, and he smiled. And over his shoulder I could see the lifeless form of my beloved stretched out on an altar dedicated to everything I had sworn to fight against.

I shook my head and threw the cup at the ward, slinging its contents at Gage as I did so. The blood spattered against the black netting and disappeared. The ward was fueled with blood magic, and it had sucked up Gage's blood like rain on a drought-ridden field. I began to rethink my assumption that Aunt Maggie's book would have anything in it to break this ward. Macgregor witches did not deal in blood magic.

Gage raised his hand, and the cup stirred from where it had fallen on the floor. It spun three times, and then it flew through the ward and into his outstretched hand. He caught it without ever looking away from my face.

"I will be back, vampire. Perhaps you will have reconsidered my offer by then."

"Don't count on it," I replied.

"It matters little to me if you join me willingly, as the rest of my coven has, or by force."

"You cannot force me, Gage."

"Yes, you seem willing enough to sacrifice yourself for your morals. But are you strong enough to sacrifice your companions as well? You will drink what I offer, Miss Craven, because the next time you throw this cup back in my face, I will take it and I will fill it with your lover's blood. I will drain them all dry before your eyes. Tell me," he said, almost sweetly, "can you sit there and watch them die when you could save them?"

"You're going to kill them anyway," I whispered.

"True, but if you drink from me, I'll bring them a swift death at the end of a stake. They'll never know what happened. If you refuse, I'll wake them just enough so that they know they are dying, slowly, and they'll know that you could have saved them, but you wouldn't. I hope that gives you something to think about."

He strode from the room, and the heavy wooden door slammed behind him, echoing through the chamber like a gunshot.

I sank to the floor and cried, my sobs muffled by the unending chanting that echoed through the chamber.

GAGE WAS TRUE to his word. After what seemed like an eternity, he returned with his entire black-robed coven in tow. They surrounded my warded prison like vultures waiting for the opportunity to fall on me and rend me to pieces. I ignored them and kept my eyes on Gage. He was the key. If he'd bonded the coven to him by blood, then his blood and his death should break the bond. I didn't know if any of them had enough magic on their own to fight us all, but I was willing to risk it. Gage's power radiated through the chamber, and I didn't feel anything that came close to it from any of the others.

Gage came to stand in front of me. I took a calming breath and squared my shoulders. One way or another, this nightmare would end here and now.

"Will you drink?" he demanded.

The gods knew I wanted to. I was weak and hungry, but his blood was tainted with evil and I wouldn't do it, couldn't do it. I gritted my teeth and shook my head.

"You know you want it, vampire," he said, his tone almost seductive. "You long to taste that coppery liquid on your tongue, don't you? And the power. Think of it. You have power of your own, Miss Craven. I can feel it, even though you have no idea how to use it. I can teach you."

I realized something in that moment, as I listened to him offer what I had already refused. Despite what he had said the last time he was here, it was important to him that I join him willingly. Whether it was to appease his sense of vengeance or vanity he needed me to come to him of my own free will. I would not give him that satisfaction.

"I am a Macgregor witch, Gage, whether or not I am worthy of the name. Your blood magic is beneath me. You use the dark arts because the Goddess has forsaken you. You have nothing to teach me."

He jerked his head back as if I'd slapped him, and then narrowed his eyes. "So be it."

Gage walked to where Michael lay and stood over him.

"Don't touch him!" I shouted. "If you harm any of them, I swear to you I will make you pay!"

He laughed. "How amusing that you continue to make threats, Miss Craven," Gage said as he pulled a long, deadly looking dagger from under his robe. "If you had any power to make good on them, you would have done so by now."

He raised one hand and passed it over my lover's face. Michael's eyes flew open, and I could see the muscles in his neck straining with the effort to move.

Gage leaned down, smiling. "Good evening, vampire."

"Who are you?" Michael asked, his voice low and hoarse. "Why can't I move?"

"I am Edmund Gage, and I have just been having a conversation with your lady. Did you know that she has all your lives in her hands, and she refuses to save you?"

"Cin? What have you done to her?"

Gage stepped back and allowed Michael to turn his head. His blue eyes focused on me, and I smiled sadly as his worried gaze raked over me from head to toe. Then, satisfied that I was unharmed, he glanced around the room.

"One simple task could save you and your friends," Gage said, drawing Michael's attention back to him, "yet she refuses. She would rather let me bleed you dry. What do you think of her love for you now?"

"Michael, no," I pleaded. "It's not—"

"Shh, *m'anam*," he said. "I trust you."

I looked at him, and my stomach clenched. He was my world, this man. I had been raised a sheltered and spoiled aristocrat, meant for nothing more in life than breeding more sheltered and spoiled aristocrats. And then I had found him. I had given up my life to save us all, and I had died in his arms. I looked into his eyes and I remembered that night, and all the others that had followed—dancing with him in the streets of Paris; making love to him with the salt of a Spanish sea still on my skin; lying in his arms under a Highland sky, watching the northern lights shimmer above us. He had taught me how to truly live, and love. I loved this man beyond all reason. I loved his body. I loved his mind. I loved the way he made me laugh and the kindness in his heart. I loved the way that he loved me like I was the other half of his soul.

I reached my hand out to him just as Gage's blade came down, slicing Michael's wrist open and spilling his blood across the cold gray stone of the altar.

I slammed my body into the ward and screamed to the gods from the depths of my soul.

And the world stood still.

NOTHING MOVED. GAGE'S hand was frozen on the downswing, that evil smile I'd come to hate was still plastered across his face. Not a breath or a heartbeat echoed through the chamber. I stared, transfixed, at the drop of Michael's blood that hung suspended in the air below his wrist.

"Three years," came a deep, definitely female voice from behind me. I spun around and was completely unprepared for whoever—or whatever—stood behind me.

She was tall, and I couldn't distinguish any of her features. She wore a cloak made entirely of black feathers. The hood framed where her face should be, but all I could see was shadow. She walked past me, through one side of the ward and out the other as though it weren't there. As she moved the shadows under that hood seemed to move with her. The feathers that made up the cloak grazed my hand as she passed, and they seemed almost alive. They were huge, black and glossy, with iridescent undertones of dark purple and green, and they brushed the floor with a soft whisper as she moved.

"Three years," she said again. "A blink of the eye, really, compared to the millennia I've witnessed. I thought I would give you time to adjust, to learn on your own." She turned and faced me again, standing between me and Michael. As she crossed her arms over her chest her feathers seemed to fluff, like an agitated bird, and then settle again. "Obviously that approach has not worked well."

I shook my head. "Who *are* you?"

She sighed. "Don't be obtuse, Cin. You called me. Whoever do you think I am?"

I had called her? My mind raced. Gage had cut Michael and I had screamed . . .

"Morrigan," I whispered.

The feathers ruffled again. "Precisely."

Morrigan, the Great Phantom Queen, war goddess,

harbinger of death. She often appeared in the guise of a raven. I had invoked her in one of my last successful spells, to summon The Righteous to me. It was how I'd met Michael. She was the goddess I prayed to the most. And she was here, standing in front of me. I fell to my knees.

"Morrigan, please, help me," I pleaded.

"Oh, for the love of Danu," she muttered as she once again walked through the ward. I looked up, but could still see nothing but shadow under the hood of her cloak. The hands that wrapped around my upper arms and jerked me to my feet, however, were very real. "Get up, child. You have no need of my help. I gave you all the power you will ever need when I created you."

"You?"

"Of course. You are all mine. Vampires, werewolves, anything that walks the night is mine. You are my warriors. There are battles to come—"

"What battles?" I asked.

She grew very still, and I cursed myself for a fool. I was probably not wise to question a goddess.

"You will know in my own good time," she said, and her words were clipped and fierce like the staccato drumbeats at a public hanging.

I dropped to one knee. "Of course. I beg your forgiveness, goddess."

"As I was saying," she continued, "I created you to feed on humans so that you would have a vested interest in protecting them, as a shepherd protects his flock."

*As a shepherd protects his flock.* I'd heard that analogy before, almost to the word. Devlin had told me that that was how the

High King viewed the symbiotic relationship between vampires and humans. Did Morrigan appear to the High King as well? If we were her creation, and he was our king, then I supposed it would be a logical assumption. It would also explain how one man had come out of nowhere, as legend had it, and challenged all comers in hand-to-hand combat until no one stood between him and control of all of our kind. It would be an easy enough thing to accomplish with a war goddess by your side.

"I created you to be virtually immortal, so you would have the power to fight what I need you to fight, and when I need you to fight it. I made you physically stronger and faster, so you would have the skills to wage the battles to come." She walked over to Michael and reached out with one pale, slender hand, running a long, shiny black fingernail down the edge of his cheek. "I created you with the capacity to love the same person for centuries, so that your long lives would not be lonely, and so that you would have something worth fighting for."

The words came softly, almost like a caress. She turned to me.

"He is beautiful. I put him in Devlin's way, you know, all those years ago. I chose him for you. He is my gift, to make up for the life you had to leave behind."

How was it that she had chosen him for me when he had been made a vampire half a century before I was even born?

"I don't understand."

"I know you don't," she said, and nothing more.

I waited for an explanation, but apparently that was all I was going to get. I knew better than to question her further. Instead, I begged for her mercy.

"Please, Morrigan, save my friends. I will give my life for theirs."

She walked over to where I knelt and reached out a hand, cupping my chin and turning my face to the dark emptiness that was her own.

"You really don't understand. As I told you before, you don't need me to save them. You are special, Cin." She leaned close. "You are my greatest weapon."

"Me? I can't even break the ward to get to Gage. I'm worthless as a witch."

She laughed and brushed past me. I watched her weave in and out of the ward, walking in circles around me.

"Tell me, Cin, do you eat as a human does?"

She already knew the answer to that, but she was a goddess and so I played along. "I *can* eat. I still enjoy the taste of human food and drink, though it gives me no sustenance."

"And can you walk in the sun? Take a morning stroll or an afternoon carriage ride through the park?"

*Only if I wanted to burst into flames,* I thought. "You know I cannot," I answered.

"Oh good, so you do realize that you are no longer human?" she said with more than a touch of sarcasm in her voice.

"Of course."

"Then why do you insist on believing that your magic must be practiced as humans practice their magic?"

"What other way is there? I practice my craft as my aunt has been teaching me, and my mother before her."

"Fine witches, the both of them, but they are not you. No vampire ever created has had the magic you have, Cin. I have given you a great deal of power, not only your own magic but the accumulated magic of all those Macgregor women who came before you. I chose you because you understand the responsibility that comes with power, it's been bred into your family for centuries, and you have the strength of character to shoulder such a burden. You are my chosen one, and it's time you ceased weeping like a child and used your power."

I opened my mouth and the closed it again, unsure of what to say to that. Before I could come up with a suitable reply, she simply vanished. A heartbeat later I felt her behind me.

"If I cannot make you understand with words," she said, and grasped my head in her hands, "then I'll try different means."

There was a nearly blinding flash of light, and then it was as if I was floating above the room, watching myself below. Gage turned and smiled at the me that was still down there, locked behind the ward. I saw myself walk through that ward, and I knew before I touched it that it wouldn't stop me. I watched my hand raise, and the knife fly from Gage's hand to mine. I felt a rush of power, as though I were in my body and yet out of it at the same time. The power wasn't Gage's or Morrigan's. It was *mine.* I felt it. I felt everything and, finally, I understood.

I knew why my magic had been so wild in those early days, and why it was so difficult for me to harness now. It wasn't that I had no control of it; it was that I didn't understand how to control it. I was raised to think of magic as a tool, something that could only be performed with the proper rituals and spells. Perhaps that's the way it worked for my human relatives, but this magic, my magic, was different. I had thought of it as something that lived inside me. I now realized that the magic *was* me. It didn't answer to herbs and potions and spells. It answered only to the force of my will. My magic had been fettered and chained all these years—by tradition, by my teachers, by my aunt Maggie—but it was free now.

I was free. I finally saw exactly who and what I was meant to be.

"There's my girl," Morrigan whispered. She took her hands from my head, and I was back in my own body again. "Now, end this," she said, and snapped her fingers. I felt her disappear an instant before time began to move again.

Gage turned to me, that arrogant smile still on his face. I called my magic and felt it rise up, filling and completing me, and for the first time it wasn't something I was trying to harness or fight.

I smiled back at Gage. I was the Devil's Witch. I was blessed by a goddess and no human wizard, no matter how powerful, could ever hope to stand against me.

I WALKED THROUGH the ward just as I had done in Morrigan's vision. There was no burning this time, no pain. The ward fell before me like a thin veil of cobwebs, not because of any spell or incantation, but because I *willed* it so. I put my hand up, and the knife flew from Gage's grasp. I caught it and felt a stirring of victory when I saw the first flicker of fear in his eyes.

"How—?"

"I warned you what would happen if you laid a hand on him, Gage," I said. "One drop of his blood is more important to me than your wretched life."

The coven stirred behind me and finally that infernal chanting stopped.

I ignored them and kept walking toward Gage.

"Keep the spells going!" Gage yelled. "She's sworn to protect humans. She won't kill me."

I cocked a brow at him. "Want to wager your life on that?"

The chanting resumed, but somewhat raggedly. When I was about five feet from Gage he conjured a ball of magic in his hand. I expected him to throw it at me, but instead he held it over Michael.

"Come no closer," he warned.

With a flick of my wrist, I snuffed the dark orb as easily as a candle. Gage roared in frustration and rushed me. I sent the knife flying into his shoulder with such force that it knocked him back against the altar. I was on him with my hand around his throat before he knew what had hit him.

"Please," he begged.

"I told you that you'd die begging for my mercy," I said, and squeezed just a bit harder.

"Cin," Michael whispered. "Don't. He's human."

I looked at my consort. I knew that look. I had once asked him to spare a life that he wanted to take. Now he was asking the same of me. Perhaps I could break the spells that held them without Gage's death. I relaxed my grip on Gage's throat . . . and felt a searing pain in my chest.

I looked down. Gage had taken his moment, pulled the knife from his shoulder and driven it into my heart. It wasn't a wooden stake so it wouldn't kill me, but by the gods it *hurt.*

"Do you feel it?" Gage asked.

I released Gage and stumbled back a few steps.

"Cin, what is it?" Michael asked. "What's wrong?"

I looked down at the knife hilt sticking out of my chest. Gage's blood had been on the knife. It was now inside me. I could feel it, the darkness in it. I felt it latch on to my own magic and spread through me like a wildfire.

I pulled the knife from my chest, dropping it to the floor.

I turned my gaze to Gage.

"You feel it, don't you?" he asked again.

"I really will kill you for this," I whispered.

"No, you won't. This is what I've been offering you, but you were too stubborn, too full of your precious morals to take it. How does it feel now, vampire?"

"It feels like evil spreading through my blood."

"Exactly," he said in triumph.

"Cin!" Michael shouted. "Fight it! Darling, please, fight it!"

"Silence," Gage snapped, passing his hand once again over Michael's face.

Michael tried to speak, but no sound came out. His eyes though, those beautiful blue eyes, were panic-stricken. I closed my eyes. I tried to fight it, but I could feel the darkness blossoming in my chest and radiating through my body. It was like the slow burn of a good whiskey, multiplied by a thousand.

"That's right," Gage said as he struggled to stand and walk to me. "Do you feel the darkness inside you now, taking you over bit by bit? It feels decadent, doesn't it, to have all that power and not be limited by morals or conscience?"

"Yes," I whispered, and opened my eyes. "But unfortunately for you my conscience and morals were the only things stopping me from doing this—" I said, and drove my fist into his chest.

I felt skin tear and bones break, not all of them his, but I didn't stop until I ripped the still-beating heart from his chest. I looked down at it and then I threw my head back and laughed.

As Gage's lifeless body sank to the ground, I turned toward

the coven. They'd abruptly stopped chanting, staring at the thing in my hand. I smiled at them and they bolted.

I willed the one door to close and lock. At first they pounded and pulled, and then they tried magic to open it. Finally, they turned back to me. I stood ready for them, soaked in Gage's blood with his heart still in my hand. The smell of their fear filled the room, mingling with the sweet scent of blood and the pungent odor of sulfur. Under the fear, though, was anger and hatred. They couldn't flee, so they would fight.

The steel-haired woman stepped forward and drew a stake from somewhere inside her robe. "She killed the master," she screamed. "She must die! Kill her! Kill her!"

The others followed her lead, and they swarmed across the floor as if someone had kicked over a nest of ants. I dropped Gage's heart to the ground.

*Let them come*, I thought, *I'm so very hungry*.

THEY FELL ON me in a blur of black-robed bodies, and I welcomed them. A black cloud enveloped me, pushing down everything I was until it alone was in control of my body. Gage's magic rode me—and it wanted blood. It wanted me to feel just how powerful I could be. My ears rang with the coven's screams of anger, and of pain.

Dimly, as though from some great distance, I heard Devlin's booming voice. "Stop her! Stop her or she'll kill them all!"

Arms like steel bands grabbed me from behind, but I would not be stopped. The magic gave me the strength to tear myself free of his grasp and I hit him with a blast so powerful that it threw him across the room. The darkness inside me reveled in the fact that I could toss a man who was nearly six and a half feet of solid muscle as though he were nothing more than a rag doll. It didn't recognize that this was Devlin, my friend, and as the black magic consumed me I couldn't bring myself to care. No matter how many of them fell by the wayside, Gage's coven seemed to keep coming at me and nothing, not Justine's pleading screams or the hands that tried to hold me back, would stop me. Gage's power had to be satisfied and the only way to accomplish that was with blood and death. Suddenly there was a face in my line of vision, blue eyes, sharp cheekbones, sensual mouth.

*Michael*, some part of me screamed softly in the darkness, *please make it stop*.

I held my hand out. As he took a tentative step toward me, a dark-robed figure rose up from the floor behind him. It was the steel-haired woman. With grim determination she raised her stake high and Michael's eyes widened in fear as I sprang toward him. I shoved him out of the way before her weapon could hit its mark. She staggered forward and the last thing she saw in this life was the fury in my eyes as I snapped her neck.

It was over.

With that final death, Gage's magic settled inside me like a nest of vipers coiled in my belly—well-fed, smug, and content. For now. I looked around. Devlin was standing a few feet away with Justine in his arms, a cloak wrapped around her that had been taken off of one of Gage's followers. Some part of me didn't understand why my friends were looking at me with something akin to horror and pity on their faces. I blinked and looked around me again.

It was carnage.

The floor was littered with bodies, twelve of them, to be

exact. Throats had been ripped out, necks twisted at odd angles. I took a step back, and my foot hit something. Turning, I looked down into Gage's slack face and blank, staring eyes. It was then I noticed that I was covered in blood. The once-white shirt was soaked with it. I raised my hands, and they too were caked with blood.

"Michael," I said softly, my hands shaking. "What have I done?"

"*Mo ghraidh*," he said and reached for me.

I stumbled backward. "Don't touch me! Oh gods, Michael, don't touch me! How can I have done this? For the love of the Goddess, why didn't you stop me?"

"We tried," he said. "Nothing short of killing you would stop you from slaughtering them all."

Michael stepped toward me again, but I kept backing up, afraid that if he touched me, the evil would taint him somehow. Panic welled within me, and I started crying uncontrollably. I had killed them, all of them. And it had felt good.

A hand touched my shoulder, and I spun around. Morrigan stood before me again. I looked at her with the horror of what I'd done gripping me.

"Morrigan," I said and raised my hands to her, palms up, as if to say *Look what I've done.*

"I know, child," she said. "I shouldn't have left you to find your way alone. This is my fault, and I'll make it right."

"What have you done to her?" Michael demanded.

I almost smiled. Only my Michael would speak to a goddess in that tone.

"I have forced her to embrace her destiny," Morrigan replied.

"*This* is her destiny?" Michael snapped, gesturing to the bodies scattered across the floor.

"Of course not," Morrigan chided. "Her power is her destiny. This was simply . . . unfortunate."

"Oh, is that all?" I asked in a small voice.

"It was the dark power riding you," she said.

"And it will do so again," I said. "It's still there, inside me. I can feel it."

"Is there nothing you can do?" Michael pleaded with Morrigan.

She nodded and turned to me. "I will make you as you were meant to be."

She reached out and put her hand over my heart. At first I felt nothing, and then what I did feel took me screaming to my knees. It was the dark magic. I had ripped it from Gage when I had taken his heart. It was like a living, evil thing that had taken over my body.

And it *wanted* me. It did not want to leave, but it was no match for a goddess.

Morrigan's power flowed through me, cleansing me, pushing all the blackness from my body. If light could be black, then that's what came out of me, a flood of bright, shining black light. And it felt as though it was trying to rip me apart as it went.

When it was over Michael was there, his arms around me, helping me to my feet.

"There's my whiskey-eyed girl again," he muttered, and pushed my hair back from my face.

The rustle of feathers made me turn in his arms. Morrigan reached out and took his wrist in her hand, the hand that was still covered in blood from the wound in my chest. I heard

Michael suck in his breath, and I glanced down at my own skin. The wound from Gage's knife was gone, healed in whatever Morrigan had done to purge the black magic from my body. She pulled her hand from Michael's wrist, and the gash Gage had made there was gone as well. Morrigan held her hand out to me, her fist closed. It took a moment to understand what she wanted. I held my hand out and she dropped a large uncut ruby into it.

"Made from your blood, and his," she explained.

"Thank you," I said, and closed my fist around the stone, holding it up to my heart.

"Goddess," Devlin spoke up from behind us, "what do we do? She's killed twelve humans."

Morrigan turned to him. "They were evil and they would have killed you. Their altar is stained with the blood of innocents and there would be more where that came from, had they lived. Do their lives truly mean so much to you?"

Devlin's face hardened. "It is not for us to decide the fate of humans."

"No," Morrigan said. "It is not."

In that moment, I realized that she had known. When she'd shown me what my magic could do, that I could stand against Edmund Gage and win, she had known what would happen.

"Why?" I asked.

Michael and my friends cast confused looks in my direction, but Morrigan understood my question.

"Because what happened here was necessary to help you become what you were created to be," she replied.

"Gage infecting me with his power, all these deaths, that was necessary to teach me how to control my magic?" I asked incredulously.

"You may not understand it now," she replied, "but one day you will."

"I pray that whatever you hoped to gain from this was worth their deaths and the nightmares that will haunt me," I said softly.

"If the lives of a dozen evil humans will make you into the warrior who will save millions of innocents then, yes, it is well worth it."

It seemed an easy thing for her to say. She didn't have to live with the nightmares of what I'd done here tonight. *Then again,* I thought as I regarded her cloaked in her own darkness, *a war goddess must carry the burden of far worse things.*

"There will be rumors," Devlin interjected. "If the High King were to find out—"

"If he takes issue with anything that's happened here," she said, "I will deal with him."

Devlin just nodded, and pulled Justine closer to him.

Morrigan turned back to me. "Dawn is approaching, and you must go. Rest today, but if I were you I'd put Venice behind me come sunset. Sara likely will not be too pleased to find her father dead, evil bastard though he was."

I nodded.

"Go with my blessing, my children," she said, and then she was just . . . gone.

I sighed and laid my head on Michael's shoulder, suddenly weary to the very marrow of my bones. All I wanted was a bath and the comfort of my lover's arms around me.

"Let's get you home, love," he said, and kissed my forehead.

"Home," I sighed. "Can we go back to England?"

"Of course," Michael replied softly.

"Sounds bloody marvelous to me," Devlin grumbled. "I've grown weary of this city."

Justine arranged her borrowed cloak more securely around her. "*Oui*," she said, "I liked Venice much better when the most interesting thing about it was keeping up with what Lord Byron was doing."

"Isn't that the truth," I murmured as Michael swept me into his arms and carried me to the door.

Jenna Maclaine is the author of the Cin Craven series. When she isn't writing, she spends her time caring for the eighty-plus animals that share her family farm in the beautiful foothills of the Blue Ridge Mountains.

You can find out more about her at www.jennamaclaine.com.

*An "ordinary" wedding is crazy enough, imagine what happens when otherworldly creatures are involved...*

FEATURES NINE OF THE HOTTEST AUTHORS OF PARANORMAL FICTION:

SHERRILYN KENYON
CHARLAINE HARRIS
JIM BUTCHER
L. A. BANKS
RACHEL CAINE
P. N. ELROD
ESTHER M. FRIESNER
LORI HANDELAND
SUSAN KRINARD

St. Martin's Griffin

EVERYONE DREAMS OF A ROMANTIC HONEYMOON WHERE TWO LOVERS CAN ESCAPE THE WORLD TOGETHER—BUT WHAT IF THE HONEYMOONERS AREN'T FROM THIS WORLD?

Featuring nine of today's hottest paranormal fiction authors:

Kelley Armstrong
P. N. Elrod
Katie MacAlister
Jim Butcher
Caitlin Kittredge
Lilith Saintcrow
Rachel Caine
Marjorie M. Liu
Ronda Thompson